Something
on the Side

CARL WEBER

Something on the Side

KENSINGTON PUBLISHING CORP.
www.kensingtonbooks.com

DAFINA BOOKS are published by

Kensington Publishing Corp.
850 Third Avenue
New York, NY 10022

All Kensington titles, imprints and distributed lines are available at special quantity discounts for bulk purchases for sales promotion, premiums, fund-raising, educational or institutional use.

Special book excerpts or customized printings can also be created to fit specific needs. For details, write or phone the office of the Kensington Special Sales Manager: Attn. Special Sales Department. Kensington Publishing Corp., 850 Third Avenue, New York, NY 10022. Phone: 1-800-221-2647.

Dafina Books and the Dafina logo Reg. U.S. Pat. & TM Off.

ISBN-13: 978-0-7582-1579-6
ISBN-10: 0-7582-1579-7

First Hardcover Printing: February 2008
First Trade Paperback Printing: January 2009
10 9 8 7 6 5 4 3 2 1

Printed in the United States of America

This book is dedicated to all the plus size sisters who love my books.

Acknowledgments

Thank you to all the booksellers and fans for supporting all of my books. And thanks to my editor Selena James and my agent Marie Brown.

1

Tammy

I love my life.

I love my life. I love my marriage. I love my husband. I love my kids. I love my BMW, and I love my house. Oh, did I say I love my life? Well, if I didn't, I love my life. I really love my life.

I stepped out of my BMW X3, then opened the back driver-side door and picked up four trays of food lying on a towel on the backseat. I had only about twenty minutes before the girls would be over for our book club meeting, but I'd already dropped off my two kids, Michael and Lisa, at the sitter, so they weren't going to be a problem. Now all I had to do was to arrange the food and get my husband out of the house. The food was easy, thanks to Poor Freddy's Rib Shack over on Linden Boulevard in South Jamaica. I merely had to remove the tops of the trays from the ribs, collard greens, candied yams, and maca-roni and cheese, pull out a couple bottles of wine from the fridge, and voilà, dinner is served. My husband was another thing entirely. He was going to need my personal attention be-fore he left the house.

I entered my house and placed the food on the island in the kitchen, then looked around the room with admiration. We'd been living in our Jamaica Estates home for more than a year now, and I still couldn't believe how beautiful it was. My kitchen had black granite countertops, stainless-steel appliances, and handcrafted cherrywood cabinets. It looked like something out of a home-remodeling magazine, and so did the rest of our house. By the way, did I say I love my life? God, do I love my life and the man who provides it for me.

Speaking of the man who provides for me, I headed down the hall to the room we called our den. This room was my husband's sanctuary—mainly because of the fifty-two-inch plasma television hanging on the wall and the nine hundred and some odd channels DIRECTV provided. I walked into the den, and there he was, the love of my life, my husband, Tim. By most women's standards, Tim wasn't all that on the outside. He was short and skinny, only five-eight, one hundred and forty pounds, with a dark brown complexion. Don't get me wrong—my husband wasn't a bad-looking man at all. He just wasn't the type of man who would stop a sister dead in her tracks when he walked by. To truly see Tim's beauty, you have to look within him, because his beauty was his intellect, his courteousness, and his uncanny ability to make people feel good about themselves. Tim was just a very special man, with a magnetic personality, and it only took a few minutes in his presence for everyone who'd ever met him to see it.

Tim smiled as he stood up to greet me. "Hey, sexy," he whispered, staring at me as if I were a celebrity and he were a star-struck fan. "Damn, baby, your hair looks great."

I blushed, swaying my head from side to side to show off my new three-hundred-fifty-dollar weave. I walked farther into the room. When I was close enough, Tim wrapped his thin arms around my full-figured waist. Our lips met, and he squeezed me tightly. A warm feeling flooded my body as his tongue entered my mouth. Just like the first time we'd ever kissed, my body felt like it was melting in his arms. I loved the way Tim kissed me. His kisses always made me feel wanted. When Tim kissed me, I felt like I was the sexiest woman on the planet.

When we broke our kiss, Tim glanced at his watch. "Baby, I could kiss you all night, but if I'm not mistaken, your book club meeting is getting ready to start, isn't it?"

I sighed to show my annoyance, then nodded my head. "Yeah, they'll be here in about ten, fifteen minutes."

"Well, I better get outta here, then. You girls don't need me around here getting in your hair. My virgin ears might overhear something they're not supposed to, and the next thing you know, I'll be traumatized for the rest of my life. You wouldn't want that on your conscience, would you?" He chuckled.

"Hell no, not if you put it that way. 'Cause, honey, I am not going to raise two kids by myself, so you need to make yourself a plate and get the heck outta here." He laughed at me, then kissed me gently on the lips.

"Aw-ight, you don't have to get indignant. I'm going," he teased.

"Where're you headed anyway?" I asked. A smart wife always knew where her man was.

"Well, I was thinking about going down to Benny's Bar to watch the game, but my boy Willie Martin called and said they were looking for a fourth person to play spades over at his house, so I decided to head over there. You know how I love playing Spades," Tim said with a big grin. "Besides, like I said before, I know you girls need your privacy."

Tim was considerate like that. Whenever we'd have our girls' night, he'd always go bowling or go to a bar with his friends until I'd call him to let him know that our little gathering was over. He always took my feelings into account and gave me space. I loved him for that, especially after hearing so many horror stories from my friends about the jealous way other men acted.

Tim was a good man, probably a better man than I deserved, which is why I loved him more than I loved myself. And believe it or not, that was a tall order for a smart and sexy egomaniac like myself. But at the 'same time, my momma didn't raise no fool. Although I loved and even trusted Tim, I didn't love or trust his whorish friends or those hoochies who hung around the bars and bowling alleys he frequented. So, before I let him leave the house, I always made sure I took care of my business in one way or another. And that was just what I was about to do when I reached for his fly—take care of my business.

"What're you doing?" He glanced at my hand but showed no sign of protest. "Your friends are gonna be here any minute, you know."

"Well, my friends are gonna have to wait. I got something to do," I said matter-of-factly. "Besides, this ain't gonna take but a minute. Momma got skills . . . or have you forgotten since last night?"

He shrugged his shoulders and said with a smirk, "Hey, I'm from Missouri, the Show Me State, so I don't remember shit. You got to show me, baby."

I cocked my head to the right, looking up at him. "Is that right? You don't remember shit, huh? Well, don't worry, 'cause I'm about to show you, and trust me, this time you're not going to forget a damn thing." I pulled down his pants and then his boxers. Out sprang Momma's love handle. Mmm, mmm, mmm, I've got to say, for a short, skinny man, my husband sure was packing. I looked down at it, then smiled. "Mmm, chocolate. I love chocolate." And on that note, I fell to my knees, let my bag slide off my shoulder, and got to work trying to find out how many licks it took to get to the center of my husband's Tootsie Pop.

About five minutes later, my mission was accomplished. I'd revived my husband's memory of exactly who I was and what I could do. Tim was grinning from ear to ear as he pulled up his pants—and not a minute too soon, because just as I reached for my bag to reapply my lipstick, the doorbell rang. The first thought that came to my mind was that it was probably my mother. She was always on time, while the other members of my book club were usually fashionably late. I don't know who came up with the phrase "CP time," but whoever it was sure knew what the hell they were talking about. You couldn't get six black people to all show up on time if you were handing out hundred-dollar bills.

Tim finished buckling his pants, then went up front to answer the door. I finished reapplying my makeup, then followed him. Just as I suspected, it was my mother ringing the bell. My mother wasn't an official member of our book club, but she never missed a meeting or a chance to take home a week's worth of leftovers for my brother and stepdad after the meeting was over. Truth is, the only reason she wasn't an official member of our book club was because she was too cheap to pay the twenty-dollar-a-month dues for the food and wine we served at each meeting. I loved my mom, but she was one cheap-ass woman.

My mother hadn't even gotten comfortable on the sofa when, surprisingly, the doorbell rang again. Once again, Tim answered the door while I fixed four plates of food for him and his card-playing friends. Walking through the door were the Conner sisters—my best friend Egypt and her older sister Isis. Egypt and I had been best friends since the third grade. She was probably the only woman I trusted in the world. That's why sometime before she left, I needed to ask her a very personal favor, probably the biggest favor I'd ever asked anyone.

Egypt and Isis were followed five minutes later by the two

ladies I considered to be the life of any book club meeting, my very spirited and passionate Delta Sigma Theta line sister Nikki and her crazy-ass roommate, Tiny. My husband let them in on his way out to his spades game. As soon as the door was closed and Tim was out of sight, Tiny started yelling, "BGBC in the house," then cupped her ear, waiting for our reply.

We didn't disappoint her, as a chorus of "BGBC in the house!" was shouted back at her. BGBC were the initials of our book club and stood for *Big Girls Book Club*. We had one rule and one rule only: If you're not at least a size 14, you can't be a member. You could be an honorary member, but not a member. It wasn't personal; it was just something we big girls needed to do for us. Anyway, we'd never really had to exclude anyone from our club. I didn't know too many sisters over thirty-five who were under a size 14. And the ones who I did know were usually so stuck-up I wouldn't have wanted them in my house anyway.

About fifteen minutes later, my cousin and our final member, hot-to-trot Coco Brown, showed up wearing an all-white, form-fitting outfit I wouldn't have been caught dead in. I know I sound like I'm hatin', but that's only because I am. I couldn't stand the tight shit Coco wore. And the thing I hated the most about her outfits was that she actually looked cute in them. Coco was a big girl just like the rest of us, but her overly attractive face and curvy figure made her look like Toccara, the plus-size model from that show *America's Next Top Model*. Not that I looked bad. Hell, you couldn't tell me I wasn't cute. And I could dress my ass off too. It's just that the way I carried my weight made me look more like my girl MóNique from *The Parkers*. I was a more sophisticated big girl.

Taking all that into account, some of my dislike for Coco had nothing to do with her clothes or her looks. It had to do with the fact that she was a whore. That's right, I said it. She was a whore—an admitted ho, at that. Coco had been screwing brothers for money and gifts since we were teenagers. And to make matters worse, she especially liked to mess around with married men. Oh, and trust me, she didn't really care whose husband she messed with as long as she got what she wanted. Now, if it was up to me, she wouldn't even be in the book club, but the girls all seemed to like her phony behind, and she met our size requirement, so I was SOL on that. I will say this, though: If I ever catch that woman trying to put the moves on my husband, cousin or not, she is gonna have some problems. And the first problem she was gonna have was getting my size 14 shoe out of the crack of her fat ass.

As soon as Coco entered the room, she seemed to be trying to take over the meeting before it even got started. She was stirring everybody up, talking about the book and asking a whole bunch of questions before I could even start the meeting. And when she and Isis started talking about the sex scenes in the book, I put an abrupt end to their conversation.

"Hold up. Y'all know we don't start no meeting this way." I wasn't yelling, but I had definitely raised my voice. "Coco, you need to sit your tail down so we can start this meeting properly."

Coco rolled her eyes at me and frowned, waving her hand at Nikki, who had already made herself a plate, asking her to slide over. Once Nikki moved, Coco sat down. Now all eyes were on me like they should be. I was the book club president, and this was my show, not Coco's—or anybody else's, for that matter. But she still had something to say.

"Please, Tammy, you should've got this meeting started the minute I walked in the door, because this book was off the damn chain." Coco high-fived Nikki.

"I know the book was good, Coco. I chose it, didn't I?" I know I probably sounded a little arrogant, but I couldn't help it. Ever since we were kids, Coco was always trying to take over shit and get all the attention. "Well, once again, here we are. Before I ask my momma to open the meeting with a prayer, I just hope everyone enjoyed this month's selection as much as my husband and I did."

Egypt raised her eyebrows, then said, "Wait a minute. Tim read this book?"

"No, but he got a lot of pleasure out of the fact that I did. Can you say chapter twenty-three?" I had to turn away from them I was blushing so bad.

"You go, girl," Isis said with a laugh. "I ain't mad at you."

"Let me find out you an undercover freak," Coco added.

"What can I tell you? The story did things to me. It was an extremely erotic read." Everybody was smiling and nodding their heads.

"It's about to be a helluva lot more erotic in here if you get to the point and start the meeting," Coco interjected, then turned to my mom. "I don't mean no disrespect, Mrs. Turner, but we're about to get our sex talk on."

"Well, then let's bow our heads, 'cause this prayer is about the only Christian thing we're going to talk about tonight. Forget chapter twenty-three. Can you say chapters four and seven?" my mother said devilishly, right before she bowed her head to begin our prayer. From that point on, I knew it was gonna be one hell of a meeting, and Tim would appreciate it later when he came home and found me more than ready for round number two.

2

COCO

The alarm on my cell phone rang, and I reached down as fast as I could, trying to silence it. By the time I stopped Chamillionaire's "Ridin' Dirty" ring tone from waking him up, I realized I had to pee. I tried to lie still and hold it, hoping I could get five more minutes of sleep, but the pressure on my bladder wouldn't let me. Besides, I knew I had to get up and outta there before he woke up. The last thing I wanted to do was talk to him now that the fun part of the night was over. Talking led to lies, and lies only led to me getting pissed off. Nobody wants to get pissed off after getting laid. So, the pressure from my bladder just made getting out of bed a little more urgent. I sat up and yawned, then stumbled through the dark hotel room to the bathroom—a reminder of the six apple martinis I drank the night before. Also reminding me of the martinis was the blaring hangover that was starting to take over my head.

Making my way into the bathroom, I sat down on the toilet without closing the door and quickly relieved myself. It felt like I peed forever. I sighed in relief. It's unbelievable how a simple bodily function like urinating can feel so good. When I finally finished, I looked in the mirror, but I couldn't see a thing, so I closed the bathroom door and flipped on the light switch. The light was like a thousand needles in my eyes, and I quickly covered my face with my arms. When my eyes adjusted to the light, I had to admit, I was embarrassed at what was staring back at me in the mirror. My weave was matted and looked like something the cat dragged home. My makeup and lipstick were completely gone. Good thing I was blessed with a pretty face, or I'd probably be looking like something out of that movie *Night of the Living Dead*.

I stared at my DDD-cup breasts, cupping them with both hands as I questioned myself, *Have they sagged?* I took a deep breath, making them appear even larger, and shook my head, dismissing the idea as fast as it had come. No, they weren't sagging; they were perfect. No saline, no silicone, no implants of any kind whatsoever—just me, one hundred percent me. I released my breasts, turning to the side as I placed one hand on my stomach so I could get a glimpse of my other great asset—my perfectly round booty. Whenever I walked down the street, all eyes were on me. I have what most guys would call a ba-dunk-a-dunk, and I used it and my titties to my advantage every chance I got. Every shirt, sweater, dress, skirt, and pair of pants I wore had been purchased just to show off my breasts and booty. There are women out there who would pay good money to have a figure like mine. Yes, there was no denying I was a thick sister with some weight on my bones, but ask any man with a pair of eyes and a dick swinging between his legs if my weight was a problem, and I could guarantee you he'd say, "Hell no!"

Shutting off the light, I opened the bathroom door and headed back into the room. I walked over to my side of the bed, searching for my personal belongings. When I had everything I came with, I started to get dressed. John was now spread out, snoring lightly and taking up most of the bed. It didn't matter, though. He'd done what I'd needed him to do, and it was time for me to go home.

I'd met John last night in the bar at the Brooklyn Marriott. I'd gone there after my book club meeting, looking for exactly what I found—free drinks and some good out-of-town dick. The only reason I'd chosen John was because he was the only man in the bar who wasn't old enough to be my father. He turned out to be a good choice. From the pounding hangover I had and the sense of fulfillment I felt between my legs, I can assure you he'd taken care of his business. The funny thing was that I might as well have called him John Doe, because I didn't even know his last name. Shoot, I couldn't be sure if his first name was really even John, for that matter. He'd probably be pretty surprised to find out my name wasn't really Lola.

I picked up my bag and headed for the door.

"Hey, where you going?" John's voice seemed to come out of nowhere.

I clutched my chest as I turned toward the bed because it was so unexpected. "Oh my God! You scared the shit outta me. You know that, don't you?"

"Sorry about that." He shifted in the bed. "You going somewhere?"

I nodded. "Home. It was nice meeting you."

I could see his white teeth shining in the dark shadows of the room. "Nice meeting you too."

I stepped closer to the bed. I wasn't sure if he could see me in the dim light. "Hey, do you think I could have a little help with cab fare?"

"Sure." He reached over for his wallet and pulled out a twenty-dollar bill.

Before he could hand it to me, I said, "I live in Long Island. It's gonna cost me at least sixty to get home."

He glanced at me skeptically, then reached in his wallet and pulled out two more twenties.

"I'm gonna look pretty cheap if I let someone drive me all the way out there and don't give him a tip." He frowned, then pulled out a ten. I quickly took the money out of his hand and shoved it into my bra. If he only knew I had driven my car and lived only fifteen minutes away. Hot-damn, looked like Momma was buying a new pair of shoes tonight.

"Look, can I get your number or something? Maybe we can do this again next time I'm in town. I had a great time." He rubbed his hand along my thigh.

I sat down on the bed, sliding my hand over the top sheet that covered his leg. My fingers caressed the imprint of his dick. It was warm and started to grow from my touch. I was tempted to pull the covers back and get one for the road. I could probably even get another fifty bucks out of him, but I knew if I got back in that bed, I wouldn't get out until sometime after the sun came up. I let go of that idea, along with his dick, with a quickness. I was like a vampire—I never let the sun catch me in a man's house or hotel room.

"Why don't you give me your number? The last thing I need is for your wife to find my number and start harassing me. No offense, but you married brothers be getting careless, and I don't need the drama. Been there, done that."

His smile disappeared. "Who said anything about me being married?"

I let out a long, aggravated sigh. *You see, this is the shit I be talking about. This is the reason I take everything I can get from a brother and keep it moving. 'Cause these niggas can't stop lying.*

"Look, let's get something straight. I had a good time with you last night. You're funny, and you actually made me come a few times, but, honey, don't think I don't know you're married. And don't even try to deny it."

"I have no idea what you're talking about. What would make you think I'm married?"

I swear to God that man gave me the most sincere look I'd ever seen—which pissed me off even more, so I got up and walked toward the door. "You know what, John? There's nothing I hate worse than a liar."

He sat up in the bed, trying to look insulted, even though he knew damn well he was busted. I'd seen it too many times before: It's always the biggest liars who will protest their innocence the loudest. "Who you calling a liar?"

"You, motherfucker! Ain't nobody else in the room." I took hold of the doorknob, opening the door slightly. "Oh, and marinate on this for a second. When I sat down next to you in the bar, you had a wedding ring on. Halfway through our conversation, it disappeared, so you might wanna tighten up your game next time you decide to lie to a sister."

He glanced down at his ring finger, then looked up at me silently. I could practically see the wheels turning in his pea brain, trying to come up with another lie. I just shook my head, and he finally buried his face in the pillow, his way of admitting he'd been busted.

I pulled the door open and walked out. Men were all the same. All they cared about was getting some. It didn't matter what game they had to run. Only difference now was that it was all I cared about, too, and I was much better at it than they were.

3

Isis

I could feel the temperature of my body rise and the space between my legs becoming moist when my sister Egypt turned her Honda Accord down my block. I'd spotted a light on in my apartment from the corner, which meant my boyfriend, Tony, was there. With any luck, he'd be lying naked in my bed, waiting for me. Trust me, I needed him to be there after discussing Mary B. Morrison's latest novel with my book club for the past two hours. Talk about turning up the heat! That woman knows she can write about some sex. I don't think any of us walked out of that book club meeting without the need for a panty liner and some companionship, if you know what I mean. Even Mrs. Turner, the sixty-some-odd-year-old mother of our book club president, Tammy, was talking about how she was going home to wake up her husband so she could get some tonight. She had us all cracking up when she picked up Tammy's phone and called ahead to make sure he took his little blue pill.

"Well, at least one of us is going to get some tonight," Egypt mumbled jealously as she pulled up behind Tony's truck to let me out. I felt sorry for my sister, but it wasn't my fault she didn't have a man. She'd had plenty of suitors over the years; it's just her standards were too damn high. She wanted someone with Russell Simmons's money and Terrence Howard's looks. The fact that she couldn't find him made her a very jealous and bitter woman.

I think she was under the illusion that she was still twenty-one and a size 10, when in reality she was thirty-four and a size 20. Now, there is nothing wrong with being a size 20—hell, I'm a size 22, pushing a 26, depending on what store I'm shopping in, so you know I can't talk—but my sister, although cute, still felt the need to try to compete for men with those skinny bitches. She wasn't interested in anyone but the unattainable brothers who were way too shallow to understand what a great catch she was.

Tony tried once to introduce her to his friend Greg, who ended up really liking Egypt, but Tony swore that after the way she treated his friend, he'd never do it again. My sister can be so stank sometimes. Do you know that she invited him out to dinner at some fancy restaurant one time, then had the nerve to order a two-hundred-dollar bottle of wine, a thirty-dollar appetizer, and the most expensive meal on the menu, then stuck him with the bill? The whole meal cost almost as much as he was making in a week, and let me emphasize again that she was the one who invited him to dinner.

"Why don't you call Greg?" I suggested. "I'm sure he'd be willing to stop by for a booty call."

Egypt raised her finger as if to chastise me, then hesitated for a second to give my suggestion some thought. The fact that she was even thinking about it was a definite giveaway. She wanted to get some tonight just as much, if not more, than I did. Eventually, though, she shook her head. "Nah. If I give Greg some, I'll never be able to get rid of him. The boy's cute and he's got some good *dick,* but he can't keep a good job."

I shrugged my shoulders and leaned over, hugging her tightly. "You mean he can't keep a six-figure job, 'cause Greg's got a good job; he works for the state."

"Whatever. You say *tomato,* I say *tomahto.* In the end, it all means the same thing, Isis."

"Which is?"

"That I can't mess with the brother if he can't keep me in the lifestyle I'm accustomed to."

"Accustomed to? Egypt, you live in Momma and Daddy's basement apartment."

"Yeah, but I don't pay no bills there. Girl, I need a man who can take care of me. Like Tim takes care of Tammy. She only works because she wants to, not because she has to."

Egypt was always comparing herself to Tammy and the life she led. It's actually pretty ironic if you ask me, because Tim was interested in Egypt when they first met, and she pawned him off on Tammy for his pretty-boy fraternity brother. Funny how things work out. Tammy and Tim have been together for more than ten years, and Egypt and the pretty boy ended up having only a one-night stand. Although Egypt and Tammy remained best friends, I knew for a fact that Egypt was more than a little jealous.

"See, that's your problem. You're not Tammy. Tammy and Tim have been together since y'all were in college, and way before his business took off. If you had stuck with your ex, Raymond, you'd probably be married to a CPA right now, living in that big house he got in Long Island, instead of that Spanish girl. You've got to work with a man, Egypt, not wait 'til he's made his money, then jump on the bandwagon like you was there all along."

She waved her hand at me and changed the subject. The fact that her college boyfriend was a successful partner in a CPA firm always annoyed her. "Hey, Isis, speaking of Tammy, you'll never guess what she asked me to do tonight."

"Girl, I ain't got no time to be playing no guessing games with you about Tammy. My man is upstairs, and I need to get to him before he falls asleep."

She reached out her hand and gently took hold of my wrist, stopping me from getting out of the car. "My God, will you calm down a second? You act like that man's dick is made of gold. Damn, this is only gonna take a second."

"Whatever." I pulled my arm free and stepped out of the car. Once outside, I leaned my head into the window. "Hurry up."

"Well, you know Tammy always gives Tim a birthday party every year, right?"

"Uh-huh."

"Well, she's not having a party this year. Guess what she wants to give him this year?"

"C'mon, Egypt, get to the point. I told you I ain't got a whole bunch of time. Tony is waiting." I glanced up at my apartment window, happy to see the lights were still on.

"Okay . . . okay . . . She decided to give him something a little more special. She's taking him to Hedonism in Jamaica."

I shifted my eyes. "Hedonism? Isn't that the place where everyone walks around nude?"

"Mmm-hmm."

An image of Tammy walking around a nudist colony came to

my mind. It wasn't a pretty image, so I quickly got rid of it. As a big girl myself, I'm here to tell you there are some things us full-figured sisters just shouldn't do, and strutting your stuff in a nudist colony is one of them.

"Oh my God, Tammy has lost her mind," I murmured.

"Tell me about it. And if you think that's something, girl, check this out," Egypt added. "She wants me to go with them."

"What?" I raised an eyebrow. I knew Tammy and Tim had money, but this didn't even sound right. And why the hell would they want to take my sister with them? "Go with them for what? What you gonna do, watch the kids while Tammy struts her fat ass around on the beach naked?"

Egypt tried to keep herself from laughing, but she couldn't. All of a sudden, she busted out laughing. I'm sure now she was the one with an image of her best friend walking around two or three hundred white people on the beach, naked in Jamaica. I know it sounds cruel, but I started laughing with her. If Egypt was telling the truth, Tammy had lost her mind.

When she finally stopped laughing, Egypt said, "Girl, you ain't right."

"Maybe, but what the hell she taking her big ass to Hedonism for, and why she want you to go?"

"She wants to give Tim a surprise for his birthday." She hesitated as if she wasn't sure she should tell me the rest of her best friend's secret. I knew it wouldn't last, because my sister was horrible at keeping secrets. All I had to do was give her a little nudge.

"So, what she need you for?"

Egypt looked around as if someone might hear our conversation. "Look, don't tell nobody . . . but Tammy asked me to be the third person. . . ."

I had a pretty good idea what she was talking about, but I didn't want to believe that Tammy was crazy enough to ask someone to do that with her husband. I needed to hear Egypt say the words, so I stood there quietly and waited for her to finish.

"The third person in a threesome! Can you believe that shit? She wants me to sleep with her husband."

"Stop lying," I snapped. "That woman does not want you to fuck her husband."

"I'm not lying, Isis. I swear. She even gave me the brochure. Look."

She reached into her bag and pulled out a pamphlet that looked like a page out of a porno magazine. A white porno magazine, I might add. Not one person in the brochure was black, and not one woman was bigger than a size 8.

"Now, is that some crazy shit or what? I mean, yeah, we talked about doing crazy shit like that when we were in college, but back then we were just kids. I thought she was joking. Tammy sounds serious now."

I stared at my sister in silence for a few seconds, wondering if she'd be foolish enough to go through with it. Seeing that Tammy went out of her way to get this brochure made me think she might just be foolish enough to go to Hedonism and make Egypt an offer like that, especially if Tim was pushing her to do it. She'd do anything to keep him happy. If he was my man and took care of me the way he took care of her, I'd probably do the same. I mean, Tim wasn't fly or anything, and I'm not really into thin men like Tammy, but there was something very attractive about the way he carried himself. Not to mention the fact that Tammy was always bragging about how big his dick was and telling us stories about how good he was in bed. Shit, after hearing all those stories, there probably wasn't one member of our book club who hadn't at least thought about how it would be to have sex with him. I'm ashamed to admit it, but I know I had. And I know my sister had, too, because she told me about one of her erotic dreams involving Tim. The real question was would my sister be down to make her erotic dream a reality? Would she be bold enough to sleep with her best friend's husband? I truly hoped not.

"Please tell me you told her no," I pleaded. "Please."

Egypt's face became very serious. "Do I look like a fool? That's my best friend, and the best way to lose your best friend is to sleep with her man, even if it's at her request. I'm just shocked that she would even ask me some shit like that. I can't even imagine sharing my man like that."

"I know that's right. Just the thought of Tony being with another woman makes my stomach turn." I glanced up at my apartment again. "Speaking of Tony, I've gotta get upstairs, sis."

"I know. Go, go, and get some for me."

I blew her a kiss, then waved as I made my way to the front door of my building. When I got into the apartment, Tony was sitting on the living room sofa, fully dressed, with a beer in his hand. Judging by the empty bottles on the coffee table, it clearly wasn't his first. I didn't mind, though, because when Tony drank, he was aggressive in bed, and aggression was exactly what I needed.

"Hey, Daddy," I purred affectionately in my little girl's voice. I walked over and sat down next to him. We kissed, and I could taste the beer on his tongue as he held me tightly. "Daddy, Momma's been thinkin' about you all day."

"I've been thinking about you, too, boo. We really need to talk about me moving in with you."

I kissed him and quickly changed the subject. "Well, we can talk about it later. Right now, I need you, baby. I need you inside of me." I reached down and caressed the part of him I needed most. He grinned, showing me the large gap in his front teeth, which, in some strange way, I found very sexy.

"You just can't get enough of me, can you?"

"No. I sure can't. Now give me what I need, Daddy."

Tony stood up, lifting my five-foot-three, two-hundred-forty-pound figure in the air without a hint of strain. I held on to his strong, broad shoulders. As he started to walk toward the bedroom, I could feel myself getting even moister with anticipation. The thought of his six-foot-two, two-hundred-seventy-pound-body lying on top of me, pounding me, or riding it from the back, was all I could think about. I couldn't wait to feel him inside of me.

I'd met Tony about two years ago at the Q-Club in Queens. I loved big men, so I was attracted to him right away. We'd taken it slow at first to get to know each other. As a matter of fact, we waited almost four months before we even had sex. Of course, you know it wasn't him who was holding out; it was me. I'm sorry, but I've got this thing about not giving up the goods until I'm sure a guy's committed. I really didn't expect Tony to stick around once I laid down the ground rules, but I was pleasantly surprised when he did.

Once we committed the act, it was on. It seemed like every time Tony and I saw each other, we had sex. I'd done things with him I'd never even dreamed about doing with other men. I'd never been so close to a man in my entire life. I loved Tony. We were so close that we'd actually gone engagement-ring shopping a few weeks ago. He didn't tell me when, but he was going to propose once he paid off the ring, perhaps even around my birthday.

Tony wanted to have at least three kids, and although I was thirty-six, I planned on giving him exactly what he wanted. I loved that man's dirty drawers, and as far as I was concerned, he was the only man on earth. Sometimes, I sat back and thought about my friends, who talked about how men didn't wanna help out, how men didn't wanna work, and how the ones who did wanna work were never around to romance you. But my Tony was like a magician. Not only did he work one job, but he worked two jobs. Although he didn't live with me, he still helped me pay my bills. And when it came to romance, I'm starting to think he invented the word, because my boo romanced me every chance he got—flowers, candy, shopping, candlelit dinners, and every six months we took a trip outta town. We'd been to Florida, California, down to Texas, and last spring we took a trip to Paradise Island in the Bahamas. Yeah, I had the perfect man, and in the next five minutes, the perfect man was about to make love to me.

Tony kicked wide the half-opened door to my bedroom, then laid me down on the bed, slowly unbuttoning his shirt. I looked up at him, admiring his husky build. His golden-brown complexion was framed by soft, round features and a clean-shaven face.

"Rough, Tony. Rough. I want it hard and rough. I don't want that gentle shit tonight. I want my Mandingo warrior. Put it on me like you just got outta jail."

"Is that what you want?" He grinned, showing that gap. "You want it rough, huh? Well, get your shit off, 'cause first I'm gonna eat that pussy like I'm a caveman; then I'm gonna fuck your ass like Shaka Zulu himself."

I shuddered with excitement. "Okay, just let me run to the bathroom." He nodded. "I'll be right back."

I jumped up from the bed and hurried to the bathroom, closed the door, and took off my clothes. I wanted to freshen up, to make sure everything was smelling good for Tony, because he loved oral sex, and I loved the way he did it to me. Normally, I wouldn't be so worried about this type of thing, but I'd been doing my share of sweating during our book club discussion. I didn't have time for a shower, but a little soap and water wouldn't hurt.

I grabbed my washrag and soaped it up good, running it under my arms and between my legs. Just as I was about to put the washrag down and run back to Tony, I heard a buzzing sound. I glanced at the floor, and my pants were moving on the tile. It scared the hell outta me until I realized that it was my cell phone, which was on vibrate, and someone was calling me. I reached down and picked it up. The caller ID read PRIVATE CALLER. I figured it was my sister letting me know she got home. Egypt never unblocked her home number.

"Hello." I could hear light breathing on the other line, but the caller hesitated to answer. "Hello," I repeated. "Look, if you're not going to say anything, then I'm gonna hang up."

I was about to close the phone when a deep voice said, "Hey, Pooh."

My heart skipped a beat because I recognized the voice right away. And only one person called me *Pooh*. It was Rashad, my former fiancé and the only man besides Tony I'd ever been in love with. We'd broken up about three years ago when he got a new job working for a record label in Atlanta. He'd asked me to move down there with him, but I refused to go unless we got married before we left. I wasn't about to quit my job and pack up my entire life without a true commitment. Well, to make a long story short, I stayed in New York.

He'd recently moved back to New York and had bumped into Egypt in the city. He'd obviously run some BS story on her because she'd given him my cell phone number about a week ago, and he'd been blowing up my phone ever since. I hadn't told Tony about him being in town yet, because I knew he was gonna flip, and I was hoping Rashad would just stop calling since I wouldn't answer when I saw his number. But now it looked like he'd resorted to blocking his number to get to me.

"Rashad? Why are you calling me?"

"Because I wanna see you, Pooh. I miss you, baby. I fucked up. I know now that I should have never left without you."

Before I could respond, Tony knocked on the door. I dropped the phone on my clothes. "You all right in there, baby? It don't take this long to take a pee."

"Ah, yeah, boo, I'm fine. I'll be right out."

"Okay, but you may have to get me warmed up again. I'm starting to lose my buzz."

"Don't worry. I'll take care of that." *Just as soon as I get this other fool off the phone,* I thought.

I turned my attention back to the phone. "Rashad, I told you before—I have a man. Please don't call me anymore," I whispered.

"Pooh, you know me. I'm not giving up. I know you still love me."

"No, I don't love you, and will you stop calling me Pooh? My name is Isis." I closed the phone, knowing he was telling the truth. He wasn't gonna give up. That was one determined man.

"I'm waiting!" Tony yelled from the bedroom.

"I know. I'm coming, baby." I decided to turn off the phone completely. If I knew Rashad, he'd definitely be calling back later. To tell you the truth, I wasn't even horny anymore. I was too concerned about how I was going to avoid Rashad and the drama I knew he was about to bring into my life.

4

Nikki

We were halfway through a rerun of *Girlfriends* and a bucket of fried chicken when the doorbell rang. I'd never seen this episode, so I didn't budge, but my girl Tiny got up from the sofa, peeked through the peephole, then glanced back at me. I knew who was there just from the look of frustration on her face. Her response confirmed it.

"It's that son of a bitch, Dwayne," she growled.

I took a long, deep breath, shifting my body on the sofa in agitation before speaking. "I knew he was gonna pull some shit like this. Why can't these stupid-ass men ever do what's right? He was supposed to pick up DJ last night before we went to our book club meeting." I sighed. "Go on and let his ass in."

Tiny hesitated and the doorbell rang again. "I don't know why you put up with this nigga's shit, Nik—"

I glared at her, quickly hushing her. "Don't, Tiny, okay? Just don't, aw-ight. I don't wanna hear it. I told you that's my baby's father. He has a right to see his son, no matter how trifling he is, so just open the damn door."

Tiny pouted but did what I asked, unlocking the dead bolt and opening the door. A few seconds later, in walked Dwayne Washington, my ex-boyfriend, my baby's daddy, a wannabe thug, and quite possibly the finest man I'd ever seen. Dwayne was six foot five with a very slim build, a baby-smooth bronze complexion, and a dick that sometimes appeared to be as long as my arm and as thick as my pudgy wrist. Oh, and Lord have mercy, did he know how use it! There was a time when I would have let him make love to me in the middle of Times Square on New Year's Eve for the entire country to see. But those days were long gone. Now the only thing he could do for me was kiss my black ass and take care of his son, 'cause I hated him. Let me reiterate that one more time, just in case I didn't make myself clear. *I hated him!!!!*

Dwayne glanced at Tiny, then shook his head, obviously disgusted by her mere presence. When he walked toward the sofa, Tiny began making faces behind his back like he was a punk. I had to look away just to keep myself from laughing in his face. Dwayne and Tiny had never gotten along. They'd actually had a couple of physical confrontations. To be quite frank, from what I could see before the fight was broken up, Tiny had won every time. Don't let her nickname fool you. Tiny wasn't tiny at all. She was a five-foot-eleven, two-hundred-fifty-five-pound bruiser who could smack fire out of you without even thinking about it.

"Where's DJ?" Dwayne demanded.

"Where's DJ?" I repeated his words with attitude, sucking my teeth for good measure. "I don't know, Dwayne. Wasn't he supposed to be with you?" He rolled his eyes at me. "Oh, that's right. Your sorry ass didn't pick him up last night, did you? You know that boy wouldn't go to sleep the entire night because you told him you'd be over here to pick him up after school. I even had Mrs. Simpson watch him over here while I was at my book club meeting, just in case you came by to get him. What kind of fucking father are you?"

"Don't start, Nikki. Don't even start. Just get my son ready to go." He folded his arms. "Besides, I sent you an e-mail."

I jumped up from my seat and quickly pointed my finger in his face. "An e-mail? Motherfucker, you know I don't check e-mail unless I'm at work."

Dwayne swatted my finger out of his face. "Get your fucking finger out my face, Nikki, before I break it off." I was about to put my finger farther in his face, but I could see Tiny sneaking up behind him, and if I didn't back off in a few seconds, we'd all be on the floor fighting, and that was the last thing I wanted to do with my son in the house. I may hate Dwayne, but my son loved him. Last time Tiny and Dwayne got into it, DJ didn't speak to her for three weeks and kept insisting that he wanted to go live with his father.

I lowered my hand and sat back on the sofa, giving Tiny the eye to back off. Unfortunately, I'd also alerted Dwayne that Tiny was behind him.

"What the fuck?" He turned toward Tiny, lifting his fists. "I know you ain't trying to sneak me, you fat bitch." Tiny just smiled, and I could see the concern on Dwayne's face as he glanced back and forth between the two of us. He knew Tiny wasn't afraid of him, and I think he was starting to realize I wasn't afraid of him anymore either. Why should I be afraid of him? I outweighed his ass by nearly fifty pounds.

"You know what, Dwayne? I've got a good mind not to let DJ go with you."

"Fine with me. I didn't really wanna sit through no damn baseball game anyway. That was your idea, remember?" Then he smirked. "I hope you have a good time explaining all this to DJ, though."

I was about to get in his face again, but just then, DJ ran into the room. "Daddy, Daddy, Daddy!" He jumped up into Dwayne's arms, kissing his father on the cheek and hugging him tightly. "You still gonna take me to the Mets/Yankees game on Saturday?"

Dwayne glanced at me. "I got the tickets right here," he said, patting his pockets. "But it doesn't look like your mother wants you to go with me for some strange reason. Isn't that right, Nikki?" My son's head swiveled toward me, his eyes looking like they were about to burst into tears. "I'm sorry, son. I was really looking forward to it too."

I hated when Dwayne did that. He was always twisting my words, trying his best to make me look like the bad guy in DJ's eyes. He knew damn well I wanted him and DJ to go to the baseball game. Shit, I was the one who went to Ticketmaster and got the damn tickets. I was just trying to make a point that he needs to keep his word—if not to me, then to our son. I shouldn't have to force him to spend time with his own son. It seemed like he was more interested in spending time with me than with DJ.

"Mommy, I wanna go with my daddy," DJ cried. He was about two seconds from a meltdown, and that was the last thing I wanted to deal with.

"Okay, DJ, okay. You can go with your father. Just let me get your stuff together."

I felt like I was being played by both of them, because as soon as my son registered my words, his tears stopped.

I got up from the sofa and walked into DJ's room. His knapsack was still packed from the day before, when Dwayne was supposed to pick him up. I walked back into the living room, and Dwayne and Tiny were staring at each other like two heavyweights getting ready to battle. I stood between them and handed DJ's bag to Dwayne.

"Now, what time are you gonna have my son back on Sunday?"

"Who says I'm bringing him back on Sunday?"

"Well, we ain't gon' be here on Saturday, and he's got school on Monday, so he needs to be here on Sunday—preferably after church."

"I'll bring him here when I'm ready."

I was about to raise my finger and start to cuss, but I knew it wasn't worth the argument. Dwayne never kept DJ more than a day or two, so he'd have him home on Sunday—that I was sure of. I leaned over and gave my son a kiss.

"I'll see you on Sunday, DJ."

"Bye, Mommy."

"Aren't you gonna say bye to Aunt Tiny?"

DJ looked at his father, then glanced over at Tiny, who was standing by the door. "Bye, Aunt Tiny," he said reluctantly.

Tiny opened the door and watched my son and his father walk out. When she closed the door, I released a sigh of relief, glad to have survived one more confrontation with that loser, even if I knew it wouldn't be the last.

5

Tammy

I glanced at my cell phone for the correct time, then nodded my head with approval. 12:57 P.M. The moment of truth would soon be at hand. I picked up the glass in front of me and gulped down what was left of my second rum and Coke. I was hoping the alcohol could give me the courage I surely needed to ask my best friend for the second time in a week what most women would never ask in a lifetime. I wanted her to be the third person in a threesome with my husband and me. She'd turned me down the first time I'd asked after our book club meeting, but she wasn't gonna turn me down this time. I wouldn't let her. See, I couldn't ask just any ol' body to be all up in the bed with me and my man. It had to be someone I trusted, and there was no one I trusted more than Egypt. I knew she'd have my best interests at heart, unlike another woman who might end up deciding to try to steal my man. Not only that, but when it was all over, Egypt would have the wherewithal to keep her mouth shut about what we'd done.

I just had to explain things to her a little differently this time, make sure she understood how important this was to me. And just to make sure she agreed to my plan, I needed to explain how we could each benefit from this little endeavor. I wasn't gonna stress her too much, but trust me, I'd be damned if she was gonna leave my house without agreeing to be a part of my husband's fortieth birthday celebration.

The doorbell rang, and I was so nervous I poured myself a shot of rum and chugged it down before answering the door. Of course, I knew it was Egypt at the door. As usual, she looked great. Her hair was freshly done in microbraids, and her red dress hugged her thick curves accordingly. A great choice, I determined.

"What's up, heifer?" I greeted her playfully the moment I opened the door.

"Nothin', ho," she said with a chuckle. We hugged, then she followed me toward the living room.

"I was having a little cocktail. You want something to drink?"

"Whatchu got?" Egypt sat on one of the bar stools while I slid behind the bar.

"Wine, rum, Hennessy, vodka . . . You name it, we got it." I looked over my shoulder when she didn't make her selection immediately known. "I'm drinkin' rum and Coke," I told her.

"Ummmm . . ." She stood, with a pudgy finger tugging at her bottom lip like the decision was so difficult. That girl loved to drink, but she never knew what to order.

"Here, why don't I make something special for you?" I gave her a knowing look and smiled. "Trust me. I know you like your drinks sweet." I gave her a devilish grin.

When she smiled back, I bent down into the liquor cabinet and emerged with a bottle of vanilla rum. I placed it on the bar and reached for the bottles of rose grenadine and peach schnapps.

"Pass me that pineapple juice from over there on your right," I asked Egypt as I filled two glasses with crushed ice.

Egypt wiggled on over to the corner of the bar and gave me the juice. I mixed the perfect combination from the four bottles, added a couple of cherries, then found two cocktail straws and extended one glass to my best friend. She accepted it with a reluctant look. This wasn't something we did very often. My friend looked like she was either starting to believe I had a drinking problem, or she believed I was up to something.

"How about a toast?" I lifted my glass, hoping to lighten the mood.

She nodded slightly, keeping her eyes locked on mine like she was searching for the answer to my unusual behavior.

"To best friends," I sang. "Nothing can come between us."

"To best friends. You damn right nothing can come between us," she repeated, and then we clinked our glasses together. I smiled, bringing my glass to my lips. Instead of doing the same,

Egypt wrinkled her nose and lowered her head to sniff the drink in the glass.

"What is this? You ain't trying to poison me, are you, girl?" she asked.

"Girl, just try it," I urged, tossing her a knowing look.

Egypt took a cautious sip, then looked up at me and smiled. She pulled the glass back to her lips again. "Mmmm." She chuckled as her sips turned into hungry gulps. "This shit is good. When'd you go to bartending school?"

"See, you should trust me more often. You know I ain't gonna steer you wrong." By the time I drank a quarter of what was in my glass, she had drained her glass and placed it on the counter.

"I think I need a refill." She burped, covering her mouth but smiling the entire time.

"You lush." I shook my head and laughed. I wasn't nervous anymore. The earlier alcohol was taking effect. So this time when I fixed her drink, I decided to take the opportunity to run my request by her again. I didn't want her to have too many drinks before I talked to her, because I knew from experience that Egypt got drunk way too easily, and I wanted her to be sure she knew what she was agreeing to.

"How long have we known each other, Egypt?" I asked as I mixed her second drink.

"I don't know. Since the third grade, I think," she murmured. She was watching me like a hawk as I mixed the liquors, probably so she could make these drinks at home.

"And you know I trust you more than anyone in the world, don't you?"

"Mmm-hmm." She was still distracted by the drink I was making, so her voice was absent of any kind of suspicion of where I was going with this.

"I'd do anything for you. You know that, don't you?"

"I'd do anything for you too." She nodded. "How much rum did you put in there?"

"About two shot glasses full," I said, then stopped mixing her drink. "If you'd do anything for me, how come when I need a big favor . . ."

She lifted her head, her alcoholic trance suddenly broken. "So that's what this is all about. You're still on this threesome thing, aren't you?"

I was afraid to answer. Should I deny that's where my question was going, or just admit it and keep trying to break down her defenses?

Before I could decide, she spoke again. "No, Tammy, that's not a favor. That's crazy, and I'm not gonna do it. So you might as well forget it."

"C'mon, Egypt," I pleaded. "You're the only person I trust."

"Tammy, I'm not sleeping with your husband. It will ruin our friendship," she argued.

"No, it won't. It's not like you *want* to sleep with Tim. I'm *asking* you to sleep with him."

"The question is, Tammy, why do you want me to sleep with Tim? Is something going on between you two that I don't know about? 'Cause, baby girl, this is not a good idea." She looked frustrated, like a mother who's tired of telling her child no for the millionth time. Maybe I should have waited until she was a little more drunk before I brought up the subject.

"What's not a good idea? Having a threesome or having a threesome with me and Tim? Don't act like you never had a threesome, Egypt, because I can remember a time in college when we were on spring break when you talked me into—"

"Oh my God, I can't even believe you brought that up." She closed her eyes as if she was ashamed. "That was different. That was fifteen years ago. We were nineteen years old, just stupid kids, cut-loose and fancy-free. I don't even remember what happened that night, I was so drunk."

I smirked. I remembered. I remembered every minute of it. That was the best night of sex I'd ever had. "Want me to remind you? I can probably still find the Polaroids."

"No, no, I don't want you to remind me. I can't even believe you still have those pictures. You need to give me those before Tim finds them."

"Tim's seen them," I confessed. Well, at least he'd seen the ones of her that didn't show my face. I never told him that I'd been in a threesome before.

Egypt's face turned bright red. "He's seen them."

"Yep. That's one of the reasons I wanna do this. It's always been his fantasy to be with two women, Egypt. I feel bad that I experienced that with someone else, but I've never done it with him. Can't you understand that?"

She shook her head. "There's just something so wrong with this, Tam. That guy was just some fine motherfucker we met on spring break. We never saw him again. I mean, you want me to get down with you and your husband? I mean, daaaaamn!" she shrieked, shaking her head like she was trying to rid her mind of the image.

"So, if he were someone else, you would do it?"

She hesitated, avoiding eye contact. "Maybe . . . if he was cute."

"My husband isn't cute?"

"No, that's not what I mean and you know it. Tim's cute."

"Then what's the problem?"

"He's your husband, dammit!"

Our conversation was going in a circle, always coming back to the fact that Tim was my husband, but I wasn't giving up. I could tell I was wearing her down. When I had first presented the idea, her answer wasn't just "No," but "Hell no!" and the conversation was dead. Now she was at least thinking about it, and I could count that as progress, even if she was still protesting. I figured I could finesse a few more reasons she should help me out, but not yet. I didn't want to show my level of desperation, even though the truth was that I had become obsessed with this. I had planned it all out in my mind, every single detail of the elegant, romantic evening the three of us would have. All I needed was for her to see the light.

I finished mixing the drink, extended it to her, then yanked it back real fast when she reached for it.

"What?" She glared at me, then looked longingly at the drink.

"You want it, huh?" I teased.

"Girl, you betta give me that good drink," she exclaimed.

"I know something else that's just as good—Tim's dick."

"See, you are truly trifling," she said with a laugh. "You need to quit!"

We made our way to the den, where the TV was on but muted. I stretched out on the chaise and took a sip from my own drink.

"So, here's how it's gonna happen, and hear me out, 'cause

I'm not talking about anything tacky. Forget that Hedonism shit. We'll get a nice suite in the city, go have dinner first, even catch a show if you want. Then we take it back to the room, and we just spend some time talking, have a few cocktails; maybe I'll even pick up a bag of weed. You know what weed does to you. We can let it happen naturally," I offered carefully.

"Girl, are you crazy?" Egypt snapped. "Let it happen naturally?" she mocked me. "What the hell is natural about a threesome with your best friend and your man? Do you even hear yourself?" Egypt raised the glass to her lips again. She looked exasperated, and for a second I thought maybe I should back off a bit, but I couldn't.

A Beyoncé video came on, and we sat there looking at it in silence. I started thinking about how badly I wanted this for Tim and myself. I'd never forgotten that threesome we had had back in college. The thought of sharing a moment like that with Tim just consumed me. It was like a mountain I needed to climb. My mind strayed to the number of men who probably wished their wives would be so thoughtful. Most women would never do this for their men, too scared that another woman could come between them. But with Egypt, I knew I didn't have to worry about that. I mean, that's my girl, and I knew for sure she wasn't the least bit interested in my man. I mean, he did step to her first when we met Tim, but she passed him right along to me. He's not even her type, so that's how I knew for certain this plan was foolproof. I was not ready to give up on Egypt yet. I'd appealed to her sense of friendship, and that didn't work, so now it was time to petition to her sense of greed.

"Well, how about this. I'll pay you. I'll give you two thousand dollars," I offered.

"Two thousand dollars?" For a fleeting moment, I think the dollar amount enticed Egypt, but her expression quickly soured. "What am I, a prostitute now? Do I look like your cousin Coco? I'm not a whore, Tammy."

"I'm not calling you a prostitute. You just said the other day that you needed a couple of grand so you could get a new car since that piece of shit you been driving keeps breaking down. All I'm doing is providing you an opportunity so you can buy another one. A favor from one best friend to another. Just like I'm asking you for a favor to help me give my husband the ultimate birthday present. This is a one-time deal, Egypt. I'm trying to create memories with my husband, to fulfill his every desire. And perhaps some of mine too."

"Girl, you done lost your mind. And I need another drink." She gulped down what was left of her drink and headed back toward the bar. I followed her. "Fix me another one of these drinks." She lifted her glass.

Since my offer didn't entice her, I upped the ante. I knew Egypt had a price. Her weakness was money; it had always been money. "I'll pay you three, no five. Five thousand dollars," I said anxiously as she sat down at the bar. I slid behind it. "With five thousand plus what you can get in trade for your car, you could buy a Lexus."

Her head snapped in my direction, her eyes as big as saucers as she pulled her focus from the screen. "Lemme get this straight. You telling me you'll give me five grand to screw your husband with you?" she asked for clarification, handing her glass to me. She was on the edge of her stool by now. Finally, I thought, I had her attention.

I nodded my head. "Yes, five grand, and I'll never ask you for another favor like this again. It's five thousand dollars for one night, Egypt."

Egypt chuckled and shook her head, like she was trying to wrap her mind around me and my offer.

"Gurrl, you are too much. Just too damn much!" she declared. I watched her body language for any sign that she might be changing her mind and nearly jumped for joy when she looked up at me with a smile. It was a small smile, but it was genuine.

"So, you gonna do it?" I asked, trying to control my excitement.

Intriguing curiosity was written all over her face, although I could tell she was trying to hide it. Even without her final answer, I knew I had won her over. Images of herself in bed with me and Tim had no doubt been replaced with images of herself behind the wheel of a sleek new Lexus. That girl had wanted a Lexus ever since Tim bought me one for my birthday in 2003.

"Five grand?" she asked.

"Five grand," I confirmed with a nod.

I waited a few more seconds. One . . . two . . . three . . . then *bam!* I had her hooked. "Girl, I may feel cheap in the morning, but for five grand, I'd fuck you, your man, and your brother if you had one!"

We both busted up laughing, and my only thoughts were, *God, I love my life.*

For the next hour, we sat there talking about the fabulously romantic evening I had planned for the three of us. It started out a bit awkwardly, but the more the liquor flowed, the easier the conversation became.

"I like flavored condoms," Egypt said, now sucking on her third Pineapple Delight, the name I'd created for my cocktail.

"Okay, that'll work. Tim really likes lingerie," I said, making sure we covered every detail. "And I don't mean that stuff from Victoria's Secret either. He likes that raunchy stuff from Frederick's of Hollywood, so you and I should go shopping," I said.

"You paying for that too?" she asked.

"Yeah, girl. Why don't we just make an entire day out of it?"

Egypt threw her hands up in surrender and leaned back a bit. "Whoa! Hold up, girlfriend. If I gotta go at it with the two of you all day long, it's gon' cost you a whole helluva lot more than five grand," she informed me, slightly slurring.

"Damn, aren't you shy?" I commented. "I wasn't talking about screwing all doggone day. I meant we, you and me, could go to the spa, go shopping, you know, the works, keep us nice and relaxed. Then we could meet up with Tim later that evening for dinner and the rest," I said.

Egypt was nodding her head. "Okay, okay, I'm feeling you on that. That sounds like a plan," she said. And for the first time since the idea had initially popped into my head, I felt at ease, because the elusive third wheel had finally agreed to come along for the ride.

A while later, as Egypt started gathering her things to go, I felt all giddy inside. I was like a kid on Christmas Eve. I walked her to the door, and we experienced an awkward moment. I had already pulled the door open, but she seemed reluctant to leave.

"Okay, so you'll let me know where and when and all of that, right?"

"I sure will," I said.

"So, what should I do in the meantime?" she asked.

"Girl, you just gotta keep it cute, and I'll handle the rest," I suggested.

Just before she stepped out, she turned to me and said, "Oh, and I'm gonna need half up front."

"Of course," I said. "Actually, why don't I get my checkbook now, before you leave. I ain't got no problem with a down payment."

Once I paid her, Egypt tucked the check into her bag and whispered, "You know, Tam, I would have probably done it for four thousand." She laughed.

I laughed along with her as I thought, *I would have paid you ten thousand.*

Hedonism was out, but a trip to Frederick's of Hollywood and the Marriott downtown was almost certain. Now that that was done, all I had to do was talk my husband into it.

6

Coco

My thighs were burning, my chest was on fire, and sweat was pouring from my body like a waterfall. I was on the butt-and-thigh-shaper machine, and my level of intensity had me pretty damn near a heart attack. But I knew I had to do what I had to do to keep this body of mine as tight as possible. The older I got, the harder it was to keep my weight under control, but I was determined to do it. I wasn't like most women in the gym. I wasn't there to lose weight, even though most of the stares and glances I got told me people thought I should do just that. Instead of trying to drop pounds, I was just trying to maintain. The saying that inside every big girl is someone skinny dying to get out simply didn't apply to me. I loved my curves and my extra cushion. I just didn't want any more than God had already blessed me with.

I sure as hell didn't care what all these skinny girls with their flat asses and nonexistent titties thought, even though they had no shame in letting me know what they thought of my full-figured curves. Every time I walked by people in the gym, conversation ceased instantly, and I'm not talking about the guys. I could take their stares. To be honest, I rather enjoyed them. It was those playa-hating women I couldn't stand. I couldn't take three steps without scornful eyes gazing up and down my body. You might think some of them were gay the way their eyes openly lingered on my breasts and ass like they had no shame. One day it was little snide comments about how "big girls" were getting too carried away, trying to be fashionable. I just smirked and kept stepping. Then last week in the shower, I could've sworn one of 'em was eyeing my ass so hard, I started to do the booty dance so she'd know I noticed her watching me. The minute I stepped out, she and another one started whispering, and I just knew they were talking about me.

Damn! I had six more reps to go, and I wasn't sure if I was gonna make it. *Come on, Coco, work it out, girl. Work it out. Keep this booty firm.* Three, four, five, six, seven, eight, damn! My legs felt like they were gonna give up on me soon.

"Eeeeer," I groaned as I finished the last two reps in the set.

"Um, 'scuse me. Can you keep it down over there? Some of us are tryin' to work out in peace," this twig next to me snarled. What the fuck was her problem? I didn't even know her. I tried to concentrate until I realized that not only was she was talking to me, but she was staring me down too. I tossed her a nasty look and moved to the next machine.

I'd had enough of these damn skinny bitches. Okay, yeah, I might have screwed a couple of their boyfriends and husbands, but if they were taking care of business at home like they were supposed to, their men would have never stepped to me in the first place.

"Eeemmm," I moaned louder than necessary.

"Are you deaf? I asked you to keep it down. I got my iPod turned all the way up, and I can still hear your groaning," she shouted at me.

I hated when people shouted at me. My momma didn't shout at me, so I wasn't about to take it from her. I looked at her while doing my standing leg curls and frowned.

"You talking to me?" I pointed at my chest.

"Yeah, she's talkin' to you," this other wench standing behind her barked. I might not have known the first one, but I knew bitch number two, not by name but by face. Her man's name was Rodney. I'd fucked his ass two weeks ago. Matter of fact, I fucked his ass so well that he treated me to an expensive lunch and paid for my hair and nails to get done. What he shoulda done was give her a couple dollars, too, 'cause her head was looking raggedy as shit, and those nails! They looked like a blind woman did them, so I know she wasn't talking shit.

"You act like you the only one working out up in here. We get tired of hearing all the grunting and goaning coming outta you," bitch number one hissed, then rolled her eyes at me. "It ain't burning that damn much. You just trying to get some attention."

"Maybe, but I pay my membership fee just like everyone else.

And I don't hear you or anyone else complaining when the guys are making the noise." I shot her skinny ass a we-can-do-this-right-now look, and she backed down right away. By the time I looked over at her friend, she had moved on to the nearby Stair-Master. Scared-ass bitches. I shook my head, chuckled, and continued my workout.

When I finished working out, I figured it was time to shower, change, and get my groove on. Oh, and I was determined to get my groove on with Rodney, skinny bitch number two's man. He and this overly muscle-bound brother behind the front desk were flirting with me before I entered the locker room. I was gonna get Rodney to take me to a nice restaurant, and if he promised to get my hair and nails done again, I'd reward him later by squeezing his head between my thighs. The boy gave excellent head.

I didn't want to take all night, so I quickly showered, gathered my things out of my locker, and was about to head out to find Rodney when a voice stopped my steps.

"Coco?" a very unfamiliar female voice called out to me. I didn't have a single friend in this gym, so I wondered who could be calling me and what the hell she wanted.

"Who wants to know?" I turned to find bitches number one and two looking at me. Bitch number one stepped to me like she didn't realize I was three times her size. She confirmed my belief that the smallest ones always barked the loudest.

"I don't 'preciate you flirting with my man. You need to step off!" She was talking with her hands.

I chuckled. She couldn't be serious. I had no idea who her man was. I'd been flirting with her friend's man, Rodney. It wasn't the first time I had been accused of flirting with some man who hadn't even registered on my radar, and this time, I had no idea who they were talking about. Like I said, I'd been flirting with Rodney.

"One of these days, you gon' fuck with the wrong one, and you not gon' get no friendly little warning," her sidekick, Rodney's girl, bitch number two, tossed in.

Normally, I would've just brushed that off and gone about my business. But when I turned to leave, additional words from bitch number one stopped me. "Besides, everybody knows you ain't nothing but a cheap, two-bit ho." She said it just as easily as if she was complimenting me on my outfit.

"What did you just call me?" I asked, unable to understand why these two were fucking with me.

Now her head started moving as her neck twisted, and her hands flew to her hips. "It don't make no sense how you be parading around here in your tight, coochie-cutting shorts and your titties damn near flopping out them barely-there tank tops. Haven't you ever heard of a goddamn sports bra?" she hissed.

That's when I realized this was nothing but tittie envy. I had more than enough to give them both some and still have plenty left over. Then there was my most bodacious booty, which I was certain didn't help matters any for the haters.

"Baby, this is a sports bra, so don't get it twisted," I corrected, sticking my triple Ds out for them to envy even more. They both looked like lifelong members of the itty bitty tittie committee. "And why y'all concerned about my titties any damn way? I don't even swing like that."

The more I looked at bitch number one—a short, rail-thin girl, flat in the front and back—the more I understood why her man would want me. Her sidekick was curvy, but in all the wrong places. She looked like an oddly shaped water buffalo with wide, thick shoulders; round midsection; and bird legs. Some people were beyond workouts, and she was definitely one of 'em.

"Keyshawn, you betta than me, girl," Rodney's girl stated. "If I knew some hoochie was pushing up on my Rodney, oh, it would be on for real!" she said, her eyes rolling up and down my body. If that bitch called me a hoochie one more time, I swear to God I was gonna tell her more about her man's dick than his doctor could.

"Look, I'm not the least bit interested in your man, whoever the hell he is," I said to Keyshawn, figuring her man must be the muscle-bound brother at the front desk with Rodney.

"You liar." Keyshawn's head snapped toward her friend. "Charmaine, tell me what happened again?" She turned her evil eyes back to me.

"I know what I saw, and as God as my witness, before she switched her big behind up in here, she stopped at the counter, leaned over, damn near knocking David in the head with those watermelons, and was all smiling up in his face. I think she might have even given him her phone number." Charmaine finished her report with a slight nod in my direction, like that was indisputable evidence because she said so. Guess she didn't notice that while I was leaning over the counter, her man's hand was feeling all over my ass.

"What did you say his name was?" I asked, my eyebrows up as my brain started working.

"His name is David Jackson. You know, as in David, the guy who owns this joint."

"Really?" I moved closer to her, then said, "Hmmm, David Jackson, huh? He's the big guy, right?"

"Mmm-hmm. That's him. Like you didn't know."

"No, actually, I didn't know. And I definitely didn't know he was the owner. I just thought he was a clerk or the manager. But that's cool 'cause it wasn't him I was flirting with." I stepped a little closer to her and pointed at her friend. "I was flirting with your girl Charmaine's man, Rodney. I guess now's as good a time as any to let her know I've been sleeping with him for the past month."

"You ain't messing with Rodney!" Charmaine shouted angrily. But I could tell from her expression that it wouldn't take much to convince her.

"If you say so." There was sarcasm all up in my voice. "But I don't know how you deal with his uncircumcised dick. I mean, I wouldn't even suck it."

I guess that was enough to convince her, because she stormed out of the locker room like a woman on a mission. So I turned my full attention back to bitch number one, Keyshawn. "Damn, it looks like Rodney's got some explaining to do, but don't worry. You can mark my words—I will screw your man too. As a matter of fact, I will not only screw him, but I'll call you so you can hear how I make him scream! Show you what a big girl can do," I blurted out. "Now, if you gonna do something, let's do it, 'cause I got shit to do. It seems my dinner partner is otherwise occupied."

I clenched both fists, taking a step closer. Keyshawn took a step back, her eyes wide in disbelief, her mouth hanging open, speechless. She didn't want any part of me.

"You'd better believe! You done fucked with the wrong one." I tossed my bag over my shoulder, grinning wickedly as I sauntered off, switching my massive behind specifically for her amusement.

7

Isis

I got up from my desk and looked around my empty work space. Everything was in order, so I was ready to go. I was one of the last people in the office, and I knew I needed to get going before Mr. Benson, the head of billing, found something else for me to do. He could spend the rest of his evening in the office if he wanted to, but these cheap-ass lawyers we worked for didn't pay salaried employees overtime, so I was outta there. Some of us had lives. I flicked the billing department phones over to our after-hours answering service, grabbed my purse, and headed for the elevator.

On the ride down the elevator, I wished I'd called my sister or one of the girls from my book club to meet me for happy hour or perhaps even dinner. A couple of drinks and some good food would have been right on time, especially since I wasn't supposed to see Tony until tomorrow. It was my own fault because I was the one who set up the rules with Tony—rules I believed would make me more desirable as a potential wife. You know the old saying, "Why buy the cow if you're getting the milk for free?" Well, nothing was free with me, so there was no casual hanging out without notice, no booty calls at two in the morning. When we saw each other, it had to be planned, or at least a phone call a few hours in advance, and tonight was not a planned night. Our next date was set for tomorrow night. Occasionally, Tony was allowed to spend the night at my place, but never, ever two nights in a row. These rules were designed to make me just slightly unattainable to him. I wanted him to get the message: If he wanted all of me, he had to marry me. Only problem was that the rules left me lonely some nights, wishing I could break them and call Tony for some on-the-spot lovin'. I hated going home alone to my boring, empty apartment.

I frowned. Who was I fooling? I should have stayed upstairs with Mr. Benson. I didn't have a life. I wouldn't have a real life until I married Tony and we started our family.

At the front of the building, I fumbled in my purse for my Metro Card as I went through the revolving door. When I looked up to exit, I stopped dead in my tracks. There was no way for me to avoid him because he—he being my ex, Rashad—was standing there blocking my path.

How the hell did he find out where I worked? I knew the answer before I even finished the thought. My sister must have told him. Egypt was always getting involved with shit she had no business getting involved in.

"Hey there, Pooh Bear. You're looking good." He smiled as I approached, like I should've been excited to see him. I hated to admit it, but he was the one who was looking good in his designer suit. Rashad was stop-and-stare gorgeous. He may be short, but he had a thick, husky body with extremely square shoulders, like a football player. I couldn't speak for anyone else, but football players turned me on, especially those big, rugged linemen. Both Rashad and Tony had been linemen back in high school and college.

"My name is not Pooh," I stated. I tried to walk around him, but he wouldn't let me pass. "What the hell do you want, Rashad?" I snarled.

He stared at me, then stuck out his tongue, making a face that made me laugh. I hated when he did that, because it always had the same effect on me. It broke my concentration even when I was mad, and despite how hard I fought it, I always seemed to laugh. How could my mind betray me so easily, especially now? I shook it off and threw him my best don't-fuck-wit'-me glare.

"Awww, c'mon now, Pooh Baby. Now, you know you ain't gotta act all like that." He was speaking to me in this sexy-ass smooth tone as he took hold of my arm. " 'Sides, you far too cute to be frowning up all like that. You and your sexy self."

It took a second for me to realize that I was falling for his shit. As much as I hated to admit it, the look he was giving me had actually taken my breath away, as images flooded my mind of the great sex that used to follow this type of flirting from Rashad. I had to put a stop to this quickly. I pulled my arm free, rolling my eyes at him to let him know I wasn't tryin' to hear nothing he had to say. Rashad was a smooth talker who had a way of making everything sound good. I swear that man could sell ice to an Eskimo. I had to keep my wits about me, otherwise I'd fall right into his trap.

"I repeat, what the hell do you want?" I hardened my tone to convince him—or was it myself?—that my attitude was not just an act.

"I know you don't wanna see me," he said, laying it on thick, batting his incredibly thick eyelashes as he spoke. "But I really need to talk to you, Pooh."

"What you need to do is get out of my way before I call the police on your ass," I snapped. If I could just keep this attitude up until I got away from him, I'd be fine.

"Damn, girl, you still ain't nothin' nice, are you?" He smiled playfully, staring at my breasts. "And mmm-mmm-mmm, you sure have been taking care of yourself. Your titties look like they got even bigger. Shit, why don't you turn around so I can check out that banging ass of yours? You know I always loved your ass."

His smirk was sexy, and the way he talked was actually a turn-on. I tried to convince myself that he was disrespecting me, but deep down inside, I knew Rashad, and he meant every word as a compliment. Damn, why'd he have to be so fine?

But he had to be up to something, and I wasn't in the mood to fall for no okeydoke, not with Tony on the verge of proposing. Jesus Christ, if he knew I was talking to Rashad, he'd kill me. Finally, as Tony entered my mind, the reality of this situation hit me, and guilt set in.

"You need to move," I said as he continued to praise the shape of my behind. "I need to get out of here, and I can't with you standing here." My words were direct and firm, and this time it was no act.

"C'mon, Pooh. You ain't seen me in a long time. Why you gotta be all nasty and shit?" He lowered his voice down to that whisper he knew always made my knees weak. And I'll be damned if this time was no exception. My attitude was forgotten just that quick, and the sex-scene memories flooded my imagination again. Those images actually gave me goose bumps on the back of my neck.

Why was I so damn weak? Did I tell you he was stop-and-stare gorgeous? I could get lost in his green eyes. Man, if I was single now, we'd be halfway to a hotel.

I sighed and threw one hand to my hip in a weak effort to regain my resolve. "How'd you even know where to find me?"

"Oh, Pooh, you know you can't hide from me," he said with a grin. God, he was making me sick with that perfect-ass smile of his. I think he knew it was working on me, and he was loving it. I frowned at him.

"You been talking to Egypt, haven't you?"

"All it took was lunch and a new Coach bag," he bragged. "Besides, your sister knows how much I really care about you, so she didn't mind giving up the info."

I shook my head and tried to brush past him, but he was still blocking my path. I couldn't wait 'til I caught up with Egypt's ass.

"Look, Rashad, what do you want? I done told you a million times, I already got a man. Remember? His name is Tony, and Tony is very good to me. He's loyal and not afraid of commitment, like someone else I know."

"I'm not afraid of commitment anymore. I know what I want."

"Too little, too late. If that was the case, you should have married me three years ago, and we wouldn't have this problem."

Rashad grabbed me, and before I could stop it, his mouth was covering mine and our tongues were having a wrestling match. I actually let myself enjoy it for a few seconds before I jerked away from him and struggled to regulate my breathing. I rubbed my lips with the back of my hand, trying to erase the violation in more ways than one.

"Does Tony make you feel like that?" He was so cocky.

"You motherfucker. I swear to God, if you ever disrespect me like that again, I'll have you arrested for assault," I threatened, knowing just how ridiculous I sounded. After all, there was no way I could deny I had enjoyed it just as much as him for a second. And Rashad knew this. What he didn't know was that I had to practically bite my tongue to keep myself from answering his question. The truth was that as much as I loved Tony, no one had ever made me feel as sexy as Rashad.

"Hold up. I wasn't tryin' to disrespect you. I was trying to show you how much I love you."

I couldn't even look him in the eyes, afraid I wouldn't be able to hide what I was feeling. And at that moment, I didn't even quite understand what I was feeling. With a sudden desperate need to escape this dangerous situation, I forced my way around him and headed down the street toward the subway.

"Yo, hold up now, Isis," he called after me. Rashad jogged to catch up and began walking alongside me. He'd called me Isis this time, which told me he'd taken my threat seriously. All I could do was hope that when I got down to the subway, he wouldn't have a Metro Card.

"Just hear me out," he begged. "That's all I want. I just want you to hear me out. It doesn't cost you anything to listen."

"Rashad, we're over," I said without slowing my pace. "What could you possibly have to say to change that?"

"Just have dinner with me and find out."

I looked in his direction and rolled my eyes. I didn't have time for his foolishness. I knew Tony would be calling me soon. The longer I spent with Rashad, the more blurry the line would become, and I didn't need any more drama.

"You gotta eat, right? Your sister told me your man wasn't coming over tonight."

I was gonna kick Egypt's ass for sure now.

"Why not let me pick up the tab? That's all I'm asking. If you have dinner with me this one last time, I swear, I won't sweat you anymore."

I stopped walking and turned to him, staring at his pretty face while I struggled with my conscience.

"C'mon, you know you want to. It's just dinner. What are you afraid of?" He smiled. I decided at that moment that I needed to have a serious talk with myself some other time, because the craziness that was going on inside me made no sense. Why did my coochie tingle when he looked at me like that? Then when he smiled, my knees acted like they were going to give out on me. And were those butterflies making my stomach churn? I was too through with myself.

"I promise, just dinner, no strings attached. And besides, I'm sorry about what happened back there. I know you didn't really wanna kiss me, but something just came over me. I started thinking about the old days. How much I miss you. I was wrong, and it won't happen again."

His voice was sincere. Almost too sincere. What was he up to? Oh, who was I fooling? I knew exactly what he was up to. But would it be all that bad to just have dinner with him? If that's what would get him to leave me alone for good, shouldn't I just go ahead and get that over with? He could try all he wanted, but he would never convince me to leave Tony for him. So it was harmless to go to dinner with him, I decided. Besides, I didn't want to go back to that lonely apartment—not yet, at least.

"Just dinner?" I asked. We had started walking again. This time my pace was slower, more like we were enjoying a stroll.

"Just dinner," he promised.

"I swear if you try anything, I'm walking out. Just dinner!" I emphasized with the point of a finger to let him know I meant business.

The first time my cell phone rang, Rashad and I were stepping off the subway after deciding we'd go to B. Smith's for dinner. I looked down and swallowed hard when I realized it was Tony's number blinking back at me. I told myself I'd call him after a while. Now was not a good time. I didn't feel like making up a lie, especially in front of Rashad. If he saw me lying to my man, it might encourage him, and I definitely didn't want to do that.

Sitting across from Rashad was like déjà vu. B. Smith's used to be our spot when we were together. Even now, looking into his eyes brought the memories rushing back, so I scanned the room and only pulled my gaze back to him when I absolutely had to.

"You still like massages?" he asked out of nowhere.

I raised an eyebrow, prepared to protest his attempt to steer our innocent dinner conversation toward his true goal, but I was interrupted when my purse began to vibrate. I pulled my cell phone out and saw that Tony was calling again. I ignored it. I tried to hide the worry lines that I was sure would soon make their way to my forehead.

"What'd you say?" I asked, my agitated state clear in my tone. The problem was, I didn't know if it was Tony's calls or what I was feeling as I sat across from Rashad that was irritating me most.

"I wanted to know if you still enjoyed massages. I took a class while I was in Atlanta." He seemed proud of himself. What the hell was he trying to do to me? Rashad used to give the best massages when we were together, so the thought that he had some training was just tempting me even more.

"You took a class?" He made me so sick. If it was even possible, Rashad seemed to get sexier by the second. This was a bad idea, a very bad idea.

As we ate dinner, I struggled to pull my eyes away from his pretty lips as they parted to allow his fork inside. Oh, how I wanted to be that fork, or even the glass that had the privilege of touching his lips. After we broke up, I had struggled so hard to forget about Rashad, and it was truly embarrassing just how fast my feelings were returning by simply being in his presence.

"Whassup?" Rashad sat staring at me. His face told me I might have missed a question while daydreaming about his lips and the things I could do with them.

"Uh-huh," I said, shaking the thoughts from my mind.

"Uh-huh what?" he asked.

"I'm sorry. What did you say?"

"I asked if Tony knows how to hit and caress your spot," he said easily.

I started fuming. While Tony was good at taking care of my needs, Rashad used to do it like he was working to perfect his craft. Oh, I missed feeling his touch, but I knew and understood that Rashad's touch came with a price. And although Tony's skills in the bedroom might not have been as polished, he was good to me and good for me.

"He does just fine, Rashad. Besides, hitting and caressing my spot isn't what a relationship is about. I love Tony, and we're getting married soon."

When the phone rang again, the number was from my apartment, which meant Tony was there. My heart started beating a little faster. I knew I had to take the call. I pushed my chair back from the table and rushed to the back of the restaurant without a word to Rashad. By the time I arrived at a quiet area, I pushed the TALK button fast enough to snatch the call before voice mail kicked in.

"Tony? Hey, babe, how are you?"

"Where are you? And why ain't you been answering your phone? I've been worried," he said suspiciously.

"Oh, babe, I'm sorry about that. At the last minute, Mr. Benson, my supervisor, called this after-work meeting at a bar." Why did I say that? Who the hell has a meeting at a bar? God, I hated lying; it just created another lie.

"At a bar?" Tony questioned.

"Yeah, I'm tryin' to get outta here as quickly as I can."

"Okay, then, why don't I come and meet you? What bar you at?"

"Oh, baby, now, that's okay. No need. We're about to leave anyway," I said, hoping to wrap up my conversation.

"Call me before you leave," he said.

"The minute I walk out the door," I promised.

It was all I could do to hang up the phone and rush back to the table. Even from the back, Rashad looked good. I needed to leave before I did or agreed to do something I'd later regret. I walked up to the table without sitting down.

"Everything all right?"

"I gotta go home. Tony's waiting."

"But we haven't finished dinner."

"Yes, we have. Rashad, I don't ever wanna see you again. I love Tony, and he deserves better than this."

I started to walk away, but he grabbed my wrist. "You deserve better than this, Pooh. I thought you said he was going to marry you."

I glared down at him. "We are getting married."

"So, where's the ring? I don't see any ring on your finger." We both glanced down at my finger.

"That's none of your business." I pulled my arm free as I walked away. I kept telling myself how much I loved Tony and how wonderful he was and how good he was to me and for me, but a small voice in the back of my mind announced the truth that my ex was definitely a force to be reckoned with, and being around him was not a good idea. It was time Tony and I had a talk.

8

Nikki

I woke up to kisses on my thighs, but I never opened my eyes. I just savored the warmth and wetness of each kiss, along with the erotic sound they made as they came closer and closer to the triangle between my thighs. Have you ever listened to the sound a kiss makes? It can be as erotic as anything you can see with your eyes. The closer the kisses came to their final destination, the more excited I became. My clitoris was starting to throb, and my lips were moist and quivering with anticipation. Foreplay was fine, but sometimes my body just needed to be touched in the right place at the right time, and this was that time. No longer able to hold back, I cradled the skin-faded head, guiding those sweet kisses exactly where I wanted them. I was now a slave to those glorious lips and that tantalizing tongue. I gasped, letting out soft moans that would soon be a chorus in my song of orgasm. The pleasure I was experiencing was so good to me that if there was a heaven, I was truly in it.

When my orgasm subsided and my body was finally mine again, I opened my eyes, still out of breath. Tiny was gazing back at me, looking more like an eighteen-year-old boy than the thirty-three-year-old woman she was. She slowly climbed up the bed, kissing me gently on the lips.

"I love you, Nikki," she whispered, rolling me gently on top of her.

I slid down between her legs, purposely avoiding her breasts. Tiny hated her breasts, but her lower body was entirely another thing. She loved for me to go down on her. I enjoyed doing it now, but it hadn't always been that way. There was a time when the idea appalled me. Then again, there was a time when the whole idea of being in a lesbian relationship sickened me. I still wasn't comfortable with calling myself a lesbian, but after a two-and-a-half-year relationship with Tiny, reality had set in. But no matter how I had once felt about lesbianism, there was no doubt about my feelings for Tiny. I loved her, and I swear I'd never been so happy with anyone in my entire life.

I could remember a time when my life looked bleak at best. I was with my ex, Dwayne, back then. DJ was only about seven months old, if my memory serves me right. I had just accomplished the impossible; I had had my son, then bounced right back to my prepregnancy weight in no time. It's still hard for even me to believe my 200-hundred-plus-pound frame was once 132 pounds with a sexy, hourglass shape. It didn't matter to Dwayne how sexy I was, though, because things quickly turned sour between us. Once the baby was born, our relationship was straight up volatile.

I'll never forget the first time he hit me. It was a Thursday, and I was having a good day. I'd taken DJ with me to the hair and nail salon. I wanted to look good for Dwayne, because I'd just come off my period, and we hadn't had sex in a week. Now, I think I said this before, Dwayne is one fine-ass man, and I knew if I didn't keep him satisfied, there'd be fifty girls waiting in the wings to take my place. So, right before he got home, I slipped into a tight little red dress and some red heels that screamed, *I don't know what you were planning, but we're having sex tonight.* Everything was perfect until Dwayne walked through the front door, and DJ started bawling like he'd lost his mind.

"What's wrong wit' my son?" He was looking at me all skeptical, like I might have done something wrong to our child. I shrugged my shoulders instead of answering him with actual words, mostly because I didn't have an answer. My back was to him, because I was tending to the baby, trying to quiet him down.

Once I got DJ settled, I turned straight into a solid right hook. I saw stars immediately, then everything went fuzzy as I dropped to the floor with a thud. I hadn't blacked out, but with the pain I was feeling in my face and head, I kinda wished I had.

"Bitch, you answer me when I'm talkin' to you!" Dwayne screamed.

"What's wrong with you? What I do?" I lay on the floor, my head spinning, stars still blurring my vision, and my heart threatening to jump from my chest.

"That's what I wanna know. What the fuck you been doin' all damn day long? Why my son up in here screaming his lungs out? I come home and you looking all fly and shit, like you been layin' up with some nigga all day. Where the fuck that dress come from anyway?" He stood over me, kicking my midsection as I cowered into a corner, struggling to block his vicious blows.

I couldn't fathom what he was saying. Was I getting beat because DJ was crying or because I looked too good?

"Pleeeease, please!" I cried, hoping the beating would stop. But instead, my pleas must have pissed him off even more. He pulled me up from the floor and slapped me two times, then shoved me back down.

"I swear if I find out you fuckin' around on me, I'ma beat you to death," he screamed, nostrils flaring and all. And before he was finished, he went upside my head one last time. I was seeing stars and colored dots by the time he was done.

Life with Dwayne from that point on was like walking on eggshells. I never knew when his ass would snap. I was scared to talk, scared to move; I was damn near scared to breathe. I lived in indescribable fear. Because I never knew what would set him off, I tried my best not to do anything that might. When he came home, I made sure DJ was clean and quiet most days. I made sure Dwayne's food was ready, and tired or not, I gave it up without as much as a single complaint, whether I felt like it or not. It was just understood.

We lived like this, right on the edge of a possible explosion, for another few months, until I finally got tired. I had come back from the mailbox in our apartment complex while, unbeknownst to me, Dwayne had been watching me from the window. Apparently, when some guy walked by and checked out my ass, I twisted it a little too much for Dwayne's taste. Then I was supposedly eyeing up some other dude near the mailbox. By the time I got into the apartment, Dwayne was waiting for me, and so were his massive hands, which found their way to my neck.

"I can't let you out my fuckin' sight for a minute!" he screamed, veins throbbing at the sides of his head. He squeezed my neck so hard, I instantly started feeling light-headed. This was so unreal to me. I started clawing at his hands, trying to get him to loosen his grip, but the more I fought, the tighter his clutch became.

"I can't believe the way you was out there shaking your fat ass for that fool to see. You so fuckin' big now, I don't understand how any man can look at your disgusting ass!" he screamed.

I had picked up some weight. Since I couldn't talk to him, because I literally lived in fear, I'd eat to calm my nerves. I found comfort in food; for a long, long time, it was my only friend. When he and DJ were sleeping, I'd find a corner and stuff myself. I didn't dare cry because he might hear, then decide to give me something to cry about. When he left the apartment, I'd try to replay in my mind the things he'd accused me of and eat while trying to figure out how I should've handled the situation differently.

After that incident, I was beaten three more times that week alone—once for spilling something on the carpet. After he yelled and scared the living shit outta me, I dropped a plate of hot wings. Dwayne swooped up from his spot in front of the TV and drop-kicked my ass. "What the fuck you all nervous about? You must got something to hide!" he accused.

Another time, he nearly choked me with the telephone cord because he claimed I was whispering when I was simply talking to the cable company. "Who the fuck you talkin' all sweet to?" he huffed as he gripped the cord, damn near cutting off my airway completely.

The last straw was when DJ was a bit older. My son could tell something wasn't right with Mommy and Daddy. I constantly saw fear in his eyes, and the shit bothered me. This last beating happened when I was giving DJ a bath. Dwayne came busting into the bathroom like an enraged bull. I had no idea why he was kicking my ass this time, but when I raised my arm to protect my face, it sent him into a fury. He started swinging and throwing blows to my midsection.

"You raise your fucking hand at me? The only motherfuckin' hand that feeds your hippopotamus ass! You fat-ass bitch!" he screeched. By then, I had gained something like forty pounds. "And don't think I don't know you picked the fucking lock I put on the fridge," he screamed, his eyes still burning with rage.

In that moment of fear and pain, something inside me snapped and said, *Why the hell are you putting up with this shit?* That night, I crept into our bedroom, eased out some of my clothes, shoes, and other items. I pulled most of DJ's things and gathered them into two large Hefty trash bags. I hid those bags in the back of our closet and waited for the right moment. That moment came two nights later, when one of Dwayne's boys called him to go out.

"You better clean this fuckin' place before I get back," he shot toward me on his way out the door.

I did something better—I called a cab and paid the driver to take DJ and me to the women's shelter, like the caseworker at the Jersey Battered Women's center had advised me to do. We pulled up at the shelter close to 1:30 in the morning, and although I had no idea what to expect, I felt free the moment I stepped out of the cab and prepared for a life without getting my ass kicked every time his temperature rose.

That was the night I met Tiny. She was working as the guard at the door. Tiny looked like a man, although it was obvious by her huge breasts that she wasn't. Sometimes I thought she even wanted to be a man, although she denied it. But one thing was for damn sure—she didn't love like one. She had been the best thing to happen to me in a long time. Our friendship began innocently enough. She'd look out for DJ and me, bringing us all types of sweets and pies from the kitchen. When I was bored, I'd sit in the shelter lobby, and Tiny and I would talk about Dwayne and the beatings he'd given me. One day, when she up and called me beautiful, I looked around curiously, because I just knew she wasn't talking to me. Tiny must've sensed my lack of self-esteem, because from there on out, she'd go out of her way to compliment me. We quickly became fast friends, and slowly she helped restore my faith in myself. Although, I was still eating like food was going out of style.

Once I'd started getting child-support checks from Dwayne, I was scared to cash those suckers. I feared he'd be able to track me down and come beat my ass for old time's sake. By then, DJ and I had moved into some transitional apartments set up by the shelter. We were waiting on my Section 8 to come through; then I would get a place of my own. It was nothing to see Tiny hanging out, playing with DJ, who she affectionately nicknamed "li'l man," and it was even more common for her to be catering to my every need. One night, we were watching videos, and my head kept itching. It was obvious I needed to do something. If I'd continued scratching, I was sure to draw blood soon. Tiny looked at me and said, "Lemme wash your hair for you."

It struck me as an odd request at first, but I shrugged and said, "You a hairdresser or something?"

"Nah," she said. "But it's obvious it's bothering you, and I want to help make you feel better."

I had never experienced anything so sensual in my life. When she touched me, it was like electric shocks raced through my veins. We were just at the kitchen sink, but I felt something burning deep in me. I had no idea she was about to try to help me put out that flame . . . until she kissed me gently on the lips.

"You ever been with a woman before?" she asked.

I trembled as I shook my head. With conditioner still in my hair, Tiny led me to the bedroom. I turned to her and smiled nervously. Then, before I could make another move, her lips covered mine. She loved me like I was something precious and worthy of pleasure. There was nothing rough about what she did; it was sensual, almost poetic in a way. I'd had sex before, but that was the first time I'd ever made love. I felt ashamed when I realized the agonized moaning sounds were coming from me.

"I care about you so much. I've dreamed of this moment from the first time I laid eyes on you and your son," she admitted. As we lay in the afterglow of lovemaking, I really felt loved. And to this day, she'd been working overtime to make sure that feeling lasted.

Tiny and I had come a long way. I remember it took a whole year before I was even able to give her half as much pleasure as she'd given me, and never once did she complain. And now that we had been together for more than two years, there were times I could barely remember what my life had been like without her.

"I love you, too, Tiny," I whispered back as I lowered my head to show her just how much.

9

Isis

You know how they say guilt can eat you alive? When I walked up to my front door after going to that restaurant to have dinner with Rashad, I was so guilt-ridden, I could barely think straight. I had already sprayed myself with a body mist just in case Rashad's cologne was still lingering on my clothes. I'd thought up a restaurant in case Tony asked exactly where I'd been. But still, I was worried sick that he was gonna trip me up and I was gonna get caught in a lie.

When I unlocked the front door, I was nowhere near prepared for what I was stepping into. Forget about the dimmed lights; a red hue blanketed the room, and candlelight flickered all around me. My mouth fell wide open as I looked around in shock.

"Oh . . . my . . . God," I murmured.

With mixed emotions, I gazed around the room, and my heart felt heavy. I was pleasantly surprised by what I saw but was still feeling bad about what I'd done. My eyes started watering. I couldn't believe what I was seeing. When that song by Robin Thicke, "Lost Without U," came on, I felt weak in the knees. My place had been transformed into a quaint little love nest. Tony had taken it to a whole 'nother level.

A few minutes after I had taken in the scene, Tony appeared in the doorway wearing an apron, of all things. He looked sexy holding a pan in his hands. At that moment, I don't think I'd ever loved him more.

"I didn't even hear you come in." He smiled. I chuckled and put my things down near the door.

"Baby," I wailed. "You did all of this for me?"

"Why you think I was hounding you like that? I couldn't just come flat out and tell you hurry up and get your ass home. I was just trying to surprise you," he said as he placed the pan onto the table.

That's when I noticed to what extent he'd gone for this surprise. Not only had he changed out the lightbulb, but he also had a chocolate and red place setting, a small glass bowl with red roses as a centerpiece, and a bottle of wine sitting in an ice bucket.

"Oh, Tony!" I cried.

"C'mon, I know you gotta be hungry," he said.

"Oh God, you just don't know!" I lied, shaking my head. The guilt tried to creep back in, but I refused to give in to it.

Tony held up a finger. "Wait, I forgot something," he said before dashing back into the kitchen. This gave me a chance to closely inspect the table. Everything was on point. He had the red-and-chocolate-colored napkin with a matching place mat, my song on repeat, and candlelight. I wanted to kick myself for even thinking about giving up this good man of mine.

The sad thing was, I knew Tony was a good man. He may not have been able to rock my world the same way Rashad could, but he made up for his shortcomings in many other ways. Case in point, as I gazed around the gorgeous room. I counted this as another example of just how good he could be.

A few minutes later, instead of sitting across from me at the table, Tony was in a chair right next to me.

"Open up," he said as he lifted the fork of blackened catfish and wild rice into my waiting mouth.

I bit down on the heavenly food and savored every single grain of rice and piece of fish.

"Aren't you gonna eat?" I asked between forkfuls.

"It's all about you tonight, babe, besides, I nibbled while I cooked." He smiled.

I chewed and chewed, shaking my head and marveling at his culinary skills.

"Baby, everything"—I looked around the room—"everything is so beautiful. The food, oh, I just can't believe it," I said before he shoved another forkful of food into my mouth.

"C'mon, now, eat. I don't want your bathwater to get cold," he said easily, like that was just the way he rolled.

My eyes opened wide, and my face broke into a grin.

"My bath?" I asked, bewildered and ecstatic at the same time.

Tony nodded easily, as if it was just another day in the neighborhood. Talk about Mr. Too Damn Good.

"And after that, I'm going to rub you down from head to toe. I mean, it's all about you tonight," he said. I opened up wide to take another forkful.

The thing was, this VIP treatment was nothing new. Tony was so good to me, and I knew for certain that I wanted to spend the rest of my days with him. But I wanted to do it right. I had wasted too much time with Rashad only to end up empty-handed, and I damn sure didn't want that to happen again. I told myself I'd learned from that mistake and that's why I was holding out on this good man of mine. Tony would have to come correct, no ifs ands or buts about it; he had to do right by me if he wanted a future with me.

When I realized he was looking at me all cockeyed, I figured I must've missed something.

"Huh?"

"I said, are you ready to get in the tub?"

"Oh yeah," I said. He stood and pulled out my chair. When he took me by the hand and led me into my own bathroom, I felt weak all over again.

The bathroom was all aglow in flickering candlelight. Rose petals were scattered everywhere, and I could still hear my favorite song playing on repeat. Again, I gazed around the room in sheer delight and smiled when I brought my focus back to Tony.

He kissed my lips as he reached for the buttons on my shirt.

"I don't want you to lift a finger tonight. I want to undress you, wash you, then rub your body until you fall off to sleep," he said.

He unbuttoned my shirt, then removed my bra, kissing each of my nipples like he missed them terribly. Then he stood behind me, unbuckled my slacks, and allowed them to fall to the floor. I stepped out of them, and he rolled my panties off my hips and down my thighs.

"You are so beautiful," Tony said as he gazed longingly at my body. "You're so fine, from head to toe!"

When he extended a hand for me to take, I gladly accepted and stepped into the warm water.

"Aaaahhhh," I sighed, sitting down in the tub. Heaps of lavender-scented bubbles surrounded me.

Tony sat at the edge of the tub and stuck his hand in with the face towel.

"Did you enjoy dinner?" he asked.

I looked into his eyes, hoping he could see evidence of how much I appreciated what he'd done for me.

"Baby, you put your foot in that food," I declared.

"Good. I love taking care of you, you know that, right?"

"I love when you do," I said.

When Tony took the towel and squeezed it dry, then started rubbing my shoulders, I wanted to take him right then and there. I felt so good, so relaxed and so in heat.

Tony washed my back, beneath my arms and breasts, and between my thighs. Although I didn't think we'd make it out of the bathroom without something jumping off, he surprised me by keeping it clean.

He helped me out of the bath, wrapped my body in a large bath towel and dried me carefully, like he wanted to make sure he didn't miss a spot. After lotioning my body, Tony reached into a Victoria's Secret bag and pulled out lingerie he had selected specifically for our night.

"I thought you'd look good in this," he said as he pulled out the dainty outfit and held it up for me to see. It was a chocolate silk halter babydoll with a matching thong.

"That's real nice," I said, still feeling relaxed from my warm bath.

I strutted around a bit, making sure his eyes were getting their fill.

"You look so fuckin' sexy," he said as I pranced around the room. My man had planned and executed a perfect night, and I wanted to show him how much I truly appreciated his efforts.

Tony was lying back on the bed with his hands behind his head. I could see his erection from where I stood.

"Baby, if I lived here, you would come home to this kind of treatment every night," he said easily.

"Every night?" I asked skeptically.

"Every fuckin' night! This ain't shit!" Tony said.

I allowed the idea to roll around in my head for a while. Quite surely he'd get tired of doing all of this. Maybe this was just his way of luring me in; then just like Rashad, once he got me, his ass would start acting up.

"You're a queen and you deserve this kind of treatment on the regular," he declared.

His words went straight to my brain. I wanted the picture he was painting for me, but I didn't want the bits and pieces he was trying to offer. I wanted it all.

"Your life at home would be the shit if I lived here," he said, looking around the room. Robin Thicke was still crooning in the background. I felt myself getting wet. "I could take care of you the way you deserve, pay the bills, fix shit, do whatever you need done."

I wanted Tony to move in—there was no doubt about that—but I wanted him to move in as my husband. I did not want to go down the same road with him that I did with Rashad. If he wanted me, he'd have to go where no man had ever gone—straight to the altar. I was not about to accept anything less.

When I crawled onto the bed and started lathering his face with kisses, he held me up so we could be eye to eye.

"Let me treat you the way you deserve. We need to go ahead and do this," he said passionately. With the candlelight, soft music, and silk against my skin, I might've fallen for that, but I knew he needed to do more. I looked him dead in his eyes and said, "I love you, Tony, you know I do, but you know how I feel. Why would you want to buy the cow if you could keep gettin' the milk for free?"

He shook his head and sucked his teeth, but I didn't care. He knew I was telling the truth.

"I ain't trying to shack up just for sake of having a man. I done told you already, it ain't goin' down like that. If you want this, I'm gonna need a ring," I stressed.

Tony rolled his eyes and sighed.

"You know what?" I continued. "This was nice tonight, it really was, but I'm gonna need you to tell me just exactly where we stand. I'm serious; this is getting too deep." I pulled back a bit.

He grabbed me and pulled me closer. "You will have your ring soon. Believe that!"

My eyes lit up, but I tried not to show my excitement.

"You promise?" I asked cautiously.

"Mark my word. You will have your ring soon. I promise baby, I promise," he said.

10

Tammy

God, do I love my life, I thought as I walked into my bedroom, looked around, and smiled. Everything was perfect. The Godiva chocolate-covered strawberries were on a plate next to the bed. The vanilla-scented candles were strategically placed throughout the room. The silver standing ice bucket I picked up from Bloomingdales last year had one bottle of Moët in it, and I had another in the fridge. I wasn't sure how much backup I'd need. I also had sexy, slow music playing on the stereo. Last but not least, I had a small bottle of baby oil on his night table, just in case he wanted to take things in a different direction. That's right—if you haven't already figured it out, I'd do anything for my man.

I approached my nightstand to retrieve the stereo remote. Once I adjusted the music to the perfect level, I lit each of the candles, then pulled the thick drapes closed, darkening the room even more. I called Tim on his cell to see exactly how much longer I'd have to wait for him to arrive.

"Hey, baby," he said.

"Hi, you." I sighed into the phone, then paused to see if he would pick up on the vibe I was sending.

"What's wrong?" he asked.

"Just a little frustrated. You know how I get when I'm about to go on my period."

"Uh-ohhh, sounds to me like Terrible Tammy's back in town," he teased, although he wasn't far from the truth.

"Ummmm, she is, and she's been real, real naughty," I cooed. I got so horny when my period was about to come on. Believe it or not, I probably masturbated five or six times a day when I was PMSing.

"I like it when you're naughty." He sounded so sexy when he said that. I just wanted to jump through the phone and rip off his clothes.

"I know. That's why I'm calling. I wanted you to know the kids are asleep and that I'll be up in our room waiting. I need you, Daddy. I need you bad."

I could hear Tim's breathing getting heavier. Then he said, "Don't start without me. Please, don't start without me. I'm twenty minutes away, but I can make it in ten. Just don't start without me."

"I can't promise, baby, but I'm gonna try. I need you, Daddy. I need you to put out this fire between my legs."

"Don't worry. I'ma put it out. Shit, girl, you got my shit hard as steel." I could hear the excitement in his voice. "What you wearing?"

"Whatever you want, Daddy," I said.

"Surprise me." I could almost see his sexy little grin.

"Okay, then, I'll surprise you. Now let me get ready for you. I'll see you in a few."

"I'll be right there," he said before I ended the call. Once I hung up, I walked around the room, sprinkling rose petals all over the bed, floor, and furniture, then rushed to the shower. I used my Victoria's Secret blushing body wash to clean myself thoroughly. Once I was clean, I wrapped myself in a large bath sheet and lathered my skin with moisturizer. I followed up with the sparkling cream that made my plus-sized body glitter.

I thought about the things I did to spice up our marriage. I didn't want to be one of those wives miserable because all she could get was the same ole humdrum dick. Tim and I tried to keep things as interesting as possible; I bought sex toys galore, and he stayed on top of the hottest flicks. I also made sure we starred in a few of our own from time to time. We had a good, spontaneous sex life, and that's what kept us wanting each other.

Once my body was greased up and ready to go, I opened the "special" closet and ran my eyes over my various outfits, wigs, and stacked heels. I kept all of my supplies in this closet. You'd be surprised by all the kinky shit we'd accumulated over the years. I may appear to be a prudish, rather conservative woman to most of the people who knew me, but when it came to my man, I was a freak in the sheets.

"Hmm, let's see. Who's Terrible Tammy gonna be tonight? Naughty schoolgirl? Wicked streetwalker? Or maybe a dominatrix. Oh, and there's always the disobedient sex slave." I flipped though the hangers and turned my nose up at my options. No, I needed something else to drive home a point. I decided no props tonight. Tonight it would be just me and the power of suggestion. So I slipped into a silky robe and waited for Tim. In about five minutes, it was gonna be on.

The moment the alarm chirped, announcing his arrival, I poured him a glass of champagne and stepped into my high-heeled slippers. I met him at the top of the stairs.

"Oh, Terrible Tammy, you're still here," he said with a smile.

"I am." I walked over and gave him a succulent French kiss. I took his bag, placed it at his feet, and helped him take off his jacket. I handed him the glass of champagne.

"Oooh, now this is the kind of greeting a brother could get used to." He took a sip of his champagne, eyeing me lustfully from head to toe.

"You hungry, Daddy?" I asked.

"Sure I am, but not for food." The devilish grin on his face made my already wet kitty even wetter. I took him by the hand and led him into our bedroom. He didn't say a word, but I could tell he was impressed as he glanced around the room. I was pleased, but my job was just beginning.

"How about we start off with me giving you a little oral pleasure?"

"Sounds like a great place to start to me."

Tim loosened his tie as he sat down on the bed. As soft music played in the background, I lifted each leg and gently took off his shoes. I unbuckled his pants and stepped back so he could get up from the bed. I pulled down his boxers and went to work.

"You weren't kidding. You are hard as steel." I lifted my head and stared at him. Tim was moaning so loudly I decided to ease up not long after I got started. No need to end the party before it really got started. "How about we play a game?"

"A game?" He looked dumbfounded. "You were just giving me the blowjob of a lifetime and you stopped because you wanna play a game?"

"Yeah, but I think you're gonna like this game. Trust me."

"I always have." We both smiled because it was true; he'd always trusted me. And I'd never given him a reason not to.

"Take off your shirt." Tim did as he was told, and I climbed onto his lap. When I straddled him, he grabbed my hips and pulled me closer. I took hold of his dick, and in no time, I was sliding up and down on his pole, grinding as I fell onto his lap.

"Damn, girl, you're dripping wet!" He moaned softly in my ear. That was the beauty of being a big girl. We big girls always have a wet pussy. Ask any man who's ever been with a big woman. We are always wet—and surprisingly flexible.

"It's all for you, Daddy," I whispered as I quickened the pace, trying a new booty-clap move I'd been practicing with my vibrator.

"Oooooh, I swear fo' God!" he swore. "You got the best pussy in the world."

His words were like music to my ears. I grinned wickedly, moving up and down his rock-hard dick. Tim had me feeling good. It took everything I had to slow things down a bit. I grabbed his head and looked him dead in the eyes. "Tim, baby, who you thinking about?"

"Huh?" His eyes widened, and he looked at me like he didn't really understand. As if he was afraid to give the wrong answer, he said tentatively, "I'm . . . thinking about you."

"I know you are, boo-boo. But it's time to play that game I was talking about."

"Aw-ight. What you want me to do?"

"I want you to close your eyes, baby." He did, and I rocked my hips slowly. "Now I want you to tell me your fantasy."

He eased up. I was hoping he was thinking. I wanted this to go the right way, and in order to make sure it did, I needed him fully on board. "I don't have a fantasy. You're my fantasy."

"Baaaaby, stop lying," I whined. I knew he was lying, because we'd talked about our fantasies before. We'd satisfied all mine, and he'd only had one. My new mission was to satisfy his. "Seriously, Tim, I want you to share your fantasy with me. This is a role-playing game."

"You sure you won't get mad?"

Now it was my turn to ease up. I needed him to see just how serious I was. "Open your eyes for a second." He did. "I promise I won't get mad. I really want to know," I stressed. "I love you, Tim. I want to know everything about you. I wanna make your fantasies come true."

"Okay, when you say my fantasy, what exactly do you mean?"

I rolled my eyes. "C'mon, Tim. I'm serious. You know what I mean. Fantasy. What's your fantasy, sweetie? If you could fulfill your wildest sexual dreams, what would it be?"

"Hmm, well, you know I've always fantasized about being with two women." He laughed nervously as he spoke. "But you'd never agree to do anything like that . . ."

"You think so, huh? Well, if you could be with any woman, who would you choose?" He turned his dark eyes to me. "Besides me," I added.

"If I could have any other woman and still have you?" He studied my face, still probably trying to figure out if I was serious. "Honestly? You really wanna know?"

"Yes, baby." I started with the booty clap again, and Tim let out a moan. "I wanna know because I want you to pretend you're fucking both of us."

Tim's face contorted. I think my words and the booty clap had him on the verge of coming. I stopped the booty clap. Now was not the time for him to have an orgasm.

"If I could have any other woman and still have you?" He repeated his own words. "Who would I choose?"

Finally, we were on the same page. I tried to hide the smile forcing its way through, then cleared my throat. I didn't want him to think he was getting off the hook.

"Yes, and still have me, baby. Momma's not leaving you!" I rubbed my hands through the hairs on his chest. He just needed a bit more coaxing.

"Okay, well, um, well, you know I like a woman with some meat on her bones. And I hear Jennifer Hudson's in town filming a new movie, and, well, if I could still have you, I'd want her too. But I swear, babe, it's not the way I want you." He shook his head. "I mean, I want you more than I want her, but you know, if I could have her and have you, too, I'd choose her too. So, Jennifer. That's who I'd want."

Jennifer Hudson? That bitch barely weighs a hundred and eighty pounds. She don't have any meat on her bones. I sucked my teeth, trying hard to hide my disappointment.

"Not a movie star, silly. Someone we know."

He hesitated, then said, "Okay, what about Coco?" far too eagerly for me. My head snapped, and before I could control it, my neck started twisting.

"Coco!" I snarled with attitude. "Coco Brown? My cousin Coco? Of all the bitches to pick, you'd pick her? Motherfucker, is you crazy? Fucking her would put both our lives in jeopardy."

Tim closed his eyes and rubbed his face with his hands. I could feel his dick shrink inside me as he sighed. I'm sure if I wasn't on top of him, he'd be in another room by now 'cause I was hot, and he knew he'd fucked up. He'd fucked up big time.

"I can't believe you wanna fuck Coco." If I had a knife, I would have driven it right through his chest. What the fuck he want with Coco Brown?

"Baby," he pleaded, "you asked me. I didn't even want to go there with you, but you all but forced me to say someone we know. I mean damn, whatchu want me to do?" He tried to get me off of him, but I deadened my weight so he couldn't move me.

"I want you to tell me you wouldn't touch Coco's nasty ass with a ten-foot pole. That's what the hell I want!" I snapped, serving up much attitude.

"Let me up, Tammy." He tried again to no avail.

"Why, so you can fuck Coco?"

"I don't wanna fuck Coco! Why you ask me some shit like this any damn way? You knew no matter who I said, you were gonna be mad," he insisted. "That's why I didn't even wanna answer that question in the first place, but no, you insisted," he snapped right back. "This is all your fault!"

"My fault." I glared at him.

"Yes, your fault! You should have never asked me that question in the first place."

His tone and previous comment snapped me back to reality. He was right. This was all my fault. Momma always said don't ask a question if you're not ready to hear the answer.

"Baby, all I'm saying is, of all my friends, of all the people we know, you gotta understand how that makes me feel. Coco is the biggest ho we know. I mean, seriously, forget about the toxic waste stamp she has plastered on her ass; she ain't nothin' but a money-hungry hooker, straight up!" I shook my head, really wounded. I shrugged one shoulder. "I mean, what does that say about me if someone like that turns you on? I'm nothing like that ho."

"Baby, baby," Tim begged. "This ain't about you. You know I don't want Coco. I don't even want Jennifer Hudson. I only want you. You." He kissed my cheek, and I started to melt. "I only want my beautiful wife. I'm sorry if I hurt you, but you've gotta believe me. You don't have a thing to worry about."

I was starting to feel bad. I gave him a half-ass smile. "Okay."

"So, you forgive me?" he asked, giving me the same puppy-dog eyes he'd probably been using ever since he was a little boy getting in trouble with his momma.

I nodded. I wanted the truth, but not that much truth. It really disgusted me to know my husband would even think about her in that way. Coco was worse than a crackhead prostitute in my book.

"I forgive you." I eased back and let some of my weight off of his chest. "So, babe, I just would've never thought she was your type."

"She's not. You're my type, remember. I married you!"

"No, baby, that's not what I'm saying. But I am curious about something."

"What's that?" he asked cautiously, looking at me like he wasn't sure what to expect from me now.

"Well, why didn't you say, um, I dunno . . . Egypt, maybe?" I raised an eyebrow and searched his face for any kind of reaction.

"Egypt?" he questioned.

"Yeah, you know. Egypt, my best friend Egypt? She's classy, not slutty, nice, and caring. Egypt." I smiled. Just maybe I was going to get the end result I wanted after all.

Tim frowned and shrugged. He shook his head. "What difference does it make? I don't want anybody but you."

"I know. We've already gone over that, but what I'm saying is if you could have any one of my friends"—I threw up a warning finger—"Coco excluded, who would it be? Think of someone who's . . ." I shrugged. "I don't know, similar to me. Someone classy, nice, and caring. Someone who's not slutty," I added, nodding.

Tim nodded at me, too, his eyes all but studying me.

"Someone classy, nice and caring, not slutty," he repeated slowly as if he was giving the matter real thought.

"Yeah, a friend of mine," I said.

"I am not going down that road." He was adamant.

"Please, baby, just tell me. I'm not gonna get mad this time. I promise."

"No, Tammy," he stated firmly. "We are not having this conversation. My evening's already been ruined. Not to mention the fact that I'm probably gonna have blue balls when this is all over."

He sat up, motioning for me to get off him. I did, lying down next to him. The moment he eased back down in the bed, I dropped the bomb and watched it explode.

"What if I can arrange for you to have both me and Egypt for your birthday?"

I waited in silence for my words to register. Tim bolted upright in the bed. He moved back a bit and looked at me like he wanted to know what I had done with his real wife. He started shaking his head before I could even explain.

"Oh, hell no! No, I ain't even falling for this one! No thanks!"

"Baby, you don't understand. I'm serious." I tried to sound as convincing as possible.

"Yeah, I'm serious too." He shook his head vigorously. "I ain't falling for it twice. I love my wife. I love you. You're the only woman I want. Your friends are cool and all—well, not even all of 'em—but either way, I don't want no parts of this conversation. Please, I'm sleepy now. I wanna go to sleep, and hopefully my real wife will be here when I wake up."

Tim may have been trying to back out because of that little Coco blowup, but the truth was he was a man. My man, but a man nonetheless, and even if he wouldn't admit it right now, I knew he was at least thinking about it. I decided to ease up a bit. A different approach was definitely needed here.

"Hmmmph. Most men would give their right arm to have their wife suggest a threesome." Out the corner of my eye, I caught an eyebrow inching up. "But then again, I'm not sure I'd want to do something like that either if I were a man. I mean, can you imagine the pressure? You don't have to worry about just one, but two women?" I held two fingers up to emphasize my position. "I could see why you wouldn't want to do that. And let's face it. We big girls, we ain't nothing nice in the bedroom. We might hurt a skinny man like you."

He rolled over to face me and sat up in the bed. "Oh, let it be known, baby, that ain't even the issue," he declared, then grabbed his crotch. "I can damn sure handle mines!"

"Well, what's the problem, then?"

"The problem? The problem is shit like that don't always go the way you plan. Besides, you don't need none of your friends hanging around, trying to move up in here with us. That's just how sure I am of mines, so trust me, you don't wanna open that box, baby," he assured me.

"Like that, huh?" I asked, getting turned on by his cockiness.

"Shit, you know what I'm working with."

"You're right, I do, and I definitely know you damn sure got enough to feed the needy, baby."

"You damn straight I do." He grabbed his crotch again and eased back down to the bed.

When he didn't say anything else, I turned to him and said, "So, babe, what's it gonna be? Me on top while she's down below? Or how about both of us down below?"

My husband looked at me with horror in his eyes. I wasn't sure what scared him most, the picture I'd just painted, or his anticipation of how I'd react if he agreed. I eased my head toward his crotch.

"What you think? Think you can handle two?"

"Oh, I can handle two." He let out a long moan as I sucked him into my mouth. "Just let me know where I have to be. Me and Mr. Johnson here will do the rest."

I looked up at him and smirked. I loved it when a plan came together.

God, do I love my life.

11

Coco

It was that time of the month. I never looked forward to its arrival, and this month was no exception. It was time to pay the rent. I woke up to find the familiar lavender envelope on the floor by my front door, but I didn't even attempt to pick it up, because I knew it was a late notice from my bitch of a landlady, Mrs. Goldman. Damn, I sure did miss the days when her husband was alive. When he came around to collect the rent, all I had to do was explain how money was tight, offer to suck his dick if he'd cut me some slack, and he'd write me a "paid rent" receipt on the spot. I had to laugh at the memory. That old man sure used to love when the first of the month rolled around. Matter of fact, whenever I bumped into him in the hall, he loved to remind me how many days until my rent was due and tell me not to worry if I was gonna be short on it. Not his wife, though. She never gave anyone a break. If your rent wasn't in by the fifth, she'd slide one of those stupid late notices under your door at daybreak on the sixth, letting you know she wanted her rent plus an extra sixty-five dollars for the late fee.

The stupid thing was that I had plenty of money in the bank to pay my rent on time. I just hated to go into my stash to pay that old fart. Paying rent was a man's job, and even though I didn't have one living under my roof, I had plenty of them waiting to help me pay my bills. It was just a matter of figuring out who was going to get the privilege of paying my rent this month. As I dressed and rushed out the door, my mind was racing with thoughts of who I was going to use and how I was going to do it to get what I needed.

The forecast called for a sunny day, so that meant the gear I was rocking was bound to turn some heads. I was wearing a tight denim mini with fringes that sat right on my thigh. If you looked close enough, you could see my sexy tattoo that read SLIPPERY WHEN WET, with an arrow pointing toward the diamond between my thighs. The skirt was complemented by a short denim jacket that barely covered my offering up top. A pair of wedges finished off my look.

I walked out of my building soaking up all the glorious sunshine as I swayed my hips. I hadn't gone ten feet before the men on the street started catcalling and throwing out compliments.

"Bones are for dogs. Real men like meat, baby, and you workin' wit' a lot," a construction worker said as I passed him and his coworkers on the street. I could feel their eyes burning a hole in the back of my skirt as I sauntered my ample hips toward the little deli at the corner.

"You killin' it, Ma!" another man said. And I was. I felt like I owned the world, or at least my part of the world, despite the late notice that was still lying on my living room floor.

By the time I grabbed my egg sandwich and coffee, I'd already settled on a plan to pay the rent. It was time to take Keyshawn's man, David, from the gym, up on his offer for dinner. Not only was I going to get my rent money from him, but I'd also extract a little revenge. At least that was my plan until I decided to seize the moment and take advantage of an even better opportunity standing right in front of me. Now all I needed to do was play my cards right, and if all went well, I'd be able to get enough for rent and then some. Like I always say, all you gotta do is think like a man.

Think like a man, girl, think like a man ... What would a man do in this situation?

An hour later, I found myself in a tight space, wondering about this very question as I tried to remain calm. I'd been in sticky situations before, but this was by far the stickiest. It's not every day a woman finds herself trapped completely naked in a man's closet with his wife standing ten feet away, but that's exactly where I was. I would've kicked myself if I wasn't so damn cramped. Why the hell didn't I just stick with the original plan? Then I'd be somewhere with that guy from the gym, getting some overdue revenge on that skinny-ass Keyshawn, instead of being in this damn closet. I squeezed my eyes shut tightly and released a silent sigh of frustration.

You see, this entire mess all started when I stepped out of the deli and ran into the infamous Jackson Brentworth. He was quite possibly one of the most famous black real estate developers in New York. Sure, David might have owned a gym or two, but that was nothing compared to what Jackson Brentworth had. I checked out Mr. Brentworth from head to toe, and I swear I saw dollar signs before my eyes. I thought my luck couldn't have been any better. But now I was starting to have serious doubts. Being locked up in a closet for twenty minutes will do that to you. Oh, how I wished I could turn back the clock to the moment before I made my move on him.

"Oh, excuse me. I'm so sorry." I had bumped into him "accidentally on purpose" as we passed each other in the doorway of the deli. He backed up a bit.

"Ah, no, pardon me. My mind was somewhere else. I'm the one who should be apologizing to you."

Jackson Brentworth was about five foot eight at best, and truthfully, he wasn't much to look at in the face. But none of that mattered to me, because he had something much sexier than looks. He had money. He was so rich that some people even called him the black Donald Trump. Jackson owned half the buildings in my neighborhood. One of his finest masterpieces was the trendy new building of lofts a mere two blocks from mine.

I'd been trying to devise a plan to reel Jackson in for the longest. I wanted one of those lofts, and it didn't matter how many times I had to fuck him to get one. But I would start slowly. Today's priority was simply to pay the rent on the place I was living in now. No reason to be greedy, right?

We'd done the smile-politely-at-each-other, exchanging brief "hellos" a few times, but I couldn't really put my mojo on him, because his wife was always around. I wasn't even sure if he knew I existed before today. So I decided right then and there that I was not about to let that moment pass me by.

"Um, wait." I smiled, my chest heaving up and down. Thank God I was wearing the denim jacket that showed the girls in the best way possible. I was chic and sexy. As I stood in front of my dream man, I commenced to working my jelly like I didn't know when I'd get another shot at him.

"Don't I know you from someplace?" I placed a finger between my lips and pretended to give the idea some thought.

When Jackson gave me a look that said he wasn't quite buying my little routine, I grinned wickedly and said, "Hi, I'm Coco."

A smile curled at the corners of his mouth, and I decided all hope was not lost after all. I stepped closer to him, and my nose was filled with the most wonderful aroma. Have you ever smelled money? Well, this man smelled like money, lots of money, and if there was one thing that turned me on like a motherfucker, it was money.

"No, I don't think we've met, but I've seen you around," he said. His voice was panty-drenching deep. If he ever decided to get out of the real estate business, he would have made a great stand-in for Barry White. "Quite a few times," he added.

So, he had noticed me. Well, thank the Lord. For a while there I thought I was slipping. Now all I had to do was get him alone, preferably in a hotel, but I might even break my own rules and bring him back to my place if I had to. Jackson was the big fish, the kind of man who could set a sister up for life. It was just a matter of putting it on him like he'd never had before, which was my specialty. Then once I had him hooked, that steady cash flow would be coming in like I had my own personal ATM.

I immediately went to work, leaning all into his personal space, allowing my breast to graze his arm just so, to gauge his reaction. Most men were one of two things, breast men or ass men. Occasionally you found a man who was both, but that was the exception, not the rule. It didn't matter which he was, of course, since I had plenty of both, but it still helped to know which of my assets to highlight when I was working on a certain man. Jackson, I determined right away, was a breast man. He was staring at my titties so hard he looked like his mouth was going to start watering any second. I knew he just wanted to reach out and touch them.

"By the way, my name's Jackson. Jackson Brentworth." We shook hands politely. "I see you have your lunch. So, where are you headed this afternoon?" He cleared his throat but never pulled his eyes back from my breasts. That's when I figured I had him just where I wanted him. I knew for sure we'd be continuing this little conversation someplace other than on the sidewalk.

"It depends," I said coyly.

"Oh, really?" An eyebrow elevated.

I nodded. "Mmm-hmm."

We stepped aside to let someone pass. Then the conversation resumed.

"So, what exactly does it depend on?" he asked.

"You."

"Me?" He pointed at himself.

"That's right. Where I'm headed depends on where you're going. For some reason, I feel like I'm destined to spend some time getting to know you. And now is as good a time as any."

His eyes lit up, and he actually licked his lips. Little did he know he had parts of my body watering now too. I had a river flowing between my thighs. That's just what the thought of all his money did to me.

"Well, I'm headed back to my apartment," he said; then, as if an afterthought, he tossed in, "My wife is gone for the rest of the day." His eyebrows were still elevated when he tossed the word "wife" out there. I figured it was now his turn to try to gauge my reaction. I never missed a beat.

"Well," I started, "since your wife is gone for the rest of the day, I guess I'm headed back to your apartment too." I sucked in a little air and subtly arched my back, making the girls look even a little bigger. His face broke into a full smile, and his eyes started to twinkle.

"So, what we waiting for?" he asked.

Neither one of us was interested in wasting time as we turned immediately and walked in the direction of his building. I was so thrilled, I could barely control my emotions. But I was not about to make an amateur move, so as we strolled to his place, I kept my cool and swayed my hips confidently, like I was accustomed to being at the side of a multimillionaire.

Jackson's apartment was nothing short of spectacular. He had taken an entire floor in his building and refurbished it into a modern living space worthy of the cover of any issue of *Architectural Digest*. As I walked around on the hardwood floors and admired the expensive decor, I couldn't help but think I had finally hit the jackpot. Everything about his space reeked of money, and I was so happy he had decided to step up in the female department as well.

"Your place is lovely." I tried to behave like such luxury was the norm for me as well.

Jackson didn't say a word at first, his piercing eyes rolling up and down my body, then back up again. No words were necessary, because we were definitely on the same page.

"You're the one who's lovely," he said, licking those lips, which, for some strange reason, were starting to look quite luscious to me. They looked so good, I wanted to gobble him and them up. But I knew I had to play this one right. This was not about to be a one-hit wonder if I could help it. I was about to bring my game to the plate.

I leaned over and kissed him. Without breaking our kiss, Jackson started moving toward a back room. His hands were already exploring my body. He was rough, but that was all right. I could do rough.

We kissed our way into his bedroom, which was just as impressive as the rest of his fabulous apartment. All the furniture was mahogany, including the canopy bed that looked like something out of a movie. I decided to put on a little show, to really make our first encounter memorable. I'd never been a stripper, but I could have been a great one. I stepped away from him and started swaying my hips seductively. My hands traveled up my thighs, along my waist, then to the girls, where I stopped to unzip my jacket. As I stood topless in front of him, he looked like he was ready to pounce on me.

"Come here," he commanded. He had the cutest little smirk.

I removed my skirt and approached him wearing nothing at all. He buried his face in my breasts and started slopping all over them.

"Oh yes!" I squealed.

"Damn, you're so sexy!" he moaned. "So sexy." He began to feast on my enlarged nipple like he was a breast-feeding child. I grabbed the back of his head, pulling him closer, then gyrated my hips even more.

"I could suck on your titties all day." He looked up at me.

"Then suck them, baby. They are all yours." I had to admit he really knew how to make the girls happy. The next question was whether or not he was any good at pleasing my kitty. Unfortunately, I wasn't going to find out. Our heads snapped toward the door when we heard what sounded like keys dangling and someone struggling to get in.

"Oh shit!" he said in a panicked whisper, and in one quick

movement, he shoved me from his lap and jumped up. "Oh my God, that's my wife!"

"So what?" I stood my ground. I didn't give a shit about his wife. I was in his bedroom, buck-ass naked, and he was acting like a scared little bitch. This was not a part of the plan. I didn't know what he was so worried about. I'd seen his wife. She couldn't whip my ass. "What you worried about? I read in the paper that you had a prenup. She ain't going nowhere." And if she did, I'd be right there to step in.

"Did it also say in the paper that she carries a nine-millimeter handgun and shot her first husband in the leg and the woman he was with in the ass?" he asked as he started scrambling to hide the evidence.

Ah, hell naw. This woman is crazy, I thought as my heart went into overdrive. I didn't know what the hell to do. I was thinking about hiding out on the balcony, but that idea went down the drain when Jackson's dumb ass quickly scooped up my clothes and shoved them under the bed.

"Why the fuck did you do that?"

"Quick. We ain't got no time to argue." He turned to me. "Get in the closet. I'll get rid of her so you can go, but be quiet!" He pointed toward a set of doors. Without putting up a fight, I rushed over there and climbed into the damn closet. When I pulled the doors, they didn't even close all the way.

I peeked through the crack in the door as his wife strolled into the bedroom and found him there. Jackson had propped himself on the bed, leaning back on his elbows. They had some sort of brief conversation, but I stopped paying attention at that point because I felt something soft and furry rubbing against my skin. I jumped. I was grateful I didn't scream, but the urge was definitely there. Shit! What the fuck? A got-damn cat! I said a quick prayer that I wouldn't sneeze or, even worse, that the cat wouldn't leave the closet and push the doors open on its way out.

When I looked back at the Brentworths, his wife, an out-of-shape woman in her fifties, took off her shirt and exposed the saggiest pair of titties I'd ever seen. All of a sudden, Jackson had a smirk on his face—the same smirk he had when he called me over to suck on my titties. That's when it hit me that these mother-fuckers were about to have sex. He was supposed to get rid of this bitch so I could come out of this closet, but instead, he was about to fuck her flabby ass. It took everything I had not to jump out that closet and smack the shit outta Jackson—that is, until I remembered his wife carried a gun.

I couldn't believe Jackson was about to sex her old ass when only moments before he was sucking on my plump, young titties like he was recovering from a famine. I was sure my juices were still sitting on his thigh. I watched as he stripped down to show off an awful pear-shaped body that gave away his age. I couldn't remember ever seeing a scrotum sack hanging as low as his. All the money in the world couldn't conceal the fact that this was one unattractive brotha once his clothes were off. How disappointing.

As I watched Jackson and his wife get it on, I was struck by how mundane their lovemaking was. She was stiff as a board, and he gave about ten, maybe eleven humps before he was squealing like he'd just bust the best nut ever known to man. They were both panting and breathing hard, like they'd just finished marathon sex. I couldn't believe how boring he was in bed. That's when I knew he'd never really be able to handle my ass, but that didn't matter. I was not about to lose out.

"I'm gonna take a quick shower," his wife said. I watched as her wrinkled ass strolled into the bathroom, then I emerged from the closet—and not a moment too soon, either, because that frigging cat was working my nerves something fierce.

Jackson's eyes were saucers when he saw me coming from the closet. "What are you doing?" he whispered, looking nervously toward the bathroom door.

"I'm gonna need some money to walk up outta here quietly," I said, wasting no time whatsoever.

He jumped up. "Please, just um, get dressed and go," he begged.

"Just go?" I practically laughed in his face. "Unh-uh. This is gonna cost you," I warned as he pulled my clothes from beneath the bed and shoved them toward me.

I stood without moving, even after he'd given me my clothes and looked at me with pleading eyes. Finally, he sighed and reached for his pants, which were on the floor.

"How much?" he asked in a defeated voice as he grabbed his wallet.

I looked over and asked, "How much is in there?"

His eyebrows shot up, and he looked like he was about to protest until we heard the water in the shower stop running. His wife was helping me out more than she would ever know. I smirked as I stood waiting with my hand on my hip.

With a horrified look on his face, Jackson opened his wallet, dug in, and pulled out a thick wad of cash. He was still shaking after he forked it over.

"Just go," he whispered, defeated.

"Honey? You say something?" his wife called from the bathroom.

"No, dear," he said, motioning with his hand for me to get out.

I grabbed my shoes and walked out of the bedroom. By the time I made it to the front door, I was able to get my skirt and jacket on. I clutched my cash tightly as I rushed out of Jackson's apartment.

It wasn't until I got outside and checked that I realized just how generous Jackson had been. Now the rent was paid for sure, plus a generous bonus for my troubles. I wanted to do a little dance when I discovered that in less than two hours time, I had earned close to three thousand dollars. What a great day it had turned out to be.

12

Nikki

"So I'll go get the pizza, then?" Tiny asked. She pulled her baseball cap down low, even though she'd just had her fade tightened up.

"Mmmm, tastes like chicken," she said as she bent down and gave me a kiss on the lips. I was snacking on those new spicy barbecue wings from Costco.

"Okay, make sure you bring cheese and peppers. Oh, and get some napkins," I yelled, sucking sauce from my fingers.

Tiny stopped at the door. Her starched jeans were sagging off her butt, and she wore a wife-beater under a white T-shirt. She was wearing the new Jordans I bought for her last week.

"Napkins?" She scowled. "We got a gang o' paper towels in the kitchen, man. We don't need no doggone napkins."

"Yeah, I know what we got, but just get some anyway, baby. And a Coke," I threw in.

She rolled her eyes, then said, "You know I don't like when you drink soda in front of DJ. It just makes him want that shit," she warned.

"But I want it." I pouted and lowered my head, batting my eyelashes at her.

When a smile curled at the corners of her mouth, I could tell she was trying not to laugh.

"Pleeeeeassse?" I begged.

Tiny gave me knowing look, smiled, then walked out the door. I knew she'd get my Coke; then I was sure she'd get some juice or lemonade for DJ so he could have a bottle to drink from too. That's just how considerate she was. I wanted her to hurry, because I knew we had two movies to try to get through. I would be fine, but Tiny's ass couldn't stay up late if her life depended on it.

There was a knock at the door five minutes after Tiny left. I knew she couldn't be back this soon, so I walked over and looked out the peephole. "Shit!" I spat. It was Dwayne.

I pulled open the door. "Hey, why didn't you call?"

"Oh, I just came up on some tickets to that Pokémon show. You know the one—"

"DJ's been dying to see?" I finished for him. Now I was excited too.

"Where is he?" Dwayne asked as I stepped aside to let him in.

"He's in his room. Tiny went to get pizza," I said.

"Well, lemme surprise him," Dwayne said, his eyes dancing and wide.

As I followed him to our son's room, I was all caught up in the feeling. DJ had been going on and on about that damn show. He had it so bad I thought he'd drive me insane before long. But things were tight, and we didn't have extra cash for such luxuries.

DJ's door was open, and he was lying on his stomach, his feet crossed at the ankles. Dwayne and I stood in the doorway and looked at him for a minute. Then I watched as Dwayne crept into the room and eased himself onto DJ's bed. My child never stirred.

"Hey, boy," Dwayne finally said. DJ jumped, and his little eyes widened.

"Daddy, what're you doing here?" he squealed happily. Then he turned to see me standing in the doorway. "Ma?"

I just stood staring at the two of them. It brought me so much joy to see my son happy. It was amazing to me how much he resembled his father each and every day.

After he acknowledged my presence, he quickly turned his attention back to Dwayne.

"So, wassup, Dad?" he asked, going into his cool big-boy mode. I was now leaning comfortably against the doorframe with my arms crossed at my chest.

"I was wondering if you still wanted to go to the Pokémon show," Dwayne asked easily.

DJ's little head snapped in my direction. His eyes begged me to confirm whether it was true. I was smiling so hard, my jaws were aching. I nodded, getting all swept up in the excitement.

"For real, Dad? For real?" he screamed.

"Yeah, man. You down or what?"

DJ turned to me again, like he needed my permission.

"What? You can go," I said.

"Ma, I want you to come with us too. Can she, Dad? Huh, can she?" he asked, still just as excited as he was when Dwayne first announced the news.

"Um . . ." I looked at Dwayne. "Um, I don't think Daddy has enough tickets for all of us, DJ," I said somberly.

"Dad, can Mom come? Pleeeeease, pleeeeeaase?" DJ asked in a whiny voice.

Dwayne looked at our son and said, "Your Momma can come if she wants. I've got an extra ticket if she wants it," he said, like I wasn't standing right there.

"Mom, come with us pleeeeeeeease." DJ turned his whining to me. Dwayne sat there looking on like he was indifferent to what was happening. I hated him for causing this problem.

"Well, what about Tiny?" I asked. I know it was stupid, but I felt so torn. I was pissed at Dwayne's feebleminded ass for even putting me in such a position. Now the great moment my son was supposed to be having had quickly turned sour for me, and it was all Dwayne's fault.

"I ain't got no ticket for Tiny," he mumbled, pissing me off even more.

I sighed.

DJ turned to Dwayne. "Dad, tell her you want her to go, even if Tiny can't. Please, Dad, tell her."

"Why don't you two boys go and have a good time? You don't want your ole boring mom hanging with the fellas," I jokingly tried to convince my son. But he wasn't going for it.

Soon, he turned away from his dad and pouted, crossing his arms at his little chest. "I just wanted us to be a real family again." His voice cracked as he tried to hold back his tears.

My heart took a nosedive the instant he said that. I shot daggers at Dwayne.

"Okay, I'll change clothes and go with you guys," I said somberly, knowing there would be hell to pay later with Tiny.

Unfortunately for me, the moment I changed and met the

guys in the living room, the front door swung open and Tiny walked in, balancing the pizza box, a tall heap of napkins, movies, and a plastic bag with a two-liter bottle of Coke and lemonade. She dropped the stuff on the coffee table, then scanned the scene before her with confusion all over her face.

"What's going on?" she asked.

I didn't have the heart to tell her, and I didn't have to.

"Tiny! Tiny! My daddy is taking Momma and me out to see Pokémon!" DJ squealed like he was sharing the greatest news possible with her.

"Is that right, li'l man?" she asked, keeping it cool for his sake. "You and your mommy?" As she said it, her eyes met mine, and I understood that was a jab at me.

I quickly averted my gaze, looking everywhere but at her face. "I was gonna leave you a note," I said, hoping she wouldn't show out in front of Dwayne.

"A note, huh?"

"Tiny we can, um, we can talk about it later," I said.

Dwayne had the audacity to announce, "The show starts in less than an hour." I knew he was probably enjoying all this tension between me and Tiny.

"Oh, my bad," Tiny said, and dramatically stepped aside, even though she wasn't blocking our path. She moved her arm in a sweeping motion, then said, "By all means, don't let me ruin this perfect family outing."

She was playing hard, but I could tell she was hurting. I wanted nothing more than to rush to her, take her into my arms, and kiss the pain away, even though I was the one causing it.

The Pokémon show was outta this world. I don't know who enjoyed it more, Dwayne and me or DJ. From the outside, anyone looking at us would've thought we were the perfect family. I knew I had trouble waiting for me at home, but for those three hours when we sat watching those characters on stage and listening to my son laugh like never before, I felt it was worth it.

"Wanna get some pizza?" Dwayne asked once the show was over.

I wanted to kick him in the teeth. He kept making things worse for me, and I didn't understand why he was doing this.

"Pizza!" DJ screamed.

I tried to kill that madness before it got out of control.

"We already have pizza at home. Remember Tiny was bringing it in when we were going out," I said firmly. Before either one could interject anything else, I said, "Now tell your daddy thanks for the show and let's get going," I said.

I think my child knew his luck had run out. He said good-bye to Dwayne and followed me without any more protest.

When we arrived at home, the apartment was eerily dark. I didn't know what I should do. I figured I'd ease in and quietly feed DJ and get him to bed; then I'd throw myself at Tiny's feet and beg for mercy. But if I thought things would go somewhat smoothly, I was about to be slapped back to reality real soon.

"I want another slice," DJ cried as I tried to keep things quiet and shuffle him into his bedroom.

"One more," I whispered harshly, waving a warning finger in his face.

After he ate the pizza, I tucked DJ in and dragged myself into my bedroom. Tiny lay on top of the still-made bed with her hands clasped behind her head.

"Hi, baby," I said cautiously when I eased into the room.

She didn't respond, but I didn't allow that to deter me. I was still determined to make peace with her. I went into the bathroom to get ready for bed, slipping on the oversized shirt I usually slept in. When I crawled into the bed and tried to snuggle up next to Tiny, she jerked beyond my reach.

"Tiny, I know you're mad—"

"Bitch, don't fuckin' touch me. I know you fucked his ass," she barked.

I was stunned silent. It was no secret that Tiny hated Dwayne, but I never expected this accusation. I needed to make her understand that I only went out with him that night to make DJ happy. But I knew there was no sense in trying to explain myself now. When Tiny got pissed about something, she stayed pissed. I turned my back to her, hoping I'd be able to fall asleep and hoping I could talk some sense into her in the morning.

13

Isis

"Sooooo," Egypt squealed, then took a sip of her Fuzzy Navel drink. I watched her expression as she savored the taste, twisting her keys around one of the fingers of her free hand. The girl was definitely full of herself today. She had good reason, though. She'd just bought herself a new Lexus. "What did you wanna tell me? 'Cause you ain't gonna believe what I got to tell you." Her keys made an annoying jingle as she continued to twist them.

I sighed. I knew I needed to confide in somebody about the whole Tony and Rashad thing, because this shit was wearing me out. But I just didn't know how to give life to the feeling, and that in itself was a clear indicator that I was headed for disaster.

"Dish it, girl. What's up?" Egypt pressed.

"Okay, well, ever since you gave Rashad my number and told him where I work, he's been sweating me." Egypt's keys stopped jingling. "I mean, he's been sweating me something fierce!"

Her eyes were looking everywhere but at my face. She knew she was wrong. That's why she couldn't look at me. I would have never done her like that. I loved my sister, but she could be a snake sometimes.

"All I can say is you better hope he don't mess things up with me and Tony." I didn't dare look up to see what Egypt might have been thinking. I was certain it would soon be all over her face. But after a few awkwardly quiet moments, I had no choice. I turned to face her. "Well, aren't you gonna say something?" I folded my arms.

"What do you want me to say?" She shrugged her shoulders. "I mean, seriously, Tony's aw-ight, but I like Rashad better. So do Momma and Daddy." She started spinning those damn keys on her finger again. "Besides, if you really wanted to get rid of

Rashad, we wouldn't even be havin' this conversation. You would've just told Tony he was in town and been done with it, end of story."

I knew she was right, but that wasn't what I wanted to hear. I made a face and waved my hand at her, rattling off a list of reasons why I should stay with Tony. They were easy to express, because I'd been going over them in my head for days as I tried to figure out what I was going to do. "Please, Egypt, you know Tony is the man for me. He's good to me and he's responsible. All Rashad is good for is great sex and a good time. He's not responsible enough to take care of me or a family. Besides, you know how much I love Tony . . . right?"

"You tryin' to convince me or yourself? 'Cause good sex and a good time sounds like enough to me." She sipped her drink, staring at me as if she was inviting me to dish even more.

"I'm not trying to convince anyone of anything. And just for the record, Tony's good in bed too." I snarled at her but instantly realized it wasn't her fault that I didn't want to face the truth. The truth was my feelings for Rashad weren't quite gone, no matter how much I tried to deny them.

"I know you claimed to be pissed when he showed up at your job, but from what you're telling me . . . or not telling me . . ." Her eyebrows inched up. "Maybe deep down inside, you were somewhat glad to see him after all."

I thought about denying it, but decided not to. I knew the truth. Just the mere fact that I felt the need to confide in Egypt told me that I was having some serious issues regarding Rashad and my feelings for him. I was scared, nearly petrified, because ever since Rashad came back into my life, I hadn't been able to think of anything else but him. That being said, I still loved Tony. Things were so damn confusing, and I was totally unable to make the decision to cut either one of them out of my life at this point.

"Maybe I was a little glad to see him, but what it all boils down to is being happy. Tony genuinely loves me. Rashad just wants what he can't have."

"Well, if you're done dishing, I've got a real confession to make," Egypt said, shaking those damn keys. I was tired of my dilemma and needed to hear someone else's dirt for a change.

But I was in no way prepared for what fell from my sister's mouth next.

"I've decided to do it." Egypt giggled and turned up her glass, still shaking those damn keys.

"I know you're not talking about what I think you're talking about. You couldn't be that stupid," I began with my finger pointed directly in her face. Egypt looked at me over the rim of her up-turned glass, as if she was hoping for more.

"Put that damn glass down!" I demanded. "And stop shaking those f-ing keys."

She started chuckling as if something I'd said was ticklish. When she placed the glass on the table, I stared her down, waiting for her to crack a smile and say she was just joking or something. But she didn't say anything, so I did the talking.

"You've decided to do what exactly?" I asked for clarification.

"You got any more of these?" she asked, tilting the glass like I wouldn't have known what she was asking for.

"Don't play with me, Egypt. What the hell did you agree to?" I was mad and she knew it.

"Oohhh-kay. Well, I've decided to help Tammy out and do the threesome with her and Tim."

My jaw felt like it had just hit the ground. "What? I can't believe what I just heard."

"Believe it! She's even paying me. Not that I'm doing it for the money, but if you must know, it's no small change she's paying. So, yes, I'm gonna do the threesome, and I have to admit I'm looking forward to it." My mouth hung open. "You gotta agree, opportunities like this don't come around every day."

"Eeeerrrr, pump your brakes!" I held up a hand to silence her. "Opportunities? Have you lost your mind right along with Tammy?"

I sat there staring at my sister, wondering what the hell was wrong with her. She couldn't be serious! She simply could not be serious. Mentally, I was counting to ten so I wouldn't go off on her.

"Yes, opportunity, Isis. Where do you think I got the money to put down on that Lexus?"

"Um, I'm gonna need you to backtrack and come again." I

was not prepared for my very straight sister to be sitting up in my face talking about having a threesome with a friend of ours, not to mention a member of BGBC.

I sat there with my arms crossed at my chest, still hoping she would crack a smile and say she was just bullshittin' me, but she never did. She just leaned back on the chaise with a very unapologetic look on her face. She sucked her teeth, then sighed and looked at me.

"Can you please make me another drink?" she asked nonchalantly. I could have smacked her.

Maybe she's drunk, I thought. *Maybe I just have to wait for her to sober up and she'll tell me the truth.*

"No, I'm not making you a drink. You've had too many as it is. Do you hear me talking to you? I need to know why the hell you talkin' about disrespecting your best friend and yourself by fucking her man!" I hissed at her. "You ain't doing them no favor. If they wanna have a threesome, let them call an escort service or some nasty fifty-dollar hooker. That's what they are for."

"Why you gotta make it sound all like that?" She frowned up her face like I was the one giving her something to act all funky about. "I mean, when you say it like that, the shit sounds foul," she exclaimed.

I slapped my forehead, my frustration at her building. "You wanna know why it sounds foul? Because it is! It's foul, and I can't believe you'd stoop so low." I was damn near hollering at her, because she was trying to front like this was no big deal. "This sounds like some ol' Coco-type shit!"

"Well, you can judge me if you want, but the truth of the matter is, I'm kinda looking forward to it. Tammy's taking me shopping, and she's paying me five grand!"

My mouth fell and my heart hurt for my sister. She seemed to be bragging about selling her ass and her soul for money. She'd done some stupid things in her life, but nothing that compared to this fiasco.

"Where the fuck is my sister?" I shook my head, staring at Egypt. " 'Cause you look like her, even sound like her, but the shit you spittin' ain't like nothing my sister would ever do," I snapped.

"Oh, you got your damn nerve! Wasn't you the same one sitting here talking about catching feelings for your ex, even though you've said before that Tony is the best thing to ever happen to you? And now you tryin'a call me a ho?" Egypt asked with major attitude.

"I didn't call you a ho!" I screamed.

"You may as well have called me a ho, talking about this some Coco-type shit. We all know Coco will sleep with anyone, so basically you calling me a ho," she said as if the weak argument was somehow proving her point.

"You know what? You can change the subject if you want!" I screamed.

Just then, the doorbell rang, probably some type of divine intervention to distract me before I killed my sister for being so stupid. I looked at Egypt and got up to get the door, still shaking my head at her foolishness.

I looked through the peephole, then jumped back as if the door was letting off electrical shock waves.

"Oh my God! It's Rashad," I whispered, stepping quickly away from the door. My heart was suddenly beating too fast.

"Damn, what's going on with you?"

"Sssssssshhh." I pulled my finger to my lips. "Be quiet."

"Girl, please. I'm sure he heard us talking. He ain't stupid," Egypt said. I couldn't believe how she was trying to put me out there.

When Rashad rang the doorbell again, I closed my eyes and took a deep breath. I was most worried because Tony had made it clear that once he finished balling, we were going out to dinner. We were supposed to go at seven-thirty. I looked at my watch. It was already six forty-five.

"You know he ain't gonna just leave, so you might as well open the door and talk to the man," Egypt said with ease. She rose from her seat. "Besides, I'm about to bounce. I don't need to sit here being judged by somebody who's got problems of her own." With that said, Egypt grabbed her purse and made a quick dash for the door.

"Move!" she demanded, like she had a reason to be irritated. I stepped aside and watched in horror as she pulled open the door with a smile and said, "Hey, Rashad. You okay? Lemme warn you, she trippin'." She tossed me a dirty look as she left.

I quickly decided it was best if I stepped outside to talk to Rashad. The last thing I needed was him all up in my place. Ain't no telling what would happen.

"What are you doing here?" I asked the moment we were alone. He had the nerve to smile, like this was a legitimate social visit.

"I wanted to see if you wanna go grab a bite," he answered easily, despite the sharp tone I was using with him.

"Yeah, but what are you doing here?" I snapped. I couldn't believe that he was just standing in front of me like there was nothing wrong with him popping up at my place. "Why didn't you call? What if Tony was here? *You* are tripping!" I was exasperated.

He looked at me with sad puppy eyes and shook his head like he couldn't comprehend my concern. "That nigga would start trippin' off something simple like that?" He shook his head again, this time like he pitied me. "That ain't no way to treat your woman. I mean, he trusts you, right?" Without giving me a moment to respond, he had the audacity, to say, "I can't believe you'd be with a man who didn't respect you."

Now it was my turn to be stunned. "You got your nerve, talking about the way to treat a woman. I guess you forgot you walked out on me." I sucked my teeth and rolled my eyes at him.

Rashad shrugged his shoulders. "Hold up, Pooh. You got me all wrong. Like I said, that ain't no way to treat your woman."

"And what's that got to do with my woman?"

My heart dropped to my feet when I heard Tony's voice. How could I not have noticed him walking up on us?

"Um, T-Tony!" I stammered.

Rashad turned, and one of my biggest fears suddenly came true. My ex was face-to-face with my man. Anything could happen at this point. All I could do was pray there were no punches thrown.

"What the hell is goin' on here?" Tony snarled, instantly mean-mugging Rashad.

"Ah, this is my um . . . Tony . . ." I was so nervous, like I was doing something far worse than I really was. "This is Rashad, my ex," I said softly.

The look Tony gave me said he was not happy to find Rashad at my place.

14

Tammy

After a day of shopping and pampering ourselves at one of New York City's swankiest spas, Egypt and I met Tim at his office for the start of his birthday celebration. From the office, we took a car service to the Ritz-Carlton, where we had a fabulous dinner at Atelier, the French restaurant inside the hotel. The hotel was small by New York City standards, but the marble floors, tasteful wood paneling, fresh floral arrangements, and elegant setting more than made up for its size. As we strolled through the small lobby and sitting room, I glanced around at the high ceilings and nice furnishings. We had to walk to the back of the sitting area and around the corner to a sort of backdoor entrance, but it was well worth it, as it provided just the right kind of intimate and private setting we needed to help kick off our special evening.

I felt a little nervous as I thought about what we were about to undertake, but not like I didn't want to do it. I think I was just so excited that it was messing with my nerves. I looked around again, glad I'd chosen such a nice and intimate hotel. I also glanced at my best friend, happy that she was there to share such a special moment with me and my husband. This was something none of us would ever forget.

We started the evening with a very special, very expensive French wine, then worked our way through seven delicious courses. The thing I loved about French restaurants was that you always felt full when you finished eating, but never stuffed, like you didn't wanna get up. Our evening had gone well so far, and I only expected things to get better. We managed to make small talk over dinner, Egypt and I chatting about our next book for our club meeting and Tim interjecting at just the right moments with enough questions to make us believe he was interested in our conversation. The three of us were far too excited for dessert, opting instead to take care of that upstairs in our room.

"I've never had French food before," Egypt said as she leaned slightly to the side so the waiter could remove her plate. She readjusted the napkin in her lap, appearing a bit fidgety to me.

"I hope you liked it?" Tim asked her.

"Mmm-hmm," she confirmed with a nod, and I was pleased.

"Honey, did you order champagne?" I asked, making sure the room would have everything we'd need. I didn't want to leave anything to chance.

"Yeah, we're good. A bottle of Moët should be waiting for us. So if you ladies are ready," Tim said, getting up from his chair. I smiled as he walked around and pulled out Egypt's chair, with his other hand reaching toward mine.

"Everyone ready?" he asked again.

I glanced at Egypt and she smiled. "Yes, baby, I think we are."

Egypt and I sat in the lobby for a few minutes while Tim stopped off at the front desk. Soon, we were led to our suite by the bell captain.

"Thank you," Tim said to the bell captain after he helped us into our room. We had a corner suite that was simply unbelievable. The living room was huge, with phenomenal views, and was extremely well decorated with gorgeous heavy drapes and lovely furniture. It even had a table with binoculars and a New York City bird-watching book. I never thought of New York City as a place to bird-watch, but you learn something new every day.

The bell captain pointed out that the view from the bedroom windows was even more spectacular. With my attention now focused on the most important part of the suite, I went to explore. The master bathroom was gigantic, as was the glass-walled shower and separate Jacuzzi tub. I imagined all three of us could fit quite comfortably in there together. But of course, that wouldn't be until after we enjoyed ourselves in the king-sized bed. Running my hand over the superfluffy down comforter, I noticed the high-thread-count sheets and extra pillows. Oh yes, the three of us were sure to be quite cozy in this luxurious bed.

As I walked into the living room with a huge smile on my face, I saw Tim tipping the bell captain and walking him to the door. "If you need anything else . . ." the elderly man said. I'm not sure, but I think he winked at Tim as he backed into the hallway. I wondered if he thought it odd, the three of us going into the room, especially since we had no suitcases, just shopping bags.

Tim immediately fixed us a drink, grinning as he passed a glass to me, then one to Egypt. I felt anxious and thrilled at the same time. We stood close to each other and made a toast.

"To trying new and exciting things," I said, hoisting my glass up to reach his and Egypt's.

"Cheers!" Egypt said.

"Here here," Tim followed up as we clanked our glasses and took sips.

Tim strolled around as if he was inspecting the room. He fumbled for a few minutes with the binoculars, then finally turned to Egypt and me.

"So, are we really gonna do this?" The expression on his face told me he was just as anxious to get things started, despite the slight hesitation I thought I sensed in his voice. I glanced at Egypt. She had the same expression. I think they were a little scared. I was, too, but that wasn't going to stop me.

"Hold that thought," I said, raising one finger. "I've got just the thing to lighten the mood."

I rushed to my purse, which I'd left in the bedroom, and pulled out a small Ziploc sandwich bag. I returned to the living room, dangling the bag in front of Egypt and Tim. Once their eyes connected with the bag and its contents, smiles stretched across their faces, and the tension in the room instantly lessened.

"Now, that's what I'm talking about," Egypt said happily.

Tim chuckled. "Damn, I ain't smoked weed in years."

I reached into the bag and pulled out a joint. Tim started scrambling. "Shit, where are matches when you need 'em?" he said. Now, that's the kind of energy and excitement I was expecting to see from him all along. It didn't take long for him to step up and let me know it would soon be on and popping.

"You know we're showing our age, don't you?" Egypt said as she went to get her purse. She came back and passed me a book of matches from the restaurant. I put the joint between my lips and fired it up.

"Why's that?" I asked, trying not to release the smoke I'd inhaled.

" 'Cause only old people smoke joints. Real weed-heads are smoking blunts."

"She's right. We are behind the times," Tim agreed. "Then again, how often do we smoke weed?"

I shrugged my shoulders, then made them laugh by exaggerating a long, hard drag with one eye shut to avoid the smoke. The weed was definitely having the desired effect on all of us. Everyone was suddenly much more relaxed, and I was the only one who had even taken a hit yet. I took another one and passed the joint to Egypt. She followed suit, holding the joint between her index finger and thumb, then passed it to Tim. He wandered into the bedroom while he took a drag, and we followed behind him.

Tim took a seat on the bed, and Egypt and I sat on both sides of him. We took turns hitting the joint and passing it until it was nothing more than a small roach.

"You want another?" I asked, feeling mellow as hell. As a plume of smoke danced from his lips up to his eyes, Tim nodded. I quickly rolled up another joint, and we passed that one around too.

As we neared the end of the second joint, I took a drag, then locked lips with Tim and blew my smoke into his mouth. He sucked it up, holding his breath for a few seconds before releasing the smoke. We all started giggling.

"Wait, do me, do me!" Egypt sang.

Tim took a drag, then leaned toward Egypt. I felt a momentary flutter in my stomach. This was the moment of truth. Now that my husband's lips were about to touch hers, I wondered if I'd feel any jealousy. But the weed had me mellow enough that my anxiety passed as quickly as it had arrived. When their lips finally touched, I watched in fascination as their contact turned into a lingering, exploratory kiss.

When they pulled back, Tim looked at me as if he wasn't sure what to expect. I simply smiled and kissed his lips again.

"So, we 'bout to do this, then," he said softly.

"Yes, baby," I answered as I got up from the bed. "We about to do this. But first Egypt and I want to change into something a bit more appealing. You don't mind, do you?"

"Hell naw!" He leaned back and held what was left of the

joint up toward us. "I'll be right here when y'all through," he said.

Egypt and I sashayed into another room, giggling at nothing in particular.

"You feeling okay?" I asked her.

"Shit, I'm feeling lovely," she declared. "I mean, lovely, like I ain't felt in a long-ass time. I feel like a kid again."

"Good, I'm glad, because . . ." I trailed off.

Egypt turned to look at me, but she didn't say anything.

"Well, I was just saying I know you didn't want to do this at first, so I wanted to make sure you're cool with it, that's all." I was giving her a chance to get out if she really wanted. "I mean, you can keep the money if you don't wanna do it. I'll understand."

"Girl, please, I'm just glad you convinced me," she said, her voice sounding totally relaxed. "I mean, you could've just given up, but no, you were persistent. And shit, I'm glad you were."

"Cool, 'cause I'm hyped as hell. I just gotta let you know," I admitted.

"You!" Egypt sucked her teeth. "Damn, girl, you just don't know. You takin' me back to my college days." She giggled as I dug into the Frederick's of Hollywood shopping bag and pulled out the lingerie we'd bought.

The scene as we prepared ourselves for Tim must have looked like something out of an amateur porn video. When I started rubbing the glitter lotion on my arms, Egypt looked up at me and said, "Here, let me help you with that."

"Okay," I said, passing her the tube.

"You look good," she commented shyly as she stroked the lotion onto my skin.

"Hmm, you don't look bad yourself," I said. "Actually, you look sexy." I giggled.

We both busted up in nervous laughter. When her hands touched my skin, I started to tingle. She rubbed me gently and carefully, as if I was fragile. Never before had a woman's touch evoked such feelings in me, but the gentleness of Egypt's caress woke something deep inside me.

"Your skin is so soft," she said, using a voice just above a whisper.

Did my nipples just stiffen? I shook it off at first; then I gave myself permission to enjoy the feel of her hands gliding over my skin.

"Real soft," she mumbled.

I squeezed lotion into my own hands and turned to face her. I started at her shoulders, then allowed my hands to move down to her chest. At first we were looking each other in the eyes until she closed hers. When she did, I allowed my eyes to travel down to her full bosom. Her nipples were large, and the sight was turning me on. I fought the urge to lap one with my tongue, figuring I'd save that action for our time with Tim.

"Ooooooh weeeee, that feels good, girl," she cheered softly.

"Your skin's soft too," I told her.

"Mmm-hmm," she moaned. By now, my hands had started massaging the top of her chest. She didn't react or stop me when I eased down a bit and felt her breast.

"Ah, ladies . . ." Tim's voice startled us, and we both jumped. Egypt's eyes snapped open.

"Damn, it was just starting to feel good," she said.

"Hmm, then we'd better get this party started, don't you think?" I smiled at her, enjoying the moisture that had gathered between my thighs as I followed her out of the room to rejoin Tim. *Hell, who knows,* I thought. *I might even allow a little Nikki and Tiny type action tonight.*

In the bedroom, Tim had prepared his own surprise for us. Soft music set the mood, along with the flickering vanilla-scented candles he'd placed throughout the room. The comforter was covered in rose petals, and Tim stood beside the bed with two glasses extended in our direction.

Egypt and I looked at each other and smiled.

"Damn, y'all look good as hell!" he said.

When Egypt started moving her hips to the music, I caught her vibe and did the same. The look of arousal on Tim's face was indescribable. From that point on, there was no turning back for any of us. We were all about to have the time of our lives.

15

Nikki

I was in the cafeteria at work, enjoying the all-you-can-eat buffet with two of my coworkers, Lisa and Kym. They'd barely touched their food because they were too busy gossiping about some new guy Human Resources had hired to work in the mailroom. They were talking about that man like a dog. I just listened while I chowed down on some shrimp lo mein. I didn't ever talk too much during lunch, simply because conversation would interrupt my meal, and I couldn't have that. I may have started overeating because of low self-esteem, but now I overate because, well . . . I just loved food. I'm sure this is gonna sound a little messed up, but in those days, bringing me a well-cooked pork chop with some onions and collard greens would get Tiny further in the bedroom with me than a dozen roses and a full body massage. Food was just comforting in a way I can't even begin to describe.

"Did you see him?" Lisa asked.

"Mmm-hmm, I saw him. And from now on, I'm locking my purse up when I leave my desk, 'cause that fool looks like a straight-up criminal."

"Girl, I can't even believe he made it through the interview process with those long-ass braids and his pants hanging down to his knees. Talk about black people taking backward steps."

I was about to get up and refill my plate when Lisa leaned in to whisper to us, "Here he comes with Leon. Look at the way he's limping. You would think his leg was broken."

Kym whipped her head around so fast she could have given herself whiplash. Obviously Lisa's whisper wasn't exactly quiet because everyone at the table next to us was also turning around to look at this man now. I was a little more subtle, but the moment I turned, my gaze connected with the most beautiful set of hazel eyes I'd seen in quite some time, lined by lashes far too thick and long to be wasted on a man. I actually had to put down my plate and sit in my seat again to regain my composure. I was beyond confused because the man walking toward us not only stunned me with his good looks, but he was also bringing a warm feeling to the happy spot between my thighs. That was something no man had done in years—not even Dwayne, and trust me, I knew what that boy could do in the bedroom. I tried to ignore the sensation going on between my legs as Mr. Bedroom Eyes approached with Leon, the mailroom supervisor.

"Whassup, y'all?" Leon greeted us. "This here is Keith. He's gonna be working in the mailroom. Keith, this is Kym, Lisa, and Nikki."

I nodded at Keith but didn't speak, too scared that my mouth might betray me the way the rest of my body had at the mere sight of this man. To distract myself from his smile, which I now knew was every bit as beautiful as his eyes, I turned my attention back to my food. "Excuse me while I go refill my plate," I mumbled as I rushed away from the table.

When I returned with a second plate, Kym and Lisa were still whispering as they watched Leon walk Keith from table to table to meet our other coworkers. I ignored their comments, too interested in checking out Keith now that he was at a safe distance. He was wearing a pair of heavily starched khakis that hung dangerously low for work attire and a button-down oxford shirt. Yes, he did look a little thuggish, but he was definitely a sexy thug. Looking at him, I had a momentary flashback to Dwayne at the height of his bad-boy days. Lord, when we were young, you couldn't tell me he wasn't the sexiest man on the planet. But if I was into guys now, Keith might have a chance at stealing that title from Dwayne.

I shook my head, as if that could rid me of all the crazy thoughts swirling around in there, and tried to focus on the conversation between Lisa and Kym.

"I got to find me a new job because this company has gone to shit. They'll hire just about any damn body, won't they?" Kym sounded disgusted.

"I swear, I felt like throwing up gang signs," Lisa chimed in, lifting her hands as if she really knew some gang signs. The two of them cackled away at their own insulting jokes until Kym finally noticed that I wasn't joining in.

"What's wrong with you?" she demanded.

"Nothin'. I just didn't see anything that was funny. Y'all always talking about uplifting the black man, but here you are tearing one down because you don't like the way he wears his clothes." They both looked like they wanted to slap me, but that was okay. They knew they were wrong. "Besides, I think he's cute."

"What?" Kym nearly gave herself whiplash for the second time.

"You must be outta your mind," Lisa commented. "But that's why you're a lesbian." She went on to explain as if it were scientific fact, " 'Cause any real dick-loving woman could see ain't nothing cute about a broken-down gangbanger. Only reason he probably even wants to work is so he won't violate his parole."

I rolled my eyes and returned my attention to my plate of food, while they continued their little joke fest at Keith's expense. Those two could be a real trip. I personally didn't see anything wrong with a man releasing his inner thug. Back in the day, I found thuggish guys pretty damn irresistible, but now that I'd been living with a woman the past few years, I guess no one was interested in my viewpoint. I was so glad when Kym's cell rang and she had to wrap up lunch. It didn't take long for Lisa to do the same.

"You comin'?" Lisa asked.

"I'm not done yet," I said with a mouthful, pointing toward the buffet. "I'm gonna go up again."

I thoroughly enjoyed my third plate of food, and by the time I was finished, I had convinced myself that my body's reaction to Keith was just a fluke. Tiny was my girl, and there was no reason to get all confused just because I saw a guy who looked good to me. By the time I finished my lunch and headed back to my cubicle, I was feeling like myself again—until I nearly bumped into Keith and Leon while they were talking outside the elevator.

"Oh, um, this is a cool place to work," I said, giving him an awkward smile. When he didn't speak, I said, "You'll like it here. Welcome," and rushed away feeling like an idiot.

For the rest of the afternoon, I tried not to think about Keith, and especially about the way I reacted to him. As for the awkward way I acted around him and the tingling feeling between my thighs, I wrote that off as a natural reaction to the fact that Tiny was still kind of giving me the cold shoulder at home. Maybe I was just starved for some affection and my hormones were mixed up. At least that was what I tried to tell myself. But when I ran into Keith once again in the break room, my hormones kicked back up into overdrive, and I knew this was no fluke.

When I opened the door, I saw Keith standing near the vending machine, pulling every knob and yanking on the coin return forcefully. There was a slight pause in my step when I saw him, but no way was I going to turn around and leave the way I wanted to. This guy's magnetism was starting to scare me. I willed myself to play it cool this time.

"Damn," I said as I entered the room, "you sure are making a lot of noise."

"Oh, sorry, Ma," Keith said. "I just used my last dollar to get this damn Twix bar," he said, then kicked the machine for good measure.

I shook my head and stifled a laugh as I watched him start pulling all the knobs again like he was going to scare that machine into giving up the candy.

"Well, that's no way to get what you want," I finally said.

"Oh yeah?" he said as he turned to look at me. I could have sworn there was a twinkle in his eye when he said, "And I suppose you have the special touch, right?"

My heart leapt into my throat. Was this fine brother actually flirting with me? But I was quick to put that idea out of my head. Dwayne had done such a number on my self-esteem that I just assumed no man could ever find my big body attractive. I was just being silly, and this man was just trying to get his snack.

"Well, I don't know about a special touch," I answered in all seriousness, hoping he couldn't guess what I'd just been thinking. "But I've had a little more experience with this machine. Let me show you." He stepped out of my way, and I reached for the machine. I jiggled the coin-return lever a couple of times, then pressed the button for the candy bar of his choice. The candy bar fell to the bottom of the machine.

"Damn, Ma, I owe you," he said as he stooped down to get his treat. As far as I was concerned, the view of his muscled back as he bent over was reward enough. This good-looking man had me so shook that I'd almost forgotten why I even came into the break room in the first place.

Keith leaned against the machine and looked at me in a way I wasn't used to from men. "So, how long you been working here?" he asked.

" 'Bout five years," I answered, all the while chanting in my head, *Remember, girl, you love Tiny. You love Tiny.*

"Five years is a long time," Keith said, his eyes still wandering casually over my shape.

"Um, yeah, but like I told you earlier, it's a cool place to work." It was so hard to act nonchalantly while his gaze was causing heat in all the right places in my body. I couldn't confirm it at that very moment, but I thought I felt a warm trail running down my left thigh.

"You okay?" he asked, giving me a curious look.

"Ah, yeah, I'm cool. I'm good," I said. "Maybe my blood sugar is just low. Let me get something out of that machine."

He moved back just far enough for me to reach the coin slot, but not far enough for me to avoid touching him. My shoulder brushed up against his chest, and I swear I felt my knees get weak. When I bent down to get my candy out of the bin, I had no doubt about where his eyes were. The sound that escaped from his throat was like some kind of moan from deep within. If it had been Lisa or Kym, they would have turned around and slapped him for such obvious sexual tones. But me, I practically wanted to thank him for the compliment.

I stood upright, gave him a smile and a quick good-bye, then got the hell out of there, resuming the chant in my head: *Remember, girl, you love Tiny. You love Tiny.*

16

Coco

I was having a late lunch at Red Lobster with this new guy when my cell started vibrating again. I didn't even have to check the caller ID, because I already knew who it was. David from the gym had been blowing me up like nobody's business. I figured it was time to flip him and get revenge against the skinny heifers from the gym.

"Terrance, hold up for a sec. I need to take this call," I said. Terrance was a dark-chocolate delight, with the whitest teeth and sexiest lips I'd ever seen on a man. To say he was pretty was an understatement; that man was fine. He said he was a fire-fighter, and I couldn't wait for him to use his chocolate hose to put out my flames. But first I had to deal with David.

"That's cool, baby. Besides, I love to see you going." He smiled as I rose from the table to walk toward the back.

I hit the TALK button on my phone, then cooed into my Blue-tooth, "David, baby, what's up?" The minute I heard his voice, I already knew what was up. He was hungry for me, and I wanted revenge against his girl, but I also wanted to add him to the list of sponsors I was already working with. It was obvious to me he was just as ready to be put into the rotation.

"What's up? What's up is I wanna see you. I wanna stop playin' around and get down to business. You got me sweating you like a groupie." His voice was stressed. "You promised we were gonna get together this afternoon."

"Did I? Sorry, boo. It's just I'm a busy woman," I purred. "How about tomorrow?"

"How about today? Tomorrow ain't promised to any of us, and I don't wanna die missing out on a chance to be with you." He was straightforward and to the point. He wanted some ass.

"What about your girl Keyshawn? Not that I give a shit, but how's she gonna feel about you being with me?"

"Man, fuck Keyshawn! I got a chance to be with a real woman." I liked the way he talked, but we'd see if he felt the same way later on that night.

I chuckled. "So, Keyshawn ain't a real woman?"

He tried to clean it up. "Look, what I mean is . . ." At least he tried for a second. "Ah, fuck no, she ain't a real woman. At least not compared to you."

I smiled, glad to see I was talking to a smart man.

"Look, Coco, I wanna see you. I mean, I felt like we connected over the past couple of days on the phone, and well, I wanna see if we can make a run of it."

"Hold on, David. Let's get something straight so we both understand each other." I cleared my throat. "I'm not exclusive to anyone, and I'm not looking to fall in love."

"No problem. I understand. I ain't looking to fall in love either." I let out a faint laugh. Men are a trip. They all act like they can't fall in love, but six months from now when I don't want nothing to do with him, he'd be on suicide watch, talking about how he can't live without me.

"You sure? Because once you get some of this, I promise you it can become like a bad habit. A very expensive habit."

When he didn't respond, I took that as a sign that he wasn't concerned about the expense. "So, when you talking about hooking up?" I asked.

"How about right now? I got a couple of people I'm training, but I'll cancel them if I have to." He wasn't playing! He really wanted to get in my drawers bad. His boy Rodney must have told him how good it was. Speaking of Rodney, I was gonna have to talk to him about getting my hair and nails done later in the week.

"Damn. Well, I just arrived at this restaurant . . . on a date, actually," I said, testing him. Again, he didn't seem bothered by what I had to say. But while he didn't seem jealous that I was on a date, he was still pressed to get with me in a hurry.

"Well, why don't you come up with some excuse to leave so we can get together?" he said.

Oh, he wanted some of this bad, and knowing that made me sure I could get whatever I wanted out of this guy. The question was, what did I want in return for giving him some? Cash was always nice, I thought.

"You real aggressive. I like that," I said.

"Aw-ight, then, dig it," David said. "Why don't you shake that sucka and let me show you a real good time?"

I glanced over at Terrance. I was really looking forward to fucking his fine ass. "I don't know, David. This guy I'm with was gonna help me pay for this sofa I was trying to get." Sometimes it amazed me how well I could lie.

"Help you out? What was he gonna do, give you a hundred dollars? Baby, you ditch this guy and I'll buy the damn sofa for you, even throw in the love seat if you want."

Without any hesitation, I said, "I'll call you when I get in my car."

I walked back to the table regretting what I was about to do. But as fine as Terrance looked, I was a practical woman, and I knew I had to look at the bigger picture. It had to be done.

"Terrance, sweetie, I'm so sorry, but an emergency has come up. Is there any way we could do this again some other time?"

He looked up at me through doe-shaped eyes, and suddenly I just wanted to nestle his head between my soft pillows. There was something about this man that made me want to strip down right away. But sexy or not, Terrance wasn't about to give up the loot the way I knew David would. I put my best regretful look on my face.

"Well, can I drop you somewhere?" he asked, not trying to conceal his disappointment.

I shook my head. "Naw, thanks. I have my car. Just promise me we'll be able to hook back up again."

"Oh, you ain't even gotta worry about that," he assured me as he stood. "And I don't believe in waiting to be called up to bat, so either put me in the game or send me home, coach."

"Don't worry, baby. I'm definitely gonna put you in the game," I acknowledged with a smile. "You on my starting five for sure."

As I walked out of the restaurant, I kept it cute in case Terrance was still watching me. I was almost certain he was, so I put on a show that would entertain him and most likely catch a few additional eyes.

The minute I slipped behind the wheel of my car, I called David.

"Hey, boo," I said happily as soon as he answered. Sometimes before these guys get a taste, they get to thinking and get flaky with the money.

"Hey!" He sounded enthusiastic, so I felt a little less worried about getting what he'd promised me.

"So, I take it you dropped that loser, right?" he asked.

"Mmm-hmm. Let's meet at the Crowne Plaza on Baisely," I said, trying to move this show forward.

"Damn, girl, I like your style," he said, a chuckle still lingering in his voice.

"Just make sure you go to the bank before you get there. That sofa I want cost a thousand dollars, and no offense, but I don't take checks from anyone."

"No problem," he replied without hesitation. Probably glad I didn't bring up that love seat he volunteered to throw in. "Just make sure you bring the condoms."

"Honey, I never leave home without them," I said, liking this guy more and more. He was no-nonsense. I couldn't stand a man who was all about playing games and putting on some kind of act when we both knew what kind of arrangement it was we were looking for. "I'll see you in about twenty minutes."

I sat in my car parked near the driveway of the Crowne Plaza Hotel for about five minutes before David arrived. I watched him go inside, then pulled my car in front of the hotel and stepped out to turn my keys over to the valet. The moment I did, my phone rang.

"We're on the fourth floor," he said. "Room four-thirty-one; turn right when you get off the elevator. It's the last room on the right side."

"I'll see you soon," I said sweetly.

I rode the elevator up, and right before I stepped in front of room 431, I dialed a number on my cell, feeling smug. Getting Keyshawn's cell number wasn't as hard as you might think. I'd snatched it off a sign-up sheet for Pilates the day Keyshawn and her friend pissed me off. Apparently she was the instructor of the Saturday morning class. When I copied her cell number, I didn't think I'd be putting it to use so quickly, but I was definitely ready to roll.

When Keyshawn answered, I recognized her voice right away

and said, "Whatever you do, don't hang up! I'm about to teach you a valuable lesson on who not to fuck with." I knocked on the door.

"David, honey, open up," I said.

"David? Who the fuck is this?" Keyshawn's voice sounded panic-stricken.

"You hard yet?" I asked as David pulled open the door and stepped aside for me to enter. I flipped my hair over my shoulders, making sure it covered the wireless earpiece through which Keyshawn would still be able to hear everything. Now, if only she would stop screaming at me in my damn ear, I thought as I admired the room.

It was nice, done in earth tones—cream, browns, and beige. What I liked most was the very inviting king-sized bed, which was all but calling out to me.

"Damn, you look good enough to eat," he greeted, which set off another tirade of curses in my earpiece. I knew for sure that Keyshawn wasn't hanging up now.

Enjoying this little game, I put on some dramatics and shuddered with excitement. "Well, get your knife and fork 'cause I'd love for you to eat me."

David stepped closer, reaching for me, but I lifted my hand like a crossing guard stopping traffic.

"I guess you forgot about my sofa, huh?"

"No, I didn't forget nothing." He reached in his pocket and handed me a fistful of bills. I didn't even bother to count it. I just stuffed the money in my bag. The last thing I was worried about was him shorting me.

"I like a man who keeps his word," I said, knowing each word was like a knife in Keyshawn's heart. "And a very generous man at that."

"Question is, are you a woman who keeps hers? 'Cause there could be lots more where that came from if we get along."

"Oh hell no! Bitch, who the fuck is this?" I heard Keyshawn screaming as I watched David take off his shirt and flex his huge muscles. I liked athletic bodies, but truthfully, I wasn't really into muscle-bound guys. They always seemed to be lacking in the performance area. Probably all those steroids they be pumping.

"Well, before we get started, let me tell you the dos and don'ts." As I tried to explain my rules, I had to work hard to concentrate above the noise going on in my ear. Keyshawn sounded like she was about to lose her damn mind. But being all about the business at hand, I managed to tune her out. "First off, I'll go down on you if you go down on me. I love for my titties to be grabbed from behind as I'm bent over, getting fucked doggy-style. And if you go anywhere near the booty hole, you better be ready to go and buy the rest of the living room furniture I need, 'cause it's gonna cost you." I crossed my arms over my chest and asked him, "Think you can handle that?"

"Bend over and find out." We both laughed at his little joke, but Keyshawn sure as hell wasn't finding any of this funny.

"What the . . . ? Bitch, I know you ain't talking to my David!" she protested, though I had no doubt she knew damn well that it was her precious man getting ready to give it to me good. And I was gonna love every minute of it, knowing I'd gotten this bitch back for fucking with me at the gym. And the thousand bucks in my bag was a nice little bonus for all my troubles.

"Dave, you think you can handle my rules?" I asked again, just in case she didn't hear him the first time.

"Hell yeah," he confirmed. "I can do anything you want. I've been dreaming about that ass of yours ever since you first showed up at the gym."

I walked up on him and stood in his face. "Really? What else you been dreaming about, Daddy?" Damn, I wished I had turned down the volume on my earpiece a little before I made the call. This girl was screaming so much I thought I might end up with some hearing loss.

"I've been dreaming about rubbing my dick between them big-ass titties of yours." He grabbed a handful of my breast. I released a moan, kissing his cheek.

"Well, what's with all this talking? Let's get this party started." I stepped out of the jumpsuit I was wearing so David could get a view of my lace bra and matching thong. His eyes looked like they were ready to pop from his head when he took in the sight before him. I could hear some sort of scuffling on Keyshawn's phone.

"Well, aren't you gonna say anything?" I unhooked my bra, cupping the girls.

"Th-they're beautiful," was all he could manage to stutter as he stood there mesmerized.

I moved the pillows from the head of the bed and started to set them up the way I needed, but I almost lost my cool for a minute when I heard a different voice on my earpiece.

"Oh damn, Keyshawn. I know who that is! It sound like that fat bitch from the gym." Once I recognized the second voice as belonging to that other wench from the locker room, Rodney's girlfriend, I was actually relieved. Now I knew for sure that both of them would get the message loud and clear with every moan they were about to hear—I was not the one they should have been trying to play with.

I stretched across the pillows with my pelvic area slightly elevated and spread my legs. David crawled between my thighs, staring at the girls like they were made of gold.

"Come on, David," I invited. "I want to properly introduce you to the best place on earth."

"The best place on earth?" he mocked. "They look like the best place in the universe to me." He planted warm, wet kisses on each of them.

"Oh shit, David, that feels so good!" I purred. "But I wanna feel your tongue downtown."

"You ain't said nothin' but a word," David replied.

"That can't be my David." I heard Keyshawn's voice again. She actually sounded like she might be close to tears in spite of trying to act tough. "He don't even like eating pussy like that."

I decided she must not know her man too well, 'cause from the way he was acting with me, not only did he like eating pussy like that, but he loved it! David buried his head between my thighs, snatched off my thong, then slopped his face between my lips.

"Ssssss, ooooh, yes!" I cried. "Yes!"

When he used his fingers to separate my lips and reveal my swollen clit, I just about wanted to do a play-by-play for his girl. But he was just getting started. David did this move with his tongue that nearly took my breath away. He drilled his tongue into me, then sucked in my clit, holding it between his lips.

"Oh God! Oh God, David!" I cheered.

After David repeated that move a few times, I came so hard, I'm sure my screams could be heard on the next floor. Hmmmm, I thought, maybe I needed to give the muscle-bound types another chance.

"Now it's time for me to do you," I said, eager to return the favor.

"You evil bitch! You evil bitch!" Keyshawn cried in my ear.

"C'mon, David, bring me that pretty dick of yours. I'll bet you didn't know I was on a liquid diet, huh?" I actually had to stifle a laugh when I heard the way Keyshawn started to hyperventilate.

David eased off the bed and dropped his pants and drawers. His dick wasn't huge, but it sure as hell was curved. It almost looked like a hockey stick.

His rod was even harder when I deep-throated him in one smooth move. With my eyes focused on his, I tried to suck the life from him.

"Jesus, girl. Jeeees-sus!" When he grabbed the back of my head, moving me back and forth, I tightened my grip around his muscle.

"Goddamn, Coco!" I had him crying like a sissy. Superhead didn't have shit on me. "Oh damn! Suck it, girl. Suck this big ol' dick."

The fact that Keyshawn could hear us made my pussy even wetter. It was almost like she was watching, and I had been known to enjoy giving a performance or two in my lifetime. I pulled up off the dick and assumed the position, lying on my stomach across the pillows.

"Come on, baby. Give me that dick from the back." He was on top of me in a flash, and within no time, I had him screaming like a lovesick little bitch.

"Oooh, this is the best pussy I ever had!" He was enjoying himself so much that I knew this was gonna be quick, and I was right. He barely lasted five minutes, but that was okay. I'd achieved my goal. Those five minutes must have felt like an eternity to Keyshawn, who was bawling in my ear the whole time.

After he had his orgasm, he rolled over next to me on the bed. I said sweetly, "You know, David, I've always wanted to get fucked in the Crowne Plaza Hotel. I didn't even realize they had one down here by Kennedy Airport."

He looked at me and gave some answer, but I didn't even hear him. I was listening to Keyshawn say, "Crowne Plaza at Kennedy? Uh-huh. C'mon, girl, we're out!" just before she disconnected the call. I figured I could get a good twenty minutes more of dick before they got there, and I was determined to make the best of it. Maybe this time he wouldn't be so quick and I'd be able to get mine again.

"You ready to go again?" I asked David.

His dick was hard in an instant, and he was not reluctant at all to show me just how ready he was. But just like the first time, he got his with a quickness and collapsed onto my back.

There was no time for cuddling if my plan had worked the way I wanted, so I nudged him off me, and he stretched out on his back, his jimmy glistening limply on his thigh. I wore him and his muscle out.

"I'll be right back," I said as I scooped up my clothes and headed toward the bathroom. He didn't bother to answer, and I knew he was already on his way into that postsex slumber I was so good at putting on a brother. By the time I tiptoed out of the bathroom, I heard light snoring, so I kept moving to the front door and pulled it open.

"Hold the door," I called out to a couple who was just stepping into one of the elevators. I stepped one foot into the elevator but stopped when I heard Keyshawn's voice. I stuck my head out and turned to see her and her girl coming out of the next elevator.

"I'ma find this bitch, I swear, if David is really here," I heard her friend say.

"Oh, don't trip," I said gleefully out the elevator door. "You ain't gonna do shit to me. But if you're looking for David, he's in the last room on the right, four-thirty-one. I left the door open for you, and um, just in case you don't believe I was there, you'll find a royal blue thong on the floor at the foot of the bed. I left it there after David ripped it off. Oh, and, boo, while I just finished fucking your man, if you don't already know, I am not to be fucked with."

Just as the two heifers began to charge at me, I released my hand from the door and pulled my head back inside the elevator, thoroughly enjoying the sound of their angry screams as the doors closed in their faces. Besides, they couldn't have beat me anyway.

I hadn't, but before I could answer, she started dishing the dirt. "Chile, that room was the bomb. And the view! Oh my God, the view. I've never been to a hotel so damn nice and plush."

As she rambled on about the decor, I tuned her out, focusing instead on the image I couldn't get out of my head. All I could do was picture her and Tammy fucking Tim. Then things got worse, and my mind started wandering to the dark side. It was like I couldn't control myself. I wondered what Tim was working with. Was he really as big as Tammy said he was? He didn't walk like he was carrying anything major, and he didn't act all cocky like you'd think a big-dick man might. He was just Tim, plain ol' Tim. Tammy's husband, for God's sake!

"Is he working with anything down there?"

Egypt's words brought me back from that dark place. "He's hung like a horse, and he knows how to work it like he's getting paid for his services. Seriously, Isis, that man's got not only the best dick I've ever had, but the biggest," she swore, raising her hand to God.

I sat back in my chair, stunned.

"Shut the fuck up," I murmured. "You lying? Not Tim!"

Egypt gave an exaggerated nod and a wicked smile, confirming that it was in fact the truth.

"Yes, Tim. Girl, I don't even know how to explain it, except that Tim is da mothafuckin' man!" she testified. "I mean, he is the man for real!" She held her hands at least a foot apart. "And he's thick as your wrist!"

I crossed my arms in front of me, glancing at my wrist as I shook my head in disbelief. "Tim?" I asked. "Tim, Tim? Tammy's Tim?" I don't know why I kept asking. Maybe I thought that if I asked often enough, she'd admit that she was lying. I just couldn't believe it. I really didn't know how I would ever face Tammy or her husband again with this new information about him. Tim with a big dick and skills. Who would have thunk it? Damn, I always thought Tammy was lying, or at least exaggerating.

"Are you sure, Egypt? Tim? For real?"

"Yep. Tammy's Tim!" Egypt confirmed. "I can hardly believe it myself. Matter of fact, if I wasn't there, I'd think it was a lie."

"That big, huh?" I questioned like a broken record, this time holding my hands apart the same way she had.

"Yep, very well endowed," she said.

"Very well?"

She reached over and actually moved my hands apart another inch farther. "A monster."

I was still trying to wrap my head around that concept, but the next words that fell from her mouth were just as astonishing.

"The only thing I don't like about him is . . ." She stopped talking, and I had to restrain myself from taking her by the throat for leaving me in such suspense.

"What?" I demanded. "What?" I was louder this time.

She was looking up in the air again. "I just can't believe Tammy would be with a man who won't go down."

"Huh?" I was able to catch my mouth before it fell to the floor this time. "What do you mean he won't go down?" I asked. Tim's mythical status suddenly dropped a few pegs in my book. "Tim don't eat pussy?" I wanted to slap myself for even asking that question. I wasn't supposed to care about what Tammy's husband was or was not doing in the bedroom.

"Nope. Tammy says he won't do it."

"This is 2008. Everybody eats pussy."

"Not Tim, but Tammy says the dick's so good she don't even miss it. But make no mistake about it, if he was mine . . . huh, I woulda worked on that," she said, rolling her neck. "You know what they say. A man's like a dog. You have to train them young if you want them to be obedient." She held her hand up for a high five, but I was slow to respond because I was still digesting all this news. I'm not sure what I found most unbelievable, the fact that Tim was packing like a porn star, or the fact that in 2008 he wasn't licking the kitty.

Before I could decide which fact boggled me more, the doorbell rang. I looked at Egypt. "Damn, Tony got here quick," I said. "We'll have to continue this conversation later." She headed over to refill her wineglass while I went to answer the door.

When I opened it, my stomach lurched up into my throat. Why the hell had Rashad popped up on my doorstep once again—especially when I was expecting Tony?

"Hey, Pooh." He was smiling from ear to ear.

I poked my head out the door and looked both ways for Tony's truck. "What are you doing here?" I hissed at him. "I told you not to come by here anymore."

"I missed you, Pooh," he claimed.

I rolled my eyes. "Rashad, you have got to get out of here. I don't have time for your shit tonight. Tony's on his way over here." I turned away from him, muttering, "I swear, this cannot be happening right now." Was Rashad just trying to fuck things up between Tony and me?

The answer to that question came a whole lot faster than I needed when I heard the familiar sound of Tony's truck. I turned back to the door and watched as his truck pulled right in front of my building. Tony jumped out like a fireman responding to a six-alarm blaze.

"Oh shit!" I hissed. Rashad didn't even bother turning to see what had stolen my attention, although a part of me felt like he already knew.

"Tony, baby," I said, all but pushing Rashad to the side to greet Tony as he approached us. I tried to kiss him, but his attention was on Rashad.

"What the fuck is he doing here? Again?" he sneered.

"Um, wait, baby. Let me explain." It was clear Tony wanted an answer to his question, but I was afraid he was about to get up in Rashad's face and ask him directly.

"Egypt's here," I offered. I put a hand on Tony's chest and tried to distract him, but his focus would not be broken. He glared at Rashad, who was now leaning in my open doorframe as if he, and not Tony, belonged there. "She came to borrow my blouse."

"What the fuck does that have to do with his ass?" Tony's nostrils were flaring. I felt the nervous sweat start beading along my forehead.

I knew it. I just knew it, I thought desperately. *I knew something was going to happen tonight, but never did I suspect it would be this.*

The last time Tony had bumped into Rashad it hadn't been good. They'd almost come to blows before I convinced Rashad to leave. Something told me this encounter was going to be worse. By now, Tony was all but shoving me to get to Rashad. I just wanted Rashad gone, but he was looking for trouble—he'd been looking for it since the moment he showed up at my office that day.

"Babe." I tried to calm my own voice, hoping that would defuse the situation before things got out of control. But my soothing words did very little to help as Tony put his hands on my shoulders and moved me to the side.

"I'm sick of this shit. This nigga keep disrespecting me," Tony muttered. I couldn't hold him back any longer.

When Rashad stepped up to Tony, I just wanted to fall out.

"No!" I cried.

"Whassup, nigga?" Tony said, throwing his hands in the air.

Soon they were circling each other outside my front door. I felt myself getting hot. I didn't know what to do. I didn't want this to happen, but there was absolutely nothing I could do to stop it.

"He was leaving. I swear to you, I only opened the door because Egypt came to borrow a blouse," I pleaded desperately, but Tony wasn't hearing me. In fact, nobody was paying any attention to me anymore.

"I don't understand why your ass keep sniffing around my woman." Tony's face was so close to Rashad's it was like he was going to open his mouth and swallow him up.

I don't remember who made the first move, but soon a scuffle began. Tony grabbed Rashad into a headlock and started flinging his body around while Rashad grabbed Tony's midsection.

Egypt finally came running from the kitchen. "What's go—" She stopped midsentence when she saw Tony's uppercut connect with the left side of Rashad's jaw. Rashad went flying into nearby bushes, and Tony pounced on him.

"Do something!" Egypt yelled at me.

"What am I supposed to do?" I asked, looking at the two of them tumbling from the bushes to the ground. Tony jumped up, then hauled back and kicked Rashad in the ribs so hard that I practically felt the pain it caused.

"Tony! Please, baby, please!"

I was relieved when my cries seemed to snap Tony out of his violent frenzy. He turned and took a few steps away from Rashad, who was still on the ground, cradling his injured rib cage. I headed over to check on Rashad, but before I could reach him, Tony was pouncing again, throwing punches wildly. This time when Tony pulled back, I saw the blood gushing from Rashad's nose, which I was sure was broken.

"Jesus, Tony! Are you crazy? You're going to kill him!" I

threw my body in front of Tony while Egypt leaned down to help Rashad up.

"Rashad, man, you need to get to the hospital," Egypt told him, but he seemed more interested in getting near me than getting help for his broken bones.

With one arm wrapped across his ribs and the other hand trying to slow the blood flowing from his nose, he limped toward me. The sight was pretty pathetic. Tony clearly knew he had won this fight, because he didn't even bother trying to stop Rashad. Still, I wasn't taking any chances. I kept my body between the two of them so nothing could jump off again.

"This fool don't care shit about you," Rashad managed to say. "I mean, how long y'all been together and he ain't even gave you a ring or nothing? Think about it."

"You need to go to the hospital," Egypt said gently, trying to guide him away from me.

"Yeah, take your punk ass to the hospital and get your nose fixed 'fore you get even uglier than you already are," Tony said, taunting him.

Rashad ignored him. "Pooh, I'm sorry for all the stupid shit I did to hurt you, but you know damn well I love your ass," he said.

"You need to go," I said sadly, feeling so conflicted about the whole incident. Rashad and I had had our problems in the past, but I didn't want to see him hurt and bleeding the way he was now.

"You betta listen to her, dawg," Tony said. I still had one hand on his chest, and I felt his breathing quicken, like he was preparing to attack again.

"Just stop, Tony," I told him. "He's gonna go, okay? Nobody needs to get hurt over this." As I said the words, I realized Rashad was already hurt—not just physically, but now, I believed, emotionally too.

"Go on, Rashad," I said quietly.

He let go of his rib cage and, wincing in pain, dug into his pocket. I nearly fell out when I saw what he held in his hand as he struggled to get his beaten body down onto one knee. He looked down at the one-carat diamond solitaire I had once worn, then given back to him.

"I'm ready," Rashad said as he looked up into my eyes, which were dangerously close to releasing a flood of tears after all this drama. "I'm tired of this ole bullshit. Pooh, I want you to be my wife. We can go down to the courthouse right now if you want to."

For a brief second, everything else around us disappeared as I stared at Rashad and tried to process what had just happened. Then Tony's laughter broke the spell. I turned to look at Tony, who reached into his pocket and produced a ring twice as large and brilliant as the one Rashad had presented to me.

"What? What now, nigga? What?" Tony said to Rashad, still laughing loudly.

Though a small part of me felt bad for Rashad's obvious humiliation, I couldn't help but smile at Tony and the glittering stone he held out to me.

"This ain't the way I planned this shit, but, Isis, you know I'm ready, baby. So what's up? You taking that nigga or you marrying me?"

I stifled the small sigh that wanted to escape. This moment wasn't happening anything like I had dreamed it would. I had expected to hear heartfelt words about how much he loved me, how he couldn't live without me. But then again, I'm sure the circumstances weren't exactly how Tony had planned them either. He had no way of knowing Rashad was going to be there to mess up our special moment. His rough proposal was probably just because he was still hyped up in macho mode after his fight. Then it dawned on me—what if Tony hadn't planned on proposing at all today? What if he was only giving me this ring to embarrass Rashad?

"Are you sure about this?" I asked.

"Isn't this the ring we been looking at together, baby?" he asked. I nodded. "Then you know I'm for real, right? Didn't I tell you it was gonna happen? Have I ever let you down?" he asked.

"No."

"Then who's it gonna be? Why don't you tell him once and for all that you 'bout to be *my* wife? Tell him to take his punk-ass little diamond chip and step off."

I held out my shaking hand and waited for Tony to slip the

ring on my finger. Once the gorgeous gem was where it belonged, I jumped into Tony's arms and covered him with kisses.

"C'mon, Rashad. You really need to go get that checked out," I heard Egypt saying.

By the time Tony and I broke our kiss, Egypt and Rashad were halfway to her car. I wanted to call out to Rashad, but what would I say? It wasn't like I was going to apologize for saying yes to Tony's proposal. This was my moment. Sure, I felt bad that Rashad got his ass beat, but it wasn't like I invited him to my house. I even tried to give him fair warning to get lost before Tony showed up. As I turned my attention back to my fiancé, I hoped Rashad had finally gotten the message and this would be the last I saw of him.

18

Nikki

I was sitting at my desk wrapping up a phone call with a customer when I heard the mail cart coming up the hall. Never before had the sound of the mail cart triggered any kind of emotions in me, but as I sat there listening, something in my stomach came to life. I told myself since I wasn't sure who was going to be behind it, there was no need for me to start acting up, but I didn't have to wait long before Keith peered around the corner of my cubical.

"Yo, Nik, I'm not interrupting anything, am I?" he asked.

I jumped a little, then turned in my chair, smiling. "Nah, just filling out a report on the last call I took. How are you?"

He smiled, then said, "I'm aw-ight." He looked around nervously before speaking again. "So, um, Nik, can a brotha holla at'chu for a second about somethin'?"

I nodded and he leaned in close to me. For a split second, I thought he was going to try to kiss me, but his face stopped about a foot from mine. There weren't enough words to begin to explain what I was feeling with him standing so close to me, staring at me with those bedroom eyes of his. I tried to play it cool, to keep it cute and not act like men made me nervous, especially young, sexy, thugged-out fine-ass men. I could handle it; I could handle him, I thought. *Did his eyes twinkle when he just smiled at me?* I shook my head, hoping to make the thoughts disappear.

I was so glad when he spoke again because that meant I didn't have to. "Yo, Nik, check it. You think you'd be interested in going out to lunch with me today? My treat, know what I'm sayin'?"

The butterflies immediately came to life and started kicking things up in the pit of my stomach as I tried to decipher whether or not he had just asked me out on a date. But it didn't take long for me to realize he did. Where all this had come from I don't know, but there he stood, right in front of me, right in my cubical, waiting for me to decide whether I'd go out with him.

"So, Ma, whassup? We goin' to eat or what?"

My heart nearly stopped. I sat there frozen, with a breath trapped in my throat, threatening to end life as I knew it. I looked around the office, as much as I could without moving my head. But despite where my eyes traveled, they still came back to Keith and his looming question.

"Um . . . I'm ah . . . well, it depends," I finally managed. I could see a tiny sigh of relief coming from him, proving that he was in fact nervous.

"Oh, so what does it depend on?" He straightened up, looking around again. I tried to see if he was becoming irritated with me. If he was, he didn't let it show. He waited calmly, even smiling every so often. He was so hard, yet so soft at the same time.

"Well"—I took a deep breath—"it depends on whether this would be a date or just two coworkers going out to eat."

For a moment, we were both silent. I wasn't sure what he was waiting on, but I was determined to wait him out. Finally, he looked down at me. "Why does that matter?"

"Um, well, it does. I'm in a relationship." There, I'd said it! I admitted why I could not go out to lunch or anything else with him. I was seeing someone, but he didn't need to know exactly who I was seeing.

"Oh, wow! Well, um, in that case, it's just two coworkers, two friends going out to grab some lunch. Is that cool? I'm not trying to move in on dude's turf." He threw his hands up innocently, as if to prove just how harmless he really was.

I could hardly believe the conversation I was having with him. Keith was fine, I had determined. Forget about cute, he was fine! I just didn't know how to touch the topic that could not be ignored. When he didn't ask about who I was seeing, I didn't offer any details. It wasn't like I was embarrassed to admit Tiny was my lover, but I just wasn't ready to have that discussion with Keith. No man had looked at me that way in years. Despite my size, he seemed to be genuinely interested in me, and that thought made me wet despite how much I tried to deny the feelings.

"So, what now? Cat got your tongue?" he asked jokingly. I

reluctantly pulled myself away from my thoughts as I watched his gaze roll up and down the length of my body. Good Lord, this cannot be happening to me.

"Umm, no." I shook my head. Being so close to him made me nervous. I was like a stupid schoolgirl with a crush on the captain of the football team. "Cat? Nah, I'm cool. I'm straight," I stammered, struggling for just the right words.

He shrugged his shoulders. "Well, then whassup?"

"A simple lunch between two coworkers who are friends?" I repeated, trying my best to make his proposal sound okay, 'cause Lord knows I wanted to go.

Keith gave me a slight nod.

"Yeah, that's cool," I confirmed. "I'll meet you in front of the building at twelve."

"Bet. I'll see you at twelve."

I was still thinking about the wonderful lunch I had had when I strolled back into the office. I needed to get out, to just get away from all the stupid stuff going on at work, not to mention my confusion about what was going on with Keith. I had no idea a nice lunch would go so far toward making me feel good about myself, but that's exactly what it had done.

"You know, Ma, check it. Your man is one lucky mother-fucker, 'cause you one fine, female," he'd said, using his tongue to play with the straw and killing me softly in the process. We were sitting across from each other at a restaurant he chose.

The slang he used when he talked—"say, Ma," "whassup boo," "lemme holla at'chu"—and just thinking about the way words tumbled out of Keith's mouth with such ease was enough to make me wet. And even though I'm not blaming him, it seemed like Keith was all but tempting me with his roughneck ways. I'd already been caught a few times peeping his tattoos and a few other aspects of his body. Then there was the fact that his build seemed to be so athletic, I could barely take my eyes off him when he was sporting those wife-beaters beneath his open button-down shirts. It was like having the devil on one shoulder and an angel on the other, and I was doing very little to fight the direction I seemed to be leaning in. Yes, I was headed to hell for sure.

He was even more handsome than I first thought. It was as if up close and personal made him look even better. I knew I couldn't compliment him, because even though I was out with him, I wanted to make sure I wasn't the one trying to make a first move of any kind, no matter what it was I really wanted to do.

"So, how do you like the new job?" I asked him, trying to take the conversation in a safe direction. But Keith was persistent.

"I think you're the best thing there," he said.

I couldn't help but smile, but I tried not to be so obvious. I tried to act like his compliments were nothing new to me. I decided right then and there that I liked Keith. I wasn't sure what that meant, or if my liking him said anything about me, but I figured at least I had taken a first step.

Keith behaved himself during the rest of lunch, and I enjoyed his company and the food. Our lunch was good, and I was hoping we could go out again, like coworkers who are friends.

I was still floating on cloud nine when I stepped off the elevator and onto our floor. What I wasn't prepared for was all the commotion going on around my cubical. I frowned as I glanced toward Keith. As I walked toward my desk, Keith stopped off to talk to someone who had a work-related question for him. I was glad he had when I walked up into my workspace.

"Guuurrrl, Tiny is looking for you!" Kym announced like she was truly scared for me. She was nervously pacing in my small workspace.

I tried to remain calm. I didn't want any problems, and I damn sure didn't want Keith to get curious about what was going on. I told myself that if I remained calm, Kym would do the same, but I was wrong.

"She done brought you food for lunch and everything!" she exclaimed.

I placed my purse down and tried to assure Kym everything would be okay. I wanted desperately to believe it myself, but I just didn't know how things would work out with Keith mere feet away. I did know that if Kym didn't calm down real fast, she'd surely draw attention to us and I'd be pushed into an awkward position. I didn't want to have to explain to Keith why Kym was going nuts over Tiny showing up and looking for me. I just hoped she would get it out of her system before he rounded that corner.

"Girl," Kym continued, "Tiny is hot! I mean, she's been blowing you up and everything. Why haven't you been answering your phone? Did I mention she brought you food for lunch?"

I nodded slightly. "Yes Kym, you told me. She came here looking for me, she brought me food, and apparently she's been calling me like crazy." I shrugged my shoulders. "Well, I'm here now," I said calmly. But trust me, my insides were flipping, churning, and doing everything else. I didn't know what I'd say once I got home. But I told myself I'd just have to deal with that later. For now, I wanted to sit down and come up with some excuse that might work. I remembered each time she had called during lunch. I didn't want to turn the phone off, because I felt like she'd damn sure want to know why. Now I wished I had just answered her call and given her some excuse.

"I mean, where'd you go?" Kym asked, sounding all defeated, like it was her I'd been stepping out on by going to lunch with Keith.

I wanted to put an end to all the ranting and raving she was doing, but I wasn't quite sure how to do it without having to do more explaining.

"Okay, so Tiny came by to bring me lunch. I'll just straighten all of this out when I get home." I told her as calmly as I could.

"All I'm trying to say to you is when Tiny came and you weren't here, she was hot! I'm just trying to warn you, because I ain't never seen her that mad. Your girl was going ballistic!" Kym warned.

"I will deal with Tiny," I said.

"Who's Tiny?" I had no idea that Keith had even caught up to me. I wondered just how much of the conversation he might've overheard.

I shot Kym a knowing look and ignored Keith's question by simply saying, "I've got tons of work to do."

Kym stood with her arms crossed at her chest. Keith leaned up against the wall of my cubical, and as if I had summoned her out of nowhere, Tiny came walking into my workspace. Talk about timing.

"Oh, we were just talking about you," I said to Tiny. After a few moments of the most uncomfortable silence I'd ever experienced, I turned to Tiny and began the introductions.

"Um, Tiny," I squeaked, "this is my coworker Keith. Keith, this is Tiny," I said, searching her face for any signs that she could tell something just wasn't right. Let Kym tell it, she was about ready to rip me apart.

Tiny looked Keith up and down, frowned a bit, then nodded ever so slightly in his direction. She did this just as she leaned forward and placed a succulent kiss right on my lips. And believe me when I say this was no peck. She even managed to slide a little tongue action into the mix.

Tiny pulled back after clearly marking her territory. I'll never forget what happened next, because my heart sank to depths I never knew existed. The look on Keith's face said it all. His eyes were wide but sad. I watched as his gaze moved from Tiny to me, then back to Tiny again, and without saying a word, he turned and walked away. I could even see his shoulders slouching a bit.

Tiny turned to Kym and started up a conversation like I was no longer the focus of her manhunt. I felt bad about Keith, but the thing about it was, I still wasn't ready to admit to myself why I felt that way.

19

Tammy

"Will you fucking move?" I shouted at the cars in front of me, jamming my hand hard against the horn. If I wanted to be honest with myself, I'd admit my shitty-ass mood had nothing to do with the traffic jam I was sitting in. But it was so much easier to use this excuse than admit the truth. Not that I was sure what the word *truth* meant anymore.

I covered my face with my hands as if I could hold back all the frustration and the tears that felt ready to burst forth. It felt like the world I knew had completely come to an end, and I just wanted to cry, especially since I knew I had no one to blame but myself. What the fuck had I been thinking?

I lowered my hands and looked at the road, slamming on my brakes just in time to avoid ramming into the car in front of me. My heart was racing out of control. I saw the eyes of the man in the other car through his rearview mirror. He looked like he wanted to kill me. I just wanted to give him the finger. "I know how close I came, dammit! That's what the hell I got insurance for any damn way!" I snapped. "It's not like I hit your ass."

Tears started to stream down my face as the images I'd been seeing in my brain all day returned with a vengeance. My mind was like a DVD player on continuous loop. I kept seeing the same thing over and over and over again: Tim taking her leg and lifting it over his shoulder. I watched as he entered her slowly, moving his hips the same way he'd done to me thousands of times in the past. His penis—my penis—the one that conceived our two beautiful children, was moving deeper and deeper inside my best friend, my only true friend other than him.

"You like it? You like my dick?" he asked, pushing himself even deeper inside of her.

"Oh God, yes!" was all she kept saying.

I closed my eyes and opened them again, praying that it would be enough to earn me a few seconds of peace from the nightmare that was playing out in front of me. It was like he was all but ignoring me. I felt like last year's hot Christmas toy, tossed aside by a child who'd gotten something new and more exciting to play with.

"It's so big! Oh God it's so big!" she had cried.

I could still hear her pleasure-filled screams piercing my eardrums. And the only thing that was going through my mind was that she was full of shit. I mean, what the hell was she doing all that damn screaming and hollering for? She wasn't no damn virgin. The way she was moaning as she squirmed beneath him was enough to make me sick to my stomach. She was acting like she ain't ever had any dick before, but I knew different, much different.

"You can take it," he coached. "Doesn't it feel good?"

"Yes! Yes! It feels wonderful, but it's so big." She moaned loudly.

I wanted to smack the shit outta Tim, the way he was carrying on like he needed to handle her with such care, because she might rip from his massive offering. Oh, it was disgusting, absolutely disgusting.

I swallowed back tears that night as I watched my birthday dream for my husband turn into my own personal nightmare right before my eyes. I rubbed his back as if to say, "Hey, baby, don't forget about me," and he glanced my way, but when he did, the painstaking expression of ecstasy across his face told me I was messing up his concentration, and I just needed to wait my fucking turn. Can you believe it? My husband wanted me to wait my turn to get some of his dick. If I'd had a gun, I swear there would have been a murder-suicide.

"Oh shit, she's tight, so tight," he murmured. Then he had the nerve to look over at me and ask, "Is this what you wanted, baby?" All the while, his hips were moving, and he was dipping deeper and deeper between her thighs. "Huh, baby? Is this what you wanted?"

"Oh yes, Tim! Yes! This is just what I wanted. I'm about to come!" Egypt answered.

I wanted to holler, "He was talking to me, bitch!"

Reality set back in and the images faded. I was back in my car again, and the line of traffic started inching forward again. I shook my head, letting out a long sigh and telling myself to try to think better thoughts. For a few minutes, I did just that as I moved in the slow crawl of afternoon traffic. I needed to do something to keep my mind off the other night, or it was only a matter of time before I'd drift right back into those images. I thought about calling someone and even reached for my cell. Like magic, the phone rang before I could dial. I glanced down at the caller ID and sucked my teeth.

"Like I wanna talk to that bitch," I snarled as I watched Egypt's number dancing across the screen.

When Tim did finally give me some, Egypt had had the nerve to kneel down at my head and stuff her titty in his mouth. I was just outdone, but what could I do? Suddenly, Tim had become a talented multitasker when only moments earlier he had looked at me like I was messing up his groove by touching him when he was digging deep in her valley.

The phone finally stopped ringing and she left a voice mail.

"You ain't even gotta worry about me calling you back," I said out loud.

Finally, I arrived at my exit. I drove up 164th Street, glad to finally be nearing my house. I pulled into the garage, where I was relieved to see that Tim hadn't made it home before me. The kids were still at my mother's house from a few nights ago, so I would have some time alone—and I needed that time to get my head straight. I had to figure out how to approach the subject of our threesome without it turning into a huge fight. I had to calm myself down and think rationally.

Unfortunately, as soon as I entered the house, the tears started falling again. I still couldn't get past the fact that after our threesome, there was no doubt he was way more into her than me. And the worst part of it was that I was the one who had brought Egypt into our bed in the first place. For months, I thought about giving Tim that special gift. I thought I was being the kind of wife every man would die for—one willing to fulfill his greatest sexual fantasy. What man wouldn't want what I did for him? I was so eager to please Tim that I practically begged Egypt to do it. In fact, I had to do some work to convince Tim to go along with it too. But never once did I stop to think what might happen if they both enjoyed it more than me.

Now, two days after the threesome, it was all I could think about. They had clearly enjoyed each other more than me, and it was eating me alive. Shit, they might have been happier if I hadn't been in the room at all. Then their asses could have sexed each other all night long. What the hell was wrong with me, not being able to foresee this? How did I think I would be able to handle watching my husband with another woman without getting jealous? Was I crazy? If I wasn't already, all this nonstop turmoil in my head was sure to drive me into the nuthouse.

I dried my tears and washed my face, determined to get the thoughts out of my mind before Tim came home. For a few minutes, I succeeded. I turned on the TV and let the news headlines distract me. But when I saw the answering machine light blinking, then checked the caller ID, Egypt's number flashed on the screen, instantly returning me to my foul mood.

"Why the hell would she call here when she knew I was at work?" I paused for a moment as my thoughts took me to a place I did not want to go. Maybe the fact that I was at work was the whole point. Maybe Egypt had been calling to talk to Tim. This was not good. Either I was well on the way to becoming an insanely jealous woman, or my best friend was trying to get with my husband.

A quick flash of Tim savoring Egypt's breasts sent a fresh bolt of rage through me. It did not go unnoticed by me that he paid more attention to her breasts than he'd given mine in months. And while he had always adamantly refused when I asked, he even looked like he was considering going down on Egypt when she pushed his head in that direction. The more I thought about it, the more I realized Tim had enjoyed himself a little too much with Egypt. My mind went back to the blinking answering machine. What if Egypt had called because Tim had asked her to? Oh, this was definitely not good. This whole situation was a true mess.

I went downstairs and pulled out a stack of takeout menus, since I was in no mood to cook. As mad as I was, I might just decide to burn the whole damn house down.

The beeping front door alarm signaled Tim's arrival. I tried to swallow my attitude, knowing that starting a fight with him the minute he walked in the house was not the best way to approach this problem. The last thing I wanted to do was come off like a bitch. It would just drive him further into Egypt's waiting arms.

I tried to act as normal as possible, putting a pleasant look on my face when Tim walked into the kitchen, but it didn't seem to matter. He treated me as if I were practically invisible, going straight to the pile of mail on the counter and flipping through it. After he separated the envelopes into piles of bills and junk mail, he finally came over and gave me a quick peck on the cheek. For a moment, it looked like he wanted to say something to me but then thought better of it and headed for the refrigerator to get a drink.

"How was your day?" I asked when he turned to look at me.

He shrugged. "Pretty uneventful."

I nodded.

"What about yours?" he asked.

"Oh, it was okay," I said.

And that was the extent of our conversation before Tim walked out of the kitchen and into the den. I know I promised myself I wasn't going to let my jealousy rear its ugly head, but this bullshit small talk just wasn't going to cut it for me. I followed behind him and spoke up before he could turn on ESPN and totally tune me out.

"So, can I ask you a question?" I stepped in front of the television to make sure he couldn't ignore me.

His eyebrow went up. "Sure. What's on your mind?"

"I just wanted to know if you enjoyed the threesome."

He stared at me for a moment, and my mind raced with possibilities. Was he afraid to say he'd enjoyed it? Maybe he was trying to think of a lie so as not to hurt my feelings. This was the first time either of us had brought up the events of the other night, so I really had no idea where his head was at. "Ah, it was nice. Different."

I put on a fake smile, willing myself to stay calm. If he was going to avoid discussing this, I would pull the information out of him with a few leading questions. "Would you like to do it again?"

He paused briefly, glancing up at the ceiling as if considering his answer. But then he nodded. "Sure. Why not?"

I felt like he'd just punched me in the stomach, but I tried to keep my composure. "Okay . . . with someone new, or would you wanna do it with Egypt again?"

This time, there was no hesitation. "I think I'd like to do it with Egypt again." Another punch in my gut. And then he had the nerve to offer up some lame-ass explanation. "Bringing someone else in would just complicate things. Besides, we all had chemistry, don't you think?"

He had the nerve to grin, but I'd had enough of this little game. I wiped the smile right off his face. "Well, at least the two of you had chemistry," I said icily.

"What's that supposed to mean?" A brief look of panic crossed his face. There was no sense in sidestepping the issue anymore, so I got right to the point.

"Tim, did you enjoy Egypt more than you did me?"

His head snapped in my direction. "Are you crazy?"

I sucked my teeth as I closed in on him. "It's a simple question."

"I don't believe this shit. I knew this was gonna happen," he said with resignation. "Tammy, this was all your idea. You wanted this. This was your thing, not mine. I only did what you wanted."

I swallowed dry and hard at the truth in his words. I did want to do it. I thought it would make him happy. I figured he was like most men—he wanted to have two women at the same time. But I certainly didn't expect him to be so into her that he would treat me as if I didn't even exist.

"That's why I didn't want to do that shit in the first place!" he yelled.

"Well, I couldn't tell, the way you were all between her fuckin' thighs. You were all over her like . . ." I shrugged. "I don't know, but I'm just saying the way you were all into her, it wasn't right."

"What the fuck? Are you serious?" he yelled back at me. "I mean, are you really fucking serious?"

I placed a hand on my hip. "Do I look fucking serious?"

Tim shook his head. "You all but force me to fuck your friend, I do what you want, and now you're telling me you're mad because I did exactly what you wanted me to do? I mean, damn!" Tim really looked confused.

"All I'm saying is you didn't have to act like she was the best fucking thing since sliced bread. That's all I'm trying to say."

Tim stood glaring at me silently for a long time. Part of me understood his anger. I mean, I couldn't deny that I was the one who had set this whole thing in motion, so I had no idea why I had become so obsessed with this now. But I did know that things hadn't turned out anything like I'd imagined they would. I thought the three of us would get it on. I thought we'd turn him out and make his toes curl, have him screaming like he'd lost his mind. Then he would realize that his wonderful wife was the one responsible for the unimaginable pleasure he was receiving, and he'd be forever grateful that I'd fulfilled his biggest fantasy. I certainly didn't expect him to be so enthralled with making love to another woman right in my presence. And I totally miscalculated how much it would bother me to watch him with another woman, even if she was my best friend.

"I simply did what the hell you wanted; now you sitting here flipping out on me because of that?" Tim's voice was getting really loud now. "I'm not gonna deal with this shit. You can sit here and act like that if you want, but you're doing it alone." Tim stormed out of the room, leaving me standing there, even more upset than I was by the images of him sexing Egypt.

20

Coco

You'll never believe who tracked me down and begged me to let him take me out on the town—Jackson Brentworth, the rich developer who had me trapped in his closet while he screwed his wife a few weeks ago. I'd pretty much written him off after the way things turned out, until he called the house, asking me if I wanted to go out and have a drink. How he got my number beats the hell outta me, but then again, men like Jackson have plenty of resources. All I knew was that the man must have wanted some of this pretty bad to track down my unlisted home phone number, so I heard him out. It never surprised me that even though they knew it was gonna get them in trouble, men just couldn't resist giving me a call once they got a taste of my brown sugar. I know it sounds conceited, but my stuff's just that damn good, and I've got the references to prove it.

In Jackson's case, he barely got a chance to sniff my drawers before his wife barged in, forcing me to hide in his closet. So, when he called suggesting we go to the African Poetry Theater on Jamaica Avenue for Thursday night erotic poetry, I was pleasantly but also suspiciously surprised.

"What's the catch? Your wife gonna show up a half hour later?"

"No, nothing like that. My wife doesn't even like poetry, but I remember you saying that you do." He took a deep breath, probably annoyed at my reluctance. "Look, I know you're still upset about how things turned out at my place, but I swear, I'll make it up to you."

"I'm not sure," I whispered into the phone. I was hoping to give him the impression that I was having a hard time deciding, but my mind was made up from the get-go. The only question I had was how much he was willing to spend in order to make it up to me.

"Come on, Coco, take a chance. I promise you won't regret it."

"Well . . . I dunno." My smile widened as I thought about just how much I could get out of him by the time the evening was over. He was on the verge of begging, and men who were that desperate for some of my stuff were willing to part with plenty of loot. "I don't know, Jackson. This is really short notice, and I really don't have the proper jewelry to go with the outfit I'd like to wear." I was using my most practiced, babyfied voice. "I think I'm gonna pass."

"Well, we could always stop by Martin's on Jamaica Avenue on our way to the poetry reading. Martin Goldman happens to be my personal jeweler."

I lost my composure. "Really? Are you serious? You're going to buy me something at Martin's?" I was flabbergasted. You couldn't even get into Martin's without an appointment. He was considered the Jacob the Jeweler of New York. Ask any rapper.

"I don't see why not. A beautiful woman should have beautiful things." Jackson cleared his throat. "That is, as long as the beautiful woman remembers to take care of the man who provides her with those beautiful things."

"Sweetie, I have a memory like an elephant. I never forget anything a man does for me, and I always return the favor in spades. I'll see you around eight." I hung up, smiling broadly. Being locked up in that closet was turning out to be more beneficial than I could have even imagined.

The African Poetry Theater was a small, out-of-the-way place that looked more like a jazz club than any theater I'd been to. Instead of theater seats, the place was decked out with intimate tables for two, oversized love seats, and a long bar that took up an entire side of the room. The atmosphere was calming, and even though the place was jam-packed for the poetry reading, it didn't feel crowded at all. It also didn't hurt that Jackson had arranged for us to have a table off to the side in the front.

I could feel the heads turn as the hostess escorted us to our seats. The way people looked at Jackson, I felt like I was in the presence of royalty. I took hold of his arm proudly. I could get used to being on a rich, powerful man's arm. And I was trying to keep it cute in my sarong, which I chose so that I would fit in with the upscale poetry crowd I knew we'd be kicking it with.

Jackson didn't seem to mind being seen on a date with me either. I guess as long as we weren't actually caught naked in his bedroom, he could come up with a valid excuse for his wife. Personally, I didn't really care what he told her. She was his problem. For tonight, I was the queen up in this place, and the jealous looks on the faces of the women around me made it clear that most of them wished they could take my place. But trust me, I would be defending this position fiercely. The benefits were much too good to give up.

Jackson, as promised, had had his driver stop by Martin's on our way over. I picked out a banging diamond necklace to go with my outfit, and without me even asking, Jackson added the matching bracelet. None of the jewelry had any price tags, so I didn't dare ask, but I'm sure this little date set him back at least five grand. And the night was still young, I thought with a satisfied smile. Who knows how much more I could get him to spend before it was through.

As the small band started playing some old-school music, I hummed along. A lot of people didn't know this about me, but just like I loved poetry, I loved the old artists more than those new rappers, with their no-singing behinds.

As I hummed to Billy Paul's "Me and Mrs. Jones," I wondered how much more money I could hijack from Jackson. Rent was due again in a few weeks, and I still wanted that loft. I would have to put on my A-game tonight. When I got finished with him, his wife was gonna be reduced to a roommate. She could have the title; I just wanted the man and his money.

The show began with some of the best spoken-word poets I'd ever heard. First the MC introduced the poet, and then each one was preceded by an old R & B song played before the artist came on stage. Each song matched the theme of the ensuing poem.

Suddenly, Marvin Gaye's "Sexual Healing" was played as a prelude, and several women stood up, throwing their hands in the air like they were in a sexual frenzy. The lights were dimmed dramatically, and a dark shadow slowly moved onto the stage. At first he appeared only as a silhouette. The few women around us who remained seated sat upright in their chairs. Clearly, this next performer knew how to get a woman's attention. Even I couldn't resist sitting up a little straighter in anticipation. Just his entrance alone had me curious.

When he made his way to the mic, a lone blue light shone down and revealed his face. I swore my eyes had finally witnessed the human version of heaven. The MC introduced him as Mac Reynolds. This black man had a presence that commanded respect. All the women began to scream and swoon, and he hadn't even said a word. Personally, I felt like lightning had struck me, but I had to play it cool while Jackson was sitting next to me.

Mac Reynolds was tall and bald, with smooth, dark chocolate skin and an athletic body. This brother was fine as he wanted to be. And he looked to be about my age—midthirties or so. The way he held that mic stand, I don't think a single woman in there didn't wonder what it would be like to have him touch her the same way.

"Hi, I'm Mac Reynolds and I'd like to read a poem for you." His voice came out in a rich baritone, like Melvin Franklin's from the first Temptations group, and Lord knows, that's when I knew I had to have him. I've got a thing about men with deep voices, and his just sent a vibration through my body that pushed me over the edge. His lips were so close to the mic, it looked like he was basically making love to it.

Then he broke out into his poem "Sistah." It seemed like Mac kept looking directly at me when he delivered his lines, as if his words were for me only:

> *What is a sistah? A mysterious thing,*
> *Timeless, subterranean bond*
> *Which runs beneath the veins.*

Something about those lines grabbed hold of me and sent me into a sexual fantasy so deep I could have had an orgasm right there in my seat. I was so lost in my thoughts that I didn't even hear the rest of his words and only came back to my senses when the room burst into applause at the end of his poem. Mac bowed, and almost everyone—well, at least every woman in the room—rose from their seats and gave him a standing ovation.

I was instantly infatuated with him. I didn't even want to look over at Jackson for fear that the lust was written all over my face. My decision was made. Before I left, I would find a way to make this poet mine. To hell with money. This man had my coochie soaking wet with mere words, and I just wanted to get with him and see what was possible if he was with me in the flesh. As I stood there next to Jackson, clapping until my hands stung, I felt I had been lifted to a higher plane.

A few minutes later, the intermission started. Jackson and I sat together making small talk. I put on a good performance, acting interested in whatever he said, stealing glimpses around the room whenever he looked away. If I played my cards right, I could still keep Jackson on the hook and enjoy the benefits of his wealth. He didn't need to know about my new crush on a certain poet.

When his cell phone rang, Jackson took it out and proceeded to hold a conversation in my presence. I took this to mean that he wasn't the least bit concerned with me. This was actually a relief, because it gave me a few minutes to go to the bar, where I had spotted Mac Reynolds surrounded by a group of adoring fans. I excused myself from the table and headed over there to make my presence known.

I was not about to stand around like some kind of groupie waiting for my turn in line, so I took matters into my own hands.

"Excuse me," I said as I forced my way through the throng of women.

"Who does she think she is?" I heard someone say in my wake, but I ignored her and her nasty tone. I was solely focused on getting to the center of the Mac Reynolds fan club.

When I was close enough to get a good view, I stepped back for a few minutes to watch him at work. As women approached him, he'd smile, shake a hand here or there. He even exchanged cheek kisses with a couple and gave out a few hugs. This brother was certainly smooth. I noticed, with relief, that none of the women near him seemed to be getting any kind of special treatment. In other words, none of these sistahs was his woman, so I had a good shot at getting with this ebony Adonis with no competition in my way.

Up close, his skin was even smoother and more beautiful than I'd first thought. That dark chocolate complexion and thick, wavy black hair were a stunning combination. And his teeth, they had to be veneers, because they were perfectly straight and movie-star dazzling white. I just wanted to fuck every inch of his chiseled six-foot body, no questions asked, no expectations. I just wanted to feel him deep inside me. I decided on the spot that this gorgeous man could have what no man had had in years— he could have a freebie. He didn't have to buy me a drink; just take me somewhere and fuck the hell outta me.

As women took turns chatting him up, I thought about what I could do to make a lasting impression. Every woman who had approached him so far had walked away empty-handed. He hadn't given his number to anyone or taken any numbers. Either he was picky, gay, or the right woman just hadn't approached him yet. He was just too fine for God to make him be gay, so I decided it was time for the right woman to make her presence known.

"Excuse me," I said, pushing my way past the final three women who were blocking my path to him. His eyes locked on mine, and I reached out to shake his hand, holding on to it as I said, "I loved your poetry. Is there any way I can get your autograph?"

He looked at me, taking in all of my grandness, I was certain. "Ah, yeah," he said with a slight shrug. "You can have my autograph. Sure. Why not?"

"May I use this?" I snatched a cocktail napkin from a woman who was standing nearby. The look on her face said she was shocked, but before she could tell me no, I was already extending it to Mac Reynolds. He looked at me, and I smirked to let him know that yes, I really was just that bold. Mac took the napkin from my hand and began to write on it.

I leaned closer, whispering, "Oh, and I need your number too."

He stopped writing and looked up at me; then a smile stretched across his face. But no matter how amused he was by my straightforward approach, he still said, "I'm sorry. I don't give my number out to people." He offered up a slight half-shrug, as if I was just simply out of luck. I heard a woman behind me laugh, and it took all my self-control not to turn around and confront her.

"Well, handsome. I'm not most people."

I tried not to start acting up, but I felt like he was trippin' for real. I was not accustomed to having men turn me down, regardless of what I was asking for. And as I glanced around the little place at the women who had crowded him, I knew that this night should be no exception. I was by far the best choice in there, and I didn't just mean the way I looked, but the way I was carrying it, period. The whole package. Yet he had the nerve to sit there acting like he had to think about whether he wanted to give me his number? He had to be kidding.

"What do you want my number for?" he asked.

I smiled at him, even though I was truly shocked at how difficult he was being. I couldn't believe he was actually going to make me explain it. How crass. But if that's what it was gonna take, then so be it. "I want to get to know you better."

"Is that right?" he asked, a half-smile curling at the corners of his pretty lips.

What I really wanted to do was take him into a back room somewhere and ride his face until my toes curled, then slide down and ride his stick. And his smile told me he understood that to be the case. Now that we understood each other, I was content with settling for his number. The rest, I knew for certain, would come later.

"Yup, that's right."

"Well, dig it. If you're really serious about getting to know me better, I'm here every Thursday night. Why don't you check me out?" He looked toward the table where Jackson was sitting, still talking on the phone. "And next time, why don't you leave your date at home," he said easily, as if he thought he had me pegged.

Before he turned to walk away, he looked at the bartender and said, "Oh, get her a drink, and put it on my tab."

I liked his style, I really did, and I knew at that moment that I'd be able to rock his world. Then I'd bring him to his knees and make him regret acting like he didn't want to give me his number.

"You just wait and see, Mr. Mac Reynolds," I muttered under my breath as I grabbed my double of Hypnotiq and sauntered back to my table, where Jackson was just wrapping up his phone conversation.

21

Nikki

Ain't nothing worse than a jealous woman, especially if that woman is your lover. I was learning this lesson firsthand as Tiny was showing her ass to be as jealous—no, actually more jealous—than Dwayne. I thought about the heterosexual couples I knew and wondered if Tammy and Tim or Isis and Tony went through issues like this. They probably did, but when it came right down to it, it couldn't be half as bad as I had it now. The situation was getting out of control. My home used to be my sanctuary, but now I couldn't stand to come home because of the way Tiny was constantly giving me the third degree.

It all started out as a pleasant Wednesday evening at home. Tiny got in from work first. To surprise me, she had cooked my favorite meal of shrimp jambalaya over rice with corn bread on the side. DJ was over at Dwayne's mother's house, so I could tell she was thinking of making this a romantic evening, and I was all for it. It had been a while, if you know what I mean, and I really did miss Tiny. We were sitting in the dining room, with a white tablecloth, candlelight, and the whole bit.

Unfortunately, I'd started WeightWatchers a few weeks before and had already lost ten pounds, so I wasn't trying to overeat, no matter how good the meal smelled. The corn bread alone was about a thousand calories. I tried to take a small portion of the jambalaya and cut my corn bread in half.

"How come you not eating?" Tiny demanded.

She actually looked insulted, so I scooped two more big spoonfuls onto my plate to avoid any drama. Lately, Tiny was turning every little thing into a reason for a fight. I took a taste of the jambalaya. "I'm eating. Mmm, this is good. Girl, you put your foot in this."

For a moment, Tiny seemed placated, but the peace didn't last long. After she gulped down a few more bites of food, she remarked, "I notice you been taking a lot of salads to work for lunch lately like you on some rabbit shit or something. You know I like a woman with some meat on her bones. Your pants is falling off your ass now. You gonna look up and you gonna have a flat ass up in here."

I heaved a sigh. People at work had been complimenting me on my weight loss, especially Keith, and that made me feel great, but Tiny was managing to turn it into something ugly. "Tiny, puh-lease. You know the doctor told me I need to lose a little weight. My blood pressure and my cholesterol was getting too high."

"You mean the doctor your boy Keith recommended?" I hated when she called him my boy.

"Yes, the doctor my friend Keith recommended."

"Well, Keith needs to mind his own fucking business. I like you just the way you are."

"Oh, and are you gonna like me when you're pushing me around in a wheelchair after I have a damn stroke? Don't you want me to be healthy?"

"I guess so." Tiny looked glum as she continued to eat her food. Silence fell between us. Finally, she changed the subject. "How was work today?"

"Oh, it was all right."

She looked at me skeptically and said, "You don't sound like it was all right. Is someone bugging you at work? That Keith ain't trying to put his hands on you, is he?"

I knew Tiny had the best of intentions with a question like that. She would be down at my job in a heartbeat if she thought I needed her to put someone in their place. She loved being my protector, and in the past that made me feel safe. Now it just made me feel bad. Tiny wanted to feel needed, while part of me was starting to feel like I didn't need her as much as I used to, although I still loved her.

"No, Tiny, no one's bothering me at work. I just feel bad for Keith."

She rolled her eyes at the mention of his name. "What he do?"

"Nothing, that's the point. He's a good worker as far as I can see. Comes to work on time, does his job. Kym and them are spreading really nasty rumors about him because his pants were hanging below his underwear."

"Maybe the boy should put on a belt, then," Tiny said with a smirk.

"Tiny, that's not funny and you know it. It ain't right that they discriminate against him just because of the way he dresses. What if they were on my back, because I'm with you?"

"That ain't the same thing," she protested. "He can change his clothes. You can't change being gay."

"Can't I?"

"What's that supposed to mean?" Tiny's eyes locked with mine.

I'd hit a nerve and needed a way out. "Nothing. I didn't mean nothing by it, Tiny. Please don't trip," I said as innocently as possible. "I just think it's wrong that they get on him the way they do. As long as he's doing his job, why should it matter how he's dressed?"

Suddenly, Tiny turned the conversation in a totally different direction. It was no longer about Keith's clothes. It was about me. She leaned back in her chair and folded her arms across her chest. With a hint of accusation in her voice, she said, "You sure are taking up for this dude. What is it with this Keith guy? That's all you been talking about these last few weeks."

I felt my stomach do a little flip. Was Tiny just really good at reading me, or were my feelings about Keith that obvious? "He's just a coworker," I said, hoping to sound convincing. "And it's not like I talk about him all that much. Why you exaggerating? You know I'm not even into men anymore."

"Did I say anything about you being into him that way?" Tiny asked.

She was starting to trip. "No, you didn't, but you—"

"Besides," she said, interrupting me, "maybe you are still into men. How 'bout when you went out with that nigga Dwayne?"

"Oh, be real. He's my baby's daddy. Just 'cause I gotta talk to him doesn't mean I'm into him."

"Whatever," Tiny answered. "And what about that dude at the mall last weekend? I saw the way you was looking at him."

"Tiny, what the hell is wrong with you lately? That man was just selling sunglasses. You saw his little kiosk." I threw my hands in the air. "Can't I get some sunglasses? Damn."

"I don't see what you need sunglasses for. Your eyes are pretty without them."

She had softened her tone a little, but it didn't calm me down. Her jealousy was getting out of control, and she was letting it show in the most embarrassing ways. Last weekend, she cussed out the coat-check girl at the gay bar. First, she accused me of flirting with the girl when I gave her my coat. I told her she was being ridiculous, but the next thing I knew, Tiny, with her big, buff self, stomped across the bar and scared the poor woman half to death.

"What's all this cheezing up in my baby's face? Check coats, bitch, not my woman over there."

I was so embarrassed I could have died. Some of the women in the bar were looking at Tiny and shaking their heads, as disgusted as I was by her behavior. But several others seemed to think the whole thing was funny. When I saw a few of them laughing at us, I told Tiny I was ready to get the hell out of there. But she wasn't having it. In fact, I don't think she even noticed all the bitches who were laughing, because she still had her eyes locked on the coat-check girl.

Then she dragged me onto the dance floor. As mad as I was, I still danced with her, just to avoid another embarrassing scene. Little did I know, Tiny wasn't done making fools of us that night. When she danced us as close to the coat-check room as we could get, she wrapped her arms around me and started rubbing all over my ass.

She looked at the coat-check girl and said as loud as she could, "Yeah, that's right, bitch. This ass is all mine."

I cringed at the memory of that night, how Tiny had humiliated me with her jealous behavior. Now here we were having yet another fight over someone else. This was starting to happen too often, and I didn't know how much more I could take.

"So what is it, Nikki?"

"What do you mean, what is it? What is wrong with you lately?"

Tiny's nostrils began to flare, and I could almost see steam coming out of her ears. "I don't want no surprises," she hollered, jumping up from her chair and looming over the table. "Let's get this thing out in the open. You missing a nigga going upside your head 'cause he got that dick swingin' between his legs? You can go back to that bullshit if you want to."

I refused to meet her aggression with my own. I kept my voice low and even. "You gon' have to stop all this accusing me. This is turning me off." Well, that sure was the wrong thing to say.

"Oh, so I don't turn you on no more?"

I would have tried to deny that, but she didn't give me a chance to answer anyway.

"Don't I satisfy you? What do you want me to do, Nikki? I'm not stupid. I can't take no more of this."

"Take no more of what? What are you talking about, Tiny?"

"Your trying to be slick. Don't push me, girl. I'm already on the edge. If I lose you, I don't know what I'll do." Tiny's loud breathing slowed down, and her shoulders relaxed. She was quiet for a long time as she settled back into her seat. Finally, she spoke. "I'm sorry, boo. I'm not trying to go there with you. It's just . . . I feel like something's changing between us."

I didn't answer her. Yeah, something was changing between us, but I refused to take the blame. I might have been thinking about Keith more than I should have, but it wasn't like Tiny was giving me a reason not to. I wasn't the one acting all crazy jealous all the time.

Suddenly, I heard Tiny's voice sounding scared. "Are . . . are you interested in men again?"

She stared at me with such sorrow in her eyes I wanted to cry. "It's not that I'm interested in men. I . . . I . . . just . . . I just—" She cut me off, thank God, because I didn't know what I was gonna say.

"You just what?" she demanded.

"I love you, Tiny. I swear I do, but . . ."

"But what?" Her tone was getting angrier.

"But I do fantasize about having something inside of me sometimes."

"So, in other words, you wanna be with a man?"

"No, Tiny, I didn't say that. I said I fantasize about it sometimes. Don't you fantasize about being with someone else sometimes?"

"Hell no, the only person I fantasize about is you." The way she looked at me told me that she definitely didn't understand where I was coming from and never would.

22

Isis

When the doorbell rang, I rushed to answer it with mixed feelings. I was pissed off and relieved all at the same time. I'd been calling Egypt's ass all day, trying to find out where she was and when she was coming over to help me get everything together for our book club meeting. We were supposed to be hosting the meeting together. So far, I'd done all the work, and if I knew my sister, she would show up at the last minute and take all the credit once the meeting got started. So, you know she was about to get cussed out once I opened the door.

"It's about fuckin' time! Where the hell have you been?" I hissed as I swung open the door. I lifted my finger and opened my mouth to continue my tirade, only to be shocked and embarrassed when I saw that it wasn't my sister at the door. Standing in front of me were a man and a woman carrying platters and wearing Jerk Hut uniforms.

"Ma'am?" the man stuttered. I couldn't blame him for sounding a little scared. I must have looked like a damn lunatic answering my door that way. He glanced quickly over at his coworker, raising his eyebrows in an attempt to send some unspoken message to her, like, *Be careful. Don't get too close to this crazy bitch*. But with me, he remained professional.

He quickly flicked his wrist so he could check his watch. "Um, you said you wanted us here by five-thirty. It's only five-ten by my watch."

My cheeks were hot, and I was sure they had turned the same shade of red as the goofy Jerk Hut hats these people were wearing. I was so embarrassed. "Oh, I'm so sorry." I stepped aside so he and the woman could come inside. "I thought you were someone else. Y'all come on in."

"That's quite okay," the man answered, still as polite as can be. "As long as we're not late. I don't run that type of business." Oh, so he was the owner. Now I understood why he stayed so calm when I yelled at them. A typical employee might have dumped the food on the front steps and cursed me out, but this guy had to kiss my ass no matter how rude I'd been, because he wanted the rest of his money. Guess that's one of the pitfalls of being the owner of a business.

I led the way to the kitchen and instructed them where to place the platters. Before they left, I paid for the food and gave them a good tip to make up for the way I yelled at them, then said good-bye as nicely as I could. As I looked around the apartment, I was satisfied. Everything was set up just as I wanted, and the oxtails, jerk chicken, plantains, and rice and peas from the Jerk Hut smelled heavenly. I thought about sneaking myself a plate before anyone arrived but decided against it when I spotted the time on the clock hanging on my dining room wall. I only had about twenty minutes before everyone arrived, and thanks to Egypt's no-show, I still had to get dressed.

I was just finishing my makeup when the doorbell rang, and though I hoped maybe it would be my sister finally arriving, I knew that was unlikely. Besides, at this point, I'd done all the work myself, so it didn't matter when she showed up. Actually, if she got here after the other guests, she couldn't take credit for any of the preparation, so maybe it was better if it wasn't Egypt. I pulled the door open to see Nikki standing there with a bag of carrot sticks under her arm.

"Hey, girl," she greeted.

"What's up, Nik? Come on in." I stepped aside so she could walk into the apartment. "Where's Tiny? And what's with the carrots?"

"Diet. And Tiny is right behind me. She needed to get herself together. She's upset with me." I left the door partially open, since Tiny wasn't too far behind.

"What y'all fighting about this time?" I asked curiously.

"Dick," she said flatly.

My head whipped around. "Dick, as in the nickname for Richard? Or dick, as in what swings between a man's legs?"

"Dick," she said flatly, wiggling her index finger below her waist.

"What the hell you fighting over dick for? You're both lesbians, aren't you?"

Nikki let out a long aggravated sigh. "Tiny just jealous of my friendship with one of my coworkers. She thinks I want some dick."

"Do you?" I raised an eyebrow. Nikki glanced at the door as if she was concerned about Tiny walking through it at any moment. "Well, do you?" I pushed.

She hesitated, then said, "Tiny doesn't have a dick, so why would I want some? I have a good relationship, Isis."

I wasn't sure if she was trying to convince me or herself. "Sure you do, but ain't nothing like some good dick. Especially right before your cycle comes on, it soothes the savage beast."

Nikki smiled, letting me know she knew exactly what I was saying, but it was obvious she didn't want to discuss it.

"Are we the first ones here again?" she asked, quickly changing the subject as we walked into the kitchen. She dropped her carrots and purse on the chair closest to the food.

I decided to mind my business. The last thing I wanted was for crazy-ass Tiny to walk up in the house hearing me talk to Nikki about how good dick was. I'd seen what Tiny did to Nikki's ex last year at that barbeque. I didn't want no parts of that woman's rage. "You know your people. They never on time."

"I'm sorry, but I can't claim 'em," she said with a laugh.

Tiny let herself in and announced her presence with, "BGBC in the house!" When she noticed me and Nikki standing alone, she asked, "Where the hell is everybody?"

I shrugged. "I guess they're on their way."

"Well," Tiny said as she glanced at her watch, "I suppose it's really not all that late yet. I mean, twenty minutes ain't too bad."

"Don't make no excuses for them, Tiny. This shit is trifling, and my sister's the most trifling of them all, 'cause she's supposed to be cohosting the meeting with me."

"Ah, so what are we eatin'?" Nikki asked.

With a sigh, I gestured toward the table. "Well, I ordered from the Jerk Hut over there on Merrick Boulevard. You know I love me some Jamaican food."

"Me too." Tiny started removing the covers from the food just as the doorbell rang again.

"I'll get it," Nikki announced. I followed Nikki into the living room and watched Coco as she switched and swiveled in.

"What's up, y'all?" Coco greeted, looking like a plus-size runway model in her new beige suit. Sometimes I wondered if she purposely went shopping right before our meetings, 'cause I never saw her repeat the same outfit. I knew she was a slut, but deep down, I really liked her style. She always seemed happy with herself.

A short while later, we were all helping ourselves to some drinks when Tammy showed up with her momma in tow. Tammy was wearing a nasty-looking scowl across her face. I figured it must have been that time of the month, 'cause couldn't nothing make you look that funky but PMS.

Tammy must have looked at Coco wrong 'cause out of nowhere she said, "What the hell is wrong with you? Don't be rolling your eyes at me like that."

Tammy ignored her and looked straight at me. "Where's your sister?" she asked. No "How are you?" or "Hello," just "Where's your sister?" in a condescending tone. She really was in some kind of foul mood. It was funny, but as annoyed as I was with Egypt for not showing up, I was not about to let someone else get down on her.

"I'm fine, Tammy. How about yourself?" I said with a fake smile. The room grew silent.

Tammy looked around and saw that every set of eyes was on this exchange. I guess that was the only reminder she needed to keep her composure, because she changed her attitude right quick. "I'm okay. How you doing?"

"Pretty good."

"So, where's your sister?" She brought it right back to that subject, but this time she asked nicely.

"I don't know," I answered, keeping my voice neutral. I wanted to know the same damn thing, but I wasn't about to share my frustration with Tammy, who looked like she wanted to kill somebody right about now. In fact, I was starting to wonder if maybe Tammy and Egypt had had a fight, and she was the reason Egypt hadn't answered her phone. The minute Egypt showed up, I planned to take her into a back room and find out just what the hell was going on, but for now, I would protect my family. "I haven't spoken to Egypt today," I said, hoping this would end the discussion.

"She's not answering the phone for you either?"

"Nope." I felt like I was being interrogated. Tammy mumbled something under her breath that we couldn't hear.

"You say something, Tammy?"

She shook her head, pulling out her cell phone as she walked toward the bathroom.

"I wanna get the meeting started," Coco announced. "Egypt will get here when she gets here." I was grateful that she was breaking the tension by changing the subject, but I still wasn't about to let her take over *my* book club meeting. She was some kind of control freak, and I wasn't having it.

I looked around and made sure everyone understood that I was the one in charge of decision making tonight. "Okay," I announced cheerfully. "We're missing one person, but let's get started."

This time when Tiny yelled, "BGBC in the house!" everyone roared back—well, everyone except Tammy, who had just stepped out of the bathroom looking more upset than when she walked in. Even when her mother suggested we pray, Tammy was the only one who didn't bow her head and join in. And after the prayer, when we headed to the kitchen to get our food, Tammy stayed behind, sulking in the living room.

"Why y'all get oxtails?" she complained when I carried my plate into the living room and sat down. "That shit gives me heartburn."

I just rolled my eyes and dug in to the delicious food on my plate. Oh well, I decided, she was gonna have to get over the fact that she wasn't the only one who could throw a bomb-ass book club meeting. From the sounds of the ladies still in the kitchen, no one else had any complaints about the Jerk Hut food.

"So, I see you made some word games for us to play," Tammy snapped, gesturing toward the stack of papers on the coffee table.

I nodded, but before I could ask her what the hell she was doing peeking at the games before we started, she cut me off with, "Word games. How immature."

That was it. I leaned over and put my plate on the table, ready to get up and show Tammy just how immature I could be. I think she knew it, too, because she leaned back in her chair and glanced around the room like she was looking for an escape route. I'm sure she didn't want me to mess up that face of hers, but if she kept up with that attitude, I might just have to.

"You know, Tammy," I started, but before I could give her a piece of my mind, Tammy's mother came strolling into the living room, her plate piled high with Jamaican food.

"Isis, I just love oxtails. And did I hear you mention something about word games? I just love word games. Thank you so much for inviting me to this meeting. You've done a wonderful job."

"You're welcome." I smirked at Tammy, then picked up my plate and dug in again. Whatever her problem, her Momma just saved her.

When everyone had returned to the living room, we made small talk while we ate. Our rule had always been that we couldn't discuss the book until that part of the meeting officially began. Reading black authors was serious business to us, and when we talked about a book, we all agreed that it deserved our undivided attention. Tammy sulked while the rest of us ate. I'm sure it bothered her that everyone was enjoying themselves. Tiny even headed back to fill her plate a second time.

After we finished eating, I passed out the scramble game I'd made based on the names of the characters in Mary Monroe's book *Deliver Me From Evil*. All the other members were laughing and joking as they unscrambled the names and talked about their favorite characters in the book. But Tammy kept that sour look on her face and refused to join in our conversation. After a few minutes, she sucked her teeth and balled up her paper.

I was too through with her. "What is your problem?"

"This is stupid," she mumbled.

Her momma shrugged her shoulders. "Actually, I'm done," she said with a warning glance at her daughter. I guess she'd seen enough of Tammy's bad behavior over the years to know just how to put her in her place without saying a word about it.

I just kept things moving. I was in no mood for Tammy's tantrum, and there was no way I would let it ruin my meeting.

In spite of Tammy's funky mood, as the meeting got deeper under way, the discussion became very lively. People kept shouting and interrupting each other to share their opinions about the

book that they all seemed to love. Mary Monroe had never disappointed us. I had to call the meeting to order more than a few
times to get people to take turns giving their answers.

"Look, y'all, we can sing together, but we can't talk at the
same time," I shouted over the noise, but I was excited by everyone's participation and enthusiasm. Tammy took the brief lull in
the conversation as another chance to bring up the one thing
that happened to be on her mind that night.

"Aren't y'all worried about Egypt? She should have been here
by now," she asked.

Tiny looked up. "She is missing, huh?" she said before biting
into one of the extra-large chocolate chip cookies I'd baked for
dessert.

"Yeah, but one missing member don't mean we should dis-
rupt the whole meeting," I snarled toward Tammy. "Egypt's okay.
Let's get back to the book, y'all."

But Tammy wasn't about to let that happen now that she'd
steered the topic back where she wanted it. "Well, she's your sister. How come you don't know where she is?"

It was becoming clear to me that Tammy's questions were
more than just an excuse for her needing to see her best friend.
My sister must have done something to piss her off. Join the
club, I thought. Egypt was really gonna get a piece of my mind
when I saw her. Not only had she left me alone to prepare this
whole meeting, but she'd also set off her friend, and I was the
one paying the consequences with Tammy's foul mood.

I chose to ignore Tammy's question and bring my meeting
back to where I wanted it. "Damn, I forgot to put the gifts out,"
I said, standing up.

"Gifts? What the hell you buy gifts for? I know this money's
not coming out of our treasury," Tammy sneered. I shook it off
and went about my business, heading to the bedroom to get the
gifts.

After I retrieved a bag from the top shelf in my closet, I turned
around and nearly tripped over Tammy. She had followed me
into the bedroom and closed the door behind her.

"Damn, girl," I hissed. "What is your problem?"

"I've been calling your sister all doggone afternoon. How she
not gon' show up at her own damn book club meeting?" Tammy

asked. She just didn't know I wanted my sister to show up far more than she did.

"Look. Last time I checked, Egypt and I weren't Siamese twins, so I can't speak for my sister. But I know one thing. When the meeting's at your house, you want everything to be hunky-dory, but when it's at somebody else's house, you want to ruin it for the host. But you better recognize, I am not going to let you ruin this meeting, and I would appreciate it if you would respect my house."

Tammy looked shocked that I'd called her nonsense on the carpet. She backed all the way up, and the expression on her face finally softened a little. "Isis, it's not like that, I swear," she protested.

"Whatever, Tammy."

"No, really. Your book club party is real nice."

I crossed my arms and frowned at her. I wasn't buying her half-assed compliment. Again I said, "Whatever."

"Isis, I'm not lying. I'm just in a bad mood because I'm having some issues with your sister."

"Well, that's obvious, isn't it? But that ain't got shit to do with my party, so you need to keep that to yourself. Deal with Egypt when you see her. Now, I'm tellin' you for the last time that I got no idea where she is. She's a grown woman and I'm her sister, not her mama. Whatever's going on between you two can't be that serious. I'm sure she's gonna call you."

Tammy's face crumpled, and she looked like she might cry. "You don't understand, Isis. I need to see her face-to-face to talk to her. It's the only way I'll be able to tell if she's lying about Tim."

"Lying about Tim? What would she have to lie about with Tim?"

I was confused, but only for a few seconds. Just as I started to put two and two together, Tammy confirmed my suspicions. "Isis, Egypt is having an affair with my husband."

It all made sense. Tammy wanted to find my sister because, just like I'd predicted, that stupid threesome of theirs must've gone wrong. Tammy was more than a little worried that something was going on between Egypt and her husband. Matter of fact, she seemed sure of it. And from the way my sister was raving about Tim's skills in bed, maybe Tammy really did have reason to be concerned.

But even if Egypt was doing something as dirty as having an affair with Tim, that didn't mean I felt bad for Tammy. I mean, she was only paying the logical price for planning such a stupid thing. What woman in her right mind offers her best friend up to her husband? She must've thought she had her man on complete lockdown. But if her suspicions were correct and my sister really was sexing her husband, then Tammy was getting a real lesson on the true nature of her marriage, wasn't she? And Tammy had bigger problems than she probably even realized at this point, because there was one thing I knew for sure. If my sister really had her clutches into Tim, she wasn't about to let him go, not in a million years.

As I pondered the mess Tammy had created in her marriage, my eyes fell upon something sparkling on my vanity table. It was my engagement ring, I realized with surprise. I had forgotten to put it back on after I'd finished doing my makeup. Once the guests had arrived and Tammy brought in all her drama, I hadn't even thought about the great news I had meant to share with my book club friends.

I didn't even bother to say another word to Tammy as I went to get the ring and place it back on my left hand. Her marital problems were her own, as far as I was concerned. I was getting ready to start a happy marriage with the man of my dreams, and I would never make the same mistakes as someone as foolish as Tammy.

I grabbed the bag of gifts and returned to the living room, where the other club members were undoubtedly wondering why Tammy had cornered me in my bedroom. It was clear that our lively discussion about the book was over. That heifer had ruined my whole book club meeting with her nonsense. For a split second, I considered busting her out and telling everybody about the nasty threesome she'd had with her so-called best friend and her husband. But as I looked at Tammy's mother sitting there, I realized that as mad as I was at Tammy, her mother didn't deserve to be embarrassed by her daughter's lack of judgment. I would leave it to Tammy to explain this—or hide this—from her mother some other time. For tonight, I would take the high road.

"Okay, y'all. I have gifts." I pulled out a coffee mug with Afrocentric designs and handed it to Tammy's mother. "This one is for the person who finished the word scramble first."

Tiny, Nikki, and Coco applauded politely. I handed out a few more gifts to each of them for categories like Most Talkative Member and Funniest Answers, making sure everyone got something. Even Tammy, when she came back into the living room, got a small gift, though I had to create a category for hers: Most Likely to Change the Subject. She managed to give a half-hearted smile as she accepted the notepad and pen I handed to her.

"And now we come to something special I wanted to share with you all." Once I was sure everyone was looking in my direction, I raised my left hand and wiggled my ring finger so they could see the diamond glittering there.

"Oh my, what a rock!" Nikki yelled.

"I'm engaged," I announced, like they hadn't already figured it out. Everyone got up from their seats and came to admire my engagement ring.

"Chile, what you do to earn a rock like that?" Tammy's Momma joked.

As my eyes met Tammy's, I thought, *I sure as hell didn't have to do nothing nasty like some other people, 'cause my man loves me unconditionally.* I felt like the luckiest woman in the world.

23

Tammy

On my way home, I stopped off at the liquor store for a bottle of tequila. I was so upset, I didn't even wait until I got home to open the bottle. I took a swig right in the parking lot. I knew that bitch Egypt was somewhere with Tim. After the book club meeting, I'd called her a good seven times, and still no answer. She must've been doing something she had no business doing, something she knew for sure I'd be pissed about, something I was positive had to do with my husband.

As I turned up the bottle to my mouth for the third time, I dialed Tim's number. His phone went straight to voice mail. I dialed Tim's number again, and again I got his voice mail, which meant that the bastard had turned off his phone. What the hell was going on here? I was sick and tired of this shit. I didn't understand what his problem was. He'd hung up on me when I called him from Isis's bathroom during the book club meeting. All I did was ask him where he was and if Egypt was with him. If he was innocent, all he had to do was answer the damn question. I was so pissed off, I was thinking about the best way to kill them both.

"I know one of their asses better answer the fuckin' phone or I swear to God . . ." I speed-dialed Egypt's number. After I got her voice mail again, my blood was boiling. This time, I dialed Isis's number.

"Hello?" she answered way too cheerfully.

"You heard from your sister yet?" I got straight to the point.

"Tammy, I done told you, I haven't heard from Egypt. Just like she's not calling you, she ain't called me back either. But the moment she does, I'm gonna insist she hangs up with me to call you right away, okay?" Isis snapped, like I was bothering her ass.

"Well, you ain't gotta get all indignant."

"Tammy, don't even go there. I know you're having a bad day, but I ain't got nothing to do with it."

"Maybe, but your sister does."

"You know, Tammy? I doubt that. I really do doubt it. I bet when all the cards are on the table, my sister has nothing to do with it either." Then she had the nerve to hang up in my face.

Hoping I might finally get him to answer, I dialed Tim's number again. I hit the END button the second I heard the voice mail recording. By now, I was so fuckin' mad my head was spinning. I didn't know what to do with myself. Luckily, my kids were over at Tim's mother's house for the night, so I decided, what the hell? Might as well go home and finish off the rest of the bottle of tequila. I took another swig, then put the car in gear and started slowly driving the five blocks home.

I was sitting at my kitchen table, five shots into the bottle, when to my utter shock, my cell phone rang. I jumped with a start. I could barely steady my shaking hands when I realized it was Egypt's sorry behind. I took a deep breath and pressed the button to answer the call.

"Hello?" I tried to remain calm. I wasn't going to give Egypt the satisfaction of knowing just how messed up I was over this whole situation.

"Girl, I am so sorry. My ringer must have been off since yesterday, and I see you been blowing me up something fierce," she said innocently. "What's up, everything aw-ight?"

"No, everything's not all right. And where the hell you been? And why did you miss book club meeting?" So much for keeping calm, I thought.

"Gurrrl," she began, ignoring my tone. "You're not gonna believe it, but I was getting some. And it was so good, I just had to skip book club." Her girlish squealing sounded just like any other time when we had good gossip to share. She had some damn nerve. What was she expecting me to say, "You go, girl" or something?

"You was getting some, huh?" I asked suspiciously. "From who? What's his name? Where'd you meet him?"

"Girl, I can't say right now. He asked me to keep it quiet until we're sure things are gonna work out. You understand, right?" I felt the hair on the back of my neck stand up and my heart rate doubled. How could she think I didn't know she was talking about Tim, like I was some kind of idiot?

"No, I don't understand shit. I'm your best friend," I pressed on, hoping to get her to confess so we could end this sick charade. "You know I'm not gonna tell anybody. Who is he, Egypt? Do I know him?"

"Well, kinda," she whined, making it more obvious she didn't wanna tell me. "But—look, that's my other line; it might be him. Can you hold a sec?" Without waiting for me to answer, she clicked over and left me hanging. At that very moment, I wanted to reach through the phone and strangle her ass. She claimed that she wanted to tell me, but . . . bullshit! She didn't want to say, because she was fucking my man!

Moments later, Tim came strolling through our front door carrying some flowers. I flipped my phone shut and turned my rage on Tim. He had come in with a smile on his face. I knew him well. He figured if he came in like nothing was wrong, I would just forget how he hung up on me the last time we were on the phone. Well, he was dead wrong this time. We were going to have it out. He was gonna give me some answers.

"Where the fuck have you been?" I hollered, and watched as the smile and color dropped from his face.

"You need to take some of that bass out your voice when you talk to me." Tim took on a serious tone to let me know he wasn't going to back down easy, but I didn't give a shit. I was not about to let him and Egypt make a fool out of me.

"Where the fuck have you been?" I yelled louder.

He slammed the flowers on the kitchen counter. "What is wrong with you lately? What is your problem?"

"You come waltzing up in here like nothing's wrong, and you wanna know what's my problem?" I hissed. "In case you forgot, you hung the fucking phone up in my face, then turned it off. I wanna know where the fuck you were."

Tim shook his head, looking like he was disappointed that I was too stupid to figure it out for myself. "I was right here in this house when I spoke to you. I was about to leave so I could play cards. You know, like I do every other time you have one of your book club meetings. And you didn't used to call me eight hundred times to check up on me. Or ask me if I was with your friends."

"Well, what did you expect me to do when you just hung up on me, then refused to answer my calls? Don't you know that made you look guilty as hell?"

"No, I didn't. I just know it made you look paranoid as hell. And anyway, I didn't hang the phone up on you. I lost the signal."

Lost the signal, my ass. His answer just pissed me off even more, and I sure as hell didn't believe him. "Oh, so you just lost the signal and never got it back the rest of the night, huh? 'Cause every time I called you after that, your phone went right to voice mail."

A smile broke out across his face, and I had to restrain the sudden urge to slap that grin right off.

"So, now I'm a joke?"

He had the good sense to get rid of the smile. "No, babe. I just can't believe you're mad over my cell phone. I don't even have it. I swear. I came home to change my clothes when you called; then you had me so mad that I didn't bother to call you back after I dropped the call. But I swear I didn't turn it off or purposely avoid your calls tonight. Like I said, I don't even have it with me. I must've left my phone in my other pants when I left the house."

My head tilted ever so slightly. We did tend to have bad cell phone reception in our house. I wondered if there could be any truth to his words. I wanted so badly to believe him, but then a voice in my head reminded me not to let him play me so easily. Tim must have sensed my reluctance to buy his story.

"C'mon, let's go, since you don't believe me." He pulled me by the arm and led me to our bedroom. On his side of the bed, his clothes sat in a pile on the floor. He picked up his pants and reached in the pocket. Sure enough, his cell phone was there, right where he said he had left it.

"See, here it is. I told you I left my cell in my slacks. It was an accident!"

I looked at him through narrowed eyes, still allowing my suspicions to get the best of me. Finding that cell phone hadn't proven a damn thing as far as I was concerned.

As I stared at him doubtfully, Tim pressed the power button on his cell phone. It vibrated and gave a half-ring, came on, then immediately went off.

"See?" he said smugly. "The battery must've died."

"Dead battery, my ass!" I snarled. "I know exactly what the hell is going on here," I accused. "You left that damn phone here on purpose."

Tim shot me a look. As far as I was concerned, he was just mad because his little leave-the-cell-phone plan hadn't worked as well as he'd expected. I was not fooled.

"You been fuckin' Egypt!" I spat.

The horror on his face was so dramatic, he could've won an Oscar for his performance. I prepared myself for the barrage of denials. His first move was to just play dumb.

"I've been doing what?" His eyes were huge.

"You must really think I'm stupid. You think I'm that simple, Tim? I know you been fuckin' her!" I said. "I know you been fuckin' that bitch!"

Tim shook his head, but he wasn't saying anything to deny it. He just stared at me as if he thought I was stupid.

With one fist punched into my hip bone, I stepped to his chest and pointed my index finger in his face. "You think I'm real stupid, don't you? You think I didn't notice when we were getting it on yesterday afternoon?"

"What are you talking about?" he hollered.

"I'm talking about the way you seemed so distant, so far away, like all you could think about was the fun you had with Egypt. You remember that, don't you? The way you all but ignored your wife so you could have your way with her. I know what's going on, Tim. I already know! Don't trip, though."

Tim now looked at me with sheer disgust. "I can't believe you," he hissed. "I can't believe you have no faith in me, in us, our marriage. You've become obsessed with this shit, and I'm so tired of you accusing me of doing something I didn't do that I don't know what to do! You need to remember one thing, Tammy."

"Oh yeah, and what's that?" I asked, matching his angry tone beat for beat.

"You were the one who pushed me to have that threesome

with your best friend. So even if I was fuckin' Egypt now—
which I'm not—it would be your own damn fault, wouldn't it?"

"Stop trying to turn this around on me, Tim. I know you're
fuck—"

Before I could accuse him once more, Tim threw his hands up
and headed out of the bedroom. When he reached the front doorway, he turned to me and said, "You know what? Maybe we
need to just get a divorce. 'Cause I can't live with this bullshit."
Then he turned and stomped out of the house, slamming the door.

It was like he had just punched me in the stomach. I fell to my
knees and cried hard, unable to believe how everything was
turning out. I thought that threesome would be the best thing my
husband ever experienced. Instead, I couldn't stop thinking
about it, thinking about the look on his face when he was loving
my best friend. I couldn't stop thinking that every moment he
was away from me, he must be with her. And as much as it hurt
to think my husband was having an affair, it was twice as painful
to know it was my own best friend who was betraying me. But
as mad as I was at both of them, not once had I thought about
divorcing Tim. If he had just come to me and admitted what he
and Egypt were doing, we could have found a way to work
through it and stay together. Egypt, well, that bitch was another
story. She and I would probably never be cool again, but I didn't
want to lose my husband. I loved my life, and I loved him too
much to lose it all. As the tears soaked my bedroom floor, I
imagined myself having to move out of this gorgeous house and
live alone in some crappy little apartment, struggling to make
ends meet without Tim in my life.

I must have been bawling so loud that I didn't even hear Tim
come back into the house. His gentle touch on my shoulder startled me. I lifted my head out of my hands, and the sight of him
kneeling before me immediately stopped my tears. The fire was
gone from his eyes. He no longer looked angry.

"I don't know how to make you believe me, Tammy. I love
you. I wasn't with Egypt. I haven't seen her since we were all together, and no, I'm not even feeling her like that. I just wish
you'd believe me so we can move on with our lives. Please, try to
get it through your head before this thing ruins us. I don't want
Egypt. I love you." He pulled me into his arms.

I was exhausted from the emotional outburst. Giving in and collapsing against his chest felt like a huge relief, especially since that tiny apartment I'd imagined myself living in disappeared from my mind now. Still, that little voice was nagging in the back of my consciousness. Tim sounded sincere, and my romantic side wanted to believe him, but I couldn't bring myself to completely let go of my suspicions. The truth was, if he really was fucking her, would he tell me? Of course not. I would have to play it cool for the time being, because I didn't want to risk pissing Tim off again, but I would still be keeping an eye on this situation. There was no way I was going to let some bitch like Egypt take away everything I had worked so hard to obtain.

24

Coco

The cab dropped me off in front of the African Poetry Theater almost an hour later than I had planned, and I prayed that I hadn't missed Mac Reynolds's session with the mic. I would be real pissed off if he had already performed, but I wouldn't have anyone to blame but myself. No, actually, I take that back. Jackson could take some of the blame. I'd been out with him all day, taking full advantage of his American Express Black card. Because he bought me a Christian Dior dress, which I was now wearing, I felt obligated to put a smile on his face before I left him. We'd ended up in the back of the limo, my head between his legs. Now, usually when I give head, it only takes five or ten minutes for me to bring a guy to the finish line. I have that shit down to a science. But with Jackson's old ass, what should have taken five or ten minutes ended up taking an hour, hence the reason for me showing up late at the poetry theater.

I decided that even if I'd missed his performance, I was not leaving the club that night without Mac. After what his words had done to me last week, I knew exactly what I wanted, and I was a woman accustomed to getting whatever she desired. Actually, as skilled as Mac was on stage, it was more than just desire. As far as I was concerned, any man who could make my juices flow using something as corny as poetry was exactly what I *needed*. I had been to my share of open-mic nights with brothers spitting spoken word so well they could have been auditioning for *Def Poetry,* but Mac Reynolds took things to another level. Next to him, all the others were just reciting ordinary poetry. What he was doing needed its own name, like "sexual tongue-talking" or "panty-wetting speak" or something crazy like that. Yeah, I was out on the hunt tonight, and Mac was my prey.

Before I could claim a seat, the lights dimmed like the week before, and sistahs started screaming and creaming, so I knew exactly what time it was. I stood back for a few seconds and watched in awe as he made his way onto the stage.

When Mac started his performance, he scanned the crowd. I could have sworn he noticed me, and a slight smirk appeared on his face for a second. I waved casually, even tried to make eye contact with him, but got no response. I surely did not appreciate being ignored like that, but for him, I was willing to let it slide just a little. He wasn't actually ignoring me, I told myself. He was just in the zone. So, I wouldn't take him for everything he was worth, which is how I usually did it when someone dissed me. I'd just try to get a little somethin' for myself, then let him keep the rest of his tip money.

The words pouring from his lips were pure sexual healing. As I watched him holding on to the mic, I imagined the way he would be holding me later that night, and I was in a zone of my own in no time. He brought me to such intense heights of pleasure that when his set ended and he stepped off the stage, I was even more enraged by what I saw.

"What the fuck?" My eyes nearly popped from their sockets when he slid into a chair across from a brown-skinned woman. She was thin, not too tall, with bone-straight hair, the type with sad siblings for breasts instead of my buxom happy twins. When she touched the side of his head as if to congratulate him, I noticed a wedding band. My heart sank for some odd reason, but I pulled myself together in a hurry. Why was I trippin'? After all, I only wanted a piece of that pie, not the whole damn thing. I couldn't care less if he was married. All it meant was I'd have to wait for a night when she wasn't there before I could sink my claws into him.

It didn't take long for me to grow tired of watching the intimate exchange between him and his wife, or whoever she was. I turned to go to the bar, looking around to see if there were any other possible prospects. There were some cute guys at the bar, and a couple of them looked like they might even have money. Things were definitely looking up. The only problem was that as I slid onto a barstool and checked out the men sitting near me, my mind kept returning to Mac. In spite of that skinny wench sitting next to him, my body still craved him, and like some kind of addict, I did not want to wait for my fix.

My disappointment at seeing Mac with another woman must have hung in the air around me like some sort of obnoxious perfume, because no matter how many flirtatious looks I gave, I could not get a guy to sit next to me and offer to buy me a drink. It was not one of my finest moments. It was actually so embarrassing that I was considering calling it a night. I spun the barstool around and prepared to leave, nearly crashing right into Mac. He was standing behind my barstool, looking good enough to eat. And even better, he was alone.

"I guess you really do want to get to know me better," he said easily. It wasn't really a greeting; it was just a statement. But just like everything else that came out of his mouth, the words had an effect on me. Every time I heard this brother speak, I couldn't think of anything but sex. I was sure he was smooth in between the sheets in ways I hadn't begun to contemplate. It was so rare that I met a man who was my sexual equal, but I had no doubt that here he was, living and breathing. I really didn't care who that skinny bitch was. I just knew the sun would not come up without me getting some from this man.

"That's what I said, didn't I? I want to get to know you better." I glanced over his shoulder. The woman was still sitting at the table where he'd been, but surprisingly, she seemed totally content to be sitting there alone. If that were me, I'd be searching the room to see where Mac had gone. In fact, if he was mine, I'd have a GPS system tied to that fine ass at all times.

"But I don't know how much your wife would appreciate it. Why didn't you tell me you were married?" I said, cutting to the chase.

Now, it wasn't like I was about to give up just because he had a wife. I did, however, have a problem with brothers who tried to keep their wives or girlfriends a secret. The last thing I needed was some pissed-off sistah in my face. It had happened before. One guy managed to fool me into thinking he was single for quite some time, until this homely looking chick came at me one day, screaming about how I stole her man. When I told her, "I don't steal. I only do temporary withdrawals leading to nice healthy deposits into my bank account," that crazy bitch nearly ripped out my weave. Believe me, it cost her man plenty of money to have my hair fixed after that day, and then he never got a piece of ass from me again.

I was disappointed Mac hadn't told me about his woman, but if I was being honest with myself, it was more than that. It wasn't the secret that bothered me; it was the fact that he had a woman at all. As much as I hated to admit it, I wished that Mac was single. When I saw him rush off the stage to sit with this woman, I actually felt a twinge of something resembling jealousy. I vaguely remembered such a feeling from back in my college days, when I actually let a brother break my heart. That's why the feeling took me by surprise now. And as unfamiliar as it was, it told me there was something very different and special about Mac Reynolds. I tried to shake it off and tell myself he would just be another sponsor—maybe he could make a contribution to the rent pile or something—but deep inside, that nagging feeling kept telling me it was deeper than that. For me, this was very scary.

"Why didn't I tell you I'm married?" he repeated my question with an amused smile on his face. "Oh, I don't know . . . maybe because I'm not married?"

I looked at him cockeyed. "Oh, really?" was all I said, unsure what to make of his denial. I knew what I had seen earlier, the way he and the woman stared into each other's eyes. There was something in the way they behaved that said they knew each other on an intimate level that went way beyond sex. Normally, I'd go off on a dude who was telling a big bold-faced lie, and right in my face at that, but a part of me knew that he wouldn't find that sexy and might step off.

Mac must've sensed a change in me, because he eased himself onto the barstool next to mine and tapped on the bar. The bartender came over.

"Mac the man! That was tight, real smooth tonight," the bartender said. "What can I get for you two?"

"I'll take Henny on the rocks," Mac said; then he turned to me. "And give her whatever she wants."

It took everything not to tell that bartender what I really wanted, which was Mac Reynolds down in my coochie, getting to know me a whole lot better. I looked at Mac, wondering if he knew what was going through my head at that moment, then placed my order with the bartender.

Maybe he wasn't married, I thought hopefully. It was obvious the bartender knew him well, yet he didn't show any concern over the fact that Mac was ordering me a drink while the other woman was in the room. And speaking of the other woman, I couldn't believe she hadn't come racing over to the bar to get rid of me by now. I sneaked a peek in her direction and saw that she was still sitting alone, not looking the least bit agitated by Mac's absence.

Mac's eyes followed mine in the direction of the woman. He leaned closer to me and said, "That would be my agent."

"Agent? So . . . you're not married?" I tried hard not to jump off my barstool and do a dance.

"Nope. Happily single."

The bartender returned with our drinks and placed them in front of us. I raised my glass to my lips and took a sip, silently toasting the fact that this sexy mothafucka was single and free.

Mac didn't pick up his drink. He just sat and watched me. I took this as a good sign and boldly returned his stare. He was sexy as hell, from his eyes to his lips and even his well-manicured hands. Usually I wasn't into guys who took the time to get manicures and such, but I wanted him. And at that moment, the way he looked at me, I didn't care what he did—or even how much he had.

"So, you still want my number?" he asked.

"Well, we can start there . . ." I said suggestively. I licked my lips and let my eyes travel up and down his body, resting briefly on the best parts. Much to my chagrin, my hints did nothing to entice him. He didn't start reciting his digits or even ask the bartender for a pen to write down his number. This brother really knew how to get under my skin. I wasn't used to someone playing hard to get like this, and if he didn't quit soon, he was gonna make me go off on his arrogant ass.

Luckily, before I could embarrass myself like that, his agent approached us. "Mac, I'm about to get going. Kevin is calling," she said.

I was checking out her figure, feeling confident that my luscious curves were far superior to her twiggy shape, when she looked at me and smiled. "Hi, I'm Cassandra," she said without a touch of jealousy in her voice. I returned the smile and shook her hand as I introduced myself.

"And, Mac, please get some rest tonight. This is a really important shoot tomorrow. You do good with this role and I might be able to get you some breakout work."

So, I thought with relief, it was starting to look like she really wasn't his woman. I mean, she was talking about some other guy calling her, and she was actually friendly to me. Now if I could just get Mac to stop his little game, we could do this thing.

"I'm gonna walk her out, if you don't mind," he said to me. I felt like telling him he definitely did not need my permission to show her the door. Even if she was just his agent, the fewer women hovering around tonight's dick, the better.

I nodded slightly, giving him the okay, and waved good-bye to the stick-thin woman. Whoever this Kevin guy was, I sure hoped he was calling to buy the poor girl a sandwich or something, put some meat on her bones. As they headed for the exit, I sat back and watched how damn irresistible Mac looked from behind. The view alone was enough to get my juices flowing, and I hoped that within the next hour or two, I would be able to show him just how much I appreciated his beautiful body. Yep, this was going to be one hell of a night for Mac the man.

When he returned and reclaimed his place next to me, I felt a surge of electricity flow through my veins.

"So you're an actor, huh? Now I know why you have so much presence on the stage."

"If you wanna call what I do acting, then I guess I'm an actor. Truth is, what I really wanna do is direct and produce my own films, like Spike Lee and John Singleton."

We sat for a while making small talk. I complimented him on the night's performance, asking him all kinds of questions about where he came up with his ideas, telling him how much I admired his imaginative descriptions of sex. He almost seemed embarrassed. Nonetheless, I was doing all the right things, stroking his ego the way I know a man likes it, but he never brought the conversation back to him giving me his phone number. For a while, I wondered if this man was planning to make me beg or something. But then he asked a question that was music to my ears.

"I'm about to bounce. You want a ride?"

Who needed a damn phone number now? Certainly not me, I thought happily. And if things went the way I planned, I'd be riding more than just in his car that night. I was gonna fuck this man so good, he wouldn't ever want to send me home. Hell, I was already thinking of breaking my rule and staying with him after sunrise.

Just when I thought things were already perfect, my night got even better when I saw his car. He stepped up to a straight-off-the-showroom-floor Porsche Cayenne, fully loaded, and opened the passenger door for me. As soon as I settled into the soft leather interior, my body relaxed, like I belonged in this expensive machine. I couldn't wait to get him back to his place. I wanted to show him just what I could do for him so he would want to keep me around for a long, long time.

"So where do you stay?" I asked moments after he cranked up his car.

"In Rosedale," he said, though I was hoping for more information. I wanted to know if he owned his own place or rented. Instead of offering it up, he turned to me and asked, "Where do you live?"

"Between Shea Stadium and Flushing Meadow Park." I could have been more specific with my directions, but I figured it didn't matter. I had no plans on going home tonight.

I eased back in the seat and thought about all the kinky things I wanted to do to him. I wondered if his dick was as pretty as the rest of him, and wondered what he'd think once I had it bouncing off my tonsils. The image of him in my mouth sent chills down to my toes, and I kept my eyes closed, enjoying my fantasies for a few minutes. Then Mac had the nerve to interrupt it all like an ice-cold shower.

"Which street are you on?" he asked.

I opened my eyes and felt a wave of panic as I realized we were approaching my neighborhood. Oh hell no! Did this brother really think this was gonna happen at my place? I had my standards, you know, and one rule I never broke was to let a man come home with me. Once you let them in the bed one time, most of these fools start thinking they own you. And considering the fact that at any given time I could be stringing along as many as five different guys, the last thing I needed was for one of them to pop up at my apartment whenever he felt like it. No matter how gorgeous Mac was, I was not about to change this rule for him. I could imagine how good the sex was gonna be with him, but until I'd sampled the goods and knew for sure, I couldn't take any chances.

I turned to him and said, "Um, I don't believe in bringing men home."

He turned to me and said casually, "That's okay, 'cause I wasn't asking you to."

Damn, this brother was sexy as fuck! He was so confident that he didn't even think he needed to ask if he could come up. I guess he just thought he had it like that, so damn fine that he was already sure I'd be inviting him up. And the scary thing was, the boldness of his approach made me even hotter for him.

Fine, I thought recklessly, I'd fuck him in my own bed. Mac had me so damn horny that none of my rules or standards mattered one bit. The only thing I could concentrate on was the intense pleasure I would be feeling soon. I imagined the sexy smell of his musk on my silk sheets long after he had left. Hell, depending on how good it was, I might even let him stay the whole night.

I told him which street to turn down, and Mac eased into a parking space right in front of my building. That in itself was a miracle, because there was never an open space anywhere less than half a block away. I took it as a sign that this whole thing was just meant to be.

Without a word, I undid my seat belt and practically jumped out of the car, eager to get upstairs and get this party started. I shimmied my ass in that tight dress around the front of the car, making sure he got ample view of my assets. But as I stepped onto the sidewalk, I realized the motor was still running and Mac hadn't made a move to get out of the car yet.

I stepped toward the driver's side door, about to tell him to hurry his fine ass along. But Mac lowered his window, and before I could speak, he said, "Aren't you forgetting something?" He reached his arm out to me, and I saw that he was holding a small piece of paper.

Dumbfounded, I took the paper from him and looked down at it. It was a phone number. He'd finally given me his number.

"Call me," he said with a sly smirk, then pulled away from the curb. I stood there watching his Cayenne disappear down the block. I'd never felt like a bigger fool.

"Damn. I coulda had Jackson buy me an elegant dinner to-night, but I had to waste my time on Mac Reynolds and his game-playin' ass," I muttered as I walked to my apartment trying to decide who I was going to call to put out the fire Mac had started between my legs.

25

Nikki

I clutched the sheets, then arched my back as I whispered the words I knew Tiny wanted to hear. "I'mmmm, I'mmmm coming, Tiny. I'mmmmm coming, baby, and it feels so good." Tiny pressed her lips against mine, letting her tongue explore my mouth. She rolled off of me, gasping for air when my tremors subsided.

Yes, like me, she was out of breath and hardly able to speak from the intensity of our lovemaking, but the satisfied grin on her face said more than any words she could have spoken. Ms. Tiny was very pleased with herself, and I was not about to burst her bubble. If she knew I'd just faked an orgasm, I'm sure it would ruin the uneasy truce we had reached. Tiny didn't have many pet peeves, but me faking an orgasm was definitely one of them. She felt that if you tell a lie in the bedroom, you'd tell a lie about anything. And now was not the time to set her off and have her accuse me of being a liar.

For the most part, I agreed with Tiny's theory about fake orgasms, and I rarely felt the need to fake one, but this lie served a very important purpose. I was just doing what I had to do to keep the peace, to let Tiny know that I still wanted her. For a few days after our fight at the dinner table, we barely spoke. The few times that we did, she always ended up making snide remarks about my male coworkers, particularly about Keith, and I would get pissed off.

More than once I had caught her going through my cell phone call history. When I finally confronted her about it, she admitted that she was looking for proof that I was talking to Dwayne or Keith or somebody. We ended up having a long talk about her jealousy and her fears, and I was shocked by what she told me.

Tiny seemed to be developing some serious hatred for men, mostly because she had this sense that she was going to lose me to one. And it went even deeper than that. She revealed her biggest insecurity to me—the fact that she couldn't do for me what a man could do in bed.

And that's how we ended up where we were now, in the bed, with me having just faked an orgasm because the big rubber strap-on dildo that Tiny was wearing just didn't do anything for me.

"So, can I fuck as good as a man, or what?" The conceited tone in her voice was like nothing I'd ever heard come out of her mouth. Tiny took hold of the ten-inch dildo she had strapped on, then rolled onto her side to face me. I don't know what it was about grabbing one's dick, even a rubber one, but it sure made a person think highly of their sexual performance.

I knew there was going to be trouble the minute she handed me the bag and I saw the strap-on dildo she'd purchased at the X-rated video shop on our way home from our book club meeting. We'd used toys before but never for penetration. Deep down, I hated the idea of her using this one on me, but with all the drama and accusations we'd been going through lately, I honestly felt I had no choice. Tiny was determined to show me that she was better than any man.

"So, can I fuck or what?" Tiny repeated as she gently slapped the rubber penis against my thigh.

"Better, baby. You were much better than any man."

Her grin became a devilish smirk. She was convinced. I only wished I was, too, because the entire time she had that thing in me, I felt as if we had no connection. I'm sorry, but you can't get any warmth out of a piece of rubber, so it felt just like I knew it would—Tiny lying on top of me with a giant toy stuck inside. And when it came down to it, Tiny wasn't really interested in pleasing me as much as she was interested in proving her own sexual skills. The whole scenario just kind of gave me the creeps, and it was easy to feel disconnected.

"I told you that anything a man can do I can do better." She was still holding on to that thing like it was a part of her. What I really wanted was for her to hold me, to caress me, to make me feel like she had when we first met, to make me feel special.

When it came to the emotional relationship between me and Tiny, I couldn't deny that her gut feelings were correct. It's like there was a canyon growing wider and wider between us. I knew that if it became too wide, there might be enough room for someone else to jump in between us. And by the way things were going, that someone was probably going to be Keith.

26

Tammy

I was fit to be tied as I paced back and forth waiting for Egypt to show up at my house. She was already nearly two hours late and wasn't answering her phone, which I'd called about a hundred times. This was all the proof I needed to confirm what I already knew—this bitch was avoiding me because she was sleeping with my husband. She, of course, wasn't the only one avoiding the subject. Every time I tried to talk to Tim about it, he would just accuse me of being paranoid and lately made the reference that I was crazy. We'd had so many fights at this point that I'd lost count, and in the bedroom . . . forget about it. With all the tension in the air around us, we barely had sex anymore, and when we did, it was anything but intimate or loving. My pillow was soaked with tears on many occasions because of the lack of passion between us. I truly felt like every ounce of passion he once felt for me was now being lavished on Egypt, and I hated her for it.

As far as my "friend" Egypt was concerned, her mood seemed to be the exact opposite of mine lately, which set me off even more. Whenever I called, she was always too busy to talk for long, and her voice sounded so damn giddy it made me want to reach through the phone and strangle her. A few times I invited her to come by so we could catch up—my plan was to corner her so she was forced to confess—but she was always too busy to see me, or something would come up at the last minute and she'd be a no-show like today. The closest she came to confessing was to admit that she was spending all her time with her new man, but of course she never told me who he was. She said it wasn't something she was ready to talk about yet, but I was getting her message loud and clear—especially since most of the times she was too busy with her new man were the same times that Tim was out of the house, supposedly with his boys. I was at my wit's end with both of them thinking they were playing me when I knew exactly what was going on.

That was why I was so agitated by Egypt's apparent no-show now. I had finally gotten her to agree to come over, feeding her a bunch of bullshit about how much I missed my friend, how she never made time for me anymore, blah, blah, blah. I laid it on real thick, could have won an Academy Award for my performance. Egypt actually stopped her giddy schoolgirl routine long enough to say she did feel guilty about neglecting our friendship; then she promised to make time for me today. I knew that I could exploit her feelings. If I could fill her with enough alcohol, that guilty bitch would start singing her confession. Don't ask me what my next step would be once she admitted the affair. Hell, I might just decide to kill her right then and there. All I knew is that I had been obsessed by this for so long, and I needed one of them to admit it so I could get past it and try to save my marriage. I felt like today was the day it was going to happen, until Egypt's ass decided not to show.

I heard the grandfather clock chiming in the hallway and realized she was officially two hours late. As I picked up a bottle of tequila and prepared to put it back in the cabinet, it took some restraint not to throw it against the wall. This whole situation had me so damn frustrated. I wanted to kick myself for ever coming up with the idea of giving Tim a threesome for his birthday.

The doorbell rang, causing me to nearly drop the ice bucket I was carrying to the kitchen sink. I didn't know whether to be excited or even more pissed off. This bitch had the nerve to show up two hours late and would probably act like it was nothing. For a split second, I considered just not answering the door, but there was no way I could resist. I had to get Egypt to confess, and as hard as it was to get her to make time for me, this might be my only chance.

I answered the door, pulling it open wide and struggling to keep my attitude in check. Just as I expected, she barely even made mention of the fact that she was so late.

"Heeey, girl," she said, sounding way too happy. "What you got to drink?"

I wanted to smack the black off her smug face, but I played

along. "No problem, girl. I was just starting to worry about you, that's all. I mean, that's what friends do, you know? They watch out for each other."

"Yeah," she said, totally oblivious to the true message behind my words. "I appreciate you lookin' out for me. But I'm fine."

"I can see that," I responded, sickened by the devilish grin that passed over her face. "You look like you got it good."

She headed into the kitchen and made herself comfortable on one of the barstools as she purred, "Gurrrrl, you just don't know how good I got it. He's everything I ever wanted in a man."

"Do tell," I prodded. "Who is this Superman?"

"Well . . ." She hesitated, and for a second I got excited that maybe she was going to confess right then and there. But I was disappointed when she simply said, "Let's just say that sometimes the best surprise is standing right there in front of your face, especially when you don't go looking for it."

Fine, I thought. She wanted to play coy with me, like I was too stupid to know what she was implying. I poured the first of many drinks I planned on giving her. I would have this bitch so drunk she wouldn't be able to stop talking even if she wanted to.

"C'mon, Egypt. I'm your girl. How you gonna hold out on me like this? I want all the details," I said as I slid her an apple martini.

As she took a big gulp of her drink, she shook her head. "I ain't even trying to jinx this. That's just how good he is," she bragged, her titties straining to pop out of the too-tight top. If I didn't know any better, I would think she had morphed into Coco, or at least raided her closet and taken a few lessons from her on man-stealing.

I wanted to shout, "Yeah, I remember how good he is, bitch," but I contained myself. Egypt was still too sober for me to confront her. Plus, I didn't want to come at her all angry. I needed to play the friendship card.

"Well, that's good, at least one of us is gettin' some these days," I said.

She raised an eyebrow. "What are you talkin' about? The way you used to talk, you guys fuck more than a pair of rabbits, don't y'all?" She said it as if she knew something that I didn't.

As much as I wanted to punch her in the face, I had to give

her props for a superior acting job. She actually managed to look surprised, like she couldn't believe Tim and I were having a problem.

"Yeah, well, like you said, the way I 'used to talk.' You gotta admit you and I haven't been talking much lately, Egypt. Shit's been going on I haven't been able to talk to you about."

"I know, Tammy, but come on. You gotta understand. I mean, all these years I been listening to you brag about what a great sex life you have, and I was constantly dealing with these losers out here. Now I'm gettin' some good stuff, and you don't sound even a little bit happy for me. Don't you think that's just a little selfish?"

Was this bitch for real? How dare she accuse me of being selfish when it was my husband who was giving her that "good stuff" she was bragging about? My hand actually moved toward the paring knife I'd used to cut lemon slices, and as I wrapped my fingers around the handle, I imagined the satisfaction I'd feel plunging the blade into her heart.

"Tammy? You okay?" Egypt asked, snapping me out of my murderous fantasy. I released my grip on the knife, and to my surprise, I suddenly started crying real tears.

"Oh my God, girl," Egypt exclaimed, jumping from her seat to stand next to me. She rubbed my back and asked gently, "What is going on with you? First you been blowin' up my phone nonstop the last couple of weeks, and now this."

I turned to face her, not bothering to wipe away the tears as they ran down my face. As I gathered my senses again, I realized I could use the tears to my advantage. After all, it seemed I had finally gotten Egypt's attention.

"Tim's having an affair," I said bluntly.

She pulled her hand away from my back as if she'd just touched a hot stove. If that wasn't the sign of a guilty conscience, I don't know what is. "Are you sure?" she asked, backing away from me and returning to the barstool.

"Yeah," I answered as I poured her second drink, wishing I had some rat poison or something to add to it. "He's going out all the time lately, and half the time when I call his phone, he doesn't even answer it."

Egypt shook her head and started in on the fresh drink I handed her. "Damn, that don't even sound like Tim. I always thought he was, like, the perfect man."

I bet you did, bitch, I thought. *That's why you're trying to steal him now.*

"And you know what's even worse?" I asked.

"What?"

"He acts like he don't even want to have sex with me no more. You know they always say that's one of the biggest signs that your man is getting satisfied elsewhere."

"Daaaaaaaaaayum, Tammy. I don't even know what to say, girl. When did all this start happening?" She took another long gulp of her drink. I figured it was nerves making her drink so fast, but that was a good thing. The sooner she got drunk, the sooner I could get her to admit her sins.

"It started happening like right after his birthday. Right after I gave him that threesome."

Egypt's hand flew over her mouth in shock. Maybe she was worried that I was getting a little too close to figuring out what she thought was her little secret. "You don't think . . . I mean . . . do you . . . Do you think the threesome had anything to do with this?"

"I don't know, Egypt. What do you think?" I asked, struggling to keep the sarcasm out of my voice. Fuck, yeah! Of course I thought the threesome had something to do with this.

"Well . . ." she started slowly. "I have heard people say that once you give your man permission to have another woman in the bed with you, he takes that as permission to screw any woman he wants."

Oh no, she didn't! I might have regretted ever suggesting a threesome, but no way in hell was I gonna let this backstabbing bitch put the blame on me.

"What the fuck are you trying to say, Egypt? That it's my fault Tim is screwing around now?"

"Whoa, girl." She put her hands up in a gesture of surrender. "Calm down. You know I'm not trying to say that. It's just that—"

"It's just that what? Why don't you just fuckin' admit it, Egypt?" I yelled, slamming my hand on the counter.

"Admit what? What the hell are you trippin' about?"

"Bitch, you really gonna sit here and act like you don't know what the fuck I'm talkin' about?"

"Tammy," Egypt said quietly. I could see her struggling to stay calm in the face of my tantrum, but what I really wanted was for her to go off. I wanted her to give me an excuse to whip her ass. "I don't know what's wrong with you, but I did not come over here to take this shit from you. If you got issues with your husband, then maybe you need to be talking to Tim about it."

"Talking to me about what?" Tim asked as he walked into the kitchen, startling both of us.

Egypt turned to face him. "Oh, hi, Tim," she said, sounding so casual it made me sick. "I don't know why she's taking it out on me, but your wife here is having some issues I think y'all should talk about." I watched her face to see if she was trying to send him any subliminal messages, but she played it so cool you would have thought there was nothing going on between them.

The expression on Tim's face, however, was easy to read. He looked at me, clearly disappointed. "Tammy, how long are we gonna go through this?" he asked with a sigh. "How many times do I have to tell you I'm not cheating on you with Egypt?"

"What!" Egypt's scream was so loud I wondered if she had broken any of the glasses in the cabinets. She looked at me with fury in her eyes. "Is that what this shit is about? You thought I was fuckin' Tim? You think I would risk over twenty-five years of friendship for a ride on a dick?"

She looked at him, and he just shrugged. "I don't believe this shit." She grabbed her purse, gave me one last disgusted look, then said, "I'm outta here. Call me some time when you're ready to apologize for accusing me of such bullshit."

"It'll be a cold day in hell before that happens, bitch!" I yelled at her back as she left the room. I heard the front door slam; then I turned to Tim, ready to unleash my rage on him. He wasn't having it, though. Without saying a word, he left the kitchen, and I heard the front door open, then slam once again.

"That's right!" I yelled, though I knew he couldn't hear me. "Follow behind your bitch!" I picked up the tequila, put it to my lips, and tipped the bottle upward. I didn't plan to stop drinking until I was too drunk to feel anything.

* * *

By the time Tim returned home, I had managed to finish almost the entire bottle of tequila. I was lying on the couch, watching the room spin slowly round and round. It had been a long time since I'd been this drunk, but it was good to feel numb, to forget about everything for a while. I got so wasted, in fact, that I knew something had been bothering me, but I couldn't quite recall the details. My high had just started to wear off and depression was creeping in when Tim came in and reminded me just why I had been so upset in the first place.

"What's it gonna take?" he asked easily, kneeling beside the couch where I lay.

I shook my head, wishing the memories that were slowly returning to me were just hallucinations. I kept picturing my husband having sex with my best friend, and the vision made my stomach queasy, like I was about to bring up the tequila I had just drunk. Suddenly, I recalled every ounce of pain I'd felt over the last few weeks, remembered every unanswered phone call I'd made to Egypt and Tim, and every hour I'd spent waiting for Tim to come home. I started crying.

"Tammy," Tim said softly as he stroked my hair. "Please don't cry, baby. We're gonna be fine."

"How can we, Tim?" I asked, surprised at how sober I felt all of a sudden. "How can we be fine if you won't admit you're having an affair?"

Whereas this question had provoked nothing but anger from Tim before now, this time he just smiled at me sadly. "Oh, Tammy. I don't know how to make you understand that I don't want no one but you."

"But I saw you fucking her, Tim."

Again he gave me that sad smile. "Of course you did, baby. But you were the one who brought her into our bed. Or did you forget that?"

I was so sick of everyone trying to blame me for this situation. I started to get angry, struggled to sit up on the couch, then fell back when I realized that too much motion made me feel a little woozy. "Okay, so I brought her in, but I was just trying to fulfill your fantasy. You know, give you the best birthday present you ever had. But I sure as hell didn't expect you to keep fucking her after that day."

"Tammy, I'm not fuckin' her."

"Don't lie to me, Tim. I saw how much you enjoyed it."

"Of course I enjoyed it!" he said, sounding exasperated. "What man wouldn't? But it was just one night, baby. It was a fantasy, and then the fantasy was over. I have no interest in fucking anyone but you. Don't you see that?"

I was still not convinced, but at least it was a relief that we were talking about this calmly instead of yelling at each other. I pressed him further. "Here's what I don't get: If you liked it that much, why should I believe you aren't still gettin' some on the side?"

"That's my point," he answered. "You don't seem to wanna believe this, but it is possible to fuck someone only one time, even if that one time was good."

I looked at him skeptically. Maybe I would have felt better if he didn't keep agreeing that fucking Egypt was so damn good. "How is that possible? There's no way you wouldn't want to get some more if the first time was so good."

"No way at all? Are you sure?"

"Yup. That's why I'm so pissed at y'all. Just admit you went back for more; then we can move on, Tim."

He turned the tables on me. "So, you're saying that if I let you fuck another dude and he rocked your world, you'd definitely go back for seconds?"

"No!" I protested loudly.

"You sure about that?"

"Of course I am. I love you, Tim." What the hell was he getting at?

Tim looked satisfied, like his plan had just come together the way he wanted. "Then I think it's your turn. Who do you want to sleep with?" he asked.

I flinched slightly. He couldn't be serious! What kind of man would want his woman to sleep with another man? Call me old-fashioned, but for even the most adventurous married woman, the doorway to threesomes only swung one way.

"What the hell are you talking about?" I asked.

"I want you to be with another man. Maybe then you'll see that I'm telling the truth. You granting me that fantasy only made me love you more. I'd be crazy to risk losing you. I don't want no one else but you, and I want you to believe that."

I was speechless, still trying to digest the idea that he wanted me to sleep with another man.

"So, you wanna invite another man into our bed?" He asked the question like it was as ordinary as asking if I wanted steak or chicken for dinner.

I really wanted to believe everything he was saying, that he loved only me, and he wasn't doing anything behind my back. But this little voice in the back of my head was still suspicious. Maybe this was all a setup. Maybe he thought that me sleeping with another guy would make us even and he could continue doing whatever the fuck he wanted with Egypt. Or maybe he was just playing games with me, knowing I would say no anyway. Shit, he and Egypt might have come up with this plan together after they left, just to punish me for pissing them off earlier.

Fine, I decided. If this was a game he was playing, then I would call his bluff. "Okay, Tim," I said with a hint of defiance in my tone. "If you want me to, then let's do this. Who you bringin' in the bed with us?"

He actually laughed at me, which pissed me off. "Oh no, baby. It's not gonna be like that."

See, I knew he wasn't for real. "I knew you were full of shit. Ain't no way you would let me sleep with another man." I sat up and this time felt sober enough to handle it without getting queasy.

Tim placed his hands on my shoulders to prevent me from getting up and leaving the room. "No, that's not what I meant."

"Then what the fuck do you mean? 'Cause I'm gettin' tired of this game, Tim."

"I just mean that it's not gonna be a threesome."

I sighed, becoming very tired of this whole thing. Maybe I should just drink another bottle of liquor to get my high back, I thought. "If it's not a threesome, then what the fuck are you talking about?"

"It's just gonna be you and the guy."

"Eeeeew! What, are you gonna watch or something? You are becoming one hell of a pervert. I am not about to grant you another damn fantasy, Tim."

He shook his head, and I could tell he was struggling to keep his temper in check as he explained himself. "I'm not gonna watch. I could never watch you with another guy," he admitted.

"Very smart," I replied, knowing all too well how painful it was for me to keep seeing him and Egypt together in my head.

"So I'm not gonna watch, but I'm giving you permission to have another guy in our bed."

"Yeah, right," I scoffed. "And you'll pick the guy, right?"

"Actually . . . I already have someone in mind. Do you have a problem with me picking? I mean, after all, you did kinda get to pick Egypt, didn't you?"

I grimaced, remembering that his first choice had been Coco. Now I realized that my choice of Egypt was probably just as bad as if I'd let him have his first choice. Maybe even worse.

"All right, I'll play along. Who'd you have in mind?" I asked, still not quite believing that he was serious about any of this. But strangely, a part of me was becoming a little aroused at the thought of sex with a strange man picked by my husband.

I tried to convince myself it was just the alcohol doing that to me, but whatever it was, my libido kicked into high gear when Tim told me, "I was thinking of Raoul."

Thank God I'm not a man, because I would have had an erection at this point, as an image of me fucking Raoul flashed in my head. Raoul was one of the best salesmen in our company, and he was so damn fine, there wasn't a woman in the company who didn't lust for him. He was from Brazil, swarthy-looking, with a head full of dark curls. He was a little taller than Tim but more buff, and while he didn't have an obvious swagger, you felt his confidence with every step. Tim had caught me on more than one occasion eyeing Raoul's ass when he passed by my desk in the office.

"Raoul, huh?" I asked, trying to sound casual, although my emotions were a crazy jumble now. I was surprisingly horny as I imagined Raoul standing naked and aroused before me, but I was also still feeling the sting of all the pain I'd suffered since the night of the threesome. I wanted Tim to feel some of the hurt, anguish, and humiliation I had experienced. At the same time, I loved my husband and wanted our marriage to work.

"You really think this could work? It sounds too crazy," I said.

Tim took my hands in his. "Baby, it's no more crazy than the way your ass has been acting lately."

I surprised myself by laughing. It had been ages since I'd been able to do that, and the release of tension felt so good. "What the hell," I said recklessly. "It sounds crazy, but it just might work."

Tim kissed me deeply, and I felt the same passion that used to be there before this whole mess started. It filled me with hope. Maybe this insane solution really was the key to saving our relationship. And of course it didn't hurt that I'd be getting some action with one of the hottest men I'd ever seen in my life.

Eat your heart out, Egypt, I thought. *I'm gonna be fucking fine-ass Raoul, and then I'm gonna take my husband back out of your evil clutches.*

Tim didn't notice me smirking. He was too busy pressing buttons on his cell phone, making a call. He put the phone to his ear, waited a few seconds, then spoke. "Yeah, Raoul, it's me, man. That thing we talked about at the bar tonight . . . Yeah, she said yes. You ready to do this thing?"

I grabbed the bottle of tequila and guzzled the last little bit, then lay back on the couch, trying to prepare myself mentally for what I was getting ready to do. Things had become so crazy, I thought, what could possibly happen next?

27

Isis

About two months after he gave me the engagement ring, Tony booked us a flight to Las Vegas. When he first showed me the airline tickets, I thought that maybe he was planning on taking me to one of those small chapels for a quickie wedding.

"Um, Tony," I said, trying to keep a smile on my face. I didn't want to seem ungrateful. "This is really nice, but you know that I want a big wedding, right?"

A strange look passed across his face for a brief moment before it vanished. He smiled and said, "Yeah, baby. Of course I know that. What does that have to do with—Oh, I get it. You thought I was flying you to Vegas to get married?"

I didn't appreciate the way he started laughing at me. I frowned at him. "And just what is so funny about that?"

"Nothing, baby." He pulled me closer to him and gave me a big hug. "But we've only been engaged a few weeks now. I thought we were going to wait a while before we got married." His hand traveled down my back and landed on my backside. He gave it a squeeze and said, "This li'l trip to Vegas is just so we can practice for our honeymoon."

"Oh," I said, feeling a little stupid. "I knew that." This time I laughed right along with him, enjoying the way his hand traveled boldly from my ass, along my waist, and up to my breasts. Yes, I wouldn't mind a few uninterrupted days of "practice" with Tony.

When we were in Las Vegas a couple weeks later, heading down the strip in our rented Escalade, I spotted a couple holding hands as they walked into one of those quickie wedding chapels, and I recalled that conversation. I realized that after that day, Tony and I hadn't spoken again about our wedding plans. Not a word. In fact, if it wasn't for the diamond on my finger, I might have thought we weren't even engaged. Everything had returned to status quo between us. We still saw each other only on designated nights and talked on the phone a couple times a week. That's not to say that things were bad between us. I guess I just hoped that once we were engaged, I would feel closer to Tony, that he would act more excited. Instead, the only difference in my life was that Rashad wasn't breathing down my neck. Ever since the day of that fight, Rashad had dropped off the face of the earth. I guess Tony's proposal to me had been enough humiliation to convince him to leave me alone. In a way, I still felt bad for him.

But I should stop feeling sorry for him, I decided. If he had listened to me and left when I told him to, he never would have been there to be embarrassed like he was. So, that was on him. And if I never heard from him again, that would be okay by me.

"What did you think of that show last night?" I asked Tony, trying to make small talk and take my mind off all those crazy thoughts.

"It was all right, I guess. I don't really believe in all that hypnosis shit, but it was still funny to see that old lady runnin' around the stage like a chicken."

I laughed at the memory of that woman, along with all the other audience members who had made fools of themselves simply because the hypnotist told them to act in some stupid way. I wondered if any of them were really hypnotized or if they were just a bunch of people looking for attention.

"You're looking forward to tonight's show, though, right?"

"You know I am," Tony said. We were planning to go to a show called *The Sopranos' Last Supper*. I chose this one because it was loosely based on the HBO series Tony loved to watch. It was one of those dinner shows where the actors come and talk to everyone at their tables, like the audience is just part of the plot.

"And I'm looking forward to going back to the room after the show even more," he said, suggestively stroking my thigh. We'd been having some of the best sex we'd ever had on this trip.

The Sopranos' dinner turned out to be great. When I made the reservations for the show, I knew Tony would like it, but I wasn't sure he'd actually join in the show. He'd been kind of tense the last few weeks, telling me that work was stressing him out, so I thought it might be hard for him to loosen up. But by the time we finished our second bottle of wine, he was joking and laughing with the "mobsters" like they were his best friends. I guess the actors appreciated his enthusiasm, because they kept coming back to our table to get Tony to participate. He even got up and danced with Dee Dee Diamond, a character who was supposed to be a stripper.

After the show, we sat at the bar in the hotel lobby. Tony was still hyped up from the show. "Baby, I am so glad you got us tickets to that show," he said, his speech a little slurred after two shots of tequila and a beer.

"I know, boo. I'm glad you had such a good time."

He drained the last of his beer and turned to face me, looking very serious. "What is it?" I asked, surprised by this sudden change in mood.

"Isis," he started, leaning in so close that I could smell the alcohol on his breath. "I love you."

I laughed. "Oh, you had me scared there for a minute. I love you, too, boo," I said, giving him a quick kiss.

"No, you don't understand," he said, still slurring his words. "I mean I really, really looooove you, baby. I love you enough to marry you." He picked up the glass and tried to drink some more beer, though he'd already finished every drop.

"Um, yeah, baby, I know that." I wiggled my ring finger in front of his face. "Remember this ring you gave me?" I slid the glass away from him. "Maybe you've had enough to drink, Tony."

"I wish it could be like this forever," he said, still sounding a little solemn. I assumed it was from the alcohol. Some people get really moody when they drink.

"It can be like this forever. I'm gonna make you the happiest man in the world once we're married. That's a promise."

After a minute or two of silence, Tony shouted, "That's it!" and practically fell off his barstool.

"What is it?"

"We can get married here," he said as he climbed back onto his seat. "Why wait?"

I rolled my eyes. "You have definitely had too much to drink," I said. "We already talked about this, and you know I want a big wedding. I don't want to get married in some cheesy Vegas ceremony."

Just as I said this, the bartender was bringing Tony another beer. "Did you just call our Vegas weddings cheesy?" he teased.

I knew he was only pretending to be insulted, but I still felt the need to explain myself. "Uh, no, I didn't really mean that. It's just that I want a big wedding, and my fiancé here, he—"

"Hey, man," Tony interjected. "Tell my girl that it's good luck to get married in Vegas, will you?"

The bartender chuckled, clearly amused by this conversation. "Actually, I have heard that this is the best way to get married. No searching for the perfect dress, no fighting over whether you should have beef or fish on the menu, no fussing over why your great-aunt Sally shouldn't be seated anywhere near her fat, smelly neighbor Vyolet."

"But all that planning is half the fun," I protested. "I want a big wedding where I can be the center of attention."

"Well, I didn't tell you the best part about it," the bartender said, leaning in close like he was about to share some very valuable secret with us. "Compared to some big old reception hall full of guests you don't hardly even know, getting married here is a whole hell of a lot cheaper."

"Now that's what I'm talkin' about!" Tony yelled, raising his beer in the air like he was proposing a toast and sloshing the liquid everywhere.

I crossed my arms and scowled at both of them. The bartender shrugged his shoulders and walked away smiling. He could forget about a tip from me, I decided.

Tony put his arm around my shoulder and pulled me closer to him. "Aw, c'mon, baby. You know I was just joking with you, right? If you want a big wedding, then that's what we'll do."

"Well, you're not funny," I said with a pout, though I really wasn't very mad.

After I let him apologize for a few more minutes, I turned to him, looking him straight in the eye, and said, "Tony, did you really mean it?"

"Of course I did, boo. I'm sorry I even brought up the idea. You can have a big wedding," he assured me.

"No, I mean, did you really mean it that you would marry me right here . . . tonight?"

"Isis, I would marry you right now if . . ." His words trailed off. The poor guy was so drunk at this point it looked like he was losing his train of thought. ". . . if this bartender told me he was a preacher by day."

My man was so sweet. I couldn't believe how much I loved him. After I gave Tony a long, deep kiss, I turned to the wise-ass bartender and ordered a shot for myself and one for Tony. We shared one more drink, and I made a toast to our love; then I led Tony up to our room to show him just how much I loved him.

In bed a few hours later, Tony and I were cuddling under the covers after an incredible round of lovemaking. It was like the knowledge that he was so eager to get married had unleashed a wave of passion in me.

"Damn, baby, I ain't never seen you so aggressive in bed," Tony said with appreciation. He was considerably more sober than he had been at the bar—thank God, 'cause there ain't nothing worse than trying to get busy with a man too drunk to keep it up.

"I don't know, Tony. You just did something to me tonight, you know?"

"Yeah," he joked, "I just have that effect on women. Once they see what I'm packin', they just can't control themselves."

I slapped his shoulder playfully. "No, silly. I mean, yeah, you are packin', but I'm talking about what you said at the bar. It meant a lot to me."

"Uh-huh," was his only response. He yawned, probably his way of trying to tell me he didn't feel like talking. Tony never was very talkative after sex. He was one of those guys who was snoring fifteen seconds after he came. I, on the other hand, was ready to talk now. I turned to face him, propping myself up on one elbow.

"No, I mean it, Tony. I've been thinking about what you said."

"Baby, I was really drunk at the bar. I probably said a lot of things that I don't even remember." I was so disappointed by his words. Was it possible that he had only suggested the Vegas wedding because he was drunk?

"Yes, you were drunk. But are you telling me you don't remember that you said you would marry me right here in Vegas tonight?"

The silence after my question stretched on for so long that I actually thought he might have fallen asleep. "Tony?" I nudged him, and he actually sighed before he finally answered. Now I was starting to get a little annoyed. How could he not want to talk about something as important as our marriage?

"No, Isis, of course I didn't forget that I said I would marry you. But I also remember that you said you want a big-ass wedding, not a quickie. And now that I've had more time to think about it and I'm sobered up, I decided you're right. We should wait. Now, can I get some sleep? You wore my ass out."

"But what if I changed my mind?" I asked. This got his attention, and now he was the one sitting up in bed.

"What do you mean, you changed your mind? You don't want to get married? After all this time you been begging me for that damn rock you're wearing on your finger? You have any idea how much that thing cost me?"

"Whoa, calm down, baby," I said with a laugh. "Of course I love my ring. And I love you even more." I sat up and took hold of both his hands. "Tony, what I'm trying to say is that maybe you were right. Why should we wait? I have everything I need right here. I thought it was all about being the bride, being the center of attention, but now I know that's not what matters. As long as I'm the center of your world, I have everything I need."

Now, if my life was some kind of romance novel, Tony would have pulled me into his arms to kiss me passionately; then we would have run out to find an all-night chapel where we could tie the knot immediately. Instead, I was met with total silence again.

"Well?" I asked when I could no longer stand the suspense. "Don't you have anything to say?"

"Uh, yeah . . . of course I do. It's just . . . don't you wanna wait? We shouldn't rush into this until we're sure."

"That's just it, Tony. I am sure. And I thought you were too."

"What about Egypt? You know your sister would be pissed if she wasn't there for your wedding."

"She'll get over it," I answered without missing a beat.

"Prob'ly . . . but what about your friends? Don't you want them to throw you a shower before the wedding?"

"They can still do that after our wedding."

"But you don't even have a wedding dress."

"I don't need a wedding dress. I'll just wear the white dress I brought with me." I could come up with an answer for every excuse he threw at me, but that didn't mean I wanted to keep defending my position. I was starting to get frustrated.

"You know, Tony, if I didn't know better, I'd think you were trying to talk me out of getting married, and it's really starting to hurt my feelings."

He didn't even try to deny what I'd accused him of. "Aw, c'mon, Isis. Don't be like that," was all he said.

"You know what?" I said, getting out of the bed. I found my clothes in a pile on the floor, and as I started to get dressed, I continued. "Maybe we need to just go home. You know me, Tony, and I'm not about to keep giving you the milk for free. If you gonna keep playing games, I am not playing along. So get your ass up out of the bed and take me to the airport."

Tony jumped up and raced to my side. He grabbed my hands to stop me from putting on my clothes, and as he spoke, he unhooked my bra and dropped it to the floor. "Baby, why you gotta be like this? You know I wanna marry you." He stroked my breasts as he told me, "I love you, baby."

"Prove it," I said with a pout, though my erect nipples were responding readily to his touch.

"I . . . love . . . you . . . Isis." Between each word, he placed a gentle kiss on my breasts.

As much as I wanted to stay mad, I couldn't stop the moan that escaped from my lips. If there was one thing Tony knew how to do, it was how to turn me on. "I know you love me, Tony. Now prove you wanna marry me."

"I . . . want . . . you . . . to . . . be . . . my . . . wife," he said, continuing to explore my body with his tongue.

"Tell me you'll marry me here in Vegas. I want to go home as your wife. I don't wanna wait anymore."

His tongue stopped its travels, and he stood up to look me in the eyes. "Okay, you win," he said with a sigh. "You wanna get married? We'll go to the chapel tomorrow morning, all right?"

"Really?" I squealed with delight.

"Yes, really. Now, can I get back to what I was doing?"

I grabbed his head and placed his mouth back on my breasts. "By all means, please do."

The next morning, I woke up at the crack of dawn because I was so excited about what lay ahead. By the time Tony rolled out of bed, I was already wearing my white dress, my hair was done, and I was putting the finishing touches on my makeup.

"Baby, you look beautiful," Tony said when he got out of bed and came to stand behind me.

I smiled at his reflection in the mirror. "Thank you. I wanted to look my best on the day I become Mrs. Tony Johnson."

Tony's eyes shifted away from mine for a moment, and the smile on his face looked a little forced. "Uh-huh," he said, his tone sounding flat and unenthusiastic.

"Please tell me you're not getting cold feet," I said as I turned around to face him. " 'Cause you know I told you last night I wasn't playing no more games, Tony. We either gonna do this thing today or you're gonna take me to the airport . . . and then it will be a cold day in hell before you even get a whiff of my good stuff again."

Tony grimaced like I knew he would. I could always get my way with him by threatening to cut off the sex. Not to brag, but my coochie was a powerful thing when it came to my relationship with Tony.

"Calm down, Isis. No need to go getting all worked up. Unless, of course . . ." He reached his hand down and tried to stroke between my legs, but I stopped him.

"Unh-uh. Like I said. Ain't no more of this 'til we say those vows." I had made my decision the night before, and now I planned to stick to it.

"Damn," he said. "You're serious, aren't you?"

"You know I am."

"Okay, okay." He sighed loudly. "I'm goin' to get dressed. Just stop threatening to close up shop on me. You know that's my coochie."

I smiled triumphantly as I finished my makeup and waited for him to put on his clothes so we could head on down to the chapel.

At the Chapel of the Flowers, we were not the only couple waiting to be married that morning, so the clerk told us it would be about an hour before our turn.

"That's cool," Tony said to me, sounding a little too happy about it. "Why don't we just go get some breakfast and then maybe we'll come back later?"

"No, Tony. If we leave now, the line will just be bigger when we get back."

He didn't seem to like my answer. After a few more moments of weak protests, which I shot down like a pro, he said, "Fine," plopping down into the nearest chair and folding his arms across his chest. His legs were bouncing up and down like he was nervous.

"Damn, would you just stop fidgeting?" I asked. "Look, why don't we go over there and apply for our marriage license while we're waiting?"

"Huh?" He whipped his head around to look at the window where we were supposed to get the license. There was no line.

"Our license," I repeated. "You know they ain't gonna marry us without one."

"Oh yeah." His eyes looked suddenly bright and hopeful. "I didn't even think of that. We need to get blood tests anyway, don't we? Maybe we should just wait and do this another time."

"No," I said, grabbing his hand and pulling him up from the chair. "I already asked that lady who was in line in front of us. You don't need a blood test in Nevada. Now come on." I dragged him over to the window and told the person at the counter, "Hello, we'd like to apply for our marriage license."

"Certainly. All I need is some form of ID from each of you. Then you have to sign these forms stating that you are no closer than second cousins and that neither of you has a spouse still living. If you've been divorced, you'll need to provide us with the exact date of your divorce, as well as the city and state where it was finalized."

"No problem," I stated, reaching into my purse to find my driver's license. When I looked back at Tony, he was standing perfectly still, a worried look on his face.

"What is wrong with you?" I asked.

He hesitated before answering, but finally he said, "Um, my license. I don't think I have it with me."

Now I was pissed. It was so obvious that he was stalling, and I was getting sick of it. I had watched him put his wallet in the inside pocket of his coat when he got dressed that morning, so I knew he must have his license with him.

"That's all right, sir," the clerk said. "We accept other forms of ID. You can give us a birth certificate, a pass—"

"No problem," I interrupted, and before Tony could protest, I had reached into his jacket, pulled out his wallet, and opened it up. "See, he's got his license right here." I shot Tony an accusing look. "Now, are we gonna do this today, or what?"

Tony's shoulders sagged in what I could only call a gesture of defeat. I still thought he was just having a serious case of cold feet. Nothing could have prepared me for what happened next.

"Look, Isis," he started slowly, taking a step away from me. "There's something I have to tell you."

"Oh Lord, just get it over with," I said, thinking I was prepared for the embarrassment of hearing him tell me in front of this clerk that he wanted to hold off and get married some other time.

"You don't wanna marry me now?"

"No," he answered, sounding sad. "I do want to marry you. But I can't."

I jammed my hands on my hips and demanded, "And just what the hell does that mean? You *can't* marry me? Why not?"

"I can't marry you because . . ." Sweat beads had formed on his forehead, and he wiped them away nervously before he dropped the bomb. "I can't marry you because I'm already married."

I let out a scream before I felt my knees give way, and my body crumpled to the floor.

28

Nikki

I had been a wreck since the moment I called and asked Coco to join me for lunch. I didn't know who else to turn to, but I knew for sure I needed help. In the end, it was Coco I decided to call, because if anyone knew about "sneaking-around" sex, she was definitely the master. Now, I still wasn't sure I was going to pursue anything with Keith, but my mind had been wandering a lot lately, and more than I liked to admit, it was wandering into sexual fantasies about me and Keith. I figured Coco would be a good sounding board for all my mixed-up feelings.

"Oooohweee, girl. What's wrong with you?" Coco asked when I called her earlier. I had tried to sound nonchalant when I invited her to lunch, but judging from her question, I'd done a pretty bad job of hiding my feelings.

"I dunno. I need to talk. Can you meet me for lunch today?"

"Sounds serious. You payin'?"

I chuckled. Some things never change, and Coco is one of 'em for sure. That girl is forever looking for a free meal, and the truth is, no one is better than Coco at getting them too.

"Yes, I'm paying, Coco," I said. "We both know you wouldn't have it any other way."

"Hey, I'm just making sure. Okay, then, we can meet. Where?"

Once we agreed on the time and place, I felt a little better knowing I'd be able to talk to someone soon about my dilemma. I had been keeping this thing bottled up for way too long. In just about every other area of my life, Tiny was the one I went to when I had things on my mind that I needed to discuss. But for obvious reasons, I couldn't go to her about this, and the pressure of keeping it all to myself was really starting to drive me crazy. I hoped that Coco had some good advice for me.

At the restaurant, I could hear Coco before I could see her. She sauntered up in Applebee's, yapping away on her cell phone like no one else in the world mattered.

"Naw, boo. I'm meeting my girl for lunch right now," she cooed into the phone.

Coco was wearing a navy blue miniskirt with a tight sleeveless wrap shirt, proudly displaying her curves the way a much slimmer woman might do. But it didn't matter one bit that Coco was plus-sized. My girl was working it, stepping high with a pair of four-inch stiletto slingbacks. She always looked great.

I started to feel a bit self-conscious as I sat there in my denim Capris and pink polo shirt. Surely no one had looked at me as lustfully as they were looking at her while she sauntered toward my table. Then again, Coco was an expert at drawing attention to herself. It was like a fine art she had mastered. Maybe I should think about taking some lessons from her, I thought with a small laugh. On second thought, my problems seemed big enough already. If I had Coco's flair and confidence, I might not know how to handle all that attention—whether it was from men or from women.

Coco tossed her bag onto the seat, blew me an air kiss, then slid into the booth across from me. She stuck a well-manicured finger into the air to indicate she'd be off the phone soon. I really didn't mind waiting. It gave me a few more minutes to compose my thoughts before revealing them to Coco.

"Well, maybe you should call me when you decide what you want to do," Coco said to whoever was on the phone, rolling her eyes for my amusement. "Look, boo, I need to run. I'm being rude, so holla back when you finally make a decision," she said, then abruptly clicked her phone shut.

"Now, girl," she said, resting her elbows on the table and leaning toward me. "Tell me what's up with you." Coco posed the question, but within seconds, her eyes were scanning the other restaurant patrons, no doubt sizing up the men to see who might be her next target. My first reaction was to be offended that she wasn't giving me her full attention, but then I realized it was probably better this way. It would be easier to say what I had to say if I didn't have to make eye contact.

"Well," I began, still hesitant, even though Coco's eyes were glued to a table full of handsome black men in expensive designer suits. "I don't even know how to start."

Reluctantly, Coco pulled her attention away from the table of men and looked at me. "Nikki, girl, don't do this. You brought me here to tell me something; now just spit it out, 'cause I'm not in the mood to play no guessing game."

"I know. I'm sorry," I said. "It's just . . ." Images of Tiny's face came into my mind. First I saw her angry expression the day I came home from my family outing with Dwayne. Then I saw her tearful face the night she confessed her fear of losing me. And here I was at lunch with Coco, looking for advice on what I should do about my lust for a male coworker. I hated the thought that depending on my decision, I could be getting ready to break Tiny's heart—or get myself beat if she got mad enough.

"Look," Coco snapped, bringing me out of my trance, "why don't you spare me the hassle and tell me what the hell is wrong with you. 'Cause if you can't say what you got to say, I might as well go over and introduce myself to the men at that table over there."

She was right; I needed to get to the point and do it quickly. I swallowed dryly and exhaled. "Okay, well, um, there's this guy . . ." I stopped when I saw Coco's eyes bug out. "What?" I asked, a little irritated by her reaction. I'd finally built the courage to begin, and she was bugging out before I got anywhere near the heart of the matter.

"A guy . . . as in . . . What do you mean, a guy?"

"Coco, just let me finish," I said, feeling a little testy. The need to get this off my chest was even stronger now. "When I say *guy,* I mean a *man,* Coco, in every sense of the word, and"—I leaned forward and whispered the last part—"he is so fuckin' fine."

"Excuse me?" she said, looking like she was barely able to get the words out she was so shocked.

Unlike Coco, I was having no trouble expressing myself now that my little secret was out. "I mean, my panties can't stay dry when I'm next to him. And he's like, always going out of his way to get next to me. I mean, he flirts with me, and . . ." I shrugged my shoulders. "I don't know. I think . . . Coco, I ain't had dick in three years. I ain't even thought about it, never missed it, didn't want to miss it, and here I am sweatin' this young guy."

"Are you telling me you're thinking about switching teams again?" Coco asked, leaning back in her seat and shaking her head in bewilderment. "Damn, this is some shit!"

"Who you tellin'?"

"Okay, so you want my advice, right?" she asked.

I looked up at her through pleading eyes. I wasn't sure what I wanted, but I surely did know what I needed—someone to tell me to stop fooling around and stop thinking about that young boy. I needed someone to remind me of what I already knew, that Tiny had been there for me over the years. After all, it was Tiny who had restored my faith in love. She had made me feel worthy after all the damage Dwayne had done to my self-esteem. Those were true gifts she had given me, and they should have been enough to override this unexpected desire I was feeling for sex with a man. Deep down, I knew that Tiny didn't deserve the treacherous thoughts I was having. Yet, I had chosen to seek my advice from Coco, a woman who was all about doing whatever felt good. Did I really think she would advise me to do the right thing when it came to Tiny? Or maybe I had chosen Coco because subconsciously I was looking for her to give me permission to cheat.

I felt like shit. Still, there was that little part of me that was overwhelmed with emotions each time I thought about Keith. I imagined the way he smelled, the way he walked with that sexy swagger, his smile. Everything about him was so electrifying to me.

Before Coco could begin to offer me advice, the waiter approached our table. We stopped our discussion long enough to order some drinks and listen to him tell us about the specials.

As soon as he left the table to get our drinks, Coco started chattering away. "Well, since you asked for my advice, here's what I think. Now, you know I like Tiny and all, but personally, I never did understand how you could stand to go without some dick every once in a while. I mean, I could see if you'd been a dyke all your life . . ."

I cringed at her use of the word *dyke,* because I hated the term, but I didn't interrupt her.

". . . then you wouldn't know what you were missing. But you . . . you been with men before, so you know what it feels like when you got some good dick inside of you. And I know how you lesbians do, with those toys and all, but come on. You can't tell me that it's the same having some fake-ass plastic shit up in there."

I know that's right, I thought as my mind pictured Tiny sliding that hideous rubber strap-on in and out of me. I despised that thing, and what made it even worse was the fact that lately Tiny insisted we use it every single time we made love.

"Ain't nothin' the same as having a real live man. I'm talking about good, hard, veins-throbbing dick. The real McCoy, baby!"

Just as she was talking about the veins on the side, the waiter returned to our table. He had clearly heard what Coco was talking about, because he almost dropped our drinks right in her lap. She just looked up at him with a wicked smile. I stifled a laugh. The poor guy was so flustered he didn't even ask if we were ready to order before he bolted away from our table.

"Now come on, Nikki, you can't tell me you don't miss it," Coco said.

I realized with resignation that she was absolutely right. I couldn't deny that I missed it. As she was describing it, I felt the area between my thighs spring to life, and that's when I knew I was in trouble. When I got with Tiny and fell in love, I really thought I would never be with another man, and it didn't bother me one bit. And until Keith came along, I really hadn't missed a man's touch—or at least I didn't think I'd missed it. Now I couldn't stop thinking about what it would feel like to have his hands all over my body, to feel his throbbing hardness inside of me.

"Nikki, you with me? You look like you about to have an orgasm over there or something," Coco said, louder than I would have liked.

I shook my head. "Yeah, I'm here. It's just that until I talked to you, I guess I had convinced myself that this was just a silly little crush. Now I don't know."

"So what you worried about? Ain't nothing wrong with wanting some dick, you know."

"That's easy for you to say." I sighed. "You're not supposed to be a lesbian."

"*Supposed to be?* Girl, you don't have to be anything but who you are. And if that means you're a lesbian who wants some dick, then so be it. Why you trippin' over this anyway?" she asked as she began perusing the menu.

"Because I thought I was gay, Coco," I said, a little annoyed that she was acting as if this was all so simple when it was tearing me apart. "And now I don't know what I am, 'cause I can't stop thinking about a dude."

"So maybe you should just fuck him to get it out of your system. Then you could go back to your happy little lesbian life," she suggested with a smirk.

"I'm glad you think this is funny," I said.

"Of course I think it's funny. Why are you so worked up over this? It's just sex, for God's sake. Do you, girl . . . or should I say 'do him'?" She laughed, and I couldn't help but join her.

"Look," I said when the laughter subsided, "even if I did take your advice and do this, it wouldn't be fair to Tiny. That's my biggest problem."

"Tiny? Who said she has to know anything about this?"

"Are you serious? She's always riding my ass, watching me like a hawk as it is. The second I tried to step out, I guarantee she'd know what was up."

Coco actually looked sympathetic. "Oh, my child, you have so much to learn, don't you?"

"So teach me, oh wise one," I said, using sarcasm to hide the fact that I was truly interested in her advice. I think part of me had already decided I was going to go through with this. Coco's scheming might help me avoid lots of grief with Tiny later on.

Coco grinned at me. "It's really quite simple. Fuck ol' boy at work, in a deserted conference room or a closet. . . . Or go to a quick-stay motel during lunch. That way, you ain't gotta worry about coming up with lies and double-checking your facts and shit like that. Just do it there. Rock his world, then go on home to Tiny like it was just another day at the office," she said easily.

I guess deep down I had known even before we met for lunch that this would be the type of advice Coco would ultimately offer. The girl was a true master at this shit. As I thought about her suggestions, I realized that if I could get up the nerve to hook up with Keith at work, I might just be able to get away with it.

And as I thought about working up my nerve, the waiter looked like he had finally found his again. He approached the table to take our orders. I saw a gleam in Coco's eye, and for a second I thought she was about to embarrass the poor guy with more dick conversation. But she took pity on him and waited until he was finished.

Once the waiter left the table, she said happily, "Now, let's continue our lesson. I know it's been a while, but you do remember how to work with a dick, don't you?" And without waiting for an answer, Coco's crazy ass launched into a minilecture you might call "How to Make a Man Scream 101," displaying her extensive knowledge of the subject matter. I just wasn't sure if I'd be able to put her lecture to use, because despite how I was starting to feel about Keith, I still loved Tiny, and I didn't know if I could cheat on her.

29

Coco

I knew that I was handling my job correctly when it came to Jackson, because he started blowing me up, taking me into the city for fancy dinners, springing for luxurious suites at some of New York City's finest hotels. He even took me on a shopping spree to Bergdorf's after one of my finest performances in the bedroom.

"Pick out something," he insisted. I only had to be asked once, 'cause if there is one fantasy near the top of my list, it's high-end shopping where I never have to see the bill. Of course, I knew I'd be back on my knees again later, but when one dress cost as much as four months' rent, I figured it was the least I could do for him. When the salesgirl rang up my purchases, he barely blinked at the total.

"Now we have to take you someplace nice to wear that outfit," he said on the way back to the hotel. We had very little conversation other than that, because Jackson seemed to be constantly on his cell phone. Brotha man wheeled and dealed all day long. When I started feeling a little taken for granted, I reminded myself not to take it personally. You don't become one of the richest black men in New York by working part-time. Besides, while he was doing business on the phone, it left me free to daydream about Mac.

On the nights when I wasn't with Jackson, Mac and I had quite a few late-night phone conversations. Some of them got pretty graphic, so I still expected that eventually I'd get him in bed. But I had yet to see him naked, and I was not accustomed to waiting this long for something I wanted so badly. Until Mac came to his senses and gave me some, I had to be satisfied with using my imagination. And my imagination was working on overdrive right now. I could feel my panties becoming damp, and I might have even been able to make myself come in a few minutes if Jackson hadn't hung up his phone and interrupted my thoughts.

"What kind of credit cards do you have?" He held out his hand for my wallet.

I smiled sweetly, hoping he was going where I thought he was. "Oh, the usual. Discover this, Master that."

"Limits?"

"Let's just say I'm pushing all my limits," I shot back. Hell, if Jackson wanted to pay my credit card bills, then that would be nice. As if on cue, Jackson reached into his jacket pocket and handed me a fat envelope.

"Here's a little something." I could tell by the thickness of the envelope that he'd just given me a couple thousand dollars.

"I'm gonna have to show you my appreciation in some way," I cooed, realizing that the feel of all this money in my hands was making me just as wet as my thoughts of Mac had.

That night, I gave Jackson the fuckin' and suckin' of his life. I could tell by the way he stared at me afterward that he might work out to be a huge meal ticket. And a week later, he showed me just how right I was.

Jackson called to say he had a surprise for me. Mac still hadn't made a move, so I was more than happy to get dressed and go have another expensive meal with Jackson. I knew he'd want to see all of me later, so I started my outfit with the La Perla panties and bra set from my shopping spree. Then I put on the YSL sundress he bought me with some Lanvin strappy platforms, took a twirl in the mirror, and hurried down to my car.

Jackson had given me an address that turned out to be a building in a newly gentrified, upscale neighborhood. I was surprised when I entered to find that before I even spoke, the doorman greeted me by name and buzzed Jackson to let him know I was there. I guess Jackson had given him a full description.

Jackson stepped off the elevator to greet me. The look he gave me told me he thought the money spent on my outfit was worth every penny. I did a little pose and let him enjoy the view for a few moments before I asked, "So, what are we doing tonight?" Jackson liked it when I played coy, as if I didn't know exactly what we were doing here.

"Oh," he answered, playing right along with my act, "a little of this, a little of that. But I think you'll be extremely happy by the end of the evening."

"I always am when I'm with you, Jackson," I replied as he placed his hand on my back and led me to the elevators.

When we reached the sixteenth floor, the doors opened directly into a stylish, modern apartment with stainless-steel appliances, dishwasher, and a wet bar with one of those climate-controlled wine refrigerators.

"Very nice," I murmured as I moved over to the window to check out the view. Talk about being on top of the world. This place felt like heaven.

"You like this place?"

He had to be kidding. "Like? What's not to like? It's the most beautiful apartment I've ever been in. The views . . . Hell, I could live in the kitchen," I said with a laugh. Even without furniture, you could see this place belonged in a magazine.

"Let me show you the bedroom." Jackson led me down a hallway past a wood-paneled room that I supposed was meant to be an office. He opened a door at the end of the hall. The bedroom, the only furnished room in the place, featured a king-sized cherrywood sleigh bed with matching dresser, armoire, and night tables. This was clearly not a build-it-yourself set from IKEA. This was the real thing and no doubt cost more than all the furniture I owned.

Jackson sat on the edge of the bed. "Open the closet," he told me.

I slid open the door and found some of the most beautiful clothes, coincidentally all in my size, hanging next to rows of the sexiest shoes. Manolos, Louboutins, Choos . . . you name them, they were there. I turned to Jackson, my mouth hanging to the floor. He swept his hands out.

"Coco, all this can be yours," he announced just as his cell rang. He raised his finger, motioning for me to give him a minute of privacy. "Honey, I'm working . . ." I heard him lie to his wife as I walked back into the living room.

As I stood looking around at the empty room, wishing I had a place to sit, my phone began to vibrate too. I didn't plan to answer, assuming Jackson would be done talking to his wife soon, but then I saw Mac's number on my caller ID.

"Hello."

"I been thinking about you." Mac's voice poured out smooth as buttermilk.

"Oh yeah?" I tried not to sound excited, but damn, this man did something to me.

"I got a place in the Hamptons I'm renting for the weekend. I'm gonna take the six o'clock Jitney, and I wanted you to come for the weekend."

Unfortunately, Jackson chose that moment to come strolling into the room.

"Can I call you back in five minutes?"

"Look, a simple yes or no will do. I'm not gonna sweat you to go with me."

"I know. Just let me call you back. I'm in the middle of something." I hung up as Jackson reached me. He just stood there, staring.

"What?" I damn near barked at him.

"All this," he said, sounding a little too condescending, "well, it comes with stipulations, you know, shit you can and cannot do. Other men?" He glanced briefly at the cell phone I was still holding in my hand. "This place means they no longer exist. You are to be mine and mine only, at my beck and call," he explained.

"So, I'm supposed to just sell myself so you can rent me an apartment?" I snapped. I did not like ultimatums.

"This is a condo that you will own outright in two years. It comes with a furniture budget, and I'm not talking about Jennifer Convertibles or Bob's Discount. There will also be credit cards with a ten-thousand-dollar-a-month budget, a driver on call, and an additional five thousand dollars in cash per month. All you have to do is agree to my rules."

As he spoke, I was silently calculating the dollar value of everything he had just offered to me. It was almost more than I could comprehend. Maybe it would be worth giving up everything else, I thought.

"Coco, I've slept with a lot of women, and I know you didn't get to be that good in bed by being a virgin. But I don't care who was in your past. I just want to know that if I'm giving you all of this, there will be no one but me anymore."

His eyes wandered admiringly over my breasts. "I want you, and when I want something, I am more than willing to pay for it. And as you can see, I am extremely generous," he finished.

Wow! I needed a moment to catch my breath. Here was Jackson, offering me a lifestyle so extravagant it was beyond my wildest dreams. And then there was Mac. I seriously doubted he could offer me half of what Jackson just did, but something about spending time with Mac seemed as valuable to me as all Jackson's money. Just as Jackson expected an immediate answer, Mac was also waiting for me to call him back in the next five minutes.

I hated feeling so pressured, so I came up with the only exit excuse I could think of in such a rush. "Um, I have to use the restroom. Be right back." I scurried off, leaving Jackson with an aggravated look on his face. I suppose he'd expected me to say yes without hesitation. Luckily, his phone rang before he had a chance to say anything to me.

I slipped into the bathroom and dialed Mac's number.

"Either you coming or I'm inviting somebody else," Mac blurted out.

"What?" Men usually took what they could get from me, and I made up all the rules. Now there were two of them trying to push me around on the same night.

"Coco, I made you an offer. What you gonna do?" he pressed. I was getting hot, and not in the good way. How dare he try to make me do things his way? If he wasn't so damn fine . . .

"I'm nobody's woman. I'm my own woman." I tried to sound assertive, but part of me was so afraid he might take back his offer that I knew I didn't sound very convincing.

"I guess you don't want to be my woman." Mac broke it down.

"How about you give me a minute?" I got all saucy.

"I'm a grown-ass man, Coco, and I thought you were feeling me. But I'm not into games," he added before the phone went dead.

"Coco?" I heard Jackson's voice, reminding me that I still had a serious dilemma on my hands. I wanted this apartment and all the things that came with it, but I also wanted Mac's dick, at least once.

I sashayed into the living room already feeling like I lived here. Jackson stood in the center of the room, arms crossed, looking like he wasn't going to wait long for an answer.

"So, you're asking me to be your mistress?" I asked, not sure why the idea surprised me. After all, wasn't that what I already was?

"I'm offering you a great life, Coco, where you never have to worry about money ever again."

"I've always been my own woman."

"I understand all that. Why do you think I'm making you an offer you can't refuse?"

"So, are you expecting an answer now? 'Cause I'm gonna need some time," I told him, hoping he'd be willing to grant me at least the weekend. That way I could get my groove on with Mac. After all, I hadn't even had a sample. I didn't want to say no to Jackson and give up all his money until I knew Mac was every bit as good as I imagined he would be.

"You got 'til tomorrow," he said with finality.

"I just need to be alone to think right now. You understand, don't you?" I asked sweetly, suddenly in a hurry to get out of there. "I'll take good care of you tomorrow, okay?" I said as I stroked his crotch gently.

"Tomorrow, Coco, and I mean it. After that, the offer is gone," he said as he walked me to the elevator and said good-bye.

I rushed out of the building, imagining it to be my address, my doorman, my view. As I stepped into my car, I dialed Mac's number. I didn't see any reason I couldn't have the best of both worlds, at least for one night.

"Don't hang up on me again," I purred.

"You wanna go or not?"

I knew it would be the last time he asked. How in the world did I get stuck with two men who were so damn demanding?

"Instead of the Jitney, I'll pick you up," I offered. There were a lot of things I wanted to do with Mac, but I wasn't willing to break my sunrise rule. Even for him. Besides, my car would be necessary in order to get back to the city by tomorrow to start picking out furniture for my new place. I was sure that by then I would have figured out some way to move into Jackson's condo and still keep Mac as my something on the side.

*   *   *

When I pulled up to Mac's place, he had just stepped out of the building, and I was so grateful Jackson had given me one more night. Mac wore a black T-shirt that showed off his biceps to full advantage, and my nipples rose to attention at the sight of him.

The sun began to set two hours later as we arrived at a charming beach cottage on Ninevah Beach. "So, did you say this is a rental?"

"Yeah, it belongs to some friends of mine."

"Nice friends you got."

"Sure are. You wanna take a shower?" he asked. "We have dinner reservations in forty-five minutes."

I assumed he meant we'd be taking a shower together, but he showed me to a guest room. Still, just imagining his wet, naked body had me aroused. I dressed for dinner hoping that this wasn't the bed I'd be sleeping in tonight.

Sitting across from Mac in a crowded restaurant, I could see all the women finding something to do with their eyes in his direction. If their adoring stares were any indication, any of the women, white, black, or Asian, would have gladly taken my place. But he didn't take his eyes off of me all night.

When we talked, I almost felt like I was with one of my good girlfriends instead of out with an incredibly sexy man. The men I went out with usually had no interest in talking about anything other than how much they couldn't wait to fuck me. Don't get me wrong, most of the time I was into that talk as much as they were. I mean, I knew what we were doing there, and I didn't hold any illusions about being out on a romantic date. They were out to get laid, and I was out to get paid. But with Mac, it just felt different. I found myself enjoying his company, wanting to learn more about him.

We discovered that we had some things in common. We had both been raised by our grandmothers in New York but had spent most of the summers in the South, me in Georgia and him in Virginia. We were both the youngest and the most ambitious of our siblings and the only ones without children. In a lot of ways, we had raised ourselves to want more than what we grew up around.

As we continued our getting-to-know-you conversation, it actually did begin to feel like a romantic date, and I was shocked.

It had been so long since I'd had one, I'd almost forgotten how to do it. But with Mac, it just felt natural. He slid a piece of the juiciest steak into my mouth. I washed it down with a Grey Goose lemon-drop martini, then leaned across the table to let him taste the drink on my lips. That one kiss made me hot, and I couldn't wait to get in between the sheets with him.

Mac insisted we go to a few of his favorite clubs before heading home that night. At four in the morning, we finally rolled out of the last club, sweaty and tipsy from all the club-hopping on a balmy summer night. Apparently, Mac knew his way around the jet-setting beach towns of the Hamptons.

When we got to the house, Mac took off my heels and led me to the porch swing, his big, strong arms hugging me tight. The next thing I knew, the sun began to rise, waking me. It had been years since I'd spent the night with a man, and longer since I spent that much time without having sex. In fact, I don't think it had ever happened, and I had no idea what to do.

"You awake, Coco?" Mac whispered in my ear.

"Yeah." I didn't know if I should make some excuse and get the hell out of there or what. This entire thing was new to me. I started to rise, but Mac held me tightly.

"Baby, let's watch the sun rise." His voice interrupted my need to run away, and I sat back to enjoy the dawn—no, mostly to enjoy him. Mac was proving to be different than any man I'd ever been with. After all, most men wanted to get deep inside me as quick as possible, and while Mac was interested, he certainly didn't seem rushed to hit it. With all those other men, I thought I was special because they were spending money on me, but Mac made me feel special in a way that seemed much more real.

"You comfortable?" His lips nearly kissed my ear.

"Yeah," I murmured, and I truly was. More comfortable than I'd felt in a long time.

"Coco, I may not be able to let you go." Coming from Mac, those words sounded much more romantic, but they were so similar to what Jackson had told me the night before. Both men wanted to possess me. And unfortunately, as romantic as this all was, I was still a practical girl, and I knew that there would be benefits to keeping Jackson around.

"I got to get back to the city," I said suddenly.

"Stay with me and I'll take care of all your needs." Again, his words were like an echo of everything Jackson had said, but deep inside I knew that Mac could take care of the needs of my heart, something Jackson had probably not ever considered. Then he said, "Trust me, okay?" and it just felt right. As much as I wanted to run to my car, throw it into gear, and race the hell out of the Hamptons, Mac was offering me something I knew I needed. As many men as I'd met in my life, I knew that this kind of man, making this kind of offer, wouldn't come around twice. He would only walk away once, and I didn't know if I could afford to lose him.

30

Isis

The morning after Tony's confession, I called the airline and made a last-minute reservation to get the hell out of Las Vegas. Tony had been smart enough not to try to stay in the same room with me the night before, but when he saw me checking out, he managed to find out which airline I was on and then booked himself a seat. I wanted to tell him not to waste his time or his money, but that would have meant talking to him, and there was no way I was doing that.

During the entire flight back to New York, I had to struggle to contain my rage. Even though I had requested a seat far away from him, just knowing that Tony was on the same plane made me want to get up and throw him out the emergency exit in midair. The mere sight of him pissed me off so bad that when I had to go to the bathroom, I refused to walk to the back of the plane. I'd rather hold it for the last three hours of the flight than pass by his seat and see him watching me with that sorry-ass look on his face. On the trip out to Vegas, we had sat cuddled next to each other, giggling, as his fingers did the walking beneath a blanket. Now, if he had tried to lay a finger on me, I might have snapped it right off his hand.

It felt like an eternity before the plane finally landed in New York. The moment the captain gave the okay to exit, I bolted for the door. I couldn't wait to put as much distance as possible between me and Tony. If I hadn't packed some of my most expensive outfits for our trip, I would have left my suitcase behind. But since I'd already lost so much this week—including my dignity—I refused to lose the clothes too. Tony took advantage of the opportunity and sprinted over to me in the baggage claim area.

"Yo! Isis, c'mon now. Just let me explain," he begged.

I turned my back and pretended I hadn't heard him. I didn't have shit to say to his sorry ass, and I couldn't imagine why the hell he was still trying to talk to me. Did he not know I don't fuck with married men? Obviously he hadn't gotten the fuckin' memo!

"Isis, I know you hear me," he yelled.

I saw my suitcase coming around the carousel. I slipped between a couple of muscular guys to grab the bag, knowing Tony wouldn't follow me if he had to shove these guys out of the way. Just in case he did, though, I said to the guys, "Can you make sure he doesn't follow me?" as I gestured in Tony's direction.

With my suitcase in hand, I stepped outside the airport, where there was a short line of taxis waiting. I jumped into the first one I saw and barked my address at the cabbie. I turned to look out the window. Tony had just come outside and was looking left and right, searching for me. I slid low in the backseat so he wouldn't see me inside the cab.

"Where to?" the cabbie asked like he hadn't heard me the first time.

"Hollis Avenue and 201st Street," I snapped at him, sitting up as the car pulled away from the curb.

Apparently I had gotten up too soon, because when I turned around to get one last look at Tony, I saw he was actually jumping into another cab. He must have spotted me, because the cab pulled in right behind ours, and I watched Tony gesturing wildly, pointing at my cab. I could imagine him yelling, "Follow that cab!" like he was in a movie or something. Well, this was no damn movie, I thought, and there would definitely be no romantic ending.

"Um, excuse me," I said to the driver, inching forward to read his name, which I couldn't pronounce. "You think you could lose that cab behind us?" I asked. I made eye contact with him in the rearview mirror. "It's worth an extra twenty for you."

"Sure, lady," he said in his thick accent. He stepped on the accelerator so hard, my body flew back against the seat. After weaving in and out of the slow traffic on the highway, he got off at the first exit and made a quick U-turn. He drove two blocks down, then turned into an alley. I doubted Tony's cab driver had even managed to follow us off the highway, but I was still nervous when I finally peeked out the back. We were alone in the alley, no other cab in sight.

"Good for you?" the driver asked.

"Good," I confirmed.

We left the alley, and in about thirty minutes, he pulled in front of my apartment. I breathed a sigh of relief when I realized Tony was not there. I had half expected him to have the cab drive straight to my place after we lost them on the highway. Maybe he had finally gotten the message and decided to leave me alone.

I gave the cab driver the extra twenty I promised and jumped out, lugging my suitcase as quickly as I could to my door. As soon as I was inside my apartment, I set the dead bolt and the chain. I wasn't normally so safety-conscious, but Tony had a key. Actually, I was momentarily surprised that I hadn't found him already inside the place when I got home. Then reality hit me with a sickening feeling—maybe the reason he wasn't here was because he had gone home . . . to his wife!

I started to gather up his shit. I didn't want to see anything that could remind me of his sorry ass. Only problem was that everything reminded me of him. As I was filling the Hefty trash bag, my ears perked up at what I thought was the sound of Tony's voice outside. I had this terrible mixed-up feeling—half pissed off that he was still trying to talk to me, but half proud that he wanted me so much he left his wife behind to come to my place. She must not be all that, I thought, if she couldn't keep his ass at home.

I heard his key slide into the lock in my front door, and I was no longer confused. I was just plain mad now. He had some damn nerve coming by my house with his lying ass.

When he realized the chain was blocking his entrance, Tony started pounding. "Isis! Please, baby, let me explain. Just let me explain," he pleaded.

I looked out the window and couldn't believe what I saw. Tony stopped hitting the door and was actually down on his knees as he continued to plead. But I wasn't impressed. "I'm about to call the police!" I shouted.

"Baby, you gotta let me explain," he pressed.

"I ain't gotta do shit!"

I moved away from the window, but my apartment was only

so big, so no matter where I went, I could still hear him. I paced back and forth in my living room for a few minutes while Tony continued to beg. He'd quieted down enough that there wasn't much danger of my neighbors calling the cops, but he didn't show any signs of stopping. After a while, the sound of his voice did something to me. I hated myself for it, but I actually started to cry. Just a few days before, Tony was the man I was supposed to marry, the love of my life. Why the hell had he done this to me? Why had he smashed my dreams and taken away everything I thought would be my future?

I dried my tears quickly, then flung open the door, determined to get the answers to my questions. Tony's eyes lit up as he got to his feet and stepped toward me, but I held up a hand to stop him from getting too close.

"Where the hell you think you're going? You don't need to come in here. Say what you gotta say so you can get the hell outta here."

He looked around as if he suddenly felt embarrassed about being outside. I was trippin' off his sudden pride. Never mind the fact that he was out there less than a minute before, whining and begging like a little bitch for my whole neighborhood to hear. Where was his pride when his lying ass was loving me like he was single and available?

I sucked my teeth and rolled my eyes as I leaned my body against the doorframe. "So you wanna explain, right? Well, explain this: How could you? I can't believe you'd do this shit to me," I spat.

His answer was pitiful. "I got caught up," he said with a shrug. "I don't know what to say. I just got caught up."

"That's all you got to say?" I asked with disgust, and I reached for the door, ready to close it in his face.

"Wait!" He stopped me. "Um, I mean, when we first hooked up, I thought . . ." He cast his eyes downward. "I thought I'd just hit it and quit it, you know."

It took every ounce of self-control not to reach out and slap him. It felt like he'd just ripped my heart out and stomped on it. I was supposed to be a one-night stand for him?

The horror on my face must've scared him a bit because he took a step back. "I'm not saying it's right. I'm just try'na tell you how it went down."

"Okay, so you told me, now get the fuck off my steps. I don't ever wanna see you again," I said, holding back my tears. I refused to let him see me cry now.

"That's how it started," he said, ignoring my demand for him to leave, "but that's not how I feel now."

"Oh yeah?" I asked. I hated him right now—or I should say that I *wanted* to hate him. But as mad as I was, part of me wasn't ready to let go. I still wanted to hear him say the words I knew he was about to say.

"I got caught up and fell in love. I love you, Isis," Tony said.

I couldn't bring myself to respond to those words, but they softened me enough that I wanted to continue the conversation. "What's her name?" I asked quietly. I'm not sure why, but I needed to know the details.

"Her name is Monica," he said.

"Do I know her?"

"I don't think so," he mumbled. "At least I hope not."

"What does she do?"

"She's a secretary at a school. Near where we live."

"Where the hell do you live anyway?" I growled at him, though I was equally angry with myself at this moment. How could I have been so stupid? I let myself get so caught up that I fell for one of the oldest tricks in the book. Any self-respecting woman should know what it means when a man never takes her home to his place, but Tony had me so open I hadn't even really noticed.

He lowered his head. "Please don't get mad, but I'd rather not say where I live."

I ignored his insult and pressed on with my questions. "Do you love her?"

"Baby, I love you." The sincerity in his voice was almost enough to sway me, but I forced myself to stay focused.

"I didn't ask you if you loved me. Do you love her? Do you love your wife?"

He stood there staring at me, obviously reluctant to answer. I refused to back down, though, so eventually he admitted, "I have no choice but to love her some. She's the mother of my kids."

My jaw dropped, and I exploded in anger. "Kids? Did you just say kids? As in more than one?"

He nodded silently. My head was spinning. All this damn

time, he'd been lying to me, using me, and I had fallen for all his shit. I felt so disgusted. How could he have been living this double life like it wasn't anything?

"Motherfucker, you told me you didn't have no kids. You said you wanted to have kids with me!" I screamed a lot louder than I intended to.

Again he had no words for me. My body started trembling, and I had to lean against the doorframe to keep myself upright. Just how long would this shit have continued, I wondered, if we hadn't gone to Vegas. In my shocked state, I struggled to remember why we'd even gone there. But regardless of whose idea the trip was, he was the one who had asked me to marry him! Was this all his idea of a sick joke? That's when I looked down at the fucking rock on my finger. It was glistening, as if somehow it knew it was now under my scrutiny.

Tony followed my stare and swallowed hard. "We can work this thing out, baby," he said, reaching for me.

"Don't fucking call me baby. And don't touch me." I stepped beyond his reach, but that just gave him enough room to come in. He moved quickly, stepped inside, and slammed the door shut.

"Please, please, just hear me out. I can—we can work this out. I want to be with you. I know we can work this thing out." The desperation in his voice sickened me. All this damn time, he'd been playing with my emotions, and now here he was expecting me to listen to his blubbering.

"I know we can make it, baby," he insisted. I stood by watching silently as he continued to plead. He went on about how much I meant to him, how much he loved me, how I just had to say the word and he would tell his wife it was over.

"How can you stand here after you rocked my world with your dirty little secret and expect me to stay with you?" His audacity was so overwhelming to me. It was like he was waiting for me to welcome him back into my life and my heart with open arms. Like this was just another bump in the road, and we needed to keep going. He disgusted me more than I could fathom.

"We're meant to be together. I love you," he offered up.

"You don't love me!" I screamed at him. "You can't possibly!" My nostrils were flaring, and my breathing was fast and furious.

"This is how you treat someone you love? This? Being married and hiding it from me?" I shook my head. "You don't love me. You love you. It's just that simple. That's why your selfish ass kept me on the side, then went home to your wife and kids like some kind of family man. You make me sick." I turned my back to him and took a step away, but he grabbed my arm.

"Wait! Wait, Isis, just wait," he said, then pulled me to him. Because I didn't expect him to try it, I wasn't prepared to resist when he wrapped his arms around me in a tight embrace. He kissed my neck and head as he repeated, "I love you. I swear I love you like I've never loved any other woman. I swear!"

"Your word don't mean shit to me," I said as I jerked myself away from him. "Remember you gave me your word when you was looking me in the face, promising a future with me, talking about kids and shit. Just lying!" I shook my head. "You and your fuckin' word."

"You've gotta believe me when I tell you I love you," he pressed.

I strolled over to the front door and placed my hand on the knob. "No, you gotta believe me when I tell you this," I said, pulling the door open. "Get the fuck out, and don't come back."

Tony stood frozen for a moment, and it looked like he might still try to change my mind. But finally he took a deep breath and proceeded to the door. He stopped in front of me and said, "So that's it, right? It's just gonna end like this?"

"Nah, it's not over 'til I get the last word. So, kiss my ass and lose my fuckin' number!" I slammed the door in his face and locked it, then burst into tears.

31

Tammy

Monday morning, I beat Tim out of the house. I didn't want him to get any chance to notice the new clothes I was wearing. I had always loved the way he paid close attention to my appearance—he was quick to notice a new hairdo or outfit—but today I didn't want that. Once I showed up in the office, I wanted Raoul's eyes to be all over me. I wanted him to remember how good we were together. Ever since he left late Friday night, I couldn't stop thinking about our time together. Tim and I had avoided talking about it all weekend, but even when we made small talk, I'd find my mind drifting off. I kept having sudden flashbacks of Raoul's head between my legs.

I'd always thought of myself as a one-man woman, and Tim had been that man. I was sure that I had everything I'd ever want or need right there in my husband. But after making love to Raoul, I wasn't quite sure about anything anymore. I felt that he had something Tim didn't and probably never would. Raoul had ignited a spark in me that had recently fizzled out between me and my husband.

"Hello. Hope you had a great weekend." I waved to the security guard as I breezed past him, feeling like a spring chicken. I hopped off the elevator, racing to the office an hour before anybody else would be there. Then I did something I'd never have dreamed of doing before—this seemed to be my week for stepping outside my usual boundaries. I snuck into Raoul's office and sat my butt in his chair, imagining him sitting under me.

"Damn, girl, you better catch yourself," I warned as I felt myself actually coming close to orgasm. When my eyes popped open, I caught sight of the pictures of his wife and son on his desk. Sure, she had beauty-queen looks and a perfect body— with not a lot of extra meat on her bones—but that didn't change the fact that Raoul was all over my plus-sized frame Friday night like he couldn't get enough.

"Oh, mami, you got mucho ass, and Raoul love to feel inside you," he'd said as he pumped away.

Before long, I heard voices in the hall, interrupting my little sexual fantasy in Raoul's seat. I raced to my desk in the outer office before I could be discovered. I worked for Tim three days a week, and Monday was our busiest day, so I quickly got lost in my work.

Tim brushed his hands across my shoulder as he went by. "You want some coffee, honey?"

"No, thank you," I answered without looking up from my desk. "I already had a cup." I hadn't really, but as excited as I felt over Raoul, the smallest bit of caffeine might have me bouncing around like a crazy person.

When Raoul came into the office, I felt my entire body pause. I wanted to take him right there on the floor, and I didn't care if everybody crowded around and watched. I waved and handed him the pink memo slips from clients, trying to act as if everything was normal, as if he hadn't spent hours between my legs only three nights ago. Raoul seemed to be making the same effort to act nonchalant, and I doubt anyone watching us would have noticed any difference. But when Raoul's eyes momentarily met mine, I felt the spark in me ignite into a bonfire.

When he went into his office, I had to struggle not to just sit and stare.

"Don't look, don't look, don't look," I chastised myself. Finally, I couldn't take it. I picked up the phone.

"You need any files?"

I felt like a big idiot when he casually said, "No, thanks."

While I should have been organizing, I went onto our company Web site and clicked on Raoul's picture and profile page. I could stare at him all day. I had to stop when a couple of employees almost caught me in the act.

Tammy, pull it together. I had to quit acting like a love-struck teenager instead of the married woman that I was. But it was no use. By twelve o'clock, I felt ready to attack Raoul—oh, okay, by attack, I mean fuck his brains out. I had to know if it was just me. I dialed his number again.

"Yes," he answered in his professional voice, not the deep, smoky one I dreamed about all weekend.

"Umm . . ." I began awkwardly, speaking into the phone but looking directly at him through the window in his office. "I have a question."

He leaned forward and looked at me. "I can see you from my desk." He seemed confused. "Why don't you just come into my office?"

"No, I think I'll just do it this way." I didn't trust myself to get too close to him, in case I couldn't keep my hands off.

"Okay, so ask, then," he said, sounding slightly amused by my strange behavior.

I took a deep breath and gathered the courage to speak my mind. "Did you have a good time on Friday? I mean, honestly. Did you really enjoy yourself, or did you just say that?"

"I really enjoyed myself." I wasn't convinced, because his voice still sounded tight, like we could have been discussing business instead of wild sex.

"And that's the truth?" I couldn't help myself.

"Yes, Tammy, that's the truth." When he started glancing toward the door to Tim's office, I realized why he sounded so strange. We were in the workplace, for God's sake! He was just nervous about getting busted. But I was so damn turned on by this man that this risky conversation was making me even hotter. I threw caution to the wind and pushed further.

"So, if I wasn't married, you'd do it again?"

He looked like he was about to drop the phone. "Tammy, your husband told me this was supposed to be a one-night thing to settle some score between the two of you."

"Well, I've decided to change the plans a little . . . if you're interested."

Raoul's eyes glanced nervously at Tim's door again. "Your husband is my boss. If he found out we were having this conversation, he'd fire me."

It might sound cold, but at that moment, Raoul's job security didn't matter to me. There was only one thing I cared about, and that was getting him to give me head like he did the other night.

"Would you?" I pressed him. In the back of my mind, I knew there was a small chance he could tell Tim I was propositioning him, but I was willing to take that risk.

"Tammy . . ." He sounded like he was pleading with me to stop this conversation, but I refused.

"Just answer the question, Raoul. I have just as much as you to lose."

He gave a defeated sigh. "Okay, yes, I would. But you are married, and so am I."

"So what?"

He stood up in his chair, staring at me through the glass. My boldness had shocked me, too, but I desired him in a way I had never wanted anyone before. I don't know if it was the seven orgasms he gave me, but I needed this man again.

"What are you saying, Tammy?"

"I want more. Do you want to sleep with me again?" I held my breath as I waited for his response.

He stood still for a moment, looking like he was scared to answer. I just kept my eyes locked on him through the window, hoping he understood this was not some kind of trap, and definitely not a joke. Finally, he whispered the sweetest word: "Yes."

I actually had to grab the sides of my chair to keep from jumping out of it in my excitement. Then, realizing how strange it must look for me to be talking on the phone and staring into Raoul's office, I turned my chair away from him and tried to wipe the huge smile off my face.

"When?" I asked urgently, wishing it could be right then and there. But no matter how he answered, I knew I'd figure out a way to make it happen, because I needed him.

"I'll let you know. Just answer your phone when I call."

"You don't have to worry about that," I whispered as I hung up the phone. "You don't have to worry about that at all."

Sitting across from Tim at dinner, I could barely find words to bridge the gap of silence between us. After talking about the kids and various household things, there wasn't much we could say. Of course, both of us were avoiding the real topic. There had been a definite change in our relationship ever since Tim invited Raoul into bed with me, and neither one of us had approached the other to talk about it. I don't know what Tim thought was the reason for our recent problems, but I guess he was just so glad I wasn't trippin' over Egypt anymore that he decided not to rock the boat. This was a relief, because telling Tim the truth about what was really on my mind was not something I was prepared to do.

After dinner, Tim asked me into the den, where he stood behind the bar, mixing us drinks. "We haven't done it in a while," he said before I could even take a sip from the glass he'd handed me. "Is there something wrong?"

I knew it was too good to be true. I would have been content to continue avoiding the issue forever, but it seemed that Tim had finally had enough. I guess he missed his daily blow job more than I thought. Now he was putting me on the spot. I had to think fast, find a way to appease him without telling him the truth.

"No," I answered. "Between the kids, work, and taking care of the household, things have been crazed. We'll get to it."

"But you were never too busy to get busy with me before. Hell, the only time we ever went longer than a few days was when you were pregnant with the kids. Now it's been damn near two weeks," he complained.

"I know, Tim. Just be patient with me, okay? Everything's fine. Maybe my system is just a little out of whack from all the drama we had going on with E—"

"Okay, baby." He stopped me before I could even finish her name. Just as I suspected, he did not want to go down that road with me again, now that there was finally some semblance of peace in our house—even if that peace came with a distinct lack of sex. "I'm not trying to pressure you or nothing. I just wanted you to know that I miss being with you."

"I know, Tim." I couldn't bring myself to say I missed him too.

"So, anyway," he said, "I was thinking about you today, and I got you a little something to show you how much I love you."

I got mildly excited when I saw him pull a little blue box from behind the bar, but even that feeling was short-lived. Tim knew how much I loved a little bling from Tiffany's, but today, even that box wouldn't be enough to get my motor running. Tim just didn't do it for me anymore.

"Open it," Tim pressed me, obviously certain this gift would do the trick to set things right between us. I plastered on a smile and removed the ribbon from the box. Tim had bought me a diamond eternity ring.

"Read the inscription," he suggested as I picked up the ring. It read: *May we have an eternity of bliss.* The word *bliss* was so far from what I was feeling for Tim these days that I started to feel a bit guilty. I couldn't even look him in the eyes when he said, "Put it on, honey."

I didn't want to wear it, because it would make me feel like such a hypocrite. But I wasn't ready to deal with the problems it would cause by not wearing it, so I slid it on my finger, mumbled "thank you," then leaned in to give Tim a kiss. He took that kiss as permission and pulled me close in a passionate embrace. I prayed he wouldn't feel the tension in my body, but he seemed so desperate to get some affection from me that even this stiff hug was enough to satisfy him. When we separated, he beamed at me, holding up his glass and motioning for me to raise mine.

"Well, here's to having some adult time." Tim tapped his glass against mine.

"Mmm-hmm," I answered as I tried not to look panicked. I just wasn't feeling him. I knew I had two options at this point. I could give my husband what he wanted to thank him for the gift, or I could pack my bags and leave. Really, I had no choice. I wasn't about to give up this lifestyle, and deep down I really loved him, so I would have to give him some sex. I sipped my drink slowly as I tried to figure out the quickest way to satisfy Tim without letting him see that I wasn't turned on in the least.

A blow job. A quick blow job and it will all be done, I thought.

I was about to slide to my knees when I felt my phone vibrate in my pocket. Tim looked down at it. I had begun wearing my phone on me all the time, and I don't think it had gone unnoticed by him. Again, I used our recent situation with Egypt to distract him.

"Oh, that's probably Egypt," I told him. He looked surprised, and the thought that he might still be sleeping with her was heavy on my mind. The truth was that I still didn't trust her. I had barely spoken to her since that night, but I quickly cleaned up my mistake. "Oh yeah, I didn't tell you, did I? We finally talked the other day. We worked through a lot of that shit, and I think everything's okay between us."

My phone stopped vibrating, but I wasn't about to miss this call. "Anyway, let me just go call her back real quick. I don't want her to think I'm ignoring her calls when we're just fixing our friendship."

"Oh . . . uh, yeah." He looked like he had wanted to protest at first, but Egypt's name was still a quick way to shut him up. "You should call her back," he said weakly.

I pulled my phone out of my pocket and left the room, ignoring him when he called out, "Hurry back!"

Once in the privacy of the kitchen, I flipped open my phone, smiled to myself, then dialed Raoul's number.

"Meet me at the park in ten minutes," he demanded as soon as he answered the call.

I hated to say it, but I told him, "I can't, Raoul. Tim is home." Damn, I wanted to see that man.

"I been thinking about going down on you all day. You need to meet me at the park around the corner from your house." Then he disconnected the call. The image he had painted made me groan in pleasure. No one had ever made me feel as good as Raoul did with his tongue. Shit, in all the years I'd been with Tim, I had no idea I could come as hard and as often as I did when Raoul's head was between my legs.

I walked back into the room Tim was in. "Can I ask you a question?"

"Sure, what's on your mind?"

"If I asked you to go down on me tonight, would you do it?" I felt like a crack addict in desperate need of my next fix. Raoul had just put the offer out there, and there was no way I was going to miss out. Either Tim was going to step up to the plate, or I was headed to the park.

Tim took a step back, then stared at me in bewilderment. "Where the hell did that come from?"

"I was just talking to a friend who reminded me what I was missing."

"A friend, huh? A friend called Egypt is more like it."

"Maybe. But all I wanna know is if I ask, will you at least try it?"

"Tammy, we've talked about this. It's just not something I feel comfortable doing."

"Fine. I understand." I hustled past him, grabbing my purse and heading for the front door.

"Whoa!" Tim protested. "Where you going?"

"Ah . . . ah . . . I forgot all about the snacks and drinks for the kids' lunch. We're out of everything," I said. I knew the lie was lame, but it was the best I could do on the spur of the moment.

"Come on back here. I'll go to the store later. After we're done."

"No, that's okay. There's some other things I need to get," I answered, then threw in, "and I might need to stop at Egypt's for a minute," to shut him up. "I'll be right back." I scooted out the door before Tim could complain.

I drove like a bat out of hell to the park, where I found Raoul in our usual spot. I jumped into his Cadillac Escalade, and he wasted no time flipping the seat back until it lay like a bed.

Raoul pulled up my skirt, pushed my panties aside, and started to eat me like it had been a year instead of the three days since we'd done it. The moment his lips touched my vagina, I felt it trembling under him. This man had some pussy-eating skills and could surely teach a class. I couldn't believe I had gone all these years without a man pleasing me this way. Because Tim didn't like to eat me, I always felt self-conscious about it, but Raoul told me he woke up thinking about how beautiful and tasty I was. You can't even imagine how good that made a sister feel. After I came once, he lifted his head. Raoul had turned me out to the point where I couldn't get enough.

"Don't stop. Please don't stop. I wanna come again."

"Don't worry. This has been on my mind all day long. I been waiting to taste you," he murmured before diving back into my muff for another licking. I tried to draw Raoul close to me, ready to return the favor, but he didn't budge.

"No, this is for you and only you." He returned to the task at hand. Could anyone blame me for losing interest in my husband when I found another man like this?

His tongue darted in and out, bringing me to another orgasm. Wow! Before Raoul, I didn't realize I could come so many times. I always thought multiple orgasms were just some shit women lied about.

Four orgasms later and a quick run to a convenience store, I pulled up to my house. I did a check in the rearview mirror, fix-ing my outfit and my hair so it didn't look like I had been doing what I had just done. Tim met me at the door, grabbing the bags out of my hands.

"Baby, let me carry these." He could be awfully helpful when he wanted to get laid.

As I was putting the groceries away, I tried to figure out the best way to back out of sex with my husband. If he got a whiff of me and smelled how fragrant I was, he'd know I was creeping, and it probably wouldn't take much for him to figure out with who. After the night when he invited Raoul over to sleep with me, Tim commented, with a little jealousy in his tone, on how satisfied I looked. Of course, I played it off, told him Raoul was just okay, and reassured him that nobody was better than him. But the truth was that after that first time, I couldn't get enough of my Brazilian lover. I did love my husband, but damn was I getting "addick-ted" to Raoul's pussy-licking skills.

Tim came up behind me and kissed me on the neck as I was worrying about whether I smelled too much like sex. "Come upstairs when you're finished." He spoke in that deep, I'm-about-to-fuck-the-shit-out-of-you-and-make-you-holla voice. Problem was, I had done all the hollering I could do for one day.

I lingered in the kitchen for as long as I could, until Tim finally called down the stairs and told me to hurry up. Reluctantly, I headed for the bedroom.

When I stepped inside, I saw that he had gone all out to please me. He had the mini-microwave next to the bed, ready with hot towels. There were candles, a little old-school Marvin Gaye and Tammy Terrell on the CD player, and the Kama Sutra kit of edible warming oils in different flavors. Normally, my body would tingle just seeing that Tim had gone to so much effort, but tonight my body was already satiated.

"Time to enter Tim's massage parlor." His voice had grown even deeper.

"Wow, you didn't have to do all this," I said, trying to buy myself some time.

"Baby, I'm gonna take care of all your needs tonight," Tim crooned, reaching out for my hand. The same words from Raoul would have had me dripping wet by now, but from Tim, they were just words, and they did nothing for me.

He led me over to the bed, and I protested. "Honey, I been

running all day. Why don't you let me knock some of the funk off of me?" I asked, knowing there was no way he'd miss the loud scent of my satisfied pussy.

Tim shook his head. "I like the way you smell," he said with a laugh.

Yeah, I thought, but if he liked the way I *tasted,* then we wouldn't be in this position. What kind of man neglects the most important part of a woman's body? Didn't I drop to my knees whenever we had sex, taking him in my mouth to bring him to full arousal or orgasm? I had finally learned that wanting a man to go down on me was normal, not extra, and I couldn't help but resent Tim just a little for never sharing that special gift with me.

Tim took off my tank top, rubbing the oil on my shoulders.

"Baby, you seem so relaxed."

I couldn't imagine how he thought I was relaxed when I felt like every muscle in my body was tense with worry that he was going to smell me and flip out. I had to find some way out of this.

"Ouch," I cried out.

"Did I hurt you?" Tim softened his touch.

"No, I just had a bad cramp," I lied again. There used to be a time when I couldn't imagine lying to my husband, but clearly that time had passed.

"Cramps? But your period is at least another two weeks away." He knew my schedule better than I did. Tim always said he liked to know when I was PMSing so Terrible Tammy didn't get sprung on him like some avalanche.

"I don't know if it's my period or not. I just know that these damn cramps are hurting." I winced from this imaginary pain.

"Let me get you some Midol and maybe you'll feel better in a few minutes."

"Tim, it's not like that. I'm going to sit myself in a warm bath and hope it goes away by morning." I headed into the bathroom, trying not to feel bad about the hurt and rejection on Tim's face.

32

Nikki

It wasn't something I planned; it just sort of happened. One Friday after work, a group of us went to BBQ's for drinks. For most of them, this was a regular Friday after-work thing, but if I went, I'd usually just have one drink with them, then head on home to be with Tiny and DJ. This Friday, though, the time just got away from me as we laughed and cracked jokes and had a good old-fashioned time. I wasn't really in a hurry to go home to that negativity anyway. Tiny had been acting more like a private investigator than a lover. She'd called me at least three times while I was at BBQ's, demanding to know who I was with and when the hell I was coming home. After the third call, I just turned off my phone and decided to deal with her BS later.

The other reason I was in no hurry to go anywhere was that I kept catching Keith sneaking looks at me, and I can't deny that the attention made me feel great. When his eyes met mine, I felt a spark ignite inside me, and the look on his face made me think he felt something too. That's why a few hours later, when most of my coworkers had left, I stuck around until it was only me and Keith left at the bar. He sure didn't seem to mind.

"Yo, Ma, you hungry?" Keith asked in that smooth voice of his.

"Yeah, but I'm tryin' to take some of this fat off my big behind," I joked, slapping my hip. "If I even look at the menu in here, I'll gain five pounds."

"I hope you're just dieting for health reasons." His eyes wandered appreciatively over my figure. " 'Cause you look good just the way you are, to me."

I tried to suppress my flattered smile. "Thank you. You look pretty darn good yourself." I couldn't stop blushing. "But seriously, the food in here is way too fattening for me."

"Well, I know this little place I been wanting you to try. I hear they've got low-fat soul food."

"Whatever. There is no such thing as low-fat soul food."

"You think so? Come on, I'll prove it to you." He got up off his seat and pointed to the door.

Everything sensible and loyal in me was telling me to go home to Tiny. But it was so nice to feel like the object of someone's desire that without even thinking twice, I left the bar with Keith. If Tiny knew I had let him drive her car, she would have flipped. I could only imagine what she would accuse me of. Lately, every move I made she assumed I was up to no good. But she was wrong. Sure, Keith's attention made me feel sexy, but as long as I wasn't planning on being unfaithful, what was the harm? It wasn't like I was going to sleep with him. We were just going to have dinner, right? But every time he glanced toward my thighs, I had to remind myself, *Keith's just a friend. I love Tiny. I'm gonna be good.* This internal struggle raged in my head during the whole ride to the restaurant, until Keith pulled up to a little place on Amsterdam Avenue near 135th Street.

He stepped out, then walked around to open my door, offering me his hand to help me out of the car. Even with my messed-up self-esteem, I was starting to believe Keith really liked me, and I didn't want to let that feeling go so soon. We stepped through the door, and an older, light-skinned sistah hotfooted it over to him.

"Well, hello, stranger," she hollered before pulling Keith into a bear hug.

He broke out into a huge smile. "Hey, Auntie. This is my coworker Nikki."

Even though his introduction was warm, I was a little insulted that he was describing me as a coworker when just moments before he'd been eyeing me as if he wanted to become much more. I mean, the least he could have done was upgrade me to "friend."

"I'm Aunt Gwen." She reached out toward me, and I greeted her with a handshake and a smile.

"Uh, we was kinda hungry," Keith explained. "You don't mind, do you?" He pointed toward the kitchen. I didn't expect her to reach behind the register and grab an apron, tossing it to him, but that's what she did.

"Do your thing," she said with a hearty laugh.

"You cook?" I asked.

"Does he? Girl, you are in for a treat," Aunt Gwen bragged.

If Aunt Gwen was telling the truth, I was in trouble. I reminded myself that no matter how good his food was, I was still trying to watch my weight.

"Look out for my girl," Keith said as he tied on the apron and bopped into the kitchen.

I sat in a booth and made small talk with Aunt Gwen for about half an hour while Keith cooked. He did pop his head out of the kitchen every few minutes to check on me, and I thought maybe that was why Aunt Gwen never got into anything too personal. You know, usually when you meet someone's family, you expect them to give you at least a little dirt on the person, maybe share an embarrassing story about something he did when he was younger. But she seemed determined to steer away from any conversation involving Keith. Either she was afraid he'd catch us gossiping about him, or, I realized with a hint of disappointment, she saw me as just a coworker who had no business knowing private things about Keith. I scolded myself for even wishing she saw me as something more. *You are not a single woman, Nikki.* I repeated those words in my head at least a hundred times as we waited for Keith to return.

When he finally arrived from the kitchen, he was carrying two heaping plates of soul food, the kind so good it makes you gain five pounds just from inhaling the aroma. The macaroni and cheese alone had to be five thousand calories. Aunt Gwen got up to leave us alone, and Keith set the plates down on the table and slid next to me in the booth. I tried to ignore the pulse of electricity that shot through me when his thigh brushed against mine.

"I thought I told you I was tryin' to watch my weight," I said playfully as I eyed the tempting food.

"Just trust me," he said, picking up my fork to feed me a bite of macaroni and cheese. I don't know what was more sensual— the way the creamy food melted in my mouth, or the fact that this incredibly sexy man had just fed it to me. Either way, I wanted more, so I boldly guided his hand to scoop up some more and place it in my mouth.

"Oh my God," I said, practically moaning the words. "You put your foot, your sneakers, and everything else up in this. Stop me before I eat the whole thing."

"Go ahead and eat the whole plate, girl," he said with a smile.

"I can't. I'll be ten pounds heavier by the time I leave this table."

"No, you won't," he insisted. "This is my version of healthy soul food."

I took the fork from him. "Get the hell outta here! I know this ain't no health food. Healthy food tastes like twigs and grass. This food is off the chain, Keith." I pulled a tender piece of BBQ chicken off the breast bone and sampled it, discovering that it was even better than the macaroni and cheese. "Where did you learn to cook like this?"

He winked at me, clearly pleased that I was enjoying his food. "Aunt Gwen taught me after my moms died."

"How old were you when she died?" I asked, hoping that unlike Aunt Gwen, he considered me close enough to share such personal information. He answered my question without hesitation, letting me know he didn't mind my asking.

"I was twelve. She had a stroke from her high blood pressure. That's when I went to live with my aunt Gwen."

"That must have been hard," I said.

"It was, but Aunt Gwen is a good woman."

"Seems like it. So, she taught you how to cook like this, huh?" I asked, licking barbecue sauce off my fingers. "Remind me to thank her after I'm done."

He laughed at my joke, and I continued, "But which one of you is gonna pay for the new wardrobe I'll need once this food makes my hips even wider?"

He shook his head and said, "Why do I gotta keep telling you not to worry about it?"

"I know, I know," I said after savoring a bite of collard greens. "You like a woman with something to hold on to."

"Well, yeah," he answered, "but this isn't your average soul food anyway."

"No, it sure ain't. It's been a long time since I tasted food this good."

"It's all in the seasonings. See, most people just cook with lots of fat. They think the fat's what's gonna make the food taste good. But I ain't try'na go out like my mother did, so I use low-fat cheese and cut out the lard and a lot of the salt in the recipes."

"So it's just the spices that make it taste so good?"

"Mmm-hmm."

"What spices do you use?" I asked.

"Naw, see, I can't tell you my secret."

I played along with his teasing. "That ain't fair. Why you gonna keep it all to yourself?"

Suddenly, his voice lost all its playfulness. "Nikki, if I tell you how to cook it, how am I ever gonna get you to come back here and have dinner with me again?"

I lost the ability to form a thought at this point and was unable to think of a thing to say in response to his words. All I could do was stare into his eyes. I was so lost in his warm, seductive gaze that I didn't notice he was leaning closer until his lips were practically pressed against mine. My brain kicked back into consciousness just a fraction of a second before he kissed me. I leaned away from him and turned my head slightly to the side.

Keith was still staring deeply into my eyes, but he maintained the distance I'd put between us. "Mmph!" he said with a shake of his head. "I guess you can't always have what you want."

I opened my mouth to speak, but he continued. "It's okay. You don't have to say nothing. I know you're in a relationship, and I respect you too much to step to you on some casual shit. It's just that I dig you, Nikki. If things were different—"

"But they're not. I really love Tiny," I said in response. The words were for my benefit as much as for his. During that brief seductive moment, I'd allowed my love for Tiny to be pushed so far to the back of my thoughts that I'd practically forgotten my commitment to her. It was definitely time for me to leave.

"Keith, I really think I should—"

"Yeah, you should probably go," he said. I knew he was trying to sound understanding, but he couldn't hide the frustration in his voice. "Tiny is one lucky-ass woman. Tell her I said not to mess up, 'cause I'll be waiting in the wings."

As I left the restaurant and drove home, I cursed myself for being so stupid. I should never have put myself in that position. He was just too damn tempting.

It was after midnight when I made it home. Hopefully, Tiny would be asleep. If not, I knew she'd be in one hell of a mood, since I'd turned off my phone earlier and now I was coming in so late. My stomach twitched and my heart pounded in anticipation of the fight I might be walking into. I tried to reassure myself that no matter how bad some of our shouting matches could get, Tiny was always like a big teddy bear in the end. She could talk shit and get all blustery, but she had never, ever laid a hand on me, and we always made up eventually. I took a deep breath and tried to will my heartbeat to slow down as I headed for the front door.

As soon as I put the key in the lock, Tiny yanked open the door. I lost my balance and fell inward. Rather than catch me, she stepped out of the way and watched me stumble. I looked up at her, her fists jammed onto her hips and an angry scowl on her face. But her eyes looked vulnerable, like she might almost be on the verge of tears. I almost felt guilty, until she started yelling.

"Woman, where the hell you been?"

"I was kickin' it with my friends from work," I yelled back, automatically feeling defensive. "I am grown, you know."

Tiny shook her head, heaving a deep sigh. "You have some damn nerve. No one knew where you were; then you gon' stroll your lying ass up in here like it ain't no big thing. You must be losin' your damn mind."

"I just told you where I was!" I said, wishing for once she would just let me be, let my word be the last one. But no, Tiny always had to take it one step further. She was always looking for a way to burst my bubble, to make my life difficult. The contrast between this scene and the great time I was having with Keith was almost more than I could stand.

"I called Kym and Lisa," she said accusingly, and I knew what was coming next. "They said they left you at BBQ's hours ago."

I didn't even bother to reply. Tiny was already several steps ahead of me, so I had no doubt she could bust whatever excuse I tried to spit at her. She'd probably already gotten Kym or Lisa to tell her that Keith was still there with me when they left.

To my surprise, Tiny didn't go there, didn't even mention Keith's name. "I've been about to lose my friggin' mind, worrying about you. I almost called the police." Her voice got a bit wobbly, like she was fighting to hold back tears now. "I thought something had happened to you."

I was confused by her sudden change from rage to concern, until she took a step closer and I smelled the alcohol on her breath. I wrinkled up my nose. She wasn't supposed to be drinking since she got that DUI last year. And since she had been attending her Alcoholics Anonymous meetings, she'd been dry for more than seven months. Disgusted, I pushed past her, stopping in my tracks when I caught sight of the kitchen table.

"Yeah, that's right. I cooked," she said angrily. "And if you'da brought your ass home, you mighta liked the food I made you. But no . . ." She began to carry the plates of corn bread, smothered ribs, collard greens with fatback, and sweet potatoes drenched in butter and brown sugar to the counter. One plate at a time, she dumped the food into the sink, where it landed with a thud.

"Why'd you throw it away? It looked good," I said in a weak attempt to defuse the situation.

She raised her voice to be heard above the noise of the garbage disposal as she turned it on. "Work my damn fingers to the bone trying to feed your monkey ass up in here, and that's all you can say." She mimicked me. "'It looked good!' Well, how about this? You don't have to eat shit since you on that fuckin' diet. Eat you an air sandwich."

My mind flashed for an instant back to the incredible meal Keith had prepared. Even if Tiny hadn't thrown it away, her food—smothered in fat—couldn't hold a candle to what Keith had fed to me. But, of course, I would never tell her this. In the interest of keeping the peace, I approached her and started stroking her back gently.

"Tiny, calm down. I'm sorry, okay?" I felt the muscles in her shoulders begin to relax.

"Why didn't you pick up your cell when I called you?" She still sounded agitated, but at least she wasn't yelling now.

"Tiny, I just needed some me time. Is that so bad?"

She sucked her teeth and scoffed, "Some 'you time,' huh? Well, since you *my* woman, I thought you would at least have the decency to answer your phone and tell me if you gon' be late."

I tried to reason with her. "I thought we were in a relationship. I didn't think I was a prisoner. I just needed some space."

"Well, space this," she said, her voice taking on a sinister quality. "I don't believe you've been with your friends. You've been off riding that nigga Keith's dick; that's what I think." Before I could even begin to tell her how unfair she was being, she screamed, "And don't you dare try to deny it, bitch!" In an instant, she lunged toward me and snatched me in a choke hold.

Our fights had never turned physical before, so I was totally unprepared for this attack. I didn't even have time to react before she released the choke hold and pulled my arms behind me, gripping them with one massive hand. With her other hand, Tiny reached up under my dress and grabbed my panties, trying to pull them down. Even in the best of circumstances, I would have been no match for Tiny's strength, but at least I could have tried to struggle free. Now, however, her anger seemed to have magnified her strength to superhuman levels. I was powerless and terrified.

"You lying, cheating whore! Your ass is gonna do the sniff test tonight!" By this point, her voice was so loud I wouldn't be surprised if the neighbors heard her. I pictured the police breaking down the front door and slapping the cuffs on her while I stood there with my panties lying around my knees.

"Tiny, stop!" I pleaded. "Let me go. Someone's gonna call the police."

She ignored my pleas and continued to rant about how she planned to prove I'd been cheating with Keith. "Oh yeah, I know you been fuckin'. You think just because I'm a lesbian I don't know the smell of cum? Just nasty." She tugged at my underwear again, but she couldn't pull them below my knees without bending down, which would cause her to lose hold of my arms. "You want a dick that bad? Or maybe you just want a damn thug, the kinda man who'll go upside your head and treat you like something on the bottom of his shoe."

"Let go of me!" I yelled as I struggled to loosen her grip on my wrists. "You actin' no better than some thug anyway! Just stop it!" She refused. "Dammit, Tiny, you wanna smell my panties? Just let me go and I'll give you the damn things!"

"You don't need to do that," she said. "I can get 'em myself." And with those words, she pulled so hard that my panties came off with a loud tearing sound. She waved them triumphantly in the air, so wrapped up in her accomplishment that she loosened her grip on my arms and I freed myself.

"Gimme my damn panties!" I yelled angrily, reaching out to snatch them from her. As soon as I had my hands on the material, Tiny's raised hand came down, hitting my jaw so hard that my head snapped backward. When I recovered from the shock, I managed to speak through the pain in my jaw. "You fucking bitch!" I said in a low tone full of fury. "As long as you live, don't you ever put your hands on me again. You hear me? 'Cause if you do, I swear to God you will never see me or my son again."

"Oh my God, Nikki. I'm sorry, honey." My words had their desired effect. By threatening to leave, I knew I'd just hurt Tiny every bit as deeply as her slap injured me. She broke down, slobbering like a baby. "I'm so sorry, baby. I didn't mean to hurt you." I could still smell the alcohol reeking on her breath, but when I took a few steps back to try to escape the smell, she just stepped closer, pleading for me to understand. "I don't know what came over me. I just kept picturing you with that dude. It's making me crazy to think you want something I can't give you. Don't you know I'd do anything to make you happy?"

As the tears began flowing down Tiny's anguished face, I almost felt sorry for her, and I did the same thing I'd done after every one of our fights. I gave her a hug and accepted her blubbering apology. But I realized this time was different. Tiny had hit me, something I swore I would never let anyone do again. I owed her a lot for all she had done for me, but she had just taken things to a whole other level. It was time for me to put myself first, to do what made me happy. Yes, I loved Tiny, but I loved myself more, so my happiness had to come first.

33

Coco

My body was still tingling as I lay on my back with a broad smile plastered across my face. Mac was everything I'd ever wanted in a man and something I thought I'd never find. After we watched the sun rise over the beach, we headed back inside to the bedroom, and I finally got to see what this man was working with. As hot as his poetry had made me the first night I saw him, the real thing was a thousand times better. Forget the fact that he was absolutely huge. I swear the man had me turned out after the first touch, and he kept my fire burning for hours. It was almost like a dream. I'd never met a man so skilled in the bedroom in my entire life, and let's be honest, I'd been with my share of men. The sex was so intense, we didn't even stop to eat. He just brought the food into the bedroom and incorporated it into our lovemaking. No man had ever made me feel this good—especially one who hadn't coughed up a single dime yet!

At the thought of money, Jackson's offer from the day before came rushing into my mind. Damn! He'd be expecting an answer today, and it was the middle of the afternoon already. As good as the sex with Mac was, I knew I'd be a fool to pass up Jackson's offer just yet. During the ride back to the city, I would come up with a plan to keep them both. I had to—I wasn't quite ready to give up Mac yet. I sat up in the bed and swung my legs over the side.

Mac reached out and touched my arm. "Where you goin'?" he asked in that sexy voice that got me here in the first place.

"I'm 'bout to go," I answered sweetly. One look at his naked body against the rumpled sheets, and my head was flooded with sexy images of me and Mac all twisted up like a pretzel. The last thing I wanted to do was leave this bed.

"Come back here," he said. It sounded like a command, and

normally I don't play like that, but from Mac, even that was a turn-on. I pulled my eyes away from his six-pack and looked up at his face. He was gorgeous, and his expression of sheer satisfaction let me know that he was just as whipped as I was.

"C'mon, baby. I want you here with me." His words made my heart melt in a way I couldn't even explain. Why I was feeling this way about a man I hardly knew? I could only think of one other time that I'd fallen for a man so fast, and I surely did not want to go down that painful road again.

Devon Jones was the man's name, and at the time, I thought that one day he'd make me his wife. Devon was a gorgeous hunk of a man. Not too tall, just the right height, size, and everything. He appreciated my womanly curves and truly knew how to handle them. We looked great together, and he made me feel great. I was truly a fool in love. I thought he and I would have it all.

We'd been seeing each other for close to three years when reality smacked me hard in the face. Some chick showed up, crying and bawling at my front door. At first I felt bad for the poor chile, thinking she was just at the wrong apartment.

"I know this is where he spends his time away from us," she sobbed.

I was confused. Never once did it cross my mind that she could've been talking about Devon. "Excuse me?" I asked, leaning against the doorframe and watching her sob.

"Luke. I've watched him. He leaves at all hours of the night, telling me that his sick Momma is what's keeping him away. But I've watched him leave your bed, then rush back home to me. Sometimes the sick dog wouldn't even bother to shower," she hissed.

This chick was starting to make me nervous, talking about watching someone leave my bed. I needed to get some better curtains, I thought. But it still never entered my mind that this Luke she was talking about had anything to do with me.

"Well, you can have him," she continued. "I'm tired. We just had our third child four months ago. I'm sick of going through this shit with him." She'd stopped crying by now.

I was growing tired of listening to this woman, who I was beginning to suspect had some serious mental issues. Just as I prepared to tell her she had the wrong house and the wrong guy, Devon came jogging up, out of breath.

"Crissy, I told you not to show up here," he snapped at her.

She turned to look at him and said, "Luke, you—"

"Hold up!" I yelled. "You mean you know her? What the fuck is going on here, Devon?"

"Um, yeah, baby. I was gonna tell you . . ." he began before I stepped back out of the doorway and slammed the door on both of their sorry asses.

Like a fool, though, it was only a matter of time before I let Devon sweet-talk his way back into my life. He told me that they had been married but were separated a long time ago. I even bought his story that the four-month-old she'd told me about was an accident. She had caught him off guard one night when he was drunk, seduced him, then got pregnant to try to trick him into coming back to her. I fell for his bullshit, hook, line and sinker.

Soon, he moved in with me, and despite the drama that brought him there, I was happy. I had my man, and things were good. Or so I thought, until Devon (which is what I continued to call him even though his real name was Luke) started to show his true self.

Ironically, things started to unravel on the same day that I learned I was pregnant with our child. I thought we'd have a romantic dinner and I'd tell him the news when he came home that night. Instead, he came in with his face hanging low, so I put my plans on hold to take care of my man.

"What's wrong?" I wanted to know.

It took him a while to answer, which only increased my apprehension. I was afraid he was getting ready to leave me or something. Now that I look back on it, I'm amazed at his acting job. At the time, though, he really had me snowed.

"I've got some bad news," he said, sounding devastated. "They're about to take my car if I don't get current on the payments."

Now, keep in mind I was a very different person back then. When I realized that money was his only issue, that it wasn't something wrong with our relationship, I was relieved. "That's why you're running around here acting like all hope is gone?" I asked.

I was willing to do anything to keep our little happy home together, so when he looked at me and said he needed twenty-five hundred dollars, I didn't blink an eye. I pulled out my purse and told him I'd write a check. I think back now to just how stupid I had been. Not only did I damn near wipe out my savings for him, but the very next day, I went down to the bank and added that clown to my account so he wouldn't get himself into this kind of trouble again.

In the weeks to follow, I was the one who ended up in trouble, lots of it. My money vanished quicker than I could put it into the account. And with Devon, there was always some minitragedy that needed my finances.

"My mother's Medicaid ran out. I need five hundred dollars."

"Her water heater stopped working, three hundred fifty."

"The refrigerator was already on its last leg when it just quit." That one cost twelve hundred dollars.

By the time I pulled my head out of my ass and realized what was going on, I was thousands of dollars in debt on my credit cards, and that didn't even include the card he took out in my name without my knowledge. It took a call from a bill collector to finally open my eyes. After that, I started digging and realized the damage he caused—over fifty-nine thousand dollars when you included the new car I cosigned for him.

Believe it or not, I was still so foolishly in love that I was willing to work things out with him. Besides, I was carrying his child, though I had yet to tell him about the pregnancy. I naively believed that all I had to do was confront him about his "little spending problem," and then everything would be fine between us. That's why I was so unprepared for his reaction the night I sat him down and showed him all the receipts and bank records I had dug up.

"I don't need this shit!" he screamed.

I sat in shock as he ranted and raved, rushing around the apartment, packing all of his shit. My head was spinning as I tried to backtrack and figure out what I had done wrong. By the time it was all over, his shit was packed, and he was rushing out my front door.

Days later, I realized just how much trouble I would be in if I couldn't find a way to pay off some of this debt he'd made. Hoping to talk some sense into him, I tried to call him on the cell phone I bought, but he wouldn't answer. It took a week before I finally got pissed off about the whole situation. Since he still wasn't answering my calls, I cut off the phone and told the car company I was no longer paying the note. It didn't take long for Devon to show up at my job after that.

Unfortunately for me, his loud outbursts, calling me everything but a child of God, was too much for the very nervous white people I worked with. After a few of Devon's crazy outbursts in my office and one too many warnings from my boss, I was fired.

There was nothing I could do. I packed up my shit and walked out of the office, embarrassed, pissed off, and now without a source of income. Later that night, as I sat crying to my cousin on the phone, I felt something wet between my thighs. I looked down and saw blood.

In the hospital that night, the doctors explained that the extreme stress I'd been under had caused me to miscarry. Devon had stolen all my money, made me lose my job, and now I'd lost my child. At that moment, it was like a switch went off in my brain, and the new Coco was formed. Never again would I let a man bring me down the way Devon had. I would never be a victim again. Devon had shown me that men were only good for what I could get from them, giving the least of myself in return. That had been the creed by which I'd lived ever since. And that's why, when I realized how hard and fast I was falling for Mac, I had to stop myself before I fell too far.

"Mac, it's been nice, but I really gotta go." I jumped up from the bed before he could try to stop me again. "I'll call you later," I said after I was dressed and heading out the door, feeling like I'd just barely avoided a huge mistake. I left the Hamptons and raced back to the city, praying I wasn't too late to accept Jackson's generous offer.

"Hey, it's me, Coco," I cooed into the phone as I drove home from the Hamptons.

"I been expecting to hear from you all day," Jackson barked at me.

"Sweetie, I told you I needed some time to think. This whole thing is a big step. Besides, you just told me you needed an answer today. You didn't specify a time," I said, hoping my playful tone would disarm his anger.

"Well, when I want something, I want it, and that means

don't keep me waiting." He clearly hadn't heard the word *no* too often.

It took me some time, but I talked to Jackson as I drove through Long Island, and by the time I hit the Queens border, he was calm again. Of course, it didn't hurt that I engaged in a pretty hot session of phone sex to remind him what he'd be missing if he dropped me now. He didn't have to know that everything I was describing over the phone were things I'd just finished doing to Mac that morning.

I promised to meet him for dinner at eight o'clock. That gave me just enough time to go home, take a shower, and change my clothes. I might be damn good at what I do, but I couldn't very well show up smelling like sex if I wanted to seal the deal on my new apartment tonight.

"You really want these?" Jackson dangled a set of keys at me when he met me in front of the restaurant, standing near a sparkling new black Mercedes 560.

"Your car is beautiful. You really gonna let me drive it?" I purred hopefully.

"It's not my car. It's yours." I actually had to catch my breath when I realized this beautiful machine was mine. Most men have a problem with cab fare, and here was Jackson, giving me a brand-new seventy-thousand-dollar car. I could very quickly get used to living this high off the hog.

He handed me the keys. "You want to show Daddy how happy you are with your present?"

We didn't even bother with dinner. I hopped behind the wheel of my new Mercedes and drove straight to the address where I'd met him the night before.

Once in the apartment, I got right to work, showing Jackson how much I appreciated his generosity. I unbuttoned my blouse, my breasts popping out of my top. Jackson started damn near panting. I couldn't blame him, knowing how boring his wife was in bed.

"I'm going to have to thank you the old-fashioned way," I teased as I dropped down to my knees. Unbuttoning his pants, I got right to work. Only problem was that I kept thinking about Mac and the way he had whipped it on me.

"Make me harder," Jackson breathed on me, and I realized that my daydreaming was affecting my performance. This was not the time to be thinking of Mac, I told myself. I had serious work to do here. The Mercedes was nice, but I still had to get the keys to this apartment in my hands. You know that old saying, nothing is for free. I was well aware of what it would cost to live in this beautiful place, and I was more than willing to pay that price. I got busy, concentrating on the work before me.

"What about the apartment?" I asked when he was fully satisfied a while later. Jackson smiled, clearly liking my boldness.

"I have everything right here." He removed a large manila envelope from a drawer in the nightstand and handed it to me. I opened the envelope to find house keys, two credit cards, and two envelopes of cash, one marked HOUSEHOLD and the other marked FUN. Shit, I felt like I had died and gone to heaven.

"Oooh, I can't wait to go shopping for furniture tomorrow," I squealed.

"I know, Coco," he said, sounding very pleased with himself. "And I'm glad you're so happy. Just don't forget your end of the bargain, now, and everything will work out just fine. All you have to remember is that I don't share my toys."

I felt queasy when he grabbed my ass, and I realized the true depth of what I'd just agreed to. This man, who could never make me come the way Mac had that morning, seriously expected me to give up all other men. But even more sickening was that no matter how many men I fucked, and how good they might make my body feel, it would take a hundred of them to equal one-tenth of Jackson's wealth. I wondered why I couldn't have found a man with Jackson's money and Mac's sex appeal all rolled into one.

"How about one more for the road?" Jackson asked, reaching his hands between my legs.

I placed my envelope of riches on the nightstand and got back to work. Things might get a little complicated, but I was determined to make this thing work. Somehow, I would have everything I wanted, the rich man and the real man. I had no doubt that I would come out on top.

34

Isis

It had been four long and lonely days since Tony had turned my life upside down. I suspect the only reason I stopped crying was because I didn't have a single tear left. When I got up and got a whiff of the scent coming from my armpits, I realized for the first time that I hadn't washed my ass in three days. I hadn't even bothered to brush my teeth. My mouth tasted horrible.

"Damn!" I pulled myself up from my crumpled bed, the place I'd called home ever since he left. I looked back at the crumbs that had gathered on my sheets from the cracker diet I'd been on. With no real appetite to speak of over the last few days, I didn't realize how long I'd gone without food until my stomach grumbled hard and loud.

"I'll never let a man use me like that ever again," I vowed under my breath as I moved toward the bathroom.

Despite what I knew to be true, it was still hard to believe Tony was married all along and I had no clue. He and I had been together so long, I never even thought about our shit not being real. And to imagine I chose him over Rashad. For what? Nothing. Absolutely nothing.

That's when a thought entered my mind. I smiled for the first time since misery took over my life a few days prior. I rushed to the bathroom, turned on the shower, and started scrubbing my teeth with a vengeance. I wanted to be normal again. I wanted to feel no pain, but more importantly, I wanted to feel loved and not lied to. At that moment, I knew exactly what I needed to do.

After the long, hot shower, I felt like a brand-new woman. I rushed to the closet and picked out an outfit Tony would not have approved of if we were still a couple. As a matter of fact, I wanted to do a bunch of shit he wouldn't like.

When I looked at myself in the mirror, I had to giggle at the fact that my nipples were just barely visible beneath the tube top I was wearing. But the way I was feeling, I'd probably go out naked if it wasn't against the law. I turned to look at the reflection of my butt in the tight denim skirt and liked what I saw, despite knowing that a woman my size shouldn't be wearing what I had on. I stepped into my stiletto sandals to complete the slutty look I was going for. A little MAC Viva Glam and some lip gloss gave my lips extra pout.

I was about to step out when I stopped at the door, reached under my skirt, and stepped out of my panties and left them on the floor. "Won't be needing those," I said happily.

During the drive, I rehearsed exactly what I would say and the way I'd say it. I would make sure Tony paid for the pain he caused me, and I knew there was nothing he hated more than the thought of someone else having what was his—or at least what used to be his. Shoot, I used to be glad to give it to him, I thought sadly. Either way, my mind was made up, and I was going to erase a mistake I'd made. A big mistake.

I practiced some opening lines. "I know what you're thinking . . ." Nah, that wouldn't do. I shook my head. "Um, before you say anything, just hear me out." I didn't like that one either. "I've been thinking about you just as much as you've been thinking about me." Shoot! I closed my eyes and decided I'd just wing it. Sex was sex as far as men were concerned, and that's what I was offering. Sex any way Rashad wanted it.

As I walked up to the door, I kept telling myself I was gonna fuck him right on the spot. No questions asked. The minute he opened the door, I would take his hand, slide it under my skirt, then walk in, lie down, and spread my legs as wide as humanly possible and fuck his brains out.

At his door, I took a deep breath, closed my eyes, and knocked three times before pulling my hand back. As the seconds ticked by and he still hadn't answered the door, I started losing my nerve. I knocked again a little louder. When he finally pulled the door open, he was wearing boxers, looking just as sexy as ever. I asked myself how I could've been so foolish to leave such a good-looking man. I knew Rashad had issues with commitment, but if I knew then what I know now, I would've been more than happy to take his issues.

"Ah, hey, Isis . . ." His eyes darted around, but I didn't take offense to his confused greeting. Of course he was shocked to see me. "Whassup? What you doing here?"

I licked my lips and allowed my hand to travel from my neck to my chest, ready to make my move. "Sorry for not calling first, but, um . . ." I licked my lips again and watched as Rashad's eyes traveled down to my chest. I wondered if he could tell how stiff my nipples were beneath the thin material. I wanted him to reach out and touch me, grab me, do anything to let me know I wasn't too late.

"I'm sorry. I'm so sorry," I began. Rashad shook his head like he was trying to tell me there was no need to explain, but I couldn't help myself. "I was such a fool." At first I spoke a little above a whisper, but then I started trippin' on the fact that I was still standing outside. When I had played this scenario over in my mind, I was only outside for a few seconds before he took me into his arms, wrapped himself around me, and we were inside, making up for lost time. So why were we still standing at the door now?

"I'm ready to try again," I sobbed. I didn't want to come off as this babbling mess, but I just couldn't seem to control myself. Thoughts of Tony and his betrayal were still fresh on my mind. "Can't we try again, baby? Please!"

Rashad's response was less than the enthusiastic "Yes!" I'd expected to receive. "What are you saying?" he asked in a flat tone.

I wanted to kiss his lips and make everything clear for him, but more importantly, I wanted him to know this pussy was his for the taking, free and available. But if he wanted to hear me spell out my feelings for him first, then so be it.

"What I'm saying is I was a fool to ever take him over you. I love you. I want you back, and I want to give us another chance."

He continued to stare at me blankly.

"C'mon, Rashad, you said it yourself. We were so good together. C'mon, let me make it up to you, baby," I begged.

My heart nearly stopped when I realized just what was going on. Here I was, all but throwing pussy to a man who'd recently professed his love for me, and he hadn't made a move to indicate he was down. By now, I should have been on my back with him trying to do some major damage. Instead, I was still at the door, trying to explain my way in. Something wasn't right, but still I charged forward.

"Stop playin', Rashad. I know you're still upset about Tony, but I don't want him. I want you, and I can be the woman you want me to be." I stepped closer. I even went as far as to pull down my tube top to reveal my stiffened nipple, hoping to entice him into action. But the sound of a female voice stopped me cold in my tracks. I tilted my head ever so slightly, trying to understand how this could possibly be. I know I didn't hear what I thought I was hearing.

"Shad, I know you not gonna leave me hanging like that. Who is that anyway?" There was a hesitation, then an, "Oh shit!"

My eyes nearly popped from their sockets. The voice was so familiar. I felt alarm settling in, and I was getting hot. Impulse made me shove his door wide open, and that's when I saw my sister, Egypt.

I was so confused, it hurt. She had the nerve to be wearing both his robe and an expression that told me I had interrupted something at quite a crucial moment. I couldn't help myself as I pushed my way into Rashad's place, nearly knocking him down and shoving Egypt in the process.

"You fuckin' bitch! No wonder nobody can find your ass," I hissed, balling up both my fists. "I can't believe this shit. Of all the people in the world, my own damn sister is fuckin' my man!" She stumbled back a few steps, then looked at me, bracing herself for whatever I might do next. "You think you can fuck my man, bitch?"

Suddenly Egypt stood straight up as if she'd been given some new strength and was not about to back down "Your man?" she snapped. "Let's get something straight, Isis. I'm sorry you had to find out about us this way, but Rashad is far from your man. If memory serves me correct, you told him you wanted to marry Tony. Matter of fact, you accepted the man's ring in front of his face." She smirked. "That little act made Rashad available."

I started to take my hoop earrings out of my ears. It had been a long time since I'd given my little sister an ass whippin', but going behind me and fuckin' my man meant she'd earned a good, old-fashioned beat-down.

Egypt tightened the belt on her robe as if that was going to help her. Rashad stepped in between us, looking like he was

about to referee an Evander Holyfield fight. But instead of stepping over to my side like he had recently claimed he wanted, he
moved closer to Egypt.

I looked at him and wailed, "Why, Rashad?"

He answered without hesitation. "You wanted to be with
Tony. My love wasn't good enough for you."

"Yeah, you made your decision, so I suggest you go find Tony
now," Egypt chimed in. I cut my eyes at her, and I'm sure she could
feel my anger.

"I made a mistake," I explained, some part of me still half expecting them to pull some candid-camera shit and tell me they
were just joking.

Egypt pushed up close to Rashad. "You need to tell my sister
who you wanna be with, baby."

Rashad glanced down at Egypt, then got this tight look on his
face. "I'm sorry, Isis, but Egypt is right. Sometimes in life, it's
just too little, too late."

"Too little, too late?" I was dumbfounded.

"Don't you understand English? He wants you to leave. We'd
like to get back to what we were doing." She pointed at the door.

"But . . . but what about us, Rashad? We were good together."

He placed his arm around Egypt's shoulder. "There is no us
anymore, Isis. Just me and Egypt. I think you need to go."

Egypt stomped over to the front door and held it open. Looking at the two of them was starting to make me ill. Fine. If he
wanted to fuck my sister to get back at me, then she could have
his already-been-used dick. I turned and sauntered my ass out
the door, even more mad than I was when I found out about
Tony having a wife.

35

Tammy

"Baby, that peach cobbler you made was great," Tim said as he stood in our bedroom door, rubbing a towel around his naked midsection. He'd just taken a shower.

"Thanks," I said absently, not even looking up. The truth was that I'd baked his favorite dessert simply because I felt guilty about not wanting to have sex with my own husband.

I was lying in bed reading our latest book club selection. The next meeting was supposed to be at Nikki's and Tiny's, but I heard their relationship was in trouble, so I wasn't sure if we'd even meet. Still, the book had been a good excuse to avoid Tim for a few nights. When he came to bed looking for something, I'd tell him I really had to finish the book so I wouldn't be lost during the meeting.

"What you reading?"

I glanced up. Tim stood there grinning, toweling his penis dry. This used to be our silent cue that he wanted to have sex, but I ignored him and turned back to my book. It had been weeks since Tim and I last had sex, and I knew it was because of my rendezvous with Raoul. With scenes of our incredible sex running through my head, the sight of my naked husband did nothing for me.

Poor Tim. I did feel a little guilty about denying him sex for so long, especially because he'd been acting like a dog in heat ever since the night Raoul came to our house. But whenever I started feeling too bad about what I was doing with Raoul, I reminded myself that Tim was the one who'd given me permission to sleep with his friend. Was it my fault if Raoul was willing to do the one thing Tim had refused to do throughout our marriage?

Maybe if Tim had been taking care of business properly in the first place, none of this would be happening now. At least that was what I wanted to believe.

The truth was that I might have pursued this thing with Raoul even if Tim was willing to go down on me. I just couldn't get over how this man made me feel. The first time we did it, I cried out so loudly I had to cover my mouth to keep Tim from thinking this man was murdering me. Raoul gave me my first set of multiple orgasms that night. I still remember the first time a man had brought me to orgasm, and I thought I'd never forget that moment, but multiple orgasms . . . How are you supposed to give up something like that?

"Baby," Tim said as he climbed under the sheets with no underwear on. I could see he was erect, but that didn't turn me on. There was a time when the sight of his goldenrod would get my juices flowing, but now I just felt cold. I wished I could say this was a phase I was going through, but I knew the truth. I couldn't get Raoul out of my head.

At first it was just the tongue, but now it was the whole man. He'd turned me out, and I didn't want Tim to touch me. Raoul and I had plans to meet up the next day while Tim was on a day-long business trip in New Jersey. I wanted to close my eyes and go to sleep, dreaming of my hot Latin lover.

He reached for me, but I lay there stiff as a board. Usually when he made his move, I would curl up in his arms and we'd kiss, then wind up making love in our favorite position—me on top. Tonight, though, I pushed his hand away.

"I don't feel good. I got cramps."

"Again?" he asked, and I could tell from his tone that he didn't believe me.

"Yeah," I answered without further explanation.

Tim was silent for a while, and I thought that maybe I was off the hook for one more night. But then he put his hand on my arm and said, "Tammy, I think we need to talk."

"About what?" I asked wearily.

"About what happened between you and Raoul."

I felt every muscle in my body become tense. We had never discussed that night, and I couldn't believe that all these weeks later he would bring it up. Once again, I had underestimated my husband. He was still calm, so he probably didn't know for sure that Raoul and I were hitting the sheets on the regular, but he had narrowed down the source of our problem.

"Why should we talk about that?" I asked, pretending to be bewildered. "That was like a million years ago. I did it because you wanted me to, so we'd be even. You see that I haven't brought up Egypt again since then, right?" Still, it felt like he was seeing her.

"I know," he said, "and I'm glad you don't think anything is going on with me and her anymore. But you just seem different since then."

"Different how?" I asked, scared that he was getting too close to the truth now.

"I don't know, like you're more distant. I just wanna make sure you're okay."

"I'm fine, Tim." I sighed. "Now, can we go to sleep?"

"Well, are *we* okay?"

I was so not ready to have this discussion with him. I just wanted to have my little affair, get it out of my system, then come back home. Tim would never have to know about it. I had to stop him from pushing the issue. I had no choice but to roll over on top of him to shut him up.

"Yes, Tim, we're fine. Okay?" I said, planting a kiss on his cheek.

Just that small bit of physical contact was enough to end the discussion. His hands went immediately to my ass. He slid my nightgown up above my hips, and I felt his penis spring to life beneath me. I put in a good enough performance that Tim was satisfied, but the whole time we were making love, my mind was fast-forwarding to the hours I would oon spend with Raoul.

The next day, Raoul and I each left work separately, and I parked my car in a shopping center near our job, where I waited for him to pick me up. It might sound seedy, meeting up like that in a parking lot, but I didn't care. Everything they say about those hot-blooded Latin lovers is true. I'd fallen head over heels for Raoul. I loved the way he stared into my eyes when I was talking. He seemed to hang on my every word, and damn did he make me feel like the most desirable woman in the world.

Raoul drove out to Pierre's Cuisine on Long Island, where we were seated at a table overlooking the Long Island Sound. I can't begin to tell you how many women watched us, trying to get Raoul's attention away from me, a black woman, a heavyset sistah at that. But he never took his eyes off me. He really knew how to make a woman feel like what Aretha called "a natural woman."

Raoul fed me buttered lobster from his fork. When I wiped a spot of butter from my chin, he gently held my clustered fingers together, licked the juice off my thumb, then ran his tongue around all my fingertips. He held my hand next to his and examined our bronze skin, which shimmered from the glow of the candles sitting on the center of our table. From the vase on the table, he took a long-stemmed rose and put it behind my ear like Billie Holiday's famous gardenia.

"You are beautiful, mamacita," Raoul said in his heavy accent. "You're sweeter than the nectar of this rose." He licked his lips suggestively, reminding me of L.L. Cool J's famously sexy gesture.

"Instead of some quick session today, I want us to relax in the Jacuzzi at the Continental Resort. Then you'll be nice and open like a fresh flower."

I giggled like a teenager. He didn't have to ask me twice.

Raoul continued talking in his sensuous voice. "I like how you move those succulent hips. Are you sure you're not a belly dancer?"

I blushed. I could feel my heart pounding. "You so bad," I pooh-poohed him, but I loved every word he was saying. I hoped he was telling the truth, and even if he wasn't, it sure sounded good.

"And you got young breasts. They're so nice and full, with skin like the inside of a mango—soft and supple. In my country, men would fight to get women like you. We love healthy women."

I, who usually had to be the boss with Tim during sex, was doing a meltdown and talking in a babyish tone. I almost didn't recognize my own voice. "You always make me come too much."

Raoul threw his head back and laughed with gusto. I could see his chest expanding with pride. "Oooh, mija, I love when you come. It feels like rivers gushing from Mother Earth. I thought you was gonna drown me." Raoul took my hand and put it under the table so I could feel the pulsating throb in his lap. "This is for you, mami."

"I've got something for you, too," I said coyly.

"What you got?"

"It's a surprise, baby."

"I can't get wait to get you to the Jacuzzi. Hmmph, look at you. You're so uninhibited. I want to spend the whole night in bed, loving you from head to toe."

"I can't be out too late," I reminded him, wishing I didn't have to be the one to throw cold water on our little lust-fest, even if just for a moment. "You know I told you Tim would be home tonight."

Raoul ignored the mention of my husband's name and started feeding me strawberries dipped in chocolate. With the soft classical music in the background and this gorgeous man treating me like a queen, I was getting lost in the romance. Until I heard a familiar voice screeching my name.

"Tammy? Is that you?"

I looked up to see Egypt, of all people. When Egypt recognized me, her mouth flew open. I jumped back from Raoul's embrace. There was no explaining why Raoul was feeding me chocolate strawberries. It was what it looked like. I was so busted.

Then something dawned on me. I was caught with Raoul, but what the hell was she doing with Rashad, her sister's ex? Now I understood completely. The mystery man she had been bragging about was Rashad. I had thought it was my husband she was screwing, but it turned out to be her sister's man. Well, apparently she didn't have no shame in her game, because she jumped right in my stuff without seeming the slightest bit embarrassed about who she was with.

"Tammy," Egypt snapped, her arms akimbo. "Just what the hell are you doing?"

"Not today and not here," I said, getting up and pulling her away from the table before Raoul had a chance to stop me.

Once we were alone in the ladies' room, Egypt lit into me. "Now, wait a minute, Miss High and Mighty. You been talking shit about me to everyone who will listen, and here you are fooling around with Tim's friend Raoul."

"Well, ah . . ." I couldn't even think of a lie.

"And you supposed to be my best friend. All this time you

was accusing me of fuckin' your husband, you was just using that as an excuse to throw Tim off the dirt you was doin'. You make me sick."

I couldn't just stand by and let her jump down my throat like that. I attacked back. "Well, hold up. You ain't no better than me. What the hell are you doing with Rashad?"

She smirked at me. "Don't even go there, Tammy. You know damn well that Isis and Rashad broke up years ago. They never got married. But *you* are a married woman. You ought to be 'shamed of yourself. You know this ain't right."

I did know it, but I had been living in denial ever since I started messing around with Raoul. It hurt to hear my friend speaking the truth now.

"Tim is a good man, and you are fuckin' up. I'd be less than a friend not to tell you."

I was quiet for a minute, feeling my guilt grow with each passing second. "Please, Egypt. Don't tell Tim. I can't explain it right now. I'll work this through."

My plea did not move her. She still sounded thoroughly disgusted with me when she spoke. "I don't know what has gotten into you, Tammy. It was whacked in the first place to talk about having some threesome. You know black people ain't into that wife-swapping, sharing bullshit. That's why your shit is all fucked up now."

"I know, I know," I said, pleading for her to understand. "I never should have asked you to do that. But things just got so complicated after that."

She looked skeptical. "Complicated? You are fucking around on a good man. That's pretty simple to me."

"Listen, I can't talk about this right now, but I want to explain everything to you. I need a friend, okay?"

"Hmph!" she grunted. "You need a friend, all right. And maybe an exorcism or somethin', 'cause something has sure got into you."

I accepted her abuse without attitude because I didn't want to piss her off right now. If I did, there was a chance she would tell Tim what she'd seen.

"Look, let's meet for lunch tomorrow and we'll talk," I suggested. "I need to get back to the table and tell Raoul I'm leaving. Then I'll go home to my husband."

Once she promised not to say anything to Tim, I left Egypt standing there, shaking her head.

I really did intend to go back to the table and tell Raoul I had to leave. But when I caught sight of him and we locked eyes, I knew I couldn't do what I'd just told Egypt I would. As I waltzed back to the table, I said under my breath, "I'll go home to my husband *after* I get me some."

36

Nikki

I'd been working a lot more overtime lately, because I could always use the extra pay, and because it gave me an excuse to stay away from home as much as possible. Ever since she'd hit me, I had no desire to be around Tiny. She'd been on her best behavior since then, but I sure hadn't forgotten what she did to me that night. I hadn't moved out, but my heart just wasn't in it anymore. I tried to forgive her and get past it, but after everything I'd gone through with DJ's daddy, how could I ever forget?

Every moment I spent at home with Tiny lately was like a special kind of hell. Trying to convince her I loved her and wouldn't leave her proved emotionally draining. She was constantly apologizing, begging for my forgiveness, saying she wanted everything to be the way it used to be. But I think she knew that wasn't possible. I felt like I was walking around on eggshells all the time. I was pissed at her but was also trying to be careful not to piss her off, because as many times as Tiny promised to control her temper, I suspected it would only be a matter of time before she made a habit out of putting her hands on me. That's how it went. I'd been around long enough to know that giving someone a second chance was the same as giving them permission to start kicking your ass whenever they wanted.

When my boss asked me to work overtime again on one particular Thursday, I readily agreed, looking at it as another easy excuse to avoid Tiny for a few more hours. DJ would be with his father anyway. Of course, it made my decision to stay even easier when I overheard Keith saying he planned to take the overtime too. The space between Keith and me as coworkers had collapsed, and without saying anything, we were quickly becoming something more. Each morning, I could barely wait to get dressed and go to work, and I waited for the first time he'd deliver mail on my floor. If I didn't know better, I'd believe I was holding my breath until I saw him.

I picked up the phone to let Tiny know I'd be working overtime. "Hey, baby. My boss said I got to stay late at work." Of course, my boss had given me a choice, but Tiny didn't need to know that.

"Fuck those people," she complained. "They can't fire you over that. Just come home."

"Tiny, I can't," I answered abruptly.

"But I'm cooking," she whined. Another fighting point. Tiny hated that I stuck to my diet and tried damn near every night to sabotage me by making the greasy fried foods I usually loved.

"Tiny, everybody else in the department is working overtime. How's it gonna look if I say no?" I rolled my eyes, wishing that just for once not everything had to be a fight between us.

"Shit, tell them fuckers you got a woman and a child."

"Look, I don't have a choice. I got to do it. I got to get back to work." I sighed, exhausted by the battle. "Just call me when you calm down."

"I am going to call you," she threatened.

"I'll be in the cafeteria between eight and eight-thirty; then I'll be back at my desk." I hated having to report my schedule to her like that, but it was the best way to avoid an even bigger fight later on.

She finally gave up. "All right, boo. I just miss you."

"Me too. I got to go."

I hung up the phone to find Keith leaning into my cubby, and damn, that man looked good. My body reacted at the mere sight of him these days.

"Thought you'd be long gone," he stated, his voice all smooth and deep.

"I could use the extra money for summer camp," I lied.

"What time you going to dinner?"

I looked straight into his eyes with no attempt to disguise my lust. Tonight, I wanted to have exactly what I wanted. "I'm going to dinner around eight," I told him.

He took the bait for sure. "Meet you in the lobby." He bopped away, not bothering to wait for my response. I rubbernecked, watching his pants fall a little below his butt crack. I didn't have any proof, but I knew he had to be packing some serious heat in those shorts. How the hell was I gonna keep my mind on food with his fine ass across the table?

Those two hours before dinner felt like a week. By the time eight o'clock rolled around, I couldn't pretend to play it cool. I ran into the bathroom to make sure my breasts were fully displayed. I'd lost a good ten pounds, which restored my waistline and gave me one of them big-girl hourglass shapes. I reapplied my lip gloss, all the while day-dreaming of kissing Keith in his private places.

Keith made it to the lobby before me and stood around joking with some of the other guys from the mail room. At first I almost jumped back onto the elevator. I was afraid my lust for Keith was written all over my face, and I wasn't ready to make that public.

Keith spotted me and called out before I could disappear. "Hey, beautiful, you ready?" He strutted over to me, took my hand, not caring that all his boys were staring at him. I started to feel weak in the knees with desire for him.

"Let's go get our appetites satisfied," he said, and something told me he wasn't really talking about food.

My palms started to sweat as we walked to the cafeteria. Having a man's firm and masculine hand holding mine took me back, made me remember how much I liked feeling all girly. He had the kind of hands that knew their way around a woman's body, I assumed.

"How do you stay single?" I flirted. "Or do you just like being one of them ladies' men?" I smiled, past the point of caring that I was prying.

"I'm just picky," he answered sincerely. "Chemistry is a hell of a thing. You can go looking for it, but it's one of those things that shows up when you least expect it."

"Oh yeah, like when?" I asked, feeling bold.

"Like now. You think I just want to hold your hand?"

I stopped walking and turned to him, mostly because my legs felt like jelly. "And what you plan to do about it?"

"Everything." With that, he leaned over and put those juicy lips on top of mine. My body responded like I had been in some manless desert and was in desperate need of water to quench my desire. My panties were soaked and wet.

Here we stood in front of the cafeteria, staring into each other's eyes, both of us ravenous for something other than food. As he touched the door to enter, I placed my hand over his, guiding him away.

"Oh, it's like that?" He smiled at me. I nodded my head. We race-walked back to the lobby.

As we entered the elevator, my lips fell on his, and we moved close, like hungry animals pawing all over each other. He gripped my ass, smashing me into his hard penis, and I swooned. All I wanted was this man to penetrate me, deep and hard. All the fantasies in my head were close to becoming realities, and I felt ready to explode from desire.

"I want you," Keith whispered in my ear.

"Me too." My entire body attempted to press itself into him, and that's when we felt the elevator coming to a stop. We broke apart, and I tried to fix myself up in case one of my coworkers was standing in front of the doors. The doors opened to an empty hallway, thank God, because my nipples were standing at attention.

I guided Keith to my supervisor's office, knowing that she always went home to her kids at six on the dot, no matter how much overtime the rest of us worked. As soon as I closed the door, Keith and I started grabbing for each other like we'd just been let loose after doing some serious time at Attica.

I reached to unbuckle his belt, but he slapped my hand away and flipped me around so I was facing the desk. He was taking control, and I was loving every minute of it. Keith pulled my panties down and began to finger me. It took every ounce of control to not cry out in pleasure for the entire office to hear.

I reached back to grab his dick, but he snatched both my hands, gripping them in one of his behind my back. I saw him pull a condom from his pocket right before his pants hit the floor. Less than a minute later, he entered me from the rear. Lord, have mercy, there is nothing like the fullness you feel when a man first enters you, and it felt like Keith had dick for days. It didn't take long before he was riding me past the point of pleasure. I had reached pure ecstasy.

"I want to feel it," I purred, reaching toward him. His grip tightened on my arms as he raised them even higher, pushing himself deeper into me until all I could do was moan in pleasure as I came not once but several times. I didn't realize how much I'd missed being with a real man until that exact moment. How the hell had I gone this long without a dick, without a man?

37

Coco

If there is one thing I know how to do, it's shop. Instead of sitting around staring at the walls in the new condo Jackson had gifted me, wondering how to respond to Mac's latest text message, I needed some good old-fashioned retail therapy. And now that I was able to buy without a budget, it just made things all the more exciting. For the last five or so years, I'd been jumping from dick to dick just to pay the bills, but those days were behind me. I could go anywhere I wanted—Macy's 34th Street, Bloomingdales, Barneys, and Bergdorf's—and not have to worry about screwing five Negroes to do it. I was living my *Pretty Woman* moment.

Because I was kinda feeling out of sorts, I decided to take one of my road dogs with me. I called Nikki. "Hey, heifer, what you doing today?"

"Just try'na keep Tiny off my ass, both literally and figuratively," she whispered into the phone.

"Put on something cute and roll with me into the city." We both knew that Tiny couldn't stand Nikki hanging out with me. She called me a "dick magnet" behind my back, like I'd take offense or something. But she really didn't have anything to worry about, because when Nikki was with me, I was the only one getting all the attention. In order to keep Tiny happy, Nikki spent all her time downplaying her hotness, so when we were together, she barely got hit on.

By the time I rolled up to Nikki's place in my new Mercedes, I had gotten to the other side of my funk. Driving a top-of-the-line German vehicle will lift your mood anytime.

"What time you coming back?" I heard Tiny's voice before I saw her or Nikki.

"I don't know," Nikki huffed, and I wondered how she could stand it. I ain't got nothin' against lesbians, but I've never answered to no man, so there was no way in hell I would be sweated by a woman.

I got out of the car in one of my new dresses from Bergdorf, looking fierce. Tiny didn't bother to hide the scowl on her face.

"Who you pimp out of this car?" she growled.

"Tiny, most women fuck only to wind up with broken hearts and bad attitudes. But me, I like nice things." I laughed, knowing it would piss her off. Nikki shot me a look as if to say, "Shut up, so we can get out of here."

"This car is off the chain, girl," Nikki commented before jumping in the passenger seat. I got in the driver's side, waved to Tiny, and shot out of there to save my girl from any more drama.

"What, the warden got you on lockdown or something?" My laughter stopped me from saying more, but Nikki didn't find my comment funny.

"She just making it harder for me to want to be around her ass," Nikki complained.

"Girl, better you than me."

"Can we switch subjects and talk about this ride? So, whose Mercedes you pushing?"

"Mine." I all but danced behind that wheel. "Girl, Coco done messed around and hit the lottery."

"What's his name?" she demanded.

"Jackson Brentworth," I told her nonchalantly.

It took her a second, then her eyes got big and she shouted, "Jackson Brentworth, the developer?"

I turned to her and smiled. "Mmm-hmm, that would be him."

"Oh shit! You did hit the lottery."

"Nikki, I told you a long time ago that I had a plan. And that plan was to never be broke."

"I hear you." She just had to ask, "So . . . how's the sex?"

"Not as good as I would like, but you don't get it all in one place. You either have the best sex in the world but the brother can't provide," I said, thinking about Mac, "or you get the money, and sex is part of the job description. But you know me. I plan to have both of them. 'Cause good dick is essential."

"I know that's right." Nikki gave me a knowing look that almost made me crash my new ride.

"Oh no, you didn't!" I yelled. "Oh no, you didn't fuck that young boy!"

"Oh yes, I did," she bragged. "And, honey, I can't wait to do it again."

"So you've seen the light." She nodded. "Now, I'm strictly dickly myself, so I don't know how you ever survived without one. What you planning to do about Tiny?"

Nikki scrunched up her face at me. "I ain't got that far yet. Too busy thinking about that good-ass dick. I just wish I had been able to taste it and do all those kinds of things."

"How you get that far and not take a taste?" I hollered. "What did I tell you?"

"If you won't suck it, don't fuck it." We both laughed in unison, but I stared at her seriously.

"I know, I know, but we were at work and he bent me over a desk, and . . ." She got lost in her thoughts for a minute. "Damn, that shit was good, Coco. I can't even tell you how good that shit was."

And from that moment on, I knew girlfriend was hooked on the penis again.

"Was it big?" I'm sorry, but I just had to know. Besides, I didn't see anything wrong with getting details.

She closed her eyes. "Big and thick. Oh, and did he know how to use. He wouldn't even come until I had at least three orgasms." Nikki sounded like she was getting herself all worked up, and the truth is, so was I! I was definitely going to have to call Mac after our shopping spree.

"Wow, sounds like this guy Mac I been seeing. I swear, Nikki, that man can fuck all night." I got lost in my own thoughts for a second there. "Enough about me. When you gonna see him again?"

"Hopefully Monday, at work. He invited me out this weekend, but you know that getting away from Tiny these days is like a jailbreak. It's like she got that instinct, and if I'm even thinking about Keith, she up in my stuff like she knows something." Clearly, Nikki was worried.

"You know I ain't never been one to get all tied up with another person, so I don't see why you can't just ask Tiny to move."

"You kiddin'? I can't throw Tiny out of our home. She loves

me and DJ. And after all she's done for us?" The passion in her voice had disappeared, replaced by guilt.

"See, that's why I keep my emotions out of relationships," I said. "They get all messy. Seems to me when something is over, then it's over. What's the point in dragging it out? You think Tiny gonna be less hurt in six months when she figure out you fuckin' some guy? People always get caught sooner or later. See why I stay single?"

Nikki sucked her teeth and said, "You try'na tell me this car don't have no strings attached?"

"Jackson thinks this car is a down payment on ownership of me, but . . . Well, I like to think that what he don't know ain't his business," I said with a smile.

Four hours, five stores, and two cocktails later, I dropped Nikki off and headed to Mac's place. I'd been doing a pretty good job of holding him and Jackson in check. I'd only met Mac for a few hotel-room quickies and dinner once or twice, making sure to be home in my own bed every night. Although he'd invited me, I hadn't even gone to Mac's place yet, because I didn't want to be tempted to stay. But I guess he was getting antsy. His text made it clear that we needed to have a talk today. I stashed my ride around the corner from his place and had him meet me on the street.

"What's up, Coco?" That smooth voice made me want him. I still couldn't get used to the way my entire body reacted at the sight of him.

"You tell me, baby." When a man wants to talk, it's always a good idea to let him do the talking.

He remained silent as he led me upstairs in the elevator. We kept exchanging stares, but if he wouldn't start the conversation, then neither would I. All that shifted after we entered his apartment. I didn't know exactly what kind of entertaining Mac did, but it sure did pay well. His place was laid out.

Mac pressed up in my face real close like he was going to kiss me, but instead he had one question. "You try'na play me, Coco?" Clearly, I had to be off my game not to see this coming.

"What?" I stuttered.

"You heard me. What you think, I'm some pussy hound who's so hard up all I need is a quick fuck?" My lips parted as I worked on a snappy comeback, but he placed one finger to my lips. "I don't fuck and forget, and I don't play games or women. I don't have time for bullshit. You not returning my calls, that doesn't work for me. Didn't I make myself clear when I asked you if you were ready to be my woman?" He stood so close I could feel the heat from his breath.

"This is moving kind of fast, Mac." I tried to back away a bit, but he pulled me into his personal space.

"This is real life, Coco. It moves the way it moves. I guess I should have told you that I'm an all-or-nothing kind of guy, so you need to tell me which one you want. All or nothing?"

Most men were happy with a fuck or two, and sure, some got addicted to the sex, but I could tell that that wasn't it for Mac. He wanted all of me. If he were any other man, I would have turned and run, 'cause I'm not the kind of woman to be possessed. But I'll be damned if Mac's combination of sexiness and masculinity didn't keep me rooted to the spot.

"Are you serious?" Sure, I knew the answer, but I needed to hear it anyway.

"Stop playing games. You want to keep doing what you doing, or you want to be my woman?"

I needed a plan, and fast. If I could seduce Mac, he'd forget all about this needing-an-answer thing. I leaned over and kissed him on the mouth, deep, wet, and prying, but his lips were steel and did not open for me. I pressed myself into him, my pelvis grinding close to his groin. Mac gripped my shoulders and pushed me back.

"Is that all you want? For me to fuck you? To be some piece of ass to me? Coco, I know you. We're the same, so you can't play games with me, 'cause I'm gonna know." I had made him furious.

Nobody calls me a piece of ass. I picked up my new authentic Gucci purse off the couch and headed for the door.

His voice stopped me. "If you walk out of that door, then we are done."

I froze right there. I knew this was no idle threat. Mac was truly willing to give up on all this. Was I trippin' because I hadn't had many men turn down a chance to fuck me, or was it because the thought of being without him truly hurt?

"I want to be with you, Coco, not just fuck you." I stood

there halfway between Mac and the door. The only thing I could be certain about was that I did not want to give this man up, not yet. I took a step toward him.

"I want to love you," he whispered in my ear.

"Mac, I don't know how to do this."

"I'll show you." He buried his face in my neck. That's when I heard my phone vibrate. Mac backed up. "You either gonna get that or turn it off."

So I shut off my phone, knowing Jackson would be looking for me. How the hell was I gonna pull this off? Before I could start to worry, Mac picked me up and carried me into the bedroom.

38

Isis

By the time I walked back through my door, I was lit on fire. I mean, I was beyond hot. I chose a lying, cheating snake over a man who seemed really ready to marry me, only to lose him to my can't-keep-a-man sister. Well, there was no way I was letting Tony go back to his little family like he hadn't stepped his shit-stained shoes all over my dreams. Oh, hell no. His ass was going to pay, and the wheels in my head were starting to spin with all kinds of possibilities. Did he think I took deceit lying down, like all I planned to do was crawl into a bowl of Häagen Dazs and die? Just like I didn't know what a shifty, conniving bastard he could be, he had no clue the kind of bitch I could turn into. Never underestimate the power of a woman scorned. I had dealt with too many men stepping over my body to climb onto the next woman—the one they invariably took to the altar. This time, I was out for blood. Lesson number one for Tony would be that payback is a bitch . . . and she looks just like me.

It took me a good couple of days to figure out the best way to ruin Tony's life, but once I came up with a plan, I was good to go. I wanted to thank Bill Gates, God, or whoever had created the information superhighway. I don't understand how shit got done before the Internet, but I was planning to be one with my computer until I had all the facts I needed to topple Tony's lying-ass house of cards. He was coming down, and with a quickness.

Egypt had the nerve to call to check up on me, like I really wanted to talk after catching her rank ass with Rashad. Well, I don't care how much *All My Children* or *General Hospital* you watch. In the real world, you don't climb up on the same old dick your sister had once called her own. Those were just the

rules to the game of sisterhood. Old penises were supposed to re-
tire to the dead penis cemetery and never be heard from again,
unless you wanted to dig up one of yours for your own damn
self. Never should you dig into the ghosts of penises past that belonged to your friend or even worse, family. This wouldn't be the
first time Egypt had fallen on some good dick and made a bad
choice. Unfortunately, I knew firsthand that Rashad had the
kind of dick that could make you lose your mind.

Speaking of good dick and bad choices, just me thinking
about Tony's average penis and bedroom skills made me mad all
over again. I had convinced myself I could settle for Tony and
so-so sex as long as I was married with a family. From this day
forward, I decided to put my happiness on hold until I made
Tony pay for every rotten lie he had ever told me.

"I should move in with you because my apartment is not fit
for you to step your pretty feet into," he had told me. And I
thought he was embarrassed, so I never even suggested going to
his place or trying to fix it up for him. Damn, I spent so much
time making sure he took me seriously that I never even questioned things that would be obvious to most women. Lots of
people gave up home phones and only dealt by cell, I told myself. I wanted so badly for my friends to like him that I never
questioned the fact that I hadn't met any of his. I just assumed
his job as a long-distance trucker kept him too busy to maintain
friendships. And I let him flatter me when he said, "I'm a grown-
ass man, and when I have free time, I want to spend it with you,
not hanging with a bunch of men like we're still in high school."
I bought his entire act, and now there wouldn't be a place on this
earth far enough away to keep me from destroying his life. It had
become my sole mission.

Massaging the computer keys, I typed in www.find
afriend.com. Living or dead, they promised to locate anybody. I
typed in the name "Tony Washington." In the New York City
area, there were hundreds. Since he always got to my place
pretty quickly, I figured he lived in Queens, so I narrowed my
search. Still too many to list. It figures he would have an average
name to match that average dick.

Three hours later, I still wasn't any closer to locating the
homestead of the mystery wife and four kids. The more I dug,

the less information I realized I had been privy to. "I know all about me; let's focus on you," he'd purr when I asked him questions, and my dumb ass was too happy to press him.

I looked down at the rock on my hand. I knew exactly where he had gotten the ring. We had gone shopping over at Martin's. I didn't even know he had that kind of money, but after that first down payment, it hadn't even taken him three months to get the ring. I planned to sell that ring back to the store and take myself on one of them Caribbean cruises. I also decided to use some of the money for a new mattress and fresh sheets that he'd never laid on. But before I got rid of the ring, it was going to get me the information I'd been searching for.

I took a shower and put on a beautiful white wrap top from Ashley Stewart's. It didn't cost much, but when I paired it with the right bag and shoes, you would think I had gone over to Bloomingdales on 3rd Avenue.

When I stepped into Martin's with a purpose, the salesman didn't have to ask me twice what I wanted. I removed the two-carat ring from my purse and handed it to him.

"My ex-fiancé bought me this, and I want to return it to him, but I'm not sure of his mailing address." I tried to play it cool. The salesman stared me up and down as if I might be carrying the plague or something; then he took the ring.

"Ma'am, uh, this ring must have been purchased at another establishment." He all but tossed the ring and me out of the store. He must have seen the confusion on my face, because unexpectedly, he leaned close to me, softening. "We don't sell cubic zirconia."

"CZ?" I must have shouted because everyone in the store turned in my direction. Oh no, he didn't. Lying about his wife was one thing, but giving me a fake-ass ring and having me embarrass the hell out of myself up in this store with all these white people? I wanted him to suffer.

With my eyes blinded by rage, I don't remember how I found my way home, but I tore off my clothes and sat back down at that computer. It slowly dawned on me that I did have some way to find Tony. I knew his cell phone number.

After I typed in my credit card number, I hit SEND, and a big shit-eating grin covered my face. "Gotcha!" I hollered out loud. Fourteen dollars and ninety-five cents was a small price to pay to destroy someone. The number was registered to a Mr. Tony Washington in Elmont, New York. I MapQuested the directions, threw my clothes back on, and hit it.

Not long after, I was pulling onto a tree-lined street in a middle-class neighborhood. It hit me that had Tony not been a lying snake in the grass, this would be my life, and those four kids would be calling me Mom. I slowed down as I passed a brick ranch-style house sitting back on a lawn, with both a tricycle and a scooter in the driveway. I was trying to decide what to do when a short brown-skinned woman opened the screen door.

"I'll be right back," she yelled to somebody as she jumped into her Suburban.

I stepped on the gas and followed her. A few minutes later, we pulled up into the parking lot of a Compare Foods supermarket. I found Tony's wife in the meat department, and as much as I would have rather had this moment over a latte at Starbucks, there was no time like the present. I stepped up to her.

"Excuse me?"

"Yes?" She smiled wide, like we were about to discuss the price of chuck.

"I need to talk to you about your husband."

Her hand went to her hip in a defensive position, and that friendly openness was replaced with a sneer. "What about my husband?"

"Tony and I have been dating for two years, and we went to Vegas last week to get married until I found out he was already married to you." I blurted it all out in one breath.

She stumbled back in surprise. "Bitch, I don't know who you think you talking about, but it ain't my husband." She looked ready to attack. If she put one skinny finger on me, I was about to go off. And as mad as I felt, she wouldn't have a chance.

"Tony Washington. Six feet, about two-sixty with a raised bump on his right ass cheek," I countered.

The look on her face told me I'd hit a nerve, but still she tried to deny it. "Look, I don't know who you think you messing with, but it ain't my Tony."

"I'm not try'na hurt your feelings, but if I was married to a lying, cheating, no-good dog like your husband, I would want to know."

"You better get out my face," she threatened. "I know your

type, always chasing after some married man and mad when they kick you to the curb. Tony wouldn't give your fat ass the time of day, so get outta my face with your lies."

"Well, all those nights Tony tells you he's hauling loads long-distance, he's at my house cooking me dinner, running my bath, and fuckin' my brains out." If looks could kill, I'd be one dead-ass bitch, but this sistah was hardheaded. Hell, he had convinced me he was single, so why wouldn't he convince his wife he was faithful?

"First of all, my husband works the graveyard shift as a su-pervisor at FedEx. Second of all, Tony can barely boil water, and third of all, my husband is not a chubby-chaser. He wouldn't go near your big ass." Just as I was about to lunge at her, some store manager stepped in between us.

"Mrs. Washington, are you all right?" His beady eyes darted around at me as if he were in danger.

"This woman apparently just got let out of the insane asylum. You should call the cops so she can stop harassing innocent peo-ple."

"Excuse me. You need to leave the store," he warned me.

"You try'na throw me out? You and what army?" My blood pressure was about to boil over. I grabbed a rack of lamb, clutching it to my belly.

"I have a right to shop," I yelled at him.

"Ma'am, we need you to leave the premises." Tony's wife was shielded by the manager as if he had to protect her from me. She had her hands folded and was staring me down like she really believed I had escaped from a mental ward.

"Somebody call the police," the store manager yelled out past the crowd that had gathered a noticeable distance from me.

"I never saw that woman in my life," I overheard Tony's wife telling the store manager.

"Well, I saw your husband naked for the last two years—and he did propose to me!" I reached into my purse, grabbed the fake-ass ring, and flung it at her. "Your marriage is as fake as this ring your husband gave me," I screamed.

"The cops are on their way," one of the employees yelled. Now, I was mad, but the last thing I wanted was to be hauled off to jail. I glanced toward the exit, threw down that rack of lamb, and raced out of that store as fast as I could with my pride in shambles.

Reaching the safety of my car, I tore out of that parking lot and didn't stop checking my rearview mirror until I was safely out of suburbia. Tony's wife might have won this round, but I'd be damned if I was going to give up without a fight.

39

Tammy

Raoul walked into the office, and my entire body began to tingle with anticipation. There was no way the sun could go down before I got my hands on him. And the way he kept looking at me, I knew we were on the same page. Lucky for both of us, Tim had meetings set up out of the office all afternoon and wouldn't be around the rest of the day.

My phone vibrated with a text. I knew it had to be from Raoul. Before we started fooling around, I hadn't bothered to learn that feature on my phone, so none of my friends or family ever texted me.

It read: MEET ME AT THE SPOT AFTER WORK. Once I flipped the phone shut, I couldn't get out of the office and into my car fast enough. "The spot" was our code for the short-stay motel we'd been meeting in near LaGuardia Airport. While the motel was certainly a far cry from the Four Seasons, the last thing on our mind was the quality of our surroundings. As long as the place was clean and had a big bed, then we could work with it. Hell, the sex was so good, I would have done it on a sawdust floor with him. We barely even noticed the rooms anyway. The moment we hit the door, clothes, belts, and shoes went flying every which way. Lips and hands grabbed at each other, ripping off underwear or whatever hadn't been removed.

"Kiss me," he said as soon as I entered the room, pressing his juicy wet lips onto mine. Raoul lowered himself and flipped me back onto the bed, spreading my legs wide. Oh, I thanked my yoga teacher for all those classes I'd taken over the years. People assume big women aren't flexible, but, baby, all I can say is if they saw my legs spread-eagled on that bed, they'd realize how wrong they were. Raoul licked his lips and dove deep down into my muff. This man had no issues about licking the kitty, and I was about to be transformed into a shivering mass of Jell-O.

"Oh, I'm coming . . . I'm coming . . . I'm comiiiiiiiiing!" I screamed so loud I'm sure all the other motel guests could hear me—if they weren't all here doing the same thing. As much as I loved orgasms during intercourse, they were much more explosive during oral sex. Truthfully, I'd never even really had a good orgasm until Raoul went down on me. It's a damn shame, too, because I'd always enjoyed my sex life with my husband, or at least I thought I had before I knew what I had been missing. Before I could catch my breath, Raoul was right back there, licking me into hysteria again.

"I can't help it, Tammy, but damn, you taste good," he told me before diving back down there. I don't know if it had to do with youth or that Latin thing, but Raoul had more energy, stamina, and enthusiasm than any man I'd ever been with—all five of them. As he licked, sucked, and fingered me to another orgasm, I felt sorry for all those women who had married men too young to have learned the proper oral technique and were still in the dark like I used to be.

"I could eat you all day long," Raoul panted, and I knew his words were the truth. But I wanted something else, something more, something I had never been able to do with Tim. In the world of penises, Tim qualified as an extra-big, while Raoul's dick ran more in the medium-to-large range. I had always thought bigger was better, and if there is one area black men usually have covered, it's dick size. But Raoul taught me something I had definitely been missing—a more average-sized dick allowed me to climb on top and stimulate my clitoris in such a way that damn near sent my pussy into orgasm with each grind. How could I not have known this position was so damn perfect? Tim's penis was too large to allow me to make this motion, but Raoul knew just how to move my hips so I would keep climaxing. And now that I knew the power of this position, I wanted to stay on and ride forever.

"I'm coming . . . I'm coming . . . oh, Raoul, oh . . ." I could barely keep count of the number of times I exploded. This man certainly knew how to fuck me into slumber. By the time I climbed off of him and lay my head down on the pillow, I was exhausted. Now, every woman knows she has been fucked well when she has no choice but to fall asleep. Every part of my body felt contented from the combination of wild fucking and continuous orgasms. A smile curled my lips as I fell asleep next to this sex machine Latin lover.

When I opened my eyes, the room was pitch dark. At first I forgot where I was, but then I saw Raoul stir and I remembered. I grabbed my telephone to look at the time and saw eight missed calls. It was ten past ten, and my ass was in deep trouble. Tim was gonna kill me.

"Shit!" I screamed out in panic.

Raoul popped up, wiping the sleep from his eyes. "Tam, what's wrong?"

"It's past ten o'clock at night. I didn't pick up the kids from my mother. How the hell am I going to explain this to Tim? Oh my God," I cried.

"Tim cannot find out we were together." Raoul sounded as panic-stricken as I felt. We both had so much to lose if Tim found out I'd been fucking Raoul. Not only would Raoul lose his job, but he might even have reason to fear for his life—from Tim and from his crazy-ass wife.

I scrambled out of bed, throwing on my clothes while Raoul began to gather his things. Once I had myself together, I darted to the door, throwing a quick "Talk to you later" over my shoulder on the way out.

The Airport Motel was one of those places that had parking spots right in front of the rooms. When I realized my car was not in the space where I had parked, a few doors down from our room, I stood on the curb and looked around the parking lot. In my momentary confusion, I half expected to see the car sitting in a different space, like it had just moved. By the time I heard Raoul exiting the room behind me, I realized the car wasn't there.

"My car! It's gone!" I yelled out to him.

"Where did you park?" Raoul asked. I showed him the empty spot two spaces away from his car.

"Right here. I left my car right in this space." I began to sob as I realized the depth of the trouble I was in. "Tim is going to kill me. Oh my God! What am I going to do?"

"Don't panic." Somehow, Raoul managed to stay calm.

"Do you know what Tim will do to me if he finds out I've been cheating on him?" I screamed.

"Then why did he bring me into your bed in the first place? That's almost a guarantee that your woman will cheat," Raoul said, sounding defiant even in the face of this very serious situation. Like all of a sudden he didn't care if Tim knew. But I knew he cared a hell of a lot more than he was admitting, and in my state of panic, it was pissing me off that he was acting like this was no big deal.

"Oh," I shot back, "so you don't care if you lose your job, your reputation, your wife, and everything else?"

"This is bad," he finally agreed, looking around the lot for my car the way I had done a minute earlier. "Do you think you got towed?"

"No. I never get parking tickets. I'm careful." There was only one other possible scenario, and I felt my stomach tie into knots. "Oh my God, somebody stole my car."

"I have a plan," Raoul said after a few minutes, during which I cried pretty much nonstop. "You have to go home and tell Tim somebody stole your car."

I gave him a look to let him know I thought the idea was stupid.

"It's true," he offered.

"Yeah, but how am I going to explain to the police that my car was parked at a motel when it got stolen?"

He gave the question some thought, then answered, "I got it. We'll make up a story about you being carjacked."

I didn't see how it could work but knew there wasn't really an alternative.

"When Tim sees you, he needs to be so worried for your safety that he doesn't care about the time. He'll just be so glad that you're alive." Raoul's idea actually made sense, because Tim's concern for his family came before anything else.

"Your mascara is already smudged all over your face. Now we have to find a patch of dirt and roll you in it," he continued.

"Dirt? Oh no. I have on a Diane von Furstenberg wrap dress that cost me a pretty penny. This is not a dress to be rolling on the ground in," I protested.

Raoul sounded exasperated. "Tammy, Tim has to believe some

carjackers roughed you up and threw you out of the car. You can't walk in looking like something out of a fashion magazine." As he explained, all I heard was the part about me looking like I stepped out of a fashion magazine. Even in a crisis, Raoul knew how to make me feel beautiful.

A half hour later, Raoul dropped me off a block from my house. I walked home, rehearsing my story in my head, praying it would work. But as I rounded the corner, I saw something that caused every thought to evaporate from my mind. Damn if my car wasn't sitting in the driveway looking just like I left it. I couldn't understand how it had gotten all the way from the motel to my house on its own. It was a fly car, but it damn sure didn't drive itself. I wondered for a minute if someone had stolen my car and been caught joyriding, and the police had returned it already. I knew this scenario was unlikely, but it was my best hope. I was too afraid to think of the other possibility that entered my mind. When I finally gathered the courage to go inside, hoping I could stick to the carjacking story Raoul and I had rehearsed, Tim confirmed my worst fears.

I found him in the den, sitting in his calfskin La-Z-Boy. He was so still and quiet it was frightening. Obviously, the police hadn't been here to return my car, or else Tim would have been jumping up, relieved to see me home safely.

"Tim, what is my car doing in the driveway?" I stammered.

"You mean instead of parked at the Airport Motel?" His voice was eerily calm.

I was busted, but the lies I'd created with Raoul still came tumbling out of my mouth. "Somebody stole my car. Yeah, I got carjacked." I felt desperate for him to believe me.

"You think you can just tell me anything, huh? Like I'm some goddamned idiot," Tim seethed. I had never seen him this way, and it sent shivers up and down my body.

"But, Tim, I'm telling the truth," I pleaded.

His body stiffened in that chair, but he still hadn't moved to get up. "The truth? At around six o'clock, when the children were supposed to be picked up and weren't—for the third time this week—your mother called me, worried. Dumbass me figured you got caught in traffic or ran late at the store, getting our dinner. By seven o'clock, I put worry aside and began to get suspicious." He gave a nasty smirk. "Hell, you can't blame me, can you? As long as it's been since we made love."

"We made love the other night," I shouted.

"Is that what you called it? 'Cause I could have had more fun if you handed me a sponge and some K-Y lubricant. I don't know what you call that shit the other night, but it sure as hell wasn't making love."

"Tim—"

"Don't you Tim me. The way you been acting, I was bound to wonder if there's someone else. Still, I wanted to give you the benefit of the doubt because after all, you've always been a good wife." His voice was dripping with sarcasm.

I tried to stop him before he revealed the rest of what he knew. "Tim, please listen to me—"

"Lies! I do not want to hear one more of your lies, so shut the hell up, woman." I stayed silent, waiting for the other shoe to drop. "By a quarter to eight, I contacted OnStar." My heart lurched when he mentioned the satellite security system on my car. How could I have been so stupid? Tim let out a derisive laugh. "You forgot, didn't you, that we have GPS tracking devices in the cars, in case of an emergency or if the car is actually stolen. I took a cab over to the Airport Motel, some sleazy, disgusting hovel I wouldn't walk in if I had to take a shit, but you were there with Rauol."

"Tim, you have to believe me," I cried desperately.

"Shut the fuck up!" He stood up, and I felt his anger from the fifteen feet I stood away. "You had the fuckin' nerve to accuse me of messing with Egypt, and here you are fuckin' Raoul. You make Coco look like a saint. You fuckin' whore."

"Now wait one min—" He took two steps toward me, and I shut up midsentence. I was actually afraid he was going to hit me.

"No, what you have to do is pick up those suitcases and get the fuck out of my house," he said with finality. He pointed to the matching red Tumi luggage packed and standing near the door. In the panicked state I was in, I hadn't even noticed it before.

"I am not leaving my house." I refused to let him throw me out like some common trash.

"You will pick up those bags and get out. I promise you that." His voice was still flat and emotionless.

"You can't make me," I continued to protest. "I know my rights."

"Oh yeah? Well, if you want to make this hard, then I guess I'm gonna have to tell your children what kind of slut their momma has become."

"You wouldn't dare," I challenged, hoping I was right.

"I will tell your mother, your father, all the members of the church, your book club group, everybody at work, and every damn body we ever met," he finished. "So, I suggest you get the fuck out of my house right now."

He meant every word he said. I had no choice. I picked up my bags and stepped.

40

Nikki

It had become our routine. During the past few weeks, whenever Keith and I did overtime, we'd sneak into my supervisor's office and get in a quickie before we left for our respective homes. On this particular day, I was laid out on my boss's desk with my legs wrapped around Keith's head as he licked me into ecstasy. It must have taken him two minutes flat to get me to come. He was nothing short of amazing. When I got up from the desk, I dropped down on my knees in front of him. Now it was my turn to show him my skills. I reached for his zipper, ready to release my prize, but he backed away.

"Hey, there, li'l ma. What you doin'?"

"It's my turn to show you how good I can be to you."

"Nah, I'm cool. I'm all about pleasin' you. Know what I mean?"

"But I want to do it," I said, thinking maybe he was just trying to be nice.

He reached under my arms and pulled me up. "Nah, it's not my thing, boo." His words were meant to soothe me, but all they did was confuse the hell out of me.

"What man doesn't like a blow job?"

"Look, let me show you what I like." His voice came out all smooth and hard at the same time. He kissed me and turned me around, bending me over the desk and raising my dress. I could hear his belt jiggle, and few seconds later, a condom wrapper landed on the desk in front of me. I braced myself, and he entered with one long, glorious stroke, all the while holding me down against the desk with his hand.

"Now, this is what I'm talkin' about." He dipped his tool deeper and deeper in my womb. "This is exactly what I'm talkin' about," he repeated.

"Ain't that the truth, Daddy," I purred. "Damn, you got some good dick."

Although I should have felt guilty about Tiny, my only thought was to wonder how the hell I did without this for all these years. Once again, Keith gripped my wrists in one hand, pulling me closer with the other one. It took all my willpower to stay silent as I moved my body in unison with his thrusts so that he knew exactly how good he made me feel. A good ten fabulous minutes into it, he froze, stopping all movement completely.

"No, don't stop," I whispered. "Please, I'm just about there."

"Shhhh!" Keith placed a hand over my mouth.

I ripped his hand from my mouth. "What's the matter? Why'd you stop?" I couldn't help but feel self-conscious the way he suddenly jumped away. I pulled down my dress, ready to get the hell out of dodge and forget the whole thing, but Keith held on to me.

"Dammit, Nikki, shut up and don't move," he said, and I heard the warning in his tone. That's when he pointed, and I followed his finger to the crack in the blinds. My eyes almost popped out of my head when I saw what had made him stop.

Tiny stood in front of my desk, flipping through my things. She opened my top drawers and riffled through them. I started to stand up and head for the door, but Keith grabbed me around the waist.

"Don't do it, Nikki." And that's when I came to my senses. I looked to Keith for a suggestion, because my mind had gone blank. I had no idea how I was going to get out of the building without Tiny seeing me.

"Check it. I'm gonna distract Tiny so that you can get out of here," Keith said. By the time I turned to face him, he had already put his equipment away and slipped out of the room.

I watched from the doorway as Tiny looked up and saw Keith. She sat down at my desk, staring him down.

"You seen Nikki?" Tiny didn't try to hide her dislike for Keith.

"Yeah, she was here earlier, but she went home," he said, and I couldn't believe how calm he was.

"No, she didn't." Tiny pointed at my purse, dismissing him with her condescending tone.

He scratched his head like he was surprised. "Damn, well, I thought she did."

"Then why is her bag right here, genius?" Tiny flipped him off. Any other man would have either started a fight over that disrespect, or he would have just walked away, but Keith held his ground. He was determined to distract Tiny for my sake, and I only hoped he knew how much I appreciated it.

"She probably went to the coffee shop to grab a bite. Maybe you should look for her there."

"Keith, I don't like you. I know you been sniffing 'round my woman, and I don't like it." The way Tiny was talking, I was starting to get scared. Her temper seemed to fly out of control pretty quickly these days, and the way she was talking to Keith, all I could do was hope she didn't attack.

Keith didn't seem the least bit concerned about Tiny's temper. In fact, he seemed to enjoy antagonizing her. "Look, I don't know what your problem is, but Nikki and I are friends. If you don't like it, oh well." He shrugged his shoulders.

"Well, she don't need friends like you. You think I don't know what you want?"

"So, now you know what I want?"

"Yep, sure do. You just wanna fuck her," she raged.

"Nikki is an off-the-chain woman, and fuckin' her wouldn't ever be enough," Keith growled back, and damn if I didn't get even more worried.

Tiny got up in his face. "You stay away from her. You hear? I ain't gonna tell you again."

"What, you think you scaring me? Damn, chill the fuck out and let Nikki live her life and choose her friends."

"Oh, so you think I should sit back and let her choose another loser like you? That's my woman, nigga."

"She's a grown-ass woman, and I don't see how it's any of your business who she chooses as friends." Keith spoke the words I had been wanting to say to Tiny for a long time now.

"It's my business 'cause you don't know a damn thing about Nikki," she told him.

"Yeah, well, I know she's my homie, and the kind of woman

anybody would love to go home to at night." I wondered if Keith was saying these things because he was aware that I was still listening. It felt great hearing him talk about me that way.

"Oh, that's what you think? You've known Nikki all of two months and you some kind of expert on her?" Tiny laughed in his face. "Nikki, the Nikki you see every day at work, is my own personal creation. You think that is the real Nikki?" Tiny laughed even louder, and Keith's body language made it obvious that now his temper was flaring.

"What, you her mother now? You fuckin' birthed her?"

"Yeah, bitch, I created the Nikki you see here, and without me worrying and checking up on her, she's liable to slip back into her desperate old habit of screwing a man who treats her like shit."

I knew I was supposed to be using this opportunity to sneak out of the office, but I stayed rooted in one spot, unable to believe what I was hearing from Tiny.

"You are delusional," Keith told her. "Nikki is a queen, and she deserves to be treated like one instead of you working to control her. What, you scared if she had two minutes to think without you breathing down her back she'd run the hell away from you?"

I worried that his words might have pushed Tiny over the edge. I waited for her to react.

"Oh, you think you know some shit. You know that Nikki lived with a man who treated her worse than a dog and beat her ass on the regular in front of her son?" she yelled into his ear.

"So, what, you think this is better? Checking up on her and acting like you own her?" Keith backed away. I knew he wasn't afraid of Tiny, so I assumed he was backing up to stop himself from doing what he really wanted to do—kick Tiny's ass.

Tiny continued talking about me like I was worthless. "You don't know how low Nikki was when I found her. She had been beaten into submission. If someone raised their voice, she jumped. She had spent years letting some thug Negro go upside her head. She was homeless, without any job and with nowhere to turn. You think she wants to go back to that?"

"She has a job and friends, including me, who would never let her be homeless again," he snapped. "Sounds like you trying to keep her under lock and key, but that's not gonna happen."

"What, you try'na take my woman away from me?" Tiny leaned in like she planned to hit Keith, but he didn't budge.

"I'm not tryin' to take anything. Nikki can make her own choice on that. But I'll tell you one thing, you don't deserve Nikki, because she's special."

"Well, I got her, so you might as well take your punk ass back to prison or wherever people like you belong."

It hurt to hear Tiny judging Keith the same way everyone at the office had judged him when he first came to work. Just like them, Tiny couldn't see past the baggy pants to the real Keith, and that bothered me, especially now that my feelings for him had grown.

Unlike me, Keith seemed unfazed by her insults. "Why don't you step off and let Nikki and her son have their own lives?"

"She is never going to leave me. First off, I wouldn't let her, and second, I made Nikki and she'd be nothing without me." Tiny flicked her fingers in Keith's face. "You better stop fuckin' with me, because I'm not some helpless girl you can scare."

I'd never seen Keith this mad, but the shit Tiny kept speaking made me want to jump out of the boss's office and confront her ass myself.

Tiny pushed her palm up against Keith's head. "What you gonna do now, punk?" She threw her head back and laughed. Keith psyched her out, throwing a punch near her face. Tiny reared back just as Gina, another coworker, hurried past them looking scared. Gina didn't stop to intervene, but at least her presence stopped the fight from turning into an all-out brawl. I was relieved, because the last thing I wanted was for Keith to get fired fighting over me.

"I wish Nikki knew that she deserved so much better." He no longer sounded angry, just frustrated.

"You think you better than me?" Tiny sucked her teeth all loud and ghetto.

"I'm not saying I'm better than anybody, but Nikki is a great girl who traded one abusive situation for another. Like I said, she deserves better than this bullshit." Keith scowled at Tiny.

"Let me tell you something about Nikki. She is not interested in no thug-ass bozo working in the mailroom 'cause he's too stupid to do anything else."

I watched Keith's face for a sign that he believed Tiny. I wanted him to know that she was totally wrong, that I was very interested in him.

"And just so we're clear, she is a lesbian who likes women, so stay the fuck away from my woman, bitch." Tiny spoke as if this would be the last word on the subject, but Keith wasn't letting it go that easily.

"You don't own Nikki. And just so we're clear, if I ever hear you put your hands on her, me and you gonna have a problem."

"Don't tell me how to treat my woman. Nikki belongs to me," she raged.

"Nikki is a human being, and last I checked, we can only belong to ourselves."

"Fuck you, okay? And don't stand there and tell me you ain't never put your hands on a woman," Tiny said with certainty. "I know your type, all insecure and need to act hard to feel like a man."

"I am a man, and as long as I live, I never have and never will put my hands on a woman. They don't deserve to be abused just because some idiot thinks they belong to them."

"I love Nikki." Tiny's voice sounded like it was about to break.

"Then act like it. Treat her like a queen. For some reason, she loves you, so I'm going to respect her and not really tell you how I feel," Keith finished.

"How you feel? You think I give a shit about how you feel?"

"If Nikki didn't love you, this whole thing would go another way. But she does, so I'm just letting you know that I'm her friend and I have her back. If she ever needs me, twenty-four/seven, I'm there for her." He stepped back. Keith glanced quickly toward the office where I was still hiding, and I wondered if he was just remembering that I was there.

"See those elevators?" Keith pointed toward them.

"Yeah." Tiny turned to face the elevators, her back to my boss's office, and that's when Keith waved behind his back for me to hurry out of the office.

"Nikki will probably get off one of those elevators, and when she does, try to remember that she loves you and that being with you is her choice." He started to walk away as I came toward

Tiny. I had to fix my voice to sound normal, not pissed the fuck off after hearing all the shit Tiny said about me.

"Hey, Tiny, what you doing here? I was just down in the copy room taking care of a few things." I prayed that my nervousness wasn't written all over my face.

Tiny turned to face me with a smirk. "I wanted to make sure my woman got home safe." She turned up the volume so that Keith would hear her. I glanced over Tiny's shoulder at Keith and saw his troubled expression.

"Let me grab my things." I heard the elevator chime and looked up again in time to see Keith staring at me before he stepped onto the elevator. I wanted so much to run to him and go wherever he was headed, but I couldn't, so I picked up my purse and followed Tiny out.

41

Coco

Juggling my time between Jackson and Mac for a few weeks had taken its toll on me. While Mac wore me out from all the amazing sex and great conversation, Jackson's neediness was exhausting. For the first time in my life, I had more man than even I could handle. It seemed that I was always running from Mac to Jackson, and as soon as I could get away from Jackson, I couldn't wait to jump back into Mac's arms. This man had done things to me that made my toes curl just thinking about. I would use any and every reason to be with Mac. I had even broken my own rule and started spending the whole night with him whenever Jackson was away on business.

One thing I was afraid of, though, was that all this good loving from Mac might have to end. Even though he hadn't said anything directly, I could tell he knew that something else was going on. The late-night phone calls, the unexplained absences, and the fact that I hadn't brought Mac to my place were enough to make any man suspicious.

"You awake?" Mac stirred next to me.

"Yeah, I'm awake." I pressed my body closer to him.

"You hungry? 'Cause I'm starving." Mac stretched, kissing me and bringing me closer.

We were about to start something when my cell phone buzzed with a text. Mac pulled away from me, staring into my eyes, and I could see the impatience in his gaze. Jackson's nonstop demands were wearing on my relationship with Mac. I looked at my phone on the nightstand but didn't move to check the text.

"I'm gonna make some food. You staying for dinner?" he asked, and all the sweetness had drained out of his voice. I didn't answer right away as I contemplated the phrase "skating on thin ice" that popped into my head. Giving Mac the wrong answer now might end this beautiful thing we had going. But ignoring Jackson's text for too long could mean I'd be out on the streets without my Mercedes and my monthly budget. Neither prospect was appealing to me.

Mac grabbed his pants up off the floor, still waiting for me to say something. "So, what? You staying or you going off to do whatever it is you're doing?" There was no effort to hide how angry he was at that point. I can't say I blamed him, though. I was getting tired of the whole situation myself. Every day we grew closer while I kept juggling Jackson, and it couldn't go on forever. In fact, I wouldn't be surprised if Mac ended it right there.

My phone buzzed again with a new text. Obviously Jackson wasn't taking my ignoring him too well. Looking at Mac, I knew I'd be a fool to walk out of there at that moment and expect to ever get invited back.

"Honey, I'm starving," I cooed. His face relaxed into a dangerously sexy smile. I stood up and sucked on his lips, reminding him exactly why he needed to keep me around.

When Mac headed into the kitchen, I checked my texts. Apparently, Jackson expected me to meet him at the loft at ten. Damn, didn't that man have a wife who kept close tabs on him? Every day, he would find some way to escape his wife's grip in order to have sex with me. But that wasn't even the worst of it. He needed to know my whereabouts every hour of the day. Sure, he paid the bills and kept the cash flowing, but even my momma hadn't expected no every-hour check-in when I was a teenager. When I signed on for this little agreement with Jackson, I never imagined he would keep me on such a short leash.

I texted Jackson back that I'd meet him at the spot at midnight. Hell, it wouldn't go over well that he'd be kept waiting, but he needed to learn this lesson anyway: There's some shit you can't pay for, like a black woman being on time. No matter how much money you got, there is no getting around CP time. Besides, no way was I risking losing Mac over Jackson's non-fuckin', needy ass.

Jackson texted me back that he wasn't happy with my time change, but I didn't care, and I wasn't about to budge. It was already nine, and I'd have to leave within a half hour if I wanted to be there by ten. That wasn't happening. If I tried to eat and run, Mac would surely drop me. Jackson would just have to wait.

"You wanna eat some more?" Mac asked a while later while we sat in the kitchen. He pushed the chicken pasta toward me, and I took another helping.

"Baby, you feed all my appetites." I paid him a true compliment.

"Then you shouldn't be hungry for anything else." He said it with a laugh, but I understood from the look in his eyes that his words held another meaning. If only I could make him understand that he was the only man I truly desired. It wasn't my fault, was it, that a girl had to do what she had to do to support herself?

A couple hours later, I arrived at the loft, tired and desiring to be left alone. Mac hadn't made it easy to leave him after we finished eating, and just dealing with him had sapped me of all my energy. Once we cleared away the plates, he'd taken me right there on the kitchen table, driving every inch in so deep it was like he was trying to take up permanent residence inside me. Afterward, he carried me into the bedroom and laid me down on the bed. I don't need to tell you that he was pretty damn annoyed when I sat up right away and started to get dressed. Since I had already broken my rule about spending the night, I couldn't use that as an excuse. I tried a few other lines, and Mac finally just dropped the issue and let me leave, but I could tell he saw through my flimsy excuses. He knew something was up, and I left that night worried that it might have been our last.

As beautiful as the condo was, I still didn't feel comfortable thinking of this new place as my home. As I placed my key in the lock, the door swung open, and I came face-to-face with Jackson. His expression was sheer annoyance, but the way I felt, he needed to step back and stop smothering me with demands for my time.

"Where you been?" he barked at me, checking me out from head to toe, as if my appearance would give him some clue to his question.

"Out!" I sashayed my hot ass and attitude right past him into the living room. Of course, he stayed close on my heels.

"What you mean, out?" he bellowed. With all that noise, he

should have been glad he owned the building, because if I was a paying tenant, I'da called the cops for him disturbing the peace.

I placed my hands on my hips and stared him straight in the eyes without flinching. He had already worked my last nerve, and I certainly didn't have another one. Did this buffoon really think that all the money in the world would give him ownership over me? I took a breath so I could get my words out all "Cosmo girl" instead of "girl from the hood."

"Jackson, before you met me, I had a life, and I am not the kind of woman who likes to answer to anybody."

"Take a look around you." He had the nerve to do some hand-sweeping motion like I was too dense to get his point.

"Uh-huh," I mumbled, refusing to give this tired-ass Negro any satisfaction.

"You think I provide all this so you can saunter your ass in here anytime you want like you're doing me a favor? This is my world, and I happen to own everything in this world. When I want something, I want it, and I do not appreciate being kept waiting. Not by someone I pay my hard-earned money for."

His words hurt as much as if he had just slapped me in the face. The worst part was that he had only spoken the truth. I was bought and paid for, like a piece of meat from the butcher shop. And I had signed up for this on my own. Now, instead of feeling like a savvy businesswoman who had brokered an important deal, I felt like the thing that Jackson considered me—a common street whore.

He continued his tirade and made these sentiments perfectly clear. "On every street in every borough of New York City, there is a girl like you who uses her pussy to get from men what she wants. I could have plucked any one of a million girls just like you off the streets and been shown some real respect." He either finished or had just paused to catch his breath, but I didn't give him the chance to degrade me any further.

"Then maybe you should go and find you one of them girls just like me off the streets," I challenged.

The shift in his demeanor showed that he was not used to being confronted. I can't say that he exactly started to back-pedal, but he started concentrating real hard on my breasts, which were about to pop out of my top. If there is one thing I learned about breast men, it's that they are always looking for their momma, and if their momma kept them in check in childhood . . . well, you get the point. So, instead of my threat putting Jackson off, he was getting all hard and excited. An ass man or a leg man would have been a lot quieter, less boastful than Jackson, but he would have kicked me to the curb in a second over this.

"I'm not some chump on the corner you can play, Coco," Jackson huffed, but the air had gone out of him as he considered the ramifications of losing me.

I refused to back down. "No one said you were a chump, Jackson. But maybe you need some other bitch who doesn't have a life and won't mind you treating her like your own personal sexual slave, 'cause as far as I'm concerned, slavery is dead."

"Slave? You call pushing a Mercedes, living in an eight-hundred-thousand-dollar apartment, and having unlimited funds, slavery?" he growled. "It's not asking much that I expect you to be here when I call. Shit, any other bitch would be happy to have what you have here."

As I looked around at all that I supposedly had there, I saw only what was missing—Mac. The place could be a palace, and it still wouldn't have what I needed most. Being with Mac these past weeks had changed something in me. My needs weren't just about the almighty dollar anymore. I liked having a man who worried about me, took care of me, and made me laugh, and hell yeah, the sex could not be beat. Standing in the condo with Jackson, I realized why it felt like a prison. My heart wanted to be at home with Mac.

"I thought I could do this, Jackson. I thought if I had enough money, it would make me happy." I paused, which wound up being just enough time for Jackson to add his two cents.

"This is happiness!" he boomed.

"But it's not, Jackson." I couldn't believe the words flying out of my mouth. Ever since I'd had my heart broken, I thought that money equaled happiness, that material things were enough. Now that I had access to more wealth than I'd ever dreamed of, I still felt like I had a hole in me. The only thing that made me feel real and loved was being myself with Mac.

"This is the best life you can ever have, Coco," he said with certainty. "You like money too much to try and settle for less." Powerful men can become spoiled brats when you try to take away their toys, and that's exactly what I had been for Jackson, his new toy.

"I don't want it anymore," I heard myself say the words out loud.

"You think just because you had a moment of conscience I'm gonna just let you walk away from me?" He looked ready to strike me.

"I'm in love with someone else." The words had never been clearer or more true. Instead of stepping aside, Jackson laughed in a mean, vindictive way.

"Love? The only thing you love is fucking and money. What, you think I haven't seen this before? Some woman like you who suddenly thinks she can just be in love and do without all the perks. Coco, let me tell you something about real, everyday love. It gets boring and staid. You are not a woman who ever needs to be bored. So, in a few months, if that, you'll realize that this deal is the sweetest thing you ever had going. But when you run back, I may have changed my mind."

"I won't change my mind," I protested.

He laughed at me again. "Oh yes, you will, because even if you never hung out a shingle, Coco, you're what we call a professional."

Funny, but this time, him comparing me to a prostitute didn't wound me in the slightest. Now that I'd admitted to myself that I was in love with Mac and knowing that Mac loved me made me aware of just how stupid I had been. Why had I risked something so amazing for this short, arrogant man who thought he owned me?

"Then I guess what I'm try'na tell you is I'm hanging up my shingle. Business is closed."

I turned to leave, but Jackson grabbed my arm and spun me around.

"Bitch, mark my words when I say this. You will be back, so you might as well get your ass in that bedroom, put on one of those crotchless panty outfits I bought you, and come back ready to service me." He sat down on the couch as if he actually expected me to hurry my ass into the bedroom and obey his orders. Instead, I walked into the bedroom and came back with a huge load of clothes.

"I am going to get all my stuff out of here, and if you try to stop me, I will call your wife and tell her everything. And I mean every single thing, from the beginning, when you tried to screw me on her bed and made me watch the two of you fuck. I'm sure she'd have no problem getting her half after all those years of marriage."

All the air got sucked out of him momentarily at the mention of his wife. But he didn't take long to regain his composure and tell me, "Sure. Get your things. But the car stays and so do the bank and credit cards. Oh, and you might want to leave a few things to wear for me when you come back."

I stood there for a moment, full of pride now that I had homelessness to contend with. There was only one place I wanted to be.

"Can I come in?" I stood in Mac's doorway as he blocked my entrance.

"I didn't expect you to come back." He wasn't budging.

"Do you want me to go or do you want me to stay?" My entire body shook in fear that I had pushed him too far by leaving earlier that night.

"I'm sick of this, Coco. Either you are mine and only mine, or you got to go."

I had just rejected Jackson for his efforts to own me, and here was Mac, telling me basically the same thing—he wanted me all to himself. But I'd never wanted a man more than I did at this moment. They say that love can make you desperate, and now I finally knew what that meant because I had become desperate for Mac to love me. I put my hand in his.

"I want you to be my man, Mac. I want you and only you." I leaned in and kissed his lips.

"You serious?" His killer smiled returned.

"As a heart attack. I'm all yours."

He lifted me up off the floor and swung me around.

"Uh, honey . . ." I had more news to break to him.

"Yeah?" He kissed me on the neck, breathing in my scent, which, since I hadn't had time to shower, had to be all him.

"I have a few things in the car."

As he stepped back to let me enter, he said the words I had always wanted him to say. "Welcome home, Coco."

42

Isis

I awoke to someone banging on and shaking my door like they planned to knock it off its hinges. At first I thought it was a bad dream. You know, the ones where you are naked in a crowd and a bunch of people are shouting and laughing at you. I'd been having a lot of those lately, except in my dream, the people laughing were Tony and his wife, and Egypt and Rashad. I still hadn't quite figured out how a week ago I had been headed to the altar, and today I could barely sleep all the way through the night without waking up from shitty nightmares.

Slowly it dawned on me that the noise had nothing to do with my subconscious and was very real. I got out of bed, suddenly pissed. I had listened to all that antigun rhetoric from the local politicians and opted not to buy me a good piece to protect myself. Anybody banging on my door at 2:00 A.M. deserved to have his or her ass shot to pieces. Passing a mirror on the way to the door, I did a double-take at the high scarf tied around my head a la Aunt Jemima. Wrapping my hair every night spoke volumes about my new single status.

I picked up the Louisiana slugger I kept by the door and raised it, ready to do damage. I put some bass in my voice, just in case it was some rapist stalking single women. "Who is it?"

"Isis, open this door." It was Tony. I couldn't believe he had the nerve to show up at my doorstep like I was gonna let him in. What he needed to do was take his ass home to those four liabilities and their stupid-ass momma.

"Get the hell away from my door before I call the cops," I threatened.

"Open the door!" he shouted.

"Tony, go home! I am not letting you in."

"I'm not leaving until we talk."

"Dammit, Tony, you're gonna wake the whole neighborhood." Then my curiosity got the better of me and I asked, "What do you want?" After all, he couldn't be showing up at this time of night to have a "how you doing?" conversation.

"We got to get some things straight." His voice sounded strained, like he was working hard to keep all the emotion out of it.

Even though I didn't want his lying ass in my house, I still had a few things I needed to say to him. "Give me a minute," I yelled before running into the bathroom to get my look together. I don't care how bad I felt; I wasn't about to let no lying, cheating loser see me with halitosis and a head scarf like I fell apart without his ass. Fuck him and his whole family if he thought he was going to see me looking like his dick was the only thing standing between me and sanity.

Opening the front door, I had no idea what to expect from Tony, but it sure wasn't the flashing rage in his eyes. He slammed the door behind him with such force that I backed all the way up, one eye on him, the other searching for my baseball bat.

"Bitch, have you fuckin' lost your mind?" he started.

Bitch? Tony had never even raised his voice to me, let alone called me names. I shook my head, knocking the last of the sleep out of my head, making sure I was wide awake.

"What the fuck?" I started to go off on his married ass.

"Shut the hell up and listen to me," he commanded, the veins in his neck bulging. He started moving toward me, backing me up as if to make a point.

"Don't you—" I began, but he raised his hand toward me, and my mouth went dry.

"Who the fuck do you think you are talking to my wife? Have you lost your fuckin' mind? My wife?" He was enraged. I had never been scared of Tony before, but now he had me worried.

"You don't know a goddamn thing about my wife. What makes you think it's okay for you to corner her in a grocery store and threaten her? You think your pussy is so good that you can go near my family? If you were a man, your ass would be dead right now." He was so close, I could feel his spit on my face.

For a brief moment, I felt ashamed for how I had acted in the grocery store. Then I remembered that I wasn't the one in the wrong. He should have been thinking about protecting his wife all those times his lying ass had led me to believe he planned to marry me. Thinking of Vegas, his wife, and all those times I had let him enter me when I was nothing more than a piece of ass fueled my anger until it matched his. Instead of backing away, I moved toward him, ready to do battle with the man who had broken all my dreams.

"You lying, cheating asshole," I started, jabbing a finger in his chest. "You think I give a shit about your wife? She needs to know what a dirty dog she's married to so she can put you on a shorter leash. Why should I give a damn about your wife? I thought I'd have that job."

"Have you lost your natural born mind?" he shot back. "Coming between a man and his family? This just shows how little you know about real life."

"I'll tell you what I do know—it's the last time I let some married man fuck me."

"How would you know? You got so many damn rules it's hard for a man to get close to your ass. That's not how a real marriage works. It's not some shit you read in one of your damn book club books."

I was not about to let this man sit here and insult me. It wasn't like I asked him to bring his ass to my house in the middle of the night. "Get out of my house and don't ever bring your married ass back," I hissed.

At first he narrowed his eyes and stared at me; then he took a step closer. "You just don't fuckin' get it, Isis."

"Get what? That you're a dog who just wanted to piss all over my life, mark your territory, then go back to your real life?"

"It wasn't like that." He took another step toward me. His tone had softened a little, but it was too late for him to get humble now.

"Fuck you, Tony," I spat. "Go home to your family."

"You think this shit is easy? I'm married, and you can't fuck with a man's family." By now, he had me almost pressed against the wall. If he thought I would let him make some damn excuse for his shit, he didn't know me at all.

"Go fuck your goddamn skinny-ass wife." The words snapped out of my mouth. He gave me a look like he'd beat my ass if he thought he could get away with it.

"Don't talk about my wife." His words of protection for the woman he chose over me drove me over the edge. My hand left my side, and before I could stop myself, I had slapped him across his face. The red mark swelled on his skin.

The silence that followed scared me more than if he had made some noise. In that instant, he reached up and whacked me on my cheek. The sound and the force of his hand made me gasp in shock. I raised my right arm to hit him back, but he caught my hand in his, holding it easily. Taking my other hand, he pushed my arms behind me onto the wall and held me captive. I squirmed to get free.

"Get off of me!" I yelled, wriggling in his grasp. Stubbornness made me ignore the obvious fact that I didn't come close to matching Tony. He pressed his body close to mine, still clutching my arms in his hands. Boiling with rage, I fought, except now, fighting only pressed me closer to him. I could feel my vagina starting to drip in anticipation. The fighting, coupled with our close proximity, made my juices flow into my panties, wetting them. Confusion swept through my body. I hated this man. My plans were to destroy him, not to allow him entrance into my pussy. I stopped squirming under him.

"Look at me." His voice came out as a bark, but I ignored him, instead staring at my baseball bat leaning against the couch. He bent closer, whispering into my ear. "Isis, I'm sorry. I've never hit a woman in my life."

Those words forced me to face him. "Yeah, lying to women is more your speed," I hissed.

"Look at me."

And this time I did. His body pressed even closer, sucking all the air out from between us.

"You . . . you have to go," I stuttered, confusion giving me away.

"Why?" His voice got all throaty and sexy. Fuck, what was going on with me? Could the weeks without sex have driven me to lose my good sense? Instead of fighting, I found myself staring into his eyes, as if all the heat of the moment had made me help-less.

Girl, snap out of it, I warned myself. *This man is married.* But even knowing everything I knew about Tony, my body wanted to betray me. There was breakup sex and there was makeup sex, but this was neither, so I had no idea what to do.

"Get out of my house, Tony," I yelled in his ear.

"You really want me to go?" he questioned, his voice drop-ping down into a sexier octave.

"Yes." I tried my damnedest to sound convincing.

He challenged me, "No, you don't."

"Go."

"You mean that?" He pushed his pelvis close to my groin, and before I could stop it, a murmur of pleasure escaped from my mouth.

"Go home to your wife, Tony."

"I don't want to go home to her. I want to be with you." As proof, he pressed his rock-hard dick against my thigh. Damn, had he always been that big?

"Stop." I tried to fight him, but the combination of his hot breath on my neck and his hard penis rendered me powerless. It felt like this man had whipped some kryptonite on my ass.

One more time wouldn't be the end of the world, I tried to reason with myself.

"Tell me you want me to stay and make love to you," he de-manded.

"No," I whined.

"SAY IT," he said firmly, and everything in me melted. I wanted to fuck this man. He knew it and I knew it.

"I . . ." My voice failed. His lips lightly touched the tip of my ear. An electric current shot through my body, releasing any residual fantasy that I could walk away or force him to leave. My pussy sent smoke signals to his penis, and there was no way he would release me from his grip.

"I want you to stay."

"Stay and do what?" he asked.

"And make love to me, Tony. I want you to make love to me," I begged, feeling the juice trickle down my legs. I couldn't remember ever being this turned on by Tony, but tonight, right now, I had to fuck him. I wouldn't allow myself to think about the consequences, about whether this meant we were a couple, whether he was leaving his wife. I only knew that in this moment, everything I wanted or needed was right here pressed against me. I melted into his arms and gave myself to him completely.

43

Nikki

Ever since the incident at the office with Tiny, Keith had become very protective of me. I'd described Tiny's temper to him, but now that he had seen it for himself, he was convinced that it was only a matter of time before she tried to hurt me again. I told him that after all the shit I'd been through, I wasn't fragile. I could handle it. But he said I couldn't stop him from worrying.

If Keith turned out to be right and she did put her hands on me again, Tiny and I were through. Especially after I'd heard her telling Keith that she made me. It took everything in me not to tell her that she should call my mother, and then she'd really find out who made me. But that would mean admitting that I'd heard the whole conversation between her and Keith, and it would only set her off. So, I stayed in our apartment and avoided fighting with her, hoping that somehow she'd change and stop treating me like something she owned. I was trying to give her one last shot. I didn't want to leave her unless I had no other choice. Of course, I was still meeting Keith in the boss's office every chance I got, and he was riding the subway with me every night to make sure I got home safely. He claimed it was because he was worried Tiny might hurt me, but I think it had just as much to do with wanting to spend time with me. Not that I minded, of course, because I loved every minute I got to be with him.

"I'm gonna get off with you," Keith told me one night as we reached my stop. He had to exit the station to cross over to the other side to go back downtown. He took my hand as we climbed the steps.

"I got you." He caught my arm when I nearly slipped on the wet step.

"I almost went down like a ton of bricks." I held on to him tighter.

"Told you, I ain't gonna let nothing bad happen to you," he cheesed. We both busted out laughing as we emerged from the subway, but when we turned the corner, I froze. There stood Tiny, looking madder than I'd ever seen her.

She stepped up to me, her voice booming. "What the hell this punk-ass buster doing here?" she scoffed at Keith, her stance getting more aggressive. I shifted, putting myself between them.

"Making sure you don't do something stupid," Keith said to Tiny.

"And what you gonna do? I know a pussy when I see one."

Keith was shuffling around behind me, and I could hear his breathing getting faster. In front of me, Tiny had her hands balled into fists, and she looked ready to pounce. That's when I knew I had to stop this before it got worse.

"Tiny, calm down. Keith just made sure I got home safe." I hoped that my words would end things, but talk about being all the way wrong. Tiny turned to me with such rage, I took a step back.

"You try'na protect this motherfucker? I'm your woman!" She went into pure anger mode, and I knew I was past the point of calming her down. Instead of feeling that twinge of fear, I got angry my damn self.

"Stop it, Tiny. I'm tired of this!" I shouted, not caring anymore that we were standing on a street corner acting hella ghetto.

"Stop what? Stop expecting my woman to put me first and not have some thug-ass pussy-hound sweating her?" she raged.

"You better watch yourself." Keith pointed a finger at Tiny, and I leaned back against him to try to keep him from advancing on Tiny. But it didn't matter because Tiny was just as determined to get to him. These two were itching to start hitting.

"Or what?" Tiny smashed herself against me, straining to get close enough to him to do real damage.

I took a deep breath and pushed her back. "What are you doing? You think reminding me how Dwayne used to act is gonna make me want to stay and put up with this?" I had finally reached my own breaking point.

"You comparing me with that other thug-ass punk? That your thing, Nikki? You want to be with some fake macho asshole like this Negro?" She flicked her fingers at Keith.

"It's not about Keith or Dwayne." And then I admitted what I knew. "Tiny, I heard you last week in my office when you told Keith that you made me. That I wasn't shit without you." I no longer cared about keeping the peace between us anymore.

Instead of looking even remotely embarrassed that she was busted, Tiny actually smirked at me. "So what? You want DJ to be homeless again? To live in some shelter while you get your shit together just 'cause you think you need some dick?"

She had hit me so far below the belt that my body started shaking in anger and fear. How could this person who claimed to love me be trying to use my son against me? But instead of bending to her will like I had done so many times in the past, I stood up to her. I reminded her in a deadly calm voice, "I'm not going to be homeless ever again. I'm the one who got Section eight housing. That apartment is in my name, Tiny."

She laughed. "Oh, but I'm the one paying the rent every month. Bitch, please. You think this fucking broke-ass buster gonna move in and pay your rent?"

Keith refused to take her bait this time. He leaned against a pole, letting me handle my business, but he stayed close enough in case something jumped off.

"You need me, Nikki," Tiny bragged, and for a moment, I allowed self-doubt to creep into my mind. Could I finally take care of both myself and DJ without another person as a crutch? There was no way I could be sure, but one thing I did know was that I was through being treated like this. Whether I was ready or not, I would just have to find a way to make it work without her.

"I did need you, Tiny. You saved me once, but I'm not that scared, insecure person anymore. Seems the only way you can be happy is if I stay that person I was when you met me." When the words came out, I realized it wasn't just that I didn't love Tiny anymore; I was straining to be this new person, and it threatened her too much.

Keith didn't even try to stifle his laughter. "You tell her, Nikki. You ain't need no help from her big dyke ass."

Tiny turned to him. "You think this shit is funny?"

"What I think is Nikki just broke up with you. So, bye-bye." Keith dismissed her with a wave of his hand.

"You don't know shit. Nikki, let's go home and talk about this." Tiny was trying to appear calm, but I knew that underneath, she was seething.

"Step the fuck off," Keith said, then teased, "What, you deaf? She said she don't want you no more."

"Bitch, I will kick your ass, you keep fucking with me." She took a step closer to him. "Since you too stupid to know not to get in between a couple when they handling their shit . . ." She continued moving closer, ignoring me as I begged her to back off.

Keith continued to taunt her. "It's done. Over. You the one don't know when the fuck to leave."

Tiny reached back and punched Keith, and he crumpled like a paper doll onto the pavement. She pushed past me and kicked him as he struggled to get up.

I jumped on top of Tiny and started scratching her, fighting to keep her away from Keith. Tiny spun me around, her strength turned superhuman as she flicked me off of her too easily. People gathered on the sidewalk, shouting and cheering like they had paid an entrance fee to watch us spar.

"Bitch!" Keith got up and dived into Tiny, who reared back and socked him in the side of his head. He stumbled back, holding his head and screaming out in pain. Seeing Keith in pain, I wanted to kill Tiny. I kicked my leg out, aiming at her stomach, but she moved in time, and my foot came down with a thud. She started moving toward Keith again, and I dived onto her, my arms flailing with blows. But Tiny had always been a fighter, and nothing I threw at her penetrated. I sank my teeth into the flesh of her arm, drawing blood. The crowd screamed out in approval.

Tiny held her arm, staring at me in shock. We were like wolves, circling each other. Neither of us made a move, too surprised by this turn of events to take a step and break the spell.

"Yeow!!!" Keith karate-kicked Tiny in the chin, bringing us out of our stunned state. She dived after Keith and commenced to kicking the shit out of him until he lay crumpled in a ball at her feet.

"You want some more, you pussy?" Tiny screamed at him.

I raced to his side, cradling his head in my lap. "You bully!" I shook my finger at Tiny.

She stood over us and gloated about her victory. "This the punk you expect to protect you? This what you want? Fuck you and him."

"Just go, Tiny," I said, stroking Keith's face.

"Fuck you, Nikki. This what you want? 'Cause I'm through with your ungrateful ass," she yelled at me.

"Get away from us!"

"Bitch, I hope you are happy with this asshole, 'cause I am more man than he'll ever be. I deserve a real woman and not some confused, fucked-up slut like you." Spit sprayed from her mouth as she ranted. Everything about her was ugly to me now.

I helped Keith up to his feet. "Tiny, I'm gonna be gone for a few hours, and when I get back to *my apartment,* I want you and all your shit gone."

She looked momentarily shocked by my words, like somehow she expected her victory to make me run back into her arms. But she toughened up again real quick. "No problem," she said, giving me a look filled with disgust. "And good luck with this loser. Hope he can support your trifling ass." She broke through the crowd and stomped her way back toward my place. The spectators, realizing the main event had ended, began to disperse back to their own lives.

"Is that what you want?" Keith asked, taking my hand in his.

"Yeah, I want her to leave." I stared into his battered face.

"No, I mean, do you want me to get my stuff and move in with you? I can take care of you and DJ, and I promise, Nikki, I won't ever put my hands on you." He brushed his lips on mine.

The damnedest thing happened at that moment. Instead of feeling relief that Keith wanted to rescue me and DJ, I knew I couldn't accept his offer. I had to do things differently this time unless I wanted to wind up here again. I had to make it on my own.

"Keith, that's sweet. I feel so grateful you're in my life, and I do want to see where this is going. But I need to move slowly. I have a child, and I can't keep bringing people into his life and making him believe that I'm not capable of standing on my own two feet," I explained.

"I know you can take care of yourself, but I just want to do it." Keith reached out and hugged me.

"Yeah, and a part of me wants to play that damsel in distress, but I need to be a grown-ass woman and take care of myself. I need to know that I can do it. I need that for myself, not for anybody else. I don't want to be one of those women who every few years is living with someone else 'cause I can't do the heavy lifting in my own life. My momma did that, and that's where I learned to depend on other people, but I can't anymore."

I finally realized the most important thing I needed to do to change my life. I needed to stand on my own two feet for a while, and if that meant Keith would walk away, then I'd really have to learn to be alone.

But when he spoke, his words were reassuring. "Well, I'm not gonna push you, but I want to be here if you'll let me."

"I like our friendship," I began, then smiled as I assured him, "and I am not giving up the sex. I want to see where it's going . . . but slowly."

I guess this is what people mean by setting their boundaries. Funny that at thirty-four, I was finally learning how to do that and to take care of myself.

"How slow?" Keith placed a firm hand on my ass.

"Not too damn slow," I said with a laugh, hugging him. For once, in spite of all the drama that just occurred, I felt proud of myself.

44

Coco

I hated the fact that Mac was paying all the bills. Sure, for most of my adult life I'd had men who acted as "sponsors," paying some of my bills—oh hell, paying almost all of my bills. But the difference was that I made sure to spread it around so that no one man ever believed his wallet had any power over me. I never had to answer to any of them. But now that I was living with Mac, I had cut off everyone else, and my situation didn't feel all that different from the deal I had worked out with Jackson. I'd never wanted to think of myself as the kind of woman who had nothing of her own. The kind who had to ask her man for money to buy her damn Kotex, but that's where I was now. The only real difference between this and what I had for a while with Jackson was that I loved Mac. I wasn't sure I was cut out for this, especially since the little bit of Jackson's money that I'd managed to stash was quickly dwindling. It sure wasn't going to buy me the eight-hundred-dollar outfit I was trying on in a store that used to be a regular stop during my shopping sprees.

"Damn, your body is banging," I told myself as I modeled the tight-fitting pantsuit in the dressing room. It wasn't that I couldn't afford it. It's just that with nothing coming in, I had to stop myself from indulging in a favorite pastime. Even before I had Jackson spending all his money on me, I would have bought myself the outfit to wear out at night, because it was the kind of thing that paid for itself. Men tend to get generous when you look like you don't need it. You go to a bar tore up from the floor up and all you gonna attract are broke-ass busters. Put on a little something that costs and have your weave tight, and the high rollers will spend the whole night trying to get with you.

"I have a good man who loves me," I kept telling myself as I left that store empty-handed. I knew I could get a job, but working a nine-to-five took too much time out of my day. Besides, I would never find a job that paid me half of what I needed to keep living the way I was used to. I temped at different places when I had to, but I was more the sleep-in type. Luckily, Mac liked it that way. He'd get in late from the poetry spot or auditioning, and we'd stay up all night long. I wouldn't be able to do that if I had a job.

I was amazed that I liked spending so much time with one man. Mac was the first man in years who I even wanted to go home to at night. Funny how quickly I got used to sleeping with him, and I even dug the domestic stuff. I never understood how my cousin Tammy seemed so smug all the time over one man, but now that I was with Mac, I got it.

My phone rang as I exited the store empty-handed. Thinking it was Mac, I didn't even look at the number before answering.

"Hello?"

"Hey." I didn't recognize the voice on the other end of the phone.

"Yes?" I used the serious tone I reserved for people wasting my time on the telephone, although even that seemed to be happening less now. In the last month, my phone went from buzzing and texts twenty-four/seven to barely ringing unless it was Mac or one of the girls.

"Damn, baby, I know it's been a while, but I didn't know it was like that." The brother on the other end laughed, keeping it light.

"Like what?" I joined him, feeling playful.

"Like I better not be calling for no bullshit."

"Are you?" Homeboy still hadn't gotten to the point.

"It's David from the gym." He sounded almost embarrassed that I didn't recognize his voice sooner.

"I didn't expect to hear from you again." I laughed because the last time I saw him, his skinny-ass girlfriend and her friend were about to bust him in the hotel room.

"Let's just say it took a minute to get over being used," he joked.

"Yeah, well, we kind of used each other if I'm not mistaken." I threw it out, feeling flirty all of a sudden.

"Let me commend you on your skills, though, 'cause even after I took the heat from my girl, I couldn't stop thinking about you. Granted, it's not every day you catch your man freshly laid in a hotel room, so it did take me a minute to get back to the deliciousness of the experience I had with you," he finished.

"So, you calling to see if you can get a little more of Coco?" I tried to tell these men that one time ain't enough.

"No, I'm calling 'cause I *need* more Coco. I can't stop thinking about you." His voice got all deep and sultry.

"I'm kind of off the market." A few months ago, you couldn't have paid me to believe that I'd ever say those words.

"What can I do to get you back on the market?" he offered, and I started thinking about that outfit I just tried on. I would look amazing in that pantsuit, especially the way the fabric made my ass look and the cut of the jacket in the front. It was too tempting.

"I am a little low on cash," I told him with no shame. He already knew that ain't shit from me free.

"I happen to have fifteen hundred dollars in my pocket."

"That could be the magic number," I joked, and I felt myself getting wet. The sensation was all too familiar. What was it about the combination of money and men that got my juices flowing?

"How about we meet at the Hilton by the airport?" he suggested.

"In an hour," I insisted, because Mac would be home by ten, and I wanted to be back and showered before he walked in the door.

"Damn, you look good," David complimented me when I met him at the restaurant in the hotel. He took my hand and led me over to a table in the corner, all the while staring at me like I was some goddess. I had forgotten how empowering it was to know I had this effect on men.

David's tongue all but fell out of his mouth when I removed my jacket to reveal the tightest tank with an extra-deep V for cleavage. The waiter who took my order was so busy checking out my goods that I had to tell him twice what I was drinking. Yeah, I liked the way men responded to me.

"So, what made you call me today?" I purred.

"I wanted to see you sooner, but I figured you were pissed off. I knew my girl and her friend were always giving you a tough time, but, man, you give the term, 'payback is a bitch' a whole new meaning."

"I just gave her what she deserved," I said with a smirk. If he thought I was going to apologize for messing with his relationship, he was way off base. "She didn't think you could be attracted to a full-figured girl like me." Just the memory of those skinny bitches made me want to fuck David again.

"So, you didn't want me?" He winced, and I could tell I'd bruised his ego.

"Yeah, I wanted you, but I also saw an opportunity to kill two birds with one stone, as they say." I picked up the cherry from my drink and sucked it between my lips for emphasis.

"You think we can do it again without the drama?" He grabbed my hand a little too eagerly for my taste, but then I remembered how much money he told me he was carrying. Suddenly I was calculating how long it would take me to get him off. If it was fast enough, I could still make it back to the store and buy that pantsuit before they closed.

"And you want to give me fifteen hundred reasons to do it again?" I pushed out my chest to keep his eyes on the prize.

"Of course. What I'd really like is to be naked on top of you." He pushed my hand down onto his muscular thigh. Once upon a time, I would have been impressed, but now I had to let go of images of Mac, who made David look like a puny wimp. Mac had the kind of body only a few men were fortunate to possess. That actor Djimon Hounsu, who did those underwear ads, his body was almost as sexy as Mac's.

As I agreed to David's offer, I had to keep forcing thoughts of Mac from my mind. After all, sex and love were two different things. I sure as hell didn't love David. This little rendezvous was just a means to an end, so I wouldn't have to be quite so dependent on Mac. Hell, if anything, this might help my relationship with Mac, I reasoned. Without my own money, I might end up resenting Mac for having too much control over me, and then I'd leave him. This way, I'd have a little something for myself, and

Mac and I could live happily ever after. At least that's what I kept telling myself as I allowed David to guide me to the elevator with his hands all over my ass.

"I can't wait to get you in bed." David pressed against me in the elevator. I kept thinking of the money he promised to give me and the beautiful things I could buy. Mac would love me in that suit. Dammit, I cursed myself for thinking of Mac yet again. Couldn't I keep my mind on the moment? I never had this problem before.

I slipped into the bathroom to freshen up—or at least that's what I told homeboy. Really, I just needed a moment to myself. I took off my top, letting my breasts spill out like wild children. My twins liked some freedom. Mac had told me he imagined my breasts all day long and couldn't wait to get home to them every night.

"Stop it!" I spoke to my reflection in the mirror. This was not going to work if I couldn't stop thinking about Mac. I had a sexy, horny man in the next room with a pocketful of cash and the desire for only me, and here I couldn't concentrate on anything other than Mac. I didn't want to turn into one of those women so in love that they never look out for their own interests. Or the ones whose only interests are the men they love.

Still trying to get into the right mood, I took off my short skirt only to catch sight of the belly chain Mac bought for me. He said he liked the look of jewelry against my skin. I couldn't fuck another man wearing the belly chain, so I took it off. David had probably stripped down to his birthday suit, ready to service me. I started to open the door, but I couldn't do it.

This had never happened to me. My whole life, I fucked who I wanted whenever I wanted and never gave a second thought to anybody's feelings. But this thing with Mac was different. I had told Mac every single thing about myself, and still he wanted to love me. None of the men I had slept with in the past mattered to him, and I didn't want to betray his trust. If I slept with David, it would hurt Mac, and therefore would hurt me. I dressed.

"Hey, where you going?" A bare-naked David sat up in the bed as I grabbed my purse off the dresser. I thought of taking the fifteen hundred in cash lying next to my stuff, but for once in my life, I knew the money wouldn't be worth the drama that would follow behind it. I paused at the door, looking at David, who had lied, not once but twice, to the woman he professed to love to be with me. I didn't want to turn into someone like him.

"I'm going home to my man." As I slammed the door, my head held high, I had never felt better about myself or happier about being in love.

45

Tammy

Even though I wanted to stay home—well, at my temporary place in my mother's house—my mother insisted I go out to the book club meeting with her. I think she got tired of me moping around like my life was over, but as far as I knew, it was. I had never seen Tim so angry, but then again, in ten years of marriage, I had always been a faithful wife. If the stories on *Oprah* and in *Essence* magazine about marriage were true, then we had a better relationship than most. It hadn't dawned on me while I was doing it, but now it hurt to know that the suggestion of a threesome and my affair were the main reasons our perfect life had come apart at the seams. I'd messed up my marriage and wasn't too sure it could be repaired, and when I called Raoul to get some comfort, I learned that he was also in some pretty hot water. Tim had fired him the minute he walked into the office the day after he busted me. Now Raoul was busy trying to keep his wife from learning why he lost his cushy six-figure job. Raoul and I were no good to each other at this point.

I entered the BGBC meeting at Coco's new place with my mother, hoping to put on a brave face and get the hell outta there before any of my personal business spilled out into the street. I wasn't too sure if that was possible with my mother pestering me every fifteen minutes about why I wasn't living in my house with my husband and kids. So far, I'd been able to keep her at bay with a couple of white lies, but she knew there was more to the story than I was letting on. I was afraid that she might have recruited my cousin Coco to try to force the truth out of me while we were at the meeting.

I heard Coco's big-ass mouth before she even opened the door. Nikki and she were, believe it or not, talking about somebody's great dick. I knew it couldn't have been Nikki's, since she was a straight-up lesbo, and Tiny didn't have a penis from what I could tell. I hoped they weren't gonna talk about that nonsense once I got in there, because the last thing I wanted to hear about was sex when my entire life had gone to hell because of it.

"This is nice, Coco, but what happened to your old place?" Momma asked.

"To be honest with you, I've been through a few places since I've seen you last, Auntie."

"You shoulda seen the last place she lived in, Mrs. Turner. It put this place to shame," Nikki added.

"So why'd you move? The rent too high?"

"You not gonna believe this, but Coco got a new man, and this is his place," Nikki said.

"Our place," Coco hollered, giving Nikki a high five.

That's when I noticed Coco had been arranging some shrimp cocktails and crab legs in a crystal bowl. She must have seen me watching, and she chose to rub it in my face that she could afford to serve some expensive seafood at her book club meeting.

"I hope you're hungry, Tammy, 'cause I got plenty of food," Coco bragged. She turned toward me and displayed her huge knockers, which were threatening to fling themselves out of her tight top. This ho always had to have her shit on blast, like somebody would mistake her for a man if she didn't shove her oversized watermelon breasts in someone's face.

Seeing her so domestic and happy pissed me off. After all, the only thing Coco was good for was lying on her back. I didn't need to see her all pleased with herself when my life was turning to shit.

"What you mean, she's got a man?" I joked. "Don't you mean she's sharing somebody else's man?"

Coco didn't even seem pressed that I had called her out for her man-stealing history. "Nope. This one is all mine. And I ain't about to share him with nobody," she added with a laugh. "So you can look, but don't even think of touching." She popped a shrimp in her mouth.

"Hello, hello!" Egypt hollered out on her way into the kitchen.

"We're in here," Coco yelled back.

"Why we always got to be in the kitchen? Hell, you put a

black woman's bed in the kitchen and she'd never need to leave," Egypt said, and everyone else laughed right along with her. She barely looked at me, but the satisfied look on her face was enough to make me want to knock her out. Why the hell was everyone around me so damn happy when my perfect life was in shambles?

"On another note . . ." Egypt began fanning herself. "Coco, who the hell is that fine-ass man who answered the door?"

Coco went to bragging again. "Oh, that's Mac. Isn't he cute?"

"*Cute* ain't the word," Egypt gushed. "A sister could fall in love with a man like that."

Coco winked at her.

"Girl, please. Now, you know Coco ain't in love," I chimed in. "Coco just found her a new meal ticket, that's all. Love ain't nothin' but dollar signs to her. Ain't that right, Coco?" I sat back in my chair, satisfied that I had burst her bubble.

"Tammy, I can't even be mad at you, 'cause once upon a time, you woulda been right. Before Mac, I was just wasting time waiting for him to come along," Coco shot back.

"Y'all bitches better not have started without me." Tiny's gruff voice sounded as she came toward the kitchen. She darted right over to Nikki, who didn't look too happy to see her. As a matter of fact, she walked away from Tiny. *Finally,* I thought as I watched the expression on Nikki's face, *someone as unhappy as I was.*

I watched my momma pop a shrimp into her mouth. "Mmm, these shrimps are . . . How y'all young people say it? Off the chain."

"Thank you, Auntie. I have baby lamb chops and some baby backs ribs heating up in the oven. I'll put it out and y'all can help yourselves." Coco had morphed into the perfect hostess, and it pissed me off. I can remember a time when she didn't even wanna host meetings on her turn because it was too much trouble.

"Go on, girl. This is some Tammy shit you got going on over here," Egypt raved. I wasn't sure if she was taking a personal shot at me or just speaking her mind, but either way, the comparison had me fuming. Who did Coco think she was, trying to outdo my parties?

"Sorry, baby, but I have to agree," my mother added. "These crab legs and shrimp beat anything I ever ate at your place."

I tried to contain my rage as I said, "Is that right? Well, I guess I'm gonna have to step up my game. So, next month when I host, it's on." I didn't necessarily want to have the heifers up in my house—if I was even back home by then—but I couldn't just let Coco steal my crown like this.

Coco laid out the food, and we made our plates, then headed into the living room. That's when the finest piece of dark chocolate on the planet came striding out of the bedroom, all six feet something, smooth like butter, with the body of one of those Greek statues.

"Hey, baby," he said to Coco. "I'll see you later."

He gave her a kiss, then Coco made the introductions. That man was so damn fine that I swear even Tiny, who ain't never going near a dick, did a double take. He had one of those voices that make you wanna drop your drawers, and you could tell he had some education because he spoke so well. I had only one question: What the hell was his fine ass doing with nasty Coco?

"Honey, you want me to make you something to eat before you leave?" she purred. Honey? Oh my God, I was gonna be sick.

"Nah, I'll grab something when I come home. I'm sure you ladies can't eat all this food." He smiled, and I'm ashamed to admit that I felt a tingle between my legs.

"Oh yes, we can," my momma joked as she sucked the meat off a rib bone.

"On that note, why don't you make me a plate and put it in the fridge?" He gave Coco one of those wet, juicy kisses that meant they would be having hot sex when they got together later. Back in the day, Tim used to give me kisses like that, and I'd stay wet all day until I saw him again. Coco's little domestic scene in the kitchen had pissed me off, but knowing she was getting laid by this perfect specimen sent my jealousy level through the roof.

"Good night, ladies. Nice to have met you all." Mac's smoky voice sounded damn tasty as he headed out the door. All eyes followed his tight ass as it left. By the time we turned back to Coco, she was beaming with a smile from cheek to cheek.

"Oh, hell no. That's all yours?" my momma blurted out. "Girl, niece or not, if I was twenty years younger, you'd just have to be mad at me, 'cause I'd give you a run for your money with him. That's one fine piece right there."

"Well, you'd just have to bring it, 'cause I'm willing to fight for that man." Coco laughed, but we could tell she was dead serious. Everyone else laughed with her. I fought the urge to tell her it would serve her right if someone stole Mac away, considering how many other people's men she'd fucked over the years.

After we got all the particulars on Mac—divorced, in entertainment, and owned the condo we were in—I was ready to scream. I could see that everyone was starting to view Coco differently, like snagging this man made her more worthy of our respect. Hell, she had scored past any of our expectations. I thought Coco would wind up a hooker or a stripper or something, not living with a man who was so obviously a catch. The news did nothing to help my mood. Not with my situation.

"Can we get on with the meeting?" I snapped.

"We got to wait for Isis," Nikki reminded us.

"Fuck Isis!" her own sister yelled out. "If she was coming, she would have been here by now. What she needs to do is grow the fuck up," Egypt finished.

"Now, come on, Egypt. It's not like you can blame her," I said. Even though I'd learned she wasn't having an affair with my husband, I was still pissed at Egypt. She was too damn happy for my taste, and with her sister's ex, no less!

"Tammy, you need to mind your business," Egypt shot back.

I lifted my hand like I wasn't gonna say another word.

"Wow, this book club got more drama than the book we read this month," my momma snipped, then turned to Nikki. "And I don't even wanna know what's going on between you two," she said, gesturing in Tiny's direction.

"Trust me, you sure don't," Nikki agreed, rolling her eyes at Tiny. "Some things just shouldn't be said." As long as they'd been together, it had been lovey-dovey and all that, but today it seemed like they were close to blows. And the way Nikki was looking at Tiny, she was prepared to give as good as she got. I didn't know what was going on, but it was obviously serious.

Apparently, Tiny couldn't hold back any longer, and our book club meeting turned into the ghetto version of *As the World Turns*. She jumped up out of her seat and yelled at Nikki, "I helped you support DJ, took care of you like you the damn queen of Sheba, and you wanna act like this is my fault? I'm not the one fucking some young-ass gangbanger." She clenched her fist and raised it like she was about to punch Nikki. "You know what? I should whip your—" Suddenly she looked around at all of us sitting in the circle with shocked expressions. "You know what? Fuck it." She threw her hands in the air and walked out of the room.

"BGBC in the house!" Coco shouted, but none of us joined in the chant. She tried another route to lighten the mood. "Well, Tammy, at least some of us don't have a whole bunch of drama. Right, cuz?" She stuck out her hand for me to slap like we were partners in all this happiness.

"Uh-huh. Drama-free, that's the only way to be," I answered halfheartedly. Maybe Coco didn't know that I was living with my mother, but I was sure Momma had told her that Tim and I were having problems. Bitch was probably calling me out like this, talking about "no drama" just to rub it in my face.

"You know what? People in glass houses shouldn't throw stones," Egypt snapped at me. "Some of us here know you better than that."

"I know I do," my momma added.

I don't know what her problem was, but she sure as hell was on my case. "I don't have any drama, Momma." I gave my mother a look that shut her up quick.

"So, you call fucking your husband's best friend no drama?" Egypt snapped again, and everyone in the room gasped. I wanted to kill her ass.

"Um, who fucked who?" Coco asked, sounding like she was enjoying herself. "I feel like I'm only watching half a movie."

I had to get out of there before Egypt put all my stuff out in the street. Coco was the last person I wanted to know about the threesome. For years, I'd been Miss Prim while she paraded her lack of morals around. Hell, I couldn't take that being thrown back in my face, especially today.

"Shit, the book mighta been a little boring this month, but damn, y'all," Coco joked.

"I got to go. The kids have to get up early," I lied as I stood up from my seat. Lying seemed to be the way I lived my life lately.

For once, Momma didn't jump in my shit. She didn't bust me for lying. "I'm just going to the bathroom and then we'll go, Tammy," she said.

Egypt picked up her purse. "I got stuff to do." Her ass was out the door before Momma had even gotten out of her seat.

I knew Coco would have a lot of work to do cleaning up, and I was glad. She wanted to pretend she was a domestic goddess like me; well, here was her big chance. I made sure to leave my dirty plate on the coffee table. "I'll meet you outside in the car, Momma," I said.

To Coco, I said, "I would stay and help you clean, but I do have a family to get back to." I lied again because the last thing Coco needed to learn was that her shit was working when mine wasn't.

"No worries," she said, still sounding as happy as can be. "Mac will help me clean it up." She said it like she had spent her entire life being waited on, instead of in the projects with barely anything.

"Yeah, right," I answered. "You better get to scrubbing. That man ain't gonna do nothing. Who knows how many weeks this thing is gonna last anyway?" I laughed as I sauntered toward the door.

"Damn, you need to pull back on that color green, 'cause envy ain't cute," Coco snapped as she followed me.

"All I'm doing is speaking the truth, Coco. It don't have nothing to do with jealousy. I've known you your whole life, and if there is one thing I know, it's that you can't stay with any man."

"Tammy, people change every day. The right man can do that for you. Like when a woman has a stick shoved up her ass, the right man can fuck that bad attitude right out of her," she growled, and closed the door behind me.

I laughed, knowing she was probably fuming in my wake. What had happened in my world where Coco, who had always been a low-rent tramp, had become a live-in girlfriend of a respectable, not to mention fine-as-hell, man? And here I didn't know how to get my family back. Seeing Coco live a blissed-out version of my life made me crazy. I used to go home to a man who loved me, and now I had nothing and no one, and like it or not, it was my fault.

46

Isis

I woke up happy and sore the morning after having my body ravaged by Tony. All night, he kept me coming over and over, entering me from every conceivable position until I thought I would pass out from orgasm overload. I don't ever remember him making me feel so satisfied. The ache between my legs where he insisted on delving again and again kept pulsating as if it had its own memory. Just thinking about it made me hungry to climb on top of him and go for another ride. Damn, that man made me have a bigger appetite for him than I ever had for food, and I loved me some food.

I couldn't keep my hands off of him. Reaching over, I stroked his head, replaying the vision of it bobbing up and down as he licked me into ecstasy.

Mmmm, that skin. I'd never really noticed just how smooth it was. My hands traveled down to his mouth, and all I wanted was to slide my tongue in between his lips and kiss him awake. My hands and eyes were all over his body.

I wondered how I could have given up on him so easily, but I considered myself lucky that he came back. It meant that he loved me, and I was sure he wanted to figure out some way for us to be together. As anxious as I was to get up out of my apartment, I knew Tony would probably have to move in with me at first. I didn't know much about his wife, but there aren't too many women who would let their husbands leave without making their lives miserable first. She'd take as much money as she could, and she'd probably get the house, so Tony and I would have to stay in my place and save to buy a place of our own. Considering the fact that he had four kids who would be coming to visit, we'd definitely need something bigger soon.

The thought of his kids made me realize that Tony came with a ready-made family. Becoming an instant stepmom was a little scary, but I would have to stop thinking of his kids as liabilities and recognize them as responsibilities, because obviously, loving him meant loving them. It would take some adjustment on my part, but I was willing to do it for my man's sake. I couldn't believe how quickly my life had changed.

Tony's eyes blinked awake. He stared at me as if he forgot where he had spent the night.

"Morning," I said happily.

He stretched his arms above his head. "Uuuuuuh," he yawned.

"Hungry?" I figured any man dumping a wife and leaving his four kids deserved a good meal. Besides, I needed to show him more of my domestic skills so he'd see that I'd not only make a great bed partner, but also a fabulous wife and stepmother.

"Nah, I got to get up," he said, sitting up in the bed.

I was a bit surprised by this. It left me with a sudden need to get a few things straight. After all, we really hadn't stopped to discuss anything the night before. I didn't even know what he'd told his wife. Of course, I hoped he'd said he wanted a divorce, but maybe they were only talking separation at this point. I needed to know that he was fully committing to me at this point.

"Baby, we need to talk before you go," I told him.

" 'Bout what?" He sounded annoyed, but I tried to tell myself he was just tired from all the fuckin' I whipped on him.

"I want to know what you're planning to do."

"First, I'm going to sleep for five more minutes, and then if you're deserving, I may put you back to sleep the old-fashioned way," he said with a laugh.

"Tony, I'm serious." My voice raised more than I had intended. I needed him to be on the same page with me now. There would be plenty of time for sex once we set things straight about his marriage.

"Stop trippin' on a brotha and let me rest," he complained.

"All I want to know is what you gonna do about your wife?"

He looked at me like I was simple. "What you think I'm gonna do? I'ma keep doing what I been doing." Now the annoyance in his voice came out loud and clear.

"Excuse me? You ain't leaving her?" I shouted. Normally I try to keep a cool head around my man, but it didn't take much now to turn me into an angry black woman.

"Who said anything about leaving my wife?"

"What! Then what was all this?" I gestured wildly toward our naked bodies and the bed.

"What you think this was? I mean, damn, the sex was good, baby, but that ain't got nothin' to do with me leaving my wife. Shit, I got four kids."

"I like kids," I said, feeling stupid the moment the words left my mouth.

"Isis, you know how I feel about you, but leaving my family?" He shook his head at me like the thought hadn't even occurred to him and that I must be crazy for thinking such a thing.

"Then what the fuck was this?" I asked again.

I felt myself getting hot, like a Negro-in-the-middle-of-a-deep-South summer kind of hot. Tony didn't help soothe my anger when he threw his hands up and started laughing. I'm talking the kind of wake-the-whole-damn-neighborhood, full belly kind of laughter. The kind that could make you want to kill somebody. It snapped me out of my stepmother fantasy. This shit was 'bout to be all raw.

But then I remembered what my momma always said about honey and flies, and decided to play this one sweet.

"So, this was just some one-night breakup sex thing, sweetie?" I purred in his ear.

My syrupy tone took him off the defensive. "Shit, we can do this all the time."

"How does that work?" I asked, struggling to keep my hands from flying around his throat. "You just come by whenever you can and service me sooooo good like you did last night. Is that it?"

"Shit, you whip it on me the way you did last night, and I will find a way to get up in that so much, you'll never have a chance to get horny." He laughed again.

"Won't your wife get suspicious?"

"Hell, nah. Those four kids keep her running so much she ain't got time to figure out what the hell I'm doing. Besides, at my job, we cover for each other."

I pictured him and his buddies at work and wondered how many times they'd covered for him when he came to visit me.

With a sickening clarity, I pictured him going back to them afterward and repaying their favor by sharing intimate details of our sex life. I felt so violated. Tony was gonna have to pay for this.

"How long can we do this?" I made my voice sound extra sweet.

"I will fuck you 'til your pussy can't take it," he bragged. But even his machismo couldn't drown out the sound of my biological clock running out of batteries. I'd wasted so much time on this man, who all along had only planned to keep me like some five-dollar ho. And now he still expected me to be his beck-and-call piece, a place he could dip his dick in and out of whenever he got a chance. He really expected me to be okay with him going home to his family while I grew old all alone.

"Honey, I'ma go get us something to celebrate our new arrangement," I cooed as I switched my ass off to the kitchen. Did his dumb ass think I was gonna just serve him breakfast with a celebratory glass of champagne?

Out of his view, I gripped the cold tiled countertop to stop myself from falling apart. It took every ounce of strength not to collapse onto the floor in a heap as my mind began replaying the events that brought me to this moment. In slow motion, I saw myself in Vegas, walking into the wedding chapel, ready to become happily wed. The miserable plane ride home when I felt sick, then Tony showing up at my door, pleading with me to believe how much he loved me. Cut to the jeweler trying to spare me embarrassment by telling me Tony had bought me some low-rent cubic zirconia instead of a real diamond. The motherfucker loved me so much he didn't even get me a real rock.

I felt like such a fool for letting him in the night before, falling for his bullshit once again. How could I have given in and slept with him? I had to admit to myself the sad truth that I still loved him, and I still wanted him. But even loving him didn't change the fact that right now I was madder than hell at him.

Reaching into a drawer, I pulled out what I wanted, placed it behind my back, and moved toward the bedroom.

"Baby, where's my surprise?" Tony joked, lying naked across the bed. His penis was partially erect. No doubt he was expecting to get some more action before he went home to his little family.

I approached the bed, keeping one hand behind my back. With

my other hand, I stroked my breasts and licked my lips suggestively.

"I could fuck you again," he panted.

"And then you got to go home and fuck your wife?"

"Hell, yeah." He laughed. "How you think I got four kids in
the first place?"

That little joke sent me off into a rage. I raised the knife from
behind my back and placed it to his neck before he had a chance
to react.

"So, you think I'm just some tramp you can fuck?" I
screamed at him.

His eyes grew wide with fear, and though I didn't look down
to check, I was sure his dick had shrunk to the size of a cocktail
weiner. His voice came out squeaky. "No, Isis. You know how I
feel about you. Now stop playing around."

"Oh, you think I'm playing?" I said. "Kinda like you been
playing with my feelings? Like that?"

He shook his head.

"You think I'm some dumb bitch who's gonna let you fuck
me, then go home to your wife? Is that what you thinking,
Tony?"

My eyes became blurry from the tears that had begun to
form, and in that moment, he pushed my hand away and jumped
off the bed. He scrambled around for his clothes, one hand covering his genitals to protect them from my swinging blade. I
wiped away my tears and followed close behind him, only leaving him time to grab his pants.

"If I can't have you, then ain't another bitch in the world
gonna have you!" I screamed like a madwoman, racing after
him. "You hear me, Tony? I'm not gonna play nice while you fuck
some other woman. You are supposed to be mine."

I almost caught up with him, waving the knife and trying to
do some damage to his body, but he ran around the couch, out
of my reach. He got to the front door, butt-naked, pants in hand,
then pulled it open and darted out the door to freedom.

I threw the knife on the floor and flung myself on the couch,
feeling pathetic that I had let Tony fuck me again and had liked
it enough to want to keep it going. I expected him to leave his
wife for me, and he had all but laughed in my face.

Why was this my life? I should have been having a postwedding party, surrounded by my husband and all our friends, planning my baby shower because I got knocked up on my honeymoon like any woman in her midthirties. Instead, I had been reduced to a crazy, jealous, knife-wielding woman.

47

Nikki

Keith decided to take me on our first official date. DJ was off with his father for the weekend, so I planned to make the most of this time with Keith. He was taking me to his Aunt Gwen's restaurant, and after that, who knew what would happen? The possibilities excited me.

Getting dressed for dinner, everything felt different. Butterflies flew figure eights in my stomach as I stood in front of the mirror trying to choose between four outfits. Hanging out with Keith and even having sex with him was one thing, but adding real romance to the mix had me acting as giddy as a schoolgirl. I wanted Keith to be as excited to see me as I was to be with him. I finally settled on a new pair of jeans I had recently bought. Between my diet and the breakup with Tiny, I had dropped a couple of sizes, so only a few things in my closet even fit. I put on a clingy white blouse, loving the way the color complemented my chocolate skin tone.

When the doorbell rang, I had just put the finishing touches on my face, which meant mascara and lip gloss. I guess I'm what you might call a "natural woman," but on me, less was definitely more. I felt good about the way I looked, and Keith's reaction let me know he also liked what he saw.

"Wow!" His eyes swept over me from head to toe.

"Thank you," I said, then actually blushed. I couldn't remember the last time I'd been so excited about seeing someone.

I stepped back to allow Keith into the apartment. Although we had known each other for a while now, this was his first time at my place.

"I want to see your kitchen," he insisted. I knew he wanted to find out if he could cook in my house.

I led him through the living room, and he stood in the kitchen, staring at my large collection of cookbooks. I had everything from *Spoonbread and Strawberry Wine* to *Patti Labelle's Cookbook*. Ever since I was about sixteen, I had been collecting cookbooks. Growing up poor and with a limited budget, we always ate the same foods, but in bed at night, I'd pore over the recipes, dreaming of the day when I'd be able to sample a wider array of culinary delights. Even Tiny had learned to cook some of my fantasy recipes from these books, like shrimp étouffée and chocolate soufflé.

"Damn, baby, you got yourself a collection," he said with admiration in his voice.

"I started out buying them used at library sales, and then when I got older, I joined a cookbook club where all the books are discounted. It's my vice," I said with a laugh.

Keith picked up the used Betty Crocker cookbook that resembled a three-ring binder. "So, you're like the black Betty?" He ran his tongue across his lips suggestively. "I can't wait to sample your desserts."

Suddenly, I looked at him holding that book and got what I consider one of those Oprah "aha" moments. "You ever think about taking all your recipes and making a cookbook?" The idea struck me as sheer brilliance. I continued. "Wait. Before you say anything, I would help you. If there is one thing I know, it's cookbooks, and your food is off the chain."

"Yeah, but I'd have to give up my recipes. They're sacred, yo." His posture became a little tense, so I couldn't tell if he was joking. Still, I pressed ahead.

"If we do this book and it's a best seller, investors will be throwing money at you to open a restaurant. And I don't mean some tiny place. Your food deserves to be served in a beautiful environment," I gushed.

"You think so, huh?" He relaxed a little more to the idea.

We talked about doing a cookbook all the way to Aunt Gwen's restaurant. By the time we got there, he seemed genuinely interested in the possibilities. I was happy to be the one who had put the smile on his face and opened his mind to dreams of a bigger future. I was really starting to have strong feelings about this man.

In the corner of the restaurant, Keith had set up a table with flowers and a RESERVED sign. I sat down, and he poured me a glass of red wine, then leaned in and kissed me on the cheek.

"I'm gonna try something new that would go great in the book, but you gotta tell me if it works or not." He rubbed his hands up and down my naked arm.

"We're partners, right?" Everything about this man turned me to mush.

He nodded and said, "I got a little surprise for you. I'll be back." Keith disappeared into the kitchen.

A few moments later, Aunt Gwen came into the restaurant and headed to my table. "Hey, honey, how you doing this evening?" she greeted. She had a warmth about her that reminded me of my aunts down in North Carolina.

"I'm good. I can't wait to see what Keith is making." I smiled up at her.

"So, you two a couple now?" She cut right to the point, like any of my nosy relatives would have done. In my family, secrets were nonexistent. I wasn't offended by her question, though, because I figured she was just watching out for her nephew.

"I just got out of a relationship, so we're taking it slow," I explained.

"So, you two know all about each other since you been friends for a while?" The look on her face made me wonder if there was some hidden meaning behind her question, but I tried not to read too much into it. Maybe Aunt Gwen had seen me with Tiny or something and this was her way of letting me know that she knew.

Either way, I didn't get the feeling she was trying to be hostile, so I answered calmly, "I know he's a good guy and that he's kind and thoughtful and a great listener." I could feel myself blushing.

"You two really like each other." She smiled kindly.

"A lot," I answered confidently. It felt good to be so sure that Keith did in fact like me. It wasn't like he'd said he loved me, but he just made me feel so safe and comfortable. I didn't need to hear the words to know that he considered me someone special.

"That's nice," she said, but again the look on her face didn't quite match her words.

"Yeah, since my son's father and I broke up, I didn't think I'd ever allow myself to get close to a man again. With Keith, it's like I trust him, and well . . . For me, that don't come so easy." I couldn't believe how easily I was opening up to Aunt Gwen. My new relationship with Keith seemed to be changing me in all kinds of ways.

"So, you been hurt real bad, chile?" She put her hand on mine, comforting me.

Out of nowhere, tears welled up in my eyes and spilled out on the table. "I am so sorry," I blubbered, wiping my tears with a napkin.

"You live long enough and you gonna know some hurt. It's God's way of making you strong enough to survive until the good come along." Her words were so comforting. I'd never had this kind of conversation with my own mother, and I guess I never knew how much I needed it.

"Thank you." I squeezed her hand.

"No need to thank me. The Lord always gives us what we need. I can tell you're a good person, and that chile in that there kitchen is lucky to have you."

With that, she got up and headed into the kitchen. The shouting from behind the kitchen doors was loud and sudden.

"You need to tell her everything!" Aunt Gwen's words came flying into the dining room.

"I will tell her when I'm ready!" Keith's words chilled me. What could have caused them to argue, and what was he supposed to tell me?

"Secrets and lies destroy everything good. Ain't you learn nothing already?" she yelled at him

"I got to do this my own way, and I'm not ready." Keith sounded upset, almost scared.

"This ain't the way," she warned him.

"This is my life. Mine!"

A second later, Keith burst into the dining room, ripping off his apron.

"Let's go," he barked at me.

I sat there, my eyes bugging out. This was a Keith I didn't recognize. He'd never let his temper get the best of him like this, even in the face of Tiny's verbal abuse. Something had him more upset than I'd ever seen him.

Keith saw the concern on my face and shifted. "Nikki, please. I need to get out of here," he pleaded with me.

"What was that about?" I still hadn't budged.

"Please, I'll tell you later," he promised.

We got up to leave. I saw his aunt Gwen standing in the kitchen doorway, arms folded tightly across her chest, watching us. Whatever secret Keith was hiding from me, it was enough to make sweet Aunt Gwen suddenly look very fierce.

As we walked down the block, Keith was silent, and I tried to imagine every possible scenario. What could be the worst possible secret for Keith to reveal? Had he been in jail? Was he married? Had he killed someone? I had no idea what could have caused such a rift between him and his aunt, and I prayed that it wasn't something so serious it would create the same sort of tension between me and him. And just as I thought of tension, we turned the corner and I practically ran right into Tiny.

"Nikki, I need to talk to you."

There was no way her presence in this neighborhood was an accident. "Are you following me?" I demanded.

"How else was I supposed to get you to talk to me?" she whined. "You don't answer my calls or return my texts."

"Why don't you leave her alone?" Keith was much more aggressive than usual with Tiny. She had stepped up on us at a really bad time, and with the mood Keith was in, I knew this situation could turn violent in a hurry.

Luckily, Tiny chose not to deal with him and continued talking to me. "Nikki, I love you. I know this loser ain't no good for you."

"No, Tiny, you don't know. I'm not in love with you anymore. It's over." I took Keith's hand and led him away. Tiny stood there as we passed, but fortunately she didn't try to swing at Keith.

"Nikki, you don't know him," she hollered. "But when you learn everything about him, you'll be begging me to come back!"

I refused to turn around and look at her as she continued ranting on the sidewalk. I was just glad things hadn't gotten physical. Keith and I walked in silence for a few more blocks, until we came to Sylvia's restaurant. I knew they had a new low-fat, low-sodium menu. It couldn't touch Keith's cooking, but obviously we weren't going back to Aunt Gwen's for him to cook, so this would have to do. We went in and grabbed a seat out of the way.

He placed a hand against my cheek. "We're okay, right?" Keith seemed worried.

I didn't answer him. I couldn't be sure we were okay until I knew the secret that had caused the fight with Aunt Gwen. I asked, "You gonna tell me what you and your aunt were fighting about?"

He gave me a vague answer that only confused me more. "Nikki, it's just that sometimes people change, and not everybody can truly accept that."

"You're saying your aunt doesn't accept you?"

"No . . . It's just that she thinks I'm trying to be something I'm not. But this is it. This is me, and I guess I need to know if you can accept me for me," he finished.

"Accept you? I've always had a thing for thugs," I said with a laugh.

"That's not quite it." He danced around whatever was at the heart of the matter.

"Then what is it, Keith? You can tell me anything." I took his hand in mine.

"I need you to trust me. I'll tell you everything . . . just not today," he said.

"Do you have another woman?" I needed to know that, because if he did, I could cut my losses early and move on with my life.

"Nikki, you are the only woman I think about day and night," he confessed, and looking into his eyes, I knew he was telling the truth. As long as there was no other woman in his life, I thought I could accept anything else he had to tell me. I relaxed a little and decided to give Keith the time he needed to reveal this mysterious secret.

"Okay, Keith. You tell me when you're ready." I picked up the menu. "In the meantime, let's see what Sylvia's cooking today."

48

Tammy

I turned to look at the man lying next to me. Even though it had only been a few weeks, it felt like months since we had been together. After seeing Coco and that fine-ass Mac playing house together, I was feeling extremely jealous and neglected. Some women could do without a man, but I wasn't like that. I needed to have all my needs met, mentally and physically, and that meant being with a man who made me feel complete. I stretched my hand over, cupping his tight butt, and I felt myself getting turned on all over again. Raoul woke up, smiling over at me.

"Mmmm, you want some more?" He reached over and grabbed my full breasts in his hand.

"Always." My tone turned seductive and inviting. Raoul rubbed his hands between my thighs. He picked up the remote next to the bed and flipped on the television. When he turned to me, I saw a devilish glint in his eyes.

"How about a little porn?" he asked with a smirk.

"Ooh, that's right up my alley," I purred.

The thought of porn brought my mind to Tim and how much I really missed him and the kids. Tim had turned me onto porn a long time ago. He had a huge collection of porno DVDs, many of which I had handpicked. I even went through a period where I bought cunnilingus videos, hoping they would inspire Tim. After those DVDs got no response, I gave up trying to figure out how to get Tim to like kitty-licking. At first it made me feel less than desirable, but I pushed those thoughts out of my head and decided some men were too macho to eat pussy. Then I met Raoul, and he shattered that theory for me. I still had moments where I couldn't believe I'd lived for so long without a man who would go down on me. Why couldn't Tim have just tried it once?

I'm sure my pleasurable response would have convinced him to do it forever, and it would have been him lying next to me in our bed at home, and not Raoul in some short-stay motel by the airport.

"What you like?" Raoul asked me.

"You ever seen *Super Sperminator?*" I asked.

"You like to have sex while watching porn?" Raoul sounded incredulous. He continued. "My wife hates porn."

If she was that boring, no wonder he was here with me instead of home with her. I almost felt bad for the poor woman. She had no idea the fun she was missing. Still, if he was shocked that I watched a little porn, I figured I would wait to let him know about my extensive toy collection. Tim loved when we played with toys. Dammit, why the hell did I keep thinking about Tim?

"Porn gets me hot," I told him.

"I love that you get turned on." He positioned me so that I could see the television, then he began to kiss his way down my thighs. My body tingled under his touch, and I would have done just about anything to make this man happy. I couldn't believe how passive good sex made me become.

I had become one of those women who'd do anything to please a man, and not because I had to, but because I wanted to make him really happy. It wasn't like I was ever one of those tough girls, but with Tim, I'd always felt in control, like I had no choice but to be the aggressor. With Raoul, all that control went flying out the window, and I was enjoying my new role.

"Welcome to Raoul's world," he said as he flicked the television to the adult movie screen.

"What will it be? *Butt Business, Soul Train Sister,* or *Hard the Three-Way?*"

"*Hard the Three-Way,*" I damn near shouted. Funny how I was interested in watching group sex now. My three-way with Tim and Egypt had once made me crazy jealous. But if I really thought about it, I wouldn't be getting this good sex from Raoul now if that three-way had never happened. So in some strange way, I now held a sort of fondness for the idea of ménage à trois.

The movie came on, and Raoul pushed himself closer to me, rubbing my breasts and kissing my stomach. He always told me he couldn't get enough of my silky chocolate skin. On the screen, a ruggedly built brother had his back to us, his high, tight butt cheeks turning me on as he approached a white woman seated on a sofa. Within moments, two other women, one Asian and the other black, joined them on the couch, all three women spreading their legs. The black man bent down and pleasured all three before coming up for air. As if on cue, Raoul dove down between my legs. This wasn't my first time watching porn with a lover, but I was so damn turned on I had my first orgasm in less than a minute. I closed my eyes and enjoyed the sensations as my body jerked and spasmed with pleasure.

When I finally opened my eyes again and looked at the screen, I couldn't believe what I was seeing. "Oh my God!" I screamed.

Raoul went back down, thinking I was asking for more pleasure, but I pushed him away.

"You have to see this," I said as I sat up to get a closer look.

Raoul joined me at the top of the bed. "What? He's screwing three women. You like that?" he asked, clearly mistaking my shock for arousal.

"No, I know him," I blurted out.

"You know him, know him?" Raoul's eye grew big.

"No, not like that." Without bothering to explain further, I wondered aloud, "How could he do this to her?" I couldn't take my eyes off the screen.

He tried to calm me down. "Porn is different. It's a job."

"It is not a job any man of mine would ever have. Anyway, I can't watch this one now. Let's turn on a different movie," I suggested. Raoul chose *Soul Train Sister,* and while I enjoyed the movie, he got back to work doing what he did best. As I reveled in one climax after another, I thought about how I could use my discovery to my advantage later.

49

Isis

It had been three whole days since Tony had raced out of my apartment fearing for his life. Yeah, I figured enough time had passed to put Tony off his guard. Little did he know I had a long memory, and this would only be over when I said it was. I had gathered the information that I needed to use against him and followed his wife to her work so I would know where to deliver the information when the time was right.

Tony had played me for a sucker for the last time. I was just tired of men and tired of trying to find one who would love me. Ever since I could remember, I'd been wanting some man to give me the love my own father never did. You'd think that thirty-four years later, I'd stop needing the love I didn't get in child-hood, but I hadn't. I was still craving the kind of love that made me feel worthy and valuable. I was one of those women who be-lieved I was nothing without a man. It's the kind of thinking Oprah would consider unhealthy, but after reading every self-help book I could get my hands on, I realized that there wasn't always going to be some miracle cure. So, if Tony refused to love me the way I needed him to, I was prepared to make him pay. If his wife's feelings got hurt in the process, then so be it. She needed a wake-up call anyway.

I pulled into the parking lot of the school where Tony's wife was a secretary and waited in my car. It was the end of the school day, so I watched as the kids came streaming out to board the buses. Ten minutes after the last bus pulled away from the school, adults started leaving the building, lugging briefcases full of papers to grade at home. My heart started thumping wildly when I finally spotted Monica walking toward the parking lot.

I picked up the large envelope off the passenger seat. It held enough ammunition to do a whole shitload of damage, which is exactly what I wanted. I needed revenge to complete this chapter in my life. Maybe then I could move on without a man and learn to love myself.

"Excuse me, Monica," I called to her as I stepped out of my car.

She turned her head in my direction, and as I walked closer, I watched her expression change. Obviously she remembered me from our little adventure in the grocery store. I have to give her credit, though, because instead of jumping in her car and locking the doors, she stood her ground and waited for me to approach.

When I was close enough that she could speak to me without her white colleagues overhearing us, she hissed, "What the fuck are you doing here?"

I didn't say a word. With a big smile, I presented the envelope to her.

"What the fuck is that?" she asked, refusing to touch it.

"Just a little something you might want to see."

Now, she could have just walked away at this point and refused to look inside the envelope, which is why my heart was beating so fast. My plan for revenge wouldn't work if she didn't play along. Fortunately, her curiosity got the best of her, and she snatched the envelope from my hands, mumbling something about a psycho under her breath.

Her attitude changed real quick, though, when she got a peek at the pictures inside the envelope. I'd gathered together every photo of Tony that I could find in my apartment, to prove to this woman just how well I knew her husband. As she shuffled through them, she paused for a minute at the one of me and Tony with our luggage in the airport, waiting to fly to Vegas. There was a date stamp on the bottom of the photo, so I knew she was probably doing the math in her head, recalling whatever lie he'd told her about why he was going away that week. Now she knew where his ass had really been.

With every photo she looked at, her breathing got a little quicker, and her body tensed up. Reality was hitting her hard. When she came to the first naked picture, she dropped the photos to the ground and leaned against the nearest car, probably to keep from falling over.

"You all right?" I asked, and suddenly I felt bad. Maybe I had taken things a little too far. I mean, the sister needed to know the truth, but maybe she didn't need to see the picture Tony had taken of me, kneeling on the floor in front of him, his dick in my mouth.

She looked at me and said in a weak voice, "Why?"

I didn't know if she was asking why I was showing her the pictures or why I was screwing her husband, but either way, I kinda felt like shit. "I'm sorry," I said. My apology probably couldn't make much difference now, but I felt like I needed to say something. "I just felt like you needed to know the truth. No woman deserves to be lied to that way."

"No, they sure don't," she replied sadly.

And just like that, we were no longer enemies, but two sisters bonded by our mutual pain. I suggested that we go to my car so we could sit down and talk; then I opened up to her about everything.

"When Tony and I started dating, he told me he was single," I started, then broke it down for her every detail—about the way he'd tricked me into believing all his lies and lulled me into a false sense of security while he played me. I finished my story by describing the moment when we stood in the chapel in Las Vegas and he finally told me the truth about his marriage. I stopped short of telling her about his visit three days ago, partly because I didn't want to hurt her any more than I already had, and partly because I didn't want to look like a fool—or an evil bitch—for screwing him again even after I knew he was married.

During my entire story, she had stayed mostly silent, her expressions going from shock to disgust to just plain hurt. "Don't feel bad," she finally said when I finished. "You got played good, but think how I feel. I'm his damn wife, for God's sake, and even I didn't ask the questions I should have. I missed all the classic signs."

"He's a master player, that's for sure," I agreed.

And then, a look crossed her face that I didn't expect to see. All the pain and vulnerability disappeared, suddenly replaced by strength and determination.

"You have your cell phone?" she asked.

"Yeah . . ." I hesitated, not sure what she was planning.

"Call him."

"Call him?"

"Get that motherfucker on the phone," she commanded, and

I obeyed. Things weren't turning out quite like I had expected, but this was it, my moment for revenge. From the look on his wife's face, I knew Tony was about to feel some pain himself.

I held my phone away from her when I made the call. No reason for her to see that I still had her husband's number as my number one on speed dial.

"Hi, Tony," I greeted when he picked up. I was a little surprised he answered, considering the last time I saw him I was trying to castrate him in my living room.

"What you want?" he asked angrily.

"Um . . ." I hesitated, not sure what Monica wanted me to say. "I just wanted to make sure we're still cool. I mean, we can still get together and fuck once in a while, can't we?"

To my surprise, Tony sounded excited by the idea. What a fucking dog. Less than a week ago, I was threatening to cut off his dick, but as long as I still wanted to fuck him, he was willing to come on back for more. As soon as he started telling me about all the things he wanted to do to my body, I handed the phone to Monica.

"You lying, cheating motherfucker." She all but lost her religion up in there as she served old Tony his walking papers right there on the spot.

"Don't you ever bring your ass into my house again. Yeah, you heard me. I said MY HOUSE!" She flipped the phone closed. Her body went slack, and all the fight went out of her. I knew exactly how she felt, loving a man who lied to you each and every day.

So, I had achieved my revenge. But knowing that Tony would lose his family, the one thing that meant something to him, came only as a cold comfort. Instead of the elation I expected to feel, I became even more tired. Watching Monica, a woman who obviously devoted her life to her husband and children, lose her family structure made me aware of how little I even had to lose. At least she had four children at home who loved and needed her.

It embarrassed me a little to see that she seemed to be handling Tony's betrayal much better than I had. After her initial shock, I watched her resolve strengthening and her composure coming back. I had lain in bed for days before I could even sit up straight after finding out the truth about Tony, but here this woman had just found out her husband had been cheating for three years, and one hour later, the tears were gone and she was all but humming that Gloria Gaynor anthem to all wronged women—"I Will Survive"—as she stepped out of my car.

"I'm sorry he wasted three years of your life." She actually apologized for him.

As I drove away, I glanced back in the mirror and saw Monica march toward her car, totally in control. I didn't understand why Tony would even want to be with someone like me when he had the kind of woman at home who ran circles around me in the confidence department.

Pushing my car down the freeway, I sat behind that wheel, wishing I could blink myself into bed. I just wanted to be home with the covers pulled up over me. I wanted to sleep without worrying about the morning, without waking up. I needed desperately to forget the way I was feeling all the time. I didn't see the point in getting up, showering, and going to work. I didn't want to read the next book club selection because like all the others, it would have a happily-ever-after ending. If there was one thing I knew for sure, it was that shit didn't work out happily ever after for a girl like me because I was nothing but something on the side.

50

COCO

As I left Red Lobster clutching the present Tammy gave me, I couldn't help think that she had somehow set me up. Yeah, she said she wanted to give Mac and me a gift to celebrate our new relationship, but I'd never trusted Tammy. Ever since we were kids and my mom struggled while Tammy's parents lived a comfortable middle-class life, she'd always looked down her nose at me.

When we were kids, we'd spend weekends at our grandmother's house. Tammy would always suggest things that sounded like fun to us kids but were bound to get us in some kind of trouble. As soon as I took the bait and did the deed, she'd leave me to take the fall. She always came out smelling like a rose.

"That child is pure trouble," my grandmother would rage to whoever would hear me, and there I'd be, on the hot seat, while Tammy and her perfect ponytails sat by, the picture of innocence.

When she got married and I held on to my freedom, dating whoever and whenever I wanted, she judged me any chance she got. She rarely missed an opportunity to remind me of my station in life because, after all, I was her poor, ghetto relation who would always be the town tramp, even if the town happened to be New York City.

Our grandmother used to tell us that if you live long enough, life will surprise you, and not all of it will be good. Well, I knew I had surprised Tammy when I got with Mac. And no matter how she was acting, I knew it made her jealous that I'd found a good man and was doing what she considered the "respectable thing." See, when Tammy married Tim, she was constantly rubbing it in everyone's faces, like she'd found the last good man on earth. For some reason, in order to feel good about her own life, my cousin needed to feel like shit was falling down around me.

That's why I had a bad feeling about the gift she'd given me. I kept asking myself, Why would a person who treated me as "less-than" my entire life be rolling out the red carpet suddenly?

Don't get me wrong. There were huge moments in my life when Tammy stood by me, but if I was being honest, in every one of those dramatic scenarios, I was the huge mess and Tammy rode in on her German-made automobile and rescued me. Now our roles weren't quite so well defined. Yeah, everything about this rubbed her the wrong way. She didn't seem to be able to deal with my life going well.

When I got home, I didn't bother to wait for Mac before I opened the gift. If it was just some of Tammy's bullshit, I could get rid of it before he even got home. If it was something sexy, like massage oils, I would just rewrap it and let him open it with me later. But nothing could have prepared me for what was really inside that box. Once I saw what it was, I knew I had to show it to Mac, but I damn sure wasn't gonna be wrapping it in no fancy box for him.

Two hours later, I called Mac to see what time he'd be home, to make sure he didn't miss any of the performance I had planned for him. Tonight was the night to dress in my most se-ductive teddy. I put on a champagne-colored halter nightie that barely covered my assets, slathered some Victoria's Secret gold shimmer lotion all over my body to give a little extra glow, and sprayed on some JLo perfume. I wanted to make sure all the senses were awakened.

When the doorbell rang, I took a breath, counted to ten, and then sauntered over to answer. Standing on the other side, rest-ing his arm on the doorway and looking smug, was Jackson.

"You rang?" he addressed me slowly.

"Yeah." I pasted on a smile, but my stomach began to ache. The last thing I wanted was Jackson's hands all over my body, but sometimes it's not about what I want. In fact, this entire night would be about what I needed.

"Damn, you sure know how to greet a brotha," Jackson com-mented after he'd basically undressed me with his eyes. He damn near pimp-walked past me into the living room.

"I had to show you what I'm working with," I purred, knowing it would send a woody straight to his pants.

"So, what? You come to your senses?" He ran two fingers up my middle, stopping between my cleavage.

I came straight out with the purpose of our meeting. "Maybe I decided I do need what you can offer."

"And what if the offer is no longer on the table?" He tried to act like he had the upper hand, but I was the one with the goods. I learned a long time ago the power of the pussy, and if you can throw in a kick-ass blow job, you can get a man to do anything you want. Right now, I wanted to exact some revenge on a man who had played me for a fool.

"If the offer was off the table, you wouldn't be here." I ran a hand over the swell of my breasts, licking my lips.

"So, you think you can just leave me for some other Negro and come back when it don't work?" he asked. "I told you, Coco, you had to give up all that romance for the finance. A woman like you is not made to put up with the ordinary man." This man was so damn arrogant it seemed to ooze from his pores. Normally I would have to put a man like this in his place, but this time, I didn't care how he acted. I needed him to help me carry out my plan.

"Look, I fell for someone who I thought was worthy of me, but as soon as I realized who he really was, I called you. The thing I like about you, Jackson, is that you are who you say you are. There is nothing hiding under the surface, threatening to come out and change everything. All your cards are on the table, and that's the way I like to live, out in the open." I leaned forward, knowing it would press my breasts together and give Jackson a little more incentive to make the right choice. He took the bait.

"Spill it, Coco. What is it you want?" His breathing was so rapid it sounded like he was panting.

"First, I want revenge, and you can help me get it. Second, I want you to give me everything you gave me the first time, only with a longer leash." I placed my hands on my hips and stared him in the eye to let him know that I was dead serious, and I was not interested in negotiating.

"You kiddin'?" He smirked.

"No, I'm as serious as a hard-on. I need some space. I can't go from having my entire life my way to being your slave." He raised his eyebrows at the mention of the word *slave* but didn't argue about it the way he had last time.

"I don't care if the golden handcuffs are twenty-four karat," I continued. "They're still handcuffs. So, I want you to schedule your visits. You can have four a week and no more."

He shook his head and asked, "All that for some pussy?"

"No, not *some* pussy." I lifted the hem of my teddy up above my waist. "*This* pussy."

The way he swallowed, I could tell he'd started salivating. That's when I knew Jackson would give me whatever I wanted. I grabbed his hand and prepared to move on to phase one of my revenge plan.

"Damn, girl. Where's the fire?" Jackson laughed as I shoved him into the bedroom.

It took me a few minutes to explain the benefits of doing what I needed him to do that night, but once I whipped a little Coco on him, I saw my plan coming together. I damn near threw Jackson down on the bed, then slipped his penis inside my mouth, making sure it got nice and hard. He couldn't believe I had a porno flick on the television, so when I hit PLAY and the action started, he got even more excited.

I popped my breasts out of the top of the nightie, giving him a little peekaboo. His eyes bugged out like he was about to have a heart attack. This man gave new meaning to "breast man" when he dove headfirst into my double-D cups. I climbed on top of his dick and lowered myself until he was inside of me. No, he didn't go deep like Mac, sending pulsating sensations shooting up my body, but then again, I had learned my lesson and wouldn't be craving the kind of penis that fucked with my heart. I didn't want anyone to touch me that deeply again.

"Oh God, you're going to make me come," Jackson shouted.

I jumped off of him like his penis was on fire. I hadn't laid out this perfect plan to have him ruin it by ejaculating prematurely.

"Oh no. Why'd you do that, baby?" he whined as his penis began to shrink.

I picked up the remote and paused the DVD. " 'Cause I need you to stay hard for me." I stroked his penis, watching it come back to life. Looking at the clock, I realized I needed to prevent Jackson from coming for ten more minutes.

"I could have come once, got hard and come again," he insisted, and I almost laughed out loud. Did he really think his old ass would just be able to orgasm at will like some adolescent boy? And even if he could, I was not in the position to take a chance. I had a lot riding on this night, and it was of no concern to me whether or not Jackson could fuck like a spring chicken.

"Baby, I just wanted you to slow down and enjoy this." I slipped my lips over the head of his dick, licking and sucking like it was a Tootsie Roll Pop and I had to reach the center.

"Oh shit. That feels good." Jackson grabbed my head, pushing it down the shaft. Thank God he had money and lots of it, 'cause his skills left a lot to be desired. It either took a big dick or a big bank account to get a woman to put up with bullshit, and Jackson had the bank for me to overlook his shortcomings.

When I heard the front door open, I got into position and lowered myself onto Jackson again, prepared to put on a show Mac would never forget. I released the PAUSE button on the remote and waited for the action to begin.

"Oh, Daddy, this is good!" I screamed out.

"Oh yeah. Whose pussy is this?" Jackson slapped my ass, grabbing my cheeks in his hands.

"It's your pussy. It's your pussy, Daddy." I moaned like he was giving me the fuck of my life. I really should have been nominated for my own award, because he wasn't holding it down at all.

"What the fuck?" Mac stood in the doorway, looking angry and hurt. It served him right, if you ask me.

I didn't miss a beat, continuing to bob up and down on Jackson's dick like I hadn't noticed the man I loved standing in the doorway, watching in pain. "Oh, Daddy, I love your dick," I hollered out. Mac punched the doorframe but stayed glued to the spot.

Playing his part just as I'd instructed, Jackson cupped my breasts in his hands and began to nibble on my nipples. He must have had some exhibitionist tendencies, because I swear the moment Mac entered, he seemed to get harder and hornier.

"Coco, what the fuck are you doing?" Mac yelled, stepping into the bedroom.

"I'm fuckin'," I answered as if it were the most natural thing in the world. He still hadn't taken his eyes off of us to notice the video playing. My ass flapped in the air as I continued riding up and down Jackson's dick.

"Why would you do this?" He looked hurt and vulnerable, which just made me even more pissed off at him. As soon as I'd viewed the videos from Tammy, I decided that even if I went out and fucked every man in New York City, Mac wouldn't have the right to say a damn thing about it.

"What, Big Mac?" I taunted him. "You have a problem with fuckin'? It sure don't look like you do." I gestured toward the television, where Mac could watch himself screwing some flat-chested Asian chick on the screen. I threw my head back and laughed.

Mac ran over to the TV and turned it off. "Let me explain," he begged.

I stopped in mid-grind and climbed off Jackson. He didn't complain, because I think he was enjoying this fight between me and Mac almost as much as he'd enjoyed fucking me.

"Explain what?" I asked. "That you fuck for a living? I think that about sums it up, don't you?"

"I should have told you everything."

I could see in his eyes how desperate he was for me to listen and then, of course, forgive him. Not a chance.

"You probably just came back from fuckin'," I said, refusing to give in to his emotional state. I wanted him to hurt the way that he had hurt me.

"Coco, I love you." He dropped those words as if they could stop the tide that had already started.

"Love? No, well, you don't know me enough, Mac. See, your love is bullshit. It's full of lies." I got up off the bed, pushing my breasts back into the nightie.

"Why would you do this, Coco?" he pleaded with me.

"Are you kidding? Probably the same reason you do it, Mac. For the money," I answered matter-of-factly.

Mac made a motion to reach for Jackson, who stood there smirking, delighted to watch him suffer. "You want to be with this bitch ass?" Mac asked, pointing to Jackson.

"He can afford me," I said without blinking. "And he don't need to lie to me about how he makes his money."

"Don't walk away. Let me explain." Mac gripped my shoulder.

"Hey, hands off of her," Jackson warned. "I paid too much to have you ruining my woman." Jackson was milking this. He was obviously happy to have the chance to punish Mac for "stealing" me in the first place.

"You better get the fuck out my face before I break you in two," Mac commanded.

I stepped close to Jackson as I said to Mac, "I let my guard down and got close to someone for the first time in years, and it turns out to be one. Big. Lie." I spat the words out at him.

"I told you, baby. It's not about the romance; it's all about the finance," Jackson bragged.

Mac grabbed Jackson by the collar and threatened, "Get the fuck away from her." But Jackson just shrugged him off like some annoying insect.

"I could buy you twelve times over and still get change back," Jackson said with a smirk.

"Do you think I give a shit?" Mac raised his clenched fist.

"Lay one hand on me and I'll sue you for everything you own and that includes your momma's little house in Queens that she signed over to you last March." Mac stared at him in disbelief. "Oh yeah, I know who you are, Mac Reynolds. I had you checked out the day Coco moved in here. "

Mac dropped his arms to his side and looked at me like he couldn't believe I was choosing this scrawny old man over him. Sooner or later, he'd come to his senses and realize that he'd left me no choice with his lying ass.

"Let's go," I said to Jackson.

Jackson couldn't resist one more insult. "You can't afford a woman like Coco, but don't worry. I plan to make her the best mistress ever."

As we walked toward the door, Mac's words threatened to stop me in my tracks. "I wasn't offering her money," he said quietly. "I wanted to give her my heart and a lifetime."

Some small corner of my heart was still in love with Mac, even after discovering his lies. That part of me wanted to turn around and run back into his arms. But one quick memory of the devastation I felt when I turned on the DVD and saw Mac with those women was all I needed to keep moving. At least with Jackson, I knew what I was getting and what I was sacrificing.

"Look, it ain't personal. We both got jobs to do, and since both of those jobs involve fuckin' for money, I got to go get on my back and earn my cash." I adjusted my breasts in the tight sweater I had put on.

He had the nerve to get indignant. "Doing porn is not the same thing. I call all the shots with my career, and I'm not selling myself to the highest bidder like some common whore."

"Fuck you!" I yelled at Mac as I stepped out the door. I had tried once again to love, only to be screwed, and there was no way I would ever take that chance again.

51

Nikki

I had just started cooking when the doorbell rang. Every time I heard someone at my door, I got nervous, thinking it might be Tiny, but so far she'd kept her distance. I figured this time it was Dwayne, though, since he was due to pick up DJ for their weekend together.

DJ ran past me like a lightning bolt, opening the door in a hurry.

"Hey, don't just open my door," I chastised him, but the deed was done.

"Hey, Nikki, you looking damn good." Dwayne stared me up and down, and I have to admit I appreciated the compliment.

"You packed?" Dwayne asked DJ, who scurried to his room to gather his things. I usually packed for DJ, but lately he'd taken to doing it himself. Since Tiny had moved out, DJ had become more independent, as if to prove that he and I would be fine on our own.

"Damn, Nikki, you losing all kind of weight and shit. Be careful. You about to turn back into a banger." Dwayne took off his jacket like he was about to get all comfortable and make himself at home.

"Uh, I'm expecting company." I let him know straight out that he and I would not be heading down memory lane ever again.

"Is it that dude you seeing from work?" Funny how Dwayne always seemed to know my every move. But then he continued. "I ran into Tiny."

He looked like he wanted to say something more, but I cut him off. "Yeah, well, I guess you know we over, then." For a split second, it crossed my mind that Tiny was no longer here to protect me from Dwayne the way she always had, but with my newfound confidence, I felt I could handle myself no matter what happened.

"I ain't try'na be mean or nothing, but I ain't mad at you for going back to a dude," Dwayne said. "I ain't too macho to tell you that having your woman leave you for another chick does kind of fuck with your ego."

Now, the thing was, I didn't even know Tiny when I left Dwayne. But he was no different than anyone else. People have a tendency to revise the history of their breakups and forget about the part they might have played in it. If Dwayne wanted to tell himself Tiny was the reason for our breakup, then whatever. As long as he understood that it was permanent.

"As far as me being with a chick, you love who you love, Dwayne," I reminded him.

"I get that, but to give up the basic reason men and women fit together? I don't know. It seems wrong." He'd always been clear that the idea of me with another woman was too upsetting to him.

As much as I enjoyed this civil moment with my baby daddy, I had another man on my mind, so I needed Dwayne to step. DJ must have sensed this, and he saved me from having to ask Dwayne to leave when he ran in with his backpack. Instead of checking to make sure he remembered things like his toothbrush or underwear, I hurried them out the door to continue my cooking.

It had been days since the last time I had sex, and as I cooked, it was all I could think about. Sex this, sex that. As much as I had loved Tiny, I had never daydreamed about sex with her this way. Now I was like a damn nymphomaniac, dreaming about all Keith, all the time. I imagined vivid pictures of me and him in various states of nakedness. Of course, I had to imagine what certain parts of his anatomy looked like, because we'd only ever done it in the dark or from behind. I decided that this night, I was gonna make sure we did it with the lights on so I could see every gorgeous inch of him.

Yeah, I planned to be his sexual superstar, but first I was taking the more traditional route to Keith's heart. I'd promised to try out some of his recipes to see if they turned out as good as when he cooked for me. Getting him to write down each and every step and ingredient had been the real work, but if I could convince him to give me more of his recipes, I knew the book would be destined for the *Essence* bestseller list.

As I maneuvered around my kitchen, I thought of Keith on the number two train moving toward me, and it made me even more excited. As if on cue, the doorbell rang. I slipped off the apron I had gotten as a freebie for a magazine subscription and hurried to the door.

"Hey, li'l ma." Keith was holding flowers and a bottle of wine. Just seeing him standing there, looking all sexy and thuggish, made me want to grab him and whip some loving on him.

"Yo, so how's the cooking going?" he asked me, and I wanted to tell him we should just abandon the food and heat him up in the bedroom.

"The greens are tasting almost as good as I remember, and the smothered chicken . . . Well, I'm gonna have to let you taste for yourself," I bragged.

I put the flowers in a vase and opened the bottle of wine. I don't know what it was about red wine, but damn if it didn't get me hornier. I flirted with Keith by rubbing past him every time I had to grab an ingredient, but he didn't take the bait. Maybe he was just nervous about seeing how his recipes would translate in the hands of another cook, I thought.

"You sure you put enough broth in the greens?" He kept hopping from one foot to the other, all fidgety.

"This ain't my first time in a kitchen," I joked, trying to lighten his mood.

"Um, I have something for you." Keith handed me an envelope. I assumed it was more recipes, so I set it on the counter and kept cooking.

"Ain't you gonna read it?"

"I'ma get to it later," I said. "Now stop try'na distract me, Keith. I want you to be impressed with my food." I continued working the pots and pans.

He looked at me strangely, kind of half-disappointed that I wasn't opening the envelope, but also half-relieved.

An hour and a half later, after Keith and I worked through the kinks in his recipes and ate ourselves silly, I attacked him, needing his long, hard member inside of me. If someone told me a year ago that I'd leave Tiny and be anxious to have sex with the new guy I was seeing, I would have called them insane. Yet here I was in just that situation. I couldn't get enough of Keith and his body. While it wasn't quite the "once you go black, you never go back" thing, I was amazed at how easy it was to crave the dick again, even after living as a lesbian for so many years.

I reached over to Keith, placing my hands on his waist, and started unzipping his jeans. I didn't expect him to stop me.

"Hey, what are you doin'?" he said, all the while backing away from me.

"Try'na please you, baby." I couldn't understand why he stopped at such a crucial moment.

"I'll do it." He quickly zipped up his pants.

"But I want to give you a blow job." I still didn't get his reluctance. After all, I'd never met a man who didn't want me to service him. In fact, the majority of men I'd come across would prefer a blow job over almost anything else.

"Nikki, I already told you that I'm not into blow jobs." He took my hands, staring deep into my eyes. Something just wasn't right about his constant refusal of oral sex, but I couldn't put my finger on it. Little did I know that by the end of the night, I'd know exactly what his problem was. For the time being, I still thought I could change his mind.

"That's because you never had one by me. I wanna show you my skills," I said in my most sultry voice.

"It's not my thing." He pulled me close. "I just want to be inside of you," he whispered in my ear.

As much as I wanted to complain, the idea of skipping the appetizer and going straight to dessert did appeal to me. I put my arms around his neck, kissing him passionately. He took my hand and led me into the bedroom.

When we entered the room, Keith turned off all the lights and even shut the blinds. I started to protest, but he was in between my legs so fast, licking and sucking me to ecstasy that my mind pretty much went blank.

As soon as I had my first orgasm, Keith put on a condom and entered me, pushing deeper and deeper inside. I moaned loudly and begged, "Baby, play with my titties while you're inside me." He kissed my neck and lips as his hands started exploring my breasts. This was the first time we'd done it missionary style, and I could not believe how deep he was.

"Oh, I just want you so badly." I pressed my body closer to him.

"You got me." He thrust his body closer to me, his hardness stretching me open even wider.

"I love this," I shouted.

Keith's mouth traveled to my nipples, and the sensation of his hot tongue on my breasts while he pumped deep inside me nearly sent me into a frenzy. I clung to Keith, my arms encircling his chest as we converged in a sweaty mess. That's when my hands began to travel down his back.

"Oh, baby," Keith's husky voice whispered in my ear. It felt like we were reaching new heights together.

I pumped up and down to our rhythm as he gripped my taut, thick ass cheeks. My hand slipped lower to his waist, and then stopped abruptly. I felt something thick, like a belt, in my hands.

"What the hell is this? You wearing a belt to bed?" I asked playfully, but Keith didn't seem to find anything funny. He pulled out of me in a hurry and jumped off the bed. Confused, I hit the remote on the TV to let some light into the room. I had no idea what the hell was going on at this point.

Keith was trying to grab his underwear off the floor and put them on in a hurry, but it was too late. I had already seen the one thing he didn't want me to, the one thing I could never have imagined I'd be seeing. The thing I'd felt was a belt all right, but it wasn't the kind that holds up your pants. It was holding up the big, fake-ass dick hanging between Keith's legs. And the motherfucker had the nerve to have a condom on it.

"What the fuck?" My voice raised dangerously close to glass-breaking decibels. "Oh my God. Get out. Get the fuck out!"

"Wait, let me explain," Keith said as he hastily threw on his clothes.

"Get the fuck out of my goddamned house!" I shouted at the top of my lungs. He stepped closer, and I slapped him as hard as I could. "I told you to get the fuck out my house!"

Within moments, Keith had gathered his things and was out the door. I didn't care if I never saw him—oh hell, Keith wasn't even a he!—again.

52

Tammy

When I got to my mother's place late one night after seeing Raoul, I expected a dark house. Instead, I found her sitting in the kitchen, sipping on some hot tea. Seeing her like that took me back to the days in high school, when she would wait up in just the same spot when I stayed out past my curfew.

"Hey, Momma. I'm back," I called out as I stepped into the kitchen, removing my heels.

She didn't say anything. She just stood up and grabbed another mug out of the closet.

"You don't have to do that," I told her. "I'm not in the mood for tea. I'm gonna go on to bed. I'm really tired." I didn't want to talk about why I was coming in late, or why I was still living in her house after all these weeks. She'd left the subject alone since our last book club meeting, but I could tell by the way she firmly pulled out another chair from the table that we were going to discuss it again whether I wanted to or not.

"Honey, come on over here and sit with me for a while." Her voice was calm but firm. My mother had a booming voice and was always sarcastic, but tonight she spoke to me with a softness in her voice. It was the way I'd heard her talking to my stepfather over the years.

"Now, Tammy, you know as long as I'm alive you will always have a place to call home, but I'm your mother, and I wanna know what's going on."

"Mom, it's nothing," I lied, knowing that this time she wasn't going to accept the same brief, evasive answers I'd been giving her.

"It's not nothin', Tam. It could be a lot of things, but it's definitely something. You ain't been home in over a month."

"I'll work it out." I felt my voice shaking. Had it really been that long? I'd been so busy living in denial that I hadn't noticed how much time had passed since I'd been home with my husband and my kids. My kids. Lord, I couldn't believe I hadn't seen my kids in over a month.

"Tim is like a son to me, and I love him, but you're my daughter, Tammy, and if he did something to hurt you, I want to know," she pressed. Telling my mother how my husband caught me in a motel fucking his best friend and employee wasn't what I wanted to do, but I needed to talk to someone. The words came streaming out of my mouth along with tears from my eyes.

"Momma, I messed up. We were happy with our lives, but I wanted to do more, so I pushed and pushed, and it just got worse. I am so sorry," I cried.

"I know you're sorry, baby. You talking in some kind of code 'cause you don't want to tell me what happened. Well, honey, you don't owe me any details about your marriage. That's personal business between you and Tim. But I want you to know that I'm here for you and I certainly don't judge you."

I placed my hand over hers, letting my mother know that I appreciated her.

"I done made more mistakes than I can ever remember, honey," she continued. "Your daddy and me were children who had no business thinking we could be parents. I had another husband and two more children before I met your stepdaddy and got it right. If there was an easy road and a hard road side by side, hell, your momma took the hard road. But you are different. You met Tim straight out the gate, and you two got it right, so whatever this is you going through, you gotta get to the other side . . . together."

"Momma, I call him every day. He doesn't want me anymore," I sobbed.

"If there is one thing I know, honey, it's men, and no matter what you done, no man can love you as much as Tim does, then suddenly stop. It don't work like that." She stroked my hair gently, which only sent me into louder tears.

"He's so mad at me. It's over." My words were getting lost in the hysteria of my tears.

"This is your marriage and your husband. It ain't over unless you walk away. You got two kids from that man. That ain't so easy to walk away from, and sure he's mad, but he loves you. Either you put up the fight of your life and go back there and get your family back, or you give up. But first you gotta stop running after whoever this man is you be sneaking out to see."

"You know about that?" I couldn't believe my ears.

"Girl, please, you smell like cheap hotel soap, and your skin is ashy like you just took a shower and didn't have enough time to put lotion on. Not to mention the fact that your hair is parted differently than when you left here a few hours ago." She pointed at my head. "I may be out the game, but I still know the rules. You're lucky Tim didn't catch you sooner." She stood up and kissed my head, then told me, "I'll talk to you in the morning. And I'm gonna call your husband tomorrow. I think it's time he came for a visit."

A car door slammed, and the sounds of children's laughter sent me rushing to the living room. My mother opened the front door as Tim and the kids came in. The kids rushed past my mother and into my arms as she and Tim hugged and made small talk. After a while, my mom gathered up the twins and volunteered to take them for ice cream, leaving me with Tim. One glance at his face and I wanted to rush to the car with my mom and the kids, but I also realized I needed to try working things out with my husband.

"Tim, I am so sorry," I started. But instead of listening, he began backing up as if he was ready to run. I reached out and grabbed his hand. "Baby, please. I love you."

He stopped walking toward the door, but he didn't exactly make himself comfortable. "You fucked up, Tammy," he said, leaning against the doorframe with a terrible scowl on his face. "You cheated on me, and you cheated on our family." There was nothing I could say, because he was right.

"But, Tim, I'm so sorry," I pleaded with him.

"Are you, Tammy? Are you really sorry? Because I don't know who you even are anymore. You are not the girl I married." He sounded so final.

At that moment, I saw my entire world slipping away. I was so close to losing my husband, my children, and my whole life. And as much as I liked Raoul licking and sucking me into ecstasy, I didn't love him, and I didn't want to lose my family. Whoever said you can have it all forgot to mention rule number one: Don't get caught.

"I made a mistake," I said in a last-ditch effort to explain things in a way that might make Tim forgive me. "And it started because I wanted to make you happy. I tried to be the kind of wife who fulfills all her husband's fantasies. I wanted to be better than a wife. I wanted to be your lover and the person who turns you on in every way, but somehow, it just went all wrong." The tears streamed in puddles.

Tim seemed unmoved by my words. "You fucked another man behind my back. How can I ever trust you again?"

"You brought him home to our bed in the first place. I never wanted to have another man inside of me. I just wanted you."

"How do I know you won't fuck him again?"

"I love you, Tim, and you're who I want to spend my life with." I fell to my knees at his feet, needing him to take me back.

"Tammy, I'm not the open-marriage kind of guy. Everything about me is traditional."

"I know that, and it's why I love you." I clung to his pants leg, desperate for my family to stay together.

"And if I give you another chance?" His words caused my heart to beat even faster. It was the first ray of hope he'd given me since the night he kicked me out.

"I promise to be a better wife. I will make you happy. I can." I stood up, took his face in my hands, and leaned in for a deep, soulful kiss. Instead, Tim pulled away.

"No, we're not there." He took a step backward. I started to say something, but he stopped me. "This is not an overnight thing. It's not fixed. You have a lot to prove to me," Tim informed me, but I knew that all I needed was a window of opportunity and I would find my way back into my life.

"Oh, Tim, thank you." Another wave of tears started down my face.

"You can come home . . ." he started.

"Thank you!" I interrupted him, but he held up his hand, palm facing me, to let me know he wasn't finished.

"But you stay in the guest room. As far as I'm concerned, you're only coming home for the sake of the kids."

I quickly agreed, because I really did miss my kids, and because I knew that my banishment to the guest room would only be temporary. There was one thing I knew how to do, and it was to fuck my husband. All I needed was a little bit of time, and Tim would be begging me to get back into the bedroom where I belonged. Hell, I intended to wear my sexiest nightie and start tonight, because there was no way I was going to be a guest in my own house.

53

Isis

It had been days since I'd talked to Tony's wife, and instead of feeling better because I had fucked up his life, I had sunk deeper into my funk. I couldn't shake the feeling that there was nothing in my life to make me feel whole or worth anything. My relationship with Tony had been one big lie, and I doubted there were any decent men out there, so my love life was basically over. My job was just a paycheck. I had friends, but they all had their own lives and their own dramas to deal with. And then there was my sister and my ex. Funny how after all this, my sister might end up walking down the aisle with the man I should have chosen. I was the one who couldn't tell a good man when he was right in my face. The time had come to admit that I didn't have any luck with men. Not really.

"I'm tired of always getting the scraps," I cried into my pillow, feeling like a big loser. Even the people who went on reality shows crying about their problems and making fools of themselves seemed to have more going for them than I did. At least they had the chance of becoming famous.

In less than one month, I had gone from having a life full of hope to becoming a lonely old maid who just had to accept that she wasn't the kind of person who would ever have a man love her. Tammy had Tim, who loved her dirty drawers, and Nikki dumped Tiny but still had some guy waiting in the wings to get with her. Hell, even Coco, who broke every rule of dating, was shacked up with some good-looking hottie. And then there was my sister, Egypt, who had snagged the man I could have had.

"I hate my life." The tears hit my pillow as I sobbed out loud. A couple of days ago, a neighbor knocked on my door, concerned about all the crying. I lied and told her a close relative had died, which really wasn't that far from the truth. The part of me that believed I would one day walk down the aisle and have my own family was dead. At thirty-four, my eggs were quickly aging, which meant that unless I met someone in the next year, believed his lying ass, and convinced him to marry me, who knew if I could ever have kids? Yeah, the big dreams I had were being flushed down the toilet, and there was no way I could change the tide.

"Fuuuuuuuck!" I cried out, upset that even my anger had turned to sadness. I couldn't even blame Tony for running a game on me. He saw that I wasn't really worth any commitment.

I just wanted to stay in bed until it was all over, this thing called life. Nobody deserved to keep getting kicked in the gut like a dog. One day, you just stop being able to convince yourself to get up. I had already decided that I wasn't getting up ever again, but I needed to talk to someone before I closed my eyes. I called the one person who might help me make sense of where I had gone wrong in my life.

"Hello, it's Isis. I need to talk to you," I begged.

"Why are you calling me?"

"I need to talk to you, Rashad. You're the only person who can tell me the truth."

"I can't go back into this again, Isis. I hope things work out for you."

"Please, Rashad, don't hang up!" I yelled. "If I ever meant anything to you, please just talk to me."

He sighed deep and long, but at least he was still on the line. "What?" he asked, sounding annoyed.

"I just need to know why my life is so fucked up. I wanted to hear from someone who used to love me where I went wrong and why I'm destined to end up alone."

"I don't know, Isis." He sighed again.

"Rashad, please. Tell me why I wasn't the woman you wanted to marry."

"Um, if I remember correctly, you were the one who said no when I proposed to you," he answered.

I cringed at the memory of that day. "No, Rashad. I mean before that. When I was ready to marry you, how come you just let me go? Why didn't you want to marry me then?"

"You really wanna know?" he asked, and I remained silent,

waiting to finally hear the truth. "Fine," he continued. "You were desperate and clingy. You needed guarantees that everything would turn out just the way you set up in your fantasy. Reality didn't seem to ever be enough for you."

I had spent so much time beating up on myself over the last few days that his harsh assessment of me didn't even hurt. He wasn't saying anything worse than what I'd already concluded about myself. It actually helped a little to hear it coming from Rashad.

"Wow, I'm glad you told me," was all I said.

"Mmm-hmm. Is that all you called for?" he asked, sounding anxious to get off the phone.

"Well . . . yeah. I guess. And I want you to know something too."

"What's that?"

"I'm not upset about you and Egypt. I'm happy for you two." I don't know if *happy* was really the right word for it, but I was through being mad at them. I wanted to make peace with my sister before I went to sleep.

"Maybe you should tell Egypt that," he said, and next thing I knew, I heard my sister's voice.

"Isis?" I couldn't read her tone, but I hoped she wasn't too mad at me.

"Rashad told me why it is that no man ever loves me," I cried.

"Isis, enough." Maybe she wasn't mad, but she was definitely sick of me. I couldn't blame her, though. Now that I'd taken a good, hard look at myself, I understood how I must look to her.

"You walk around letting everyone know that you're a victim," she continued. "You're not a victim; you volunteered for this. You could have had another life, but you made your choice."

"I'm sorry, Egypt. I'm so sorry." I felt myself getting extremely tired now. "I just need to go away so that no one has to deal with me anymore. It's just like when we were children. I'm a burden." My words were getting all messed up, and the snot began to run down my face. I had made a mess of things, and now it was too late to fix them.

"Egypt, I just want you to know that you've been a good sister to me. I love you," I boo-hooed.

"Isis, you got to get it together. It's not the end of the world," she said in a stern voice.

"No, I can't get it together. I'm just so tired." It took everything not to close my eyes right there.

"Of course you can get it together." She must have started taking me seriously, because now it sounded like genuine concern in her voice.

"I can't," I sobbed. "This life has been too long and too exhausting. I just want to sleep and not ever worry about messing up and making mistakes again." I felt myself getting woozy.

"You're human, sis. That's normal." She just didn't get it.

"No, it's not normal to be engaged to some guy you think you know and then you find out he's got a whole 'nother family. How would you feel if you found out your entire life was a joke?" I cried into the phone.

Egypt tried to calm me down. "Bad things happen sometimes."

"Not sometimes. Bad things happen to me all the time." As much as my sister wanted to cheer me up, I had finally learned the truth about life, and nothing she could say was going to change that fact. I balled up the sheets and blew my nose into them, then started blubbering like a baby.

"Isis, you sound a little extreme. Maybe you just need some sleep," she suggested.

"I slept for the last three days. All I want to do is sleep."

"I'll come over and we'll go to dinner," Egypt suggested. She didn't understand that it couldn't happen. I was done with simple things like breakfast, lunch, and dinner.

"No, I just need to sleep."

"Isis, I love you." Her words had a hint of desperation behind them, like she'd finally figured out what I was planning to do.

"I got to go to sleep, Egypt." I felt my head growing heavier. "Enjoy your life with Rashad, and tell Mom I love her." The phone dropped out of my hands. From a distance, I heard someone yelling my name, but it was coming through a wind tunnel or something. The bottle of pills fell out of my hand and bounced on the carpet. I watched it roll a few feet, but I felt too exhausted to pick it up. I waited for that feeling of calm to wash over me, expecting it any moment. I was so tired of hurting that I had fixed it so that it would never happen again.

54

Nikki

After I kicked Keith out, I started cleaning like a crazy person. I had called Coco to come over, but I needed something to distract me from what just happened until she got here. My mind was racing as I scrubbed and scoured everything in sight. Was every damn body someone other than who they said they were? First Tiny turned abusive, then I found out that Keith's entire identity was a lie. What the hell did this mean about me? The banging at my door interrupted my thoughts, which had to be a good thing, since I didn't even know where to begin to start dealing with all this shit.

I threw open the door and gave Coco a look that said, *Gurrrl, you won't believe this shit when you hear it.* I had given her no details over the phone, only telling her that I had kicked Keith's ass out of my house.

"We need to get ourselves some alcohol and a good place to sit first," Coco said. " 'Cause I got some shit to tell you too."

"Coco, this is serious," I whined, and as much as I hated adults who whined like cranky children, in this case, it seemed more than appropriate.

"What makes you think I ain't got my own drama going on?" she said with some serious attitude. "All hell was about to break loose over at my spot the other day, so forgive me for needing a drink."

In the kitchen, she noticed the half-full bottle of red wine left over from my dinner with Keith. "This all you got?"

I was happy to get rid of Keith's wine. I poured it down the sink and pulled out a bottle of Bacardi dark rum. "This is all I got left. When Tiny moved out, she took everything else with her."

"This'll do," Coco said, then grabbed the rum and took a

swig right from the bottle. If I didn't have my own shit going on, I would have been worried about her. Coco liked to get her drink on, but I'd never seen her down it like that. I guess she saw the look on my face, because she suddenly had a need to explain herself.

"You know, whenever you put two people together and they both got they own shit popping off, you think you got some sacred connection, but all you getting is lies when you thought you two were thick and shit." Even if I didn't completely understand her rambling, I knew what she meant. No matter how close you are to another person, you can't depend on them to tell you the whole truth.

Coco and I slipped back into the living room after I had poured us two rum and Cokes. We liked a good apple martini when we was feeling good, but when the shit hit the fan, we always reverted back to our old-school favorite. I'm sure all over the world, black folks been solving their dramas with a trusty bottle of Bacardi.

"Daaaaamn!" was all Coco said when I finished telling her about Keith being a woman. Now, for somebody like Coco, who had both seen and done her share of dirt, to be shocked, I knew I had been played.

"Ain't that some shit?" My anger began to bubble over. I hated that I seemed destined to become one of those angry black women who couldn't trust anybody to love them properly. I'd always been the hopeless romantic in the group, always believing in the power of love to heal everything. In fact, whenever I chose a book selection for the BGBC, everybody knew before they even opened it that there was going to be a happy ending. I wanted my fairy-tale finish both on and off the page, and now all those daydreams about Keith and me and the possibility of our future were fading fast.

Coco didn't seem to understand my anger. "Nikki, I hate to state the obvious, but what the hell is the big deal? You done spent all them years with Tiny, muff-diving and shit." She laughed.

"The big deal is that I thought Keith was a man, not some woman pretending to be a man." I didn't understand how she could miss my point. "And you know what pissed me off the most?" She shook her head. "The motherfucker used condoms. He was wearing a fake-ass dick but still put on a condom."

"It's rather brilliant if you think about it," she said. "That's probably why you didn't know it was fake."

"Fuck you, Coco." I was mad because she was probably right.

"Look, I ain't try'na make you mad, Nikki. I'm just sayin', it ain't like the mothafucker lied about what he did for a living or nothing." She picked up her half-full glass and finished it off in one gulp.

"Are you crazy? How is someone lying about his job worse than someone lying about his fake dick?" I asked, wondering if the whole damn world had lost its mind.

Then Coco explained to me about Mac and his real job, and I understood where she was coming from. Mac had a real dick, but it turned out he had a job that required him to stick it in all kinds of places a committed man is not supposed to be.

Coco tried to act like she was through with Mac. "I mean, let's be real, Nikki," she told me. "I saw the look on his face in those movies. It's the same damn look he gets on his face every time he be fuckin' me. How do I know he wasn't just acting with me the whole time?"

"Coco," I said sincerely, "I saw the way he looked at you at the book club meeting that night. There's no way that man is acting when he's around you. That brother loves you."

She got a faraway look in her eyes, and I knew she wanted to believe me. She wanted things to work out between the two of them, but there was still the problem of his career that he never told her about. Coco wasn't about to forgive and forget that easy.

"Girl, looks like we both found us some lying motherfuckers," she said, raising her glass.

After we had finished almost the entire bottle of rum, Coco asked, "So, why was he—I mean she—like that anyway? I mean, what makes someone start wearing a dildo in her pants?"

I just shrugged. She continued to ask questions about Keith, most of which I couldn't answer. I'd kicked him out so fast that I didn't even have time to form any questions in my head. I'd just wanted him gone. Now, though, I was a little frustrated that I had no idea why he'd done what he did. That's when I remembered the letter on the kitchen counter. I had never bothered to open it before we headed into the bedroom earlier that night.

I wasn't sure if I could stand to read it, but I went into the kitchen and brought the envelope back to Coco. "What do you think I should do with it?" I asked.

"You got to read it," was her answer.

"What? So I can read more lies?" I barked. "Motherfucker could have told me the truth. All these months of frontin', and now after I done left Tiny and broke up my home and shit, I find out it's all bullshit."

"Whoa, whoa, Keith and Tiny are two separate issues. You needed to kick Tiny's controlling ass to the curb a long time ago. In fact, the day she put her hands on you should have been her last day on earth. Maybe the only reason Keith came along was to get you to leave Tiny," she offered like some damn Oprah clone. Where the hell was my hard-ass, take-no-prisoners Coco?

"What is wrong with you?" I yelled at her. I did not want to hear that my connection to Keith was for some higher purpose in my life. I was already having a hard enough time trying to deny what I knew to be true—I had started to fall in love with Keith. And the way I had my heart ripped out, I was not in the mood to hear about any positive side to all of this.

"Hell," Coco said, "at least you got a letter instead of finding out shit from your bitchy cousin who can't stand seeing you happy." She tried to make it sound like a joke, but I could see that my girl was in pain. She loved Mac.

I knew exactly how she felt. I wanted to run away and forget everything, but like my mother always said, no matter where you go, there you are. I couldn't pretend forever that I wasn't in love with Keith. And even the fact that he had lied to me wasn't enough to make those feelings disappear instantly. I looked at the envelope in my hand, wondering if the letter inside would contain answers that might help me figure out how to move on from here.

"So, what if I read this and give Keith another chance?" I wondered out loud. "It's only a matter of time before the shit blows up in my face again."

"No one said you had to forgive Keith. I just said you should read the letter. Aren't you even curious why he lied?"

I couldn't deny that I was curious. I ripped open the envelope and began to read. I sat there in silence, slowly going over every word, every detail, as Keith, whose birth name was Karen, gave me the whole story. I read about the dark childhood Karen had

had, with an abusive father who wound up in jail for murder and a mother who hovered over her like an airplane, afraid something bad would happen to her every moment. The letter talked about how Karen felt alone in the world after her mother passed away and how none of her blood relatives would take her, so she went into the foster care system for months, having one abusive event after another heaped on her until her mother's best friend, Aunt Gwen, convinced the courts to give her custody.

The letter went on to explain how even as a little girl, she had never been interested in boys. Yeah, Karen wanted to compete with them, but she never, even in high school, wanted to have anything sexual to do with them. She fell in love with her best friend, who not only didn't return her feelings, but shunned her after her confession.

I read about so many moments of shame and isolation until her aunt Gwen put it to her: "Ain't nobody gonna love somebody who don't think they deserve to be loved." It was shortly after that when Karen decided to accept herself for who she was, and she began living her life as Keith.

Aunt Gwen accepted the change from Karen to Keith, but she disagreed with Keith's decision to keep his real identity a secret from those he got close to. That included me. He explained the argument he and his aunt had had that night at the restaurant. She told Keith he had to trust people to love him for him and that I deserved to know the truth to make my own choice. In the end, he apologized and said he was deeply afraid that the only reason I was attracted to him was because I didn't want to be gay.

I put the letter on the table and cried like a baby. Keith had poured his heart and soul into this letter, and if I had only read it when he handed it to me, instead of rushing into the bedroom, the night might have turned out quite differently. He was trying to tell me the truth, only I hadn't let him. Maybe I owed him one more chance to talk to me.

"I know what I have to do," I told Coco, and that's when I noticed the tears in her eyes.

"Me too," she said.

"You gonna call Mac? 'Cause you know I ain't letting you drive all hammered," I told her.

"Who said I was goin' anywhere?" she asked.

Now I was confused. "You just said you knew what you needed to do."

"Uh, yeah," she said sarcastically. "I just meant I need to go to the bathroom. These rum and Cokes is just runnin' through me."

I rolled my eyes at her and laughed. My girl Coco was crazy, but I was grateful to her for lightening my mood. With everything that had happened lately, I needed a good laugh. I got up and headed for the bedroom, telling Coco she could spend the night in DJ's room. I hoped I could get a good night's rest, because the next day had way too many real issues for me to scoop up off my plate.

55

Tammy

I arranged to meet Raoul one last time. There would be no sex talk, no naked bodies, no faces buried in each other's crotches. This was going to be the end of lying, cheating, and any more adulterous behavior. My real life was hanging by a thread, and if I had a chance at getting my family back, I had to let go of my affair with Raoul and act like I had some sense. I had been behaving like a dick-whipped teenager instead of a respectable wife, mother, and pillar of my community. Until I got caught, I had forgotten all about the things I stood to lose, including the only man I had ever really loved, my husband.

It took me hours to figure out where to meet and longer to choose what to wear. I didn't want to wear anything so sexy that Raoul thought I was coming on to him, but something flattering enough to remind him what he'd be missing. We met at a coffee shop not too far from the office. Luckily, even though Tim had tossed me out on my ass, he hadn't fired me. It was the one thing that made me believe I had a chance to win him and my children back, and I was not about to fuck that up for sex, no matter how good the tongue was.

Raoul showed up twenty minutes late, looking disheveled in wrinkled jeans and an old Che Guevara T-shirt. He wore a three-day-old beard and a pissed-off expression. I tried to look cheery and upbeat, like neither of us was fighting to keep our personal lives from falling apart.

"Hey." He tossed the greeting out, trying to make it appear extra casual, but I saw the look on his face, and it was the same expression he wore whenever he was about to eat me. The man still desired me; that was clear.

And despite my own inner warnings, I was starting to get turned on by the sight of him too. Before things got out of hand, I reminded myself of my purpose for meeting him here.

"We need to talk," I said.

He gave me that expression of exhaustion all men get at the sound of those four words strung together. I didn't care, though. What I planned to say needed to be said.

"About what?"

"About us. We need to stop." There, I said it.

"Why?" Raoul stared into my eyes, unblinking.

"Because this isn't good for either one of us."

"Tammy," he started, leaning in close to me, making my vagina throb with desire for him. "I want to rip off your panties and shove my tongue up your pussy until you come all over it."

It took me a moment to regain my composure before I could speak. "I can't. We can't do this anymore."

"Why? What have we got to lose now? I lost my job, and Tim told my wife, so I want to know why I should give up the best pussy I ever had," he challenged me.

He must have noticed that I wasn't sharing a similar list of problems with him, and suddenly he knew why I was ending it. "What? Has he taken you back?"

Raoul moved from his seat across the table to sit next to me. I slid away from him, but he put his hand on my thigh, under my dress.

"Stop it!" I pushed his hand away. "We have to be sorry for what we did. We hurt them!"

"I don't give a fuck anymore. Don't you get that? I've damn near lost everything, so why should I just walk away with my tail between my legs?"

I'd never seen Raoul like this. I pulled farther away from him. "I need to be back with my family. It has been fun having sex with you, but I love my husband. I love my family. I love my life." The words came out in an avalanche, but they had no effect on him.

"We didn't start this," he reasoned. "Your husband is the one who gave you to me. You think I would ever offer up the woman I love to another man? He not only gave you to me like some casual piece of ass, he let me fuck you on the same bed you sleep in at night. So, before you start acting like Tim deserves you, remember that he opened this door. We didn't."

"It's not that black and white, Raoul," I said, refusing to buy into his argument, even though it was the same one I had tried to use to explain my affair to Tim. "You don't know what I put Tim through. I started this. If it were up to Tim, there would have never been anyone but the two of us. He just tried to give me what he thought I needed." And at that moment, I realized what a huge sacrifice it had been for my husband, and I loved him even more.

"But I need you." Raoul pushed closer to me, and as much as his physical presence got my hormones going, I knew I couldn't act on my desires. I had to do the right thing to protect what was mine.

"You have to listen to me. You can work it out with your wife, Raoul, and you'll get another job." I was desperate for him to see my side of this before I gave in to my lust.

He ran his fingers up my arm. "Mami, you know you want me," he whispered close to my ear.

"Raoul, stop it!" I used the same tone I did with the kids when they were acting up and refusing to listen to reason. But he certainly wasn't behaving like my kids.

He leaned even closer, whispering in my ear. "If you give me up, then who is going to lick and suck your pussy?" His voice turned all throaty and deep. I knew I had to get out of there. Raoul ran his hand down my thigh, slipping it under my dress. I grabbed his hand before it went any farther.

"You have to stop!"

He finally heard the desperation in my voice and pulled his hand back. "Is Tim going to finally treat your pussy the way it deserves? Is he going to worship it and treat it like a fine meal? Or is he going to have you suck his dick every night until it is hard and wet and then shove it inside of you?" he asked with disgust.

I had to keep sex out of this. It wasn't about what Tim and I did in the bedroom; it was about our whole life together. "Raoul, think about the children. Our kids deserve to be raised in happy, two-parent households. I could never forgive myself if I wreck my children's childhood with this selfishness. What kind of mother would that make me?" I was past the point of caring if he knew how much I had to fight my urge for him.

"This is adult business. Children are incredibly resilient, and they will be fine," he tried to convince me, but I was a mother and knew better.

"You're just angry, but you're going to get another job, and if you focus on your wife and family, maybe you'll get another chance. Raoul, I don't want to lose my family." As the words came out of my mouth, I knew how a crack addict felt, because even though I realized he was bad for me, the desire for him wasn't lifting. I turned my body away from him, but like a drug, he knew the pull he had over me.

"You think it's going to be that easy to just walk away from this? You're telling me you don't want me to stick my fingers in your twat until you shoot that delicious liquid all over them? You want to give me a taste of what you are threatening to take away from me?" He slid his fingers up my leg and lifted the elastic of my panties.

I jumped up and damn near squashed him as I climbed over him, getting out of there. He grabbed my arm, pulling me down to his level.

"So, you go ahead and try to return to the boring sex you have with your husband. You give him my pussy and see if he can make it his again. I promise you this: Your pussy is going to be on fire tonight and every night, until I put out that fire with my tongue."

He released my hand, and I raced out of there like I had stolen something. That would definitely be the last time I saw Raoul. He had almost driven me over the edge with my need for him, and I wasn't about to let that happen again. I needed to do what I had to in order to keep my family together. I wanted to be a good wife to Tim, and tonight I would take all this pent-up sexual energy home to my husband, if he would let me. I desperately needed to forget all about Raoul, and I was praying Tim would help me.

56

Coco

In my luxurious loft apartment one night, I started feeling like one of those ladies in waiting, and it didn't sit well with me. After my drunken talk with Nikki, when I actually thought for a hot minute that I would give Mac another chance, I came to my senses and moved back into Jackson's condo and resumed my lifestyle as a pampered mistress. Unfortunately, that meant lots of time waiting for Jackson's arrival, and it certainly didn't make me feel better that I was waiting for a man who got on my goddamn nerves. He couldn't even make me come unless I was fantasizing about another man. Yeah, it might have looked all good on the outside—the Benz, the fabulous condo, and shopping whenever I wanted—but it felt empty as hell. In order to make it through most nights, I put on one of Mac's movies. Thanks to a Web site I'd discovered, I located every movie he'd ever done, including the first one where he and three other men gangbanged a woman. Yeah, I hated to admit it, but watching him serve it up to those other women didn't make me jealous; it made me hella horny.

Speaking of Mac, my phone went off as if on cue. Since I'd walked out on him, he'd been calling, texting, and e-mailing me constantly. I refused to answer, figuring sooner or later he'd get tired and step off, but the brother had stamina both in and out of the bedroom, outlasting any other man I'd ever rejected. I could have changed my number or blocked his calls, but I guess I wasn't as through with him as I wanted to be. It was actually satisfying to have him trying so hard. I'd never had a man chase me for more than a month, all day, every day. There were the guys who called every week hoping to get back in, or the brothers who dialed every day for about a week before moving on or losing interest, but never anyone as persistent as Mac.

I checked my voice mail to see what he had to say this time.

He'd kept it short and sweet. "Hey, Coco, I need to talk to you." Even on a message, Mac's voice hit me at my core. Still, I refused to call him back. I had been weak for him once, and look where it got me. There was no way I'd do that again. Besides, what could he talk to me about? Fucking in pornos and not sharing that knowledge with the woman he says he loves? At least I learned from that experience that all men are full of shit, and love is a fantasy that has more to do with sexual urges than real emotion. Maybe I just thought I loved Mac when I simply allowed myself to get dick-whipped.

"Girl, you let a man make a fool of you once, shame on you. You let a man make a fool of you twice, well, then you're just a fool," I told myself out loud. I turned back to the movie in time to see Mac enter some big-titted high-yella girl. Her entire body reacted to his entrance, and in that second, I wanted it to be me. Damn, I missed him, but wasn't no point in trying to turn a liar into an honest man.

"Hello?" Jackson's voice greeted me from the front door.

I whispered to myself, "Showtime." I turned off the DVD, threw on a robe, and went out to greet my guest.

"Um, let me see what you got under there." Jackson reached out to grab me, but I stepped away.

"It's my birthday suit, but it's not your birthday," I teased.

"Come here and let me see you under there." Again he tried to pull open my robe.

I pushed him away. I learned that if I could put Jackson off for a while, then by the time I gave him some, it would be over quick. I continued to let him chase me around, taunting and teasing him with flashes of my thigh and breast. Forty minutes later, when I let him catch me, it took ten more minutes before I had him nutting off all over the place. Lucky for me, his wife called not long after we finished and demanded he come home immediately or else she'd join him out. Yeah, I could picture his wife walking into my apartment and seeing me naked, spread-eagle, with her husband's face buried in my pussy.

"Gotta go." Jackson made skid marks like she had a tracking device on his ass, and he was about to be caught.

After he left, I took a shower, hoping it would wash the stench of Jackson off my skin. Going back to him wasn't as easy as being with him the first time, because in the interim, I had opened up my heart, and as much as I hated to admit it, the whole episode with Mac still hurt.

I got back in bed, frustrated because Jackson hadn't satisfied me. He couldn't, and truthfully didn't even try. Our entire relationship was about me satisfying him. I needed an orgasm badly, so I turned on Mac's DVD and got myself ready to get satisfaction.

Halfway to orgasm, my cell phone rang and threw off my concentration. It wasn't the phone itself that bothered me but who I knew was calling. I snatched up the phone from my bedside.

"What!" I refused to give any more than that, and he was damn lucky to even get that much out of me.

"Don't hang up," Mac begged. Just the sound of his voice sent chills up my spine. This man had the ability to make me want him even when I knew I shouldn't. It didn't help matters much that I saw him on my television screen, pumping the way he used to do to me. But I refused to give in to my base needs. I would be stronger than that.

"What the hell do you want? I have nothing to say to you."

"I want a chance to explain," he pleaded.

"Talk." I decided that since the phone gave me distance from him, I might as well hear him out.

"In person."

"I don't think so." He had some nerve asking me for anything.

"Coco, I love you, and I need to talk with you. I'm not going to give up on us until you give me a chance to speak my piece. Please!"

Oh, so he wanted a chance to speak his piece? Fine. He could have one, but it would be on my terms. We would meet in the luxurious condo provided for me by Jackson. The idea of flaunting my new life to Mac appealed to me. Yeah, he could have his say; then he'd have to realize that he was shit out of luck with me.

I gave him the address and told him now was as good a time as any. I put on one of my sexiest dresses, a Diane von Furstenberg animal-print mini that hugged my curves and made the most of my cleavage. When the doorman called to announce Mac's arrival, I poured myself a glass of wine, unlocked the door, and sat back on my chaise longue.

I knew the doorman would probably report to Jackson later that I had a man in my apartment, but I didn't care. It was just another opportunity to remind him that he didn't own me.

Mac entered looking finer than I remembered and sexier than even a screen could capture. I willed my body to stay neutral and not react to the sound of his voice or the look in his eyes. But my body betrayed me.

"Hey." His deep baritone vibrated all the way between my legs. I slammed my thighs shut, if only to remind myself that he was off-limits. I took a sip of wine, needing the liquid courage.

"What's up?" I spoke in my iciest voice, hoping it would put him off.

"Damn, Coco, you look good." He came toward me, and I had to put up my hands like a stop signal.

"Whoa!" If I let him come any closer, there was no telling what my body might do.

"I miss you." He acted like we had taken some quick break and were getting back together, not like he broke my heart and lied to me.

"Yeah, well, it's a little too late for that."

Obviously, he felt differently, because he tried to convince me we still had a chance. "Coco, I have loved you in a way I have never felt with another woman."

"Then why the hell didn't you tell me that you make your living as Mr. Porn King?" I asked with attitude, not wanting him to get any idea that he was gonna waltz into my life and all would be forgiven. I planned to rake him over the coals before tossing him out of my life once and for all.

"I planned to tell you, but it wasn't easy. You were the first woman I'd fallen in love with since getting into the business." Maybe he thought this would satisfy me, but it wasn't even close to enough.

"Didn't you think about the medical ramifications of sleeping with all those women? You put my life at risk and didn't bother to tell me, so excuse me if I don't care how hard it was for you," I huffed.

"Baby, the rules for doing a movie are tough. It ain't like I just stuck my dick into some girl who didn't have a clean bill of health. We're forced to get medical clearances. I'm clean," he announced.

"You don't know if those women you're fucking caught HIV yesterday and gave it to you today, so you could pass it on to some unsuspecting woman like me tomorrow."

"Look, I don't mean to throw stones," he said, "but you told me yourself that you've slept with over a hundred men. How many of them gave you a certificate of clean health?"

I couldn't believe he went there. "You throwing my past up in my face? At least I told you the truth about my life," I spat out.

"Yes, I should have told you. But I didn't want to lose you." He started moving close to me again, and this time I threw my hands up.

"You lied to me! You have sex for a living," I screamed at him.

"What is so different from what I do and what you do? We both fuck people for a living," he shouted back. I saw him take in my surroundings as if they proved his point. And, unfortunately, they did. But at least my sex wasn't all over the screen.

"But I stopped fucking other people when we became a couple, Mac. You didn't stop. Tell me why," I demanded.

"You don't think I can keep up my lifestyle with poetry, do you?" His words were like a cold slap of reality. As much as I hated the thought of him lying to me, I couldn't argue with his reason for doing the movies in the first place. Of all people, I understood the bottom dollar.

"It's simple," he explained. "I need the money. I don't get emotionally involved. To me, it's just a job."

"Well, how much money could they possibly pay you to do that on screen?" His place was nice, but it wasn't like his pockets were fat like Jackson's. Could porn really be a good living, or was he just lying again?

"Five thousand dollars every time I come."

As he said it, I almost choked. "Five thousand dollars?" Even I was impressed by the number. "That's no small amount of cash. How much the women get?"

"A lot more," he said with a laugh. "Why? You interested?"

"I never thought about it," I told him, and it was the truth.

"I've been thinking about making my own movies," he admitted.

"That's nice." I tried to shut off from him. Our conversation was becoming a little too casual, and I felt myself weakening.

"Coco, I love you. If you take me back, I will give up the porn and find a way to take care of us. I promise you that." Everything from the tone of his voice to the look in his eyes told me he was being honest. I moved toward him as I thought about what my life had become. How long could I keep up this ruse with Jackson? Every day it got harder to pretend I was excited by him. Someday I would feel the need to bounce, and then where would I be? I knew I couldn't keep making my money like this forever.

Even as I realized this, an idea was forming in my mind.

"What if you don't have to give up the business?" I asked.

"What do you have in mind?" He perked right up.

"Business and pleasure," I answered mysteriously.

"Whose business?" he asked.

"Ours," I answered.

"Then whose pleasure?" He moved closer to me, and this time I didn't step away.

"Ours first, and then everybody else's." I pulled him close, letting his tongue slide down my throat. Yeah, sometimes life hands you exactly what you need, and I finally figured out that Mac, me, and my new ideas were a match made in heaven. Once people got a hold of the new videos we would make, starring Mac pleasing me and maybe a bunch of other thick sisters, big girls all over the world would be opening their wallets to buy up every last DVD.

57

Isis

I heard what sounded like a banging noise, but it seemed so far away, like maybe someone was banging on another door somewhere on the other side of the apartment complex. I tried to block out the sound, but it wouldn't go away. Then I felt hands on my body, except it didn't feel like my body anymore. It felt cold and stiff.

You ever have a dream that seems so real, and when you wake up you're relieved to discover it was only a dream? Well, that's sort of what happened to me, except that instead of waking up feeling relief after my dream, I woke up into a total nightmare. When I opened my eyes, I wasn't in the peaceful place I had expected to find myself. Instead, I had landed in a hospital, with my stomach being pumped. I passed out, probably because I wasn't ready to wrap my mind around the reality of this situation.

When I came to again, I was in another room. "You're gonna be okay," Egypt kept whispering to me in that voice people adopt when they are really worried but need to convince themselves that everything is going to work out. She rubbed my hand to comfort me, but it felt like she meant to take my skin off.

I started to lift my head, but the throbbing pain in my temples made me put it back down. This must be what it feels like to get hit by a Mack truck, I thought as I focused my vision and saw that it wasn't only Egypt in the room with me. Rashad stood at the bottom of my bed, looking worried. I slammed my eyes shut, trying to block out his face. Was she crazy, bringing Rashad up in here to make me look like a bigger idiot? Next time I tried to kill myself, I planned to forget about the babbling phone call to apologize for my actions.

"Isis? You awake?" Egypt squeezed my hand. If I wasn't awake, her squeezing my fingers damn sure made it impossible to sleep. Since I could tell that there was no way to avoid this little moment, I opened my eyes.

"Y'all dead too?" Like a lot of people caught in a bad situation, I figured I better hurry up and find the humor before things got any more awkward.

"Dammit, Isis, how could you do this? You had us worried half to death." Rashad's words only made me feel worse.

Us . . . I replayed the words in my mind. Yep, his use of the word *us* made it clear that they were a couple. So, not only had I tried and failed at love, but apparently I couldn't even kill myself without some man from my past who once loved me being in the audience by my sister's side. Could it become any clearer how pathetic my life had become?

"Well, as you can see, I'm still alive, so you can leave now." I snatched my hand out of Egypt's tight grip.

"Your sister was worried about you," Rashad butted in, as if I needed to hear anything he had to say.

"Isis?" Egypt pleaded, but I turned away from both of them.

"I just want to be left alone." My words were meant to send them out the door, but, no, they didn't budge.

"We're not leaving. At least I'm not." Egypt plopped down in the chair beside my bed.

"I'ma wait outside and give you two a moment," Rashad said, and then he added, "Isis, your sister loves you."

"Egypt, you can go too," I told her. I just wanted to be alone, but nobody seemed to hear me. She sat right there as if I had invited her to stay.

"Isis, I can't lose you. Out of all the kids in our family, we've always been the closest. Remember how when we were little we insisted on sleeping together and Mommy made us get in our own beds at night, but by the morning she'd always find us in one bed?" I did remember, but I refused to go on some little nostalgia trip with her now. As far as I was concerned, my life had been one big fuckup, so there was no point in reminiscing about it now.

"You got to tell me why you did this," she said when I didn't respond to her. She started rubbing my arm.

There were so many ways I could have answered, but none of

them were the entire thing. I could talk about Tony or Rashad or any of the other men who never loved me the way I needed. Hell, I could take this all the way back to our genesis and talk about our father, who left when Mommy was pregnant. All of it sounded textbook, and no one thing was the reason, but together it had to be enough to wear anybody down.

"Is it because of Rashad?" she asked. "Isis, I swear, if the reason you hurt so much you didn't want to live anymore is because of him, then I will end it today. Ain't no man in the world worth my sister." I didn't have to look at her to know she was crying now.

"It's not because of him." As much as I wanted someone to blame, Rashad and I were over a long time ago. There was no reason to ask her to leave him now. While I might have been in pain, I couldn't stand the thought of causing my baby sister to hurt.

"Then what is it? What could make you want to kill yourself?"

Like an avalanche, all the reasons I wanted to die came rushing back to me. "Everything," I started, then began with one of the biggest reasons. "Finding out Tony had been lying to me all those years. As much as I wanted to blame him, he couldn't have played me like that unless I let him. After Rashad, I was scared of ever being hurt by a man again. That's why I set up all those rules—no spending the night, no coming over without making plans in advance, shit like that. I thought I was protecting myself, but I didn't realize it made me an easy target for Tony. I thought I was just protecting my heart, but I was giving him a way to screw me on what I thought was my schedule, then go back to his wife without me ever suspecting a thing."

"So, it's Tony?" Egypt said his name like it was a curse. "Fuck him. You deserve so much more than him." She thought those words would bring me comfort.

"It's not Tony; it's everything. What is so wrong with me that a man can't love me? Daddy didn't, and then every single man who ever loved me found some excuse not to marry me. Hell, everything has a common denominator, and in this case, I am the only thing these men have in common, so the problem has to be me. I am the one who is unlovable." As much as I wanted to be strong, I couldn't. I burst into tears.

"But you're not unlovable. I love you; the entire family loves you. You got a list of friends as long as my arm who would do anything for you. You're forever getting bonuses at work. Isis, people love you."

"Yeah, but not men." I knew what my sister was trying to do, but she didn't get it. Hell, she had a man.

"But they do," she insisted. "The only reason Rashad and I even spent time together in the first place was because he was crying over your ass. The night Tony beat him up, I took him to the hospital, and he said his biggest mistake was letting you go."

That was a nice little story she told me, but the only thing that mattered to me was the ending, and I let her know it. "But he did, Egypt. He let me go."

"Do you really want him, or do you simply need some man to drag down the aisle?" She almost sounded ready to hand him over if I said the word.

"No—and yes. If I really wanted to be with Rashad, I would have chosen him over Tony when I had the chance. But, yes, I do want to get married. Is there something wrong with that? I'm thinking that's why we're in this world, to procreate. And, yes, I went over the deep end, but everything is about the *us* and *we,* and when you are standing outside of a couple and you are an *I,* it gets lonely." It hurt to speak the words out loud. I had never admitted to anyone just how alone I felt in this world. I guess I'd felt this way for a long time. That's probably why I was so desperately seeking a man, a husband who I thought would fill that void in my life.

"But people can also be lonely in a relationship, you know." Egypt had grown so much wiser than I'd ever given her credit for.

"Yes, but it's not the same thing." I knew I was being stubborn, but I wasn't ready to let go of my pain or my anger at Tony. I wanted him to give me back the years he had stolen from me. Thinking about that jackass made me feel a little more homicidal and a lot less suicidal. Hell, I guess some would say that was a good sign. At least if I had a purpose, I could continue to be among the living. Yeah, maybe I wasn't quite done torturing Tony yet. My sister spoke, interrupting my thoughts before I could let my imagination run wild with new ideas for revenge.

"Isis, please, please don't do this again. I need you, and so do a lot of other people. And if you kill yourself, you'll be guaranteed not to ever get married."

I turned to face her. She was smiling at me through her tears. "I won't, Egypt. I was just so sad and tired."

And I no longer wanted to die. I wanted other people to die, but I wanted to be among the living. There was a lot of shit I wanted to accomplish, some of it good, like work stuff, and some of it not so good, like making sure Tony remembered what he did to me for the rest of his life. Yeah, I planned to live a long, long time.

58

Nikki

I was spending too much time every day thinking about Keith. When I was at home, I was wondering about who the hell he was, what made him that way, and how he could live a lie. When I was at work, I was busy thinking about ways to avoid him. Although his letter had moved me, and part of me really wanted to talk to him about everything, I still didn't feel ready to face him. I wanted to say I understood how difficult his life had been, but that didn't mean I understood why he chose to lie to me. I didn't know if I'd ever be able to trust him again.

Apparently, Keith didn't feel ready to talk to me either, because every time he came around my area, he kept a wide berth. If he saw me coming down the hall, he'd pretend to be busy so we wouldn't have to make eye contact. It was painful for me, and I guessed probably for him too. After a while, I noticed that he was out sick a lot more often, and management was complaining about it. As much as I didn't want to have any feelings for him, I felt bad that he might lose his job.

Well, to be honest, the thought of him losing his job was only the excuse I used for why I finally broke down and went to see Aunt Gwen. Truth was that I missed talking to Keith, and while I wasn't ready to talk to him directly, I figured talking to his aunt would be the next best thing.

"Keith's not here," Aunt Gwen said when she greeted me at the door of her restaurant. It was fairly empty, because the dinner crowd hadn't yet arrived.

"I came to see you," I explained.

She stepped out of the doorway to invite me inside, and I was relieved to see that her face held no signs of anger. I had been afraid that she would hate me for hurting Keith, but I guess I hadn't given her enough credit.

Aunt Gwen motioned for me to take a seat in a booth, and she sat down across from me. "Thank you for giving me an excuse to get offa these feets," she said with a laugh to break the tension.

I bypassed all the small talk and got right to the point. "Is he all right?"

"He's been better," she answered.

"I just wanted to make sure, because he didn't come into work today. I don't want him to lose his job."

She watched me silently for a moment, and I knew I hadn't fooled her with my supposed reason for coming to check on Keith. It was like she could read my true feelings all over my face. As confused as I still was over everything, she was able to boil my emotions down to their true essence: "You care a lot about Keith."

I nodded.

"He didn't mean to lie to you," she said, then went on to explain Keith the way only a woman who truly loved him could. "It's just that he spent so many years running from who he really is, it's hard for him to say it out loud to another human being. Especially one with the power to break him the way you can." She waited for the weight of her words to connect with me.

"But all those months . . . Why would he keep it a secret for so long? Didn't he know I wouldn't care if he was a man or a woman? How could I judge him for being a lesbian?" I lowered my voice.

"But he's not a lesbian," she explained. "Not like a girl who chooses to love other girls. Ever since he was a child, he was more boy than girl. Came out of the womb that way. In the nursery, he screamed louder than any other kid, boy or girl. He'd throw a fit if he had to wear a dress, and this was way back when he could barely walk. But his mother wanted him to be a girlie girl. She made his entire world a light shade of pink, and he hated it.

"When he got old enough, he took to hiding another set of clothes behind the radiator in the hallway. One day, I caught him and let him keep some things at my place. I loved his mother like a sister, but she didn't want to see what was obvious to me. This baby she birthed into the world didn't want no part of being a girl.

"I told him that it wasn't his fault God made him with the wrong body parts. And now that he's older, he's ready to do something about it, to make his change permanent. One of the reasons he took that job was to save up for that operation. But until that happens, it's like he's gonna be tortured. He looks at his body and wants to see something that isn't there, and he has a hard time loving what is."

She stopped talking and went back to watching me closely.

"I guess I just . . . It's not that I don't hear you," I said, "but I thought we were close. Too close for lies."

"Think about it, Nikki," Aunt Gwen said. "You met him as a man. Can you imagine how scary it must be to worry every time you meet someone that they're going to reject you once they find out the truth? Can't you see how it might just be easier to live with that lie?"

"I guess," I responded. Part of me could understand it. There were times when I first got with Tiny that I was terrified people would find out. I would meet someone new at work, or one of DJ's teachers, and we'd get along fine, but I would always be worried that their impression of me would change once they found out I was living with a woman. But once I trusted someone enough, I'd let them in on my secret. The fact that Keith never trusted me enough to tell me made me think that maybe what we had wasn't as deep as I thought.

"I used to be a hard drinker when I was younger," Aunt Gwen continued. "It wasn't a pretty sight, but when Keith's momma died, I put myself in AA and got it together. There was one thing people said to me when I started going to the meetings. You got to remember I wasn't old and wise in those days, just a young, hardheaded, hard-drinking fool. They say, 'In AA, we love you until you learn to love yourself,' and for all of these years, I been doing that for Keith." I knew without a doubt that she did love Keith very much. He was lucky to have a person like Aunt Gwen on his side.

"He's a good person, Nikki, and if you don't think you can handle loving him one day, then I need you to walk away. That child has known more hurt than any of us should in one lifetime, and he's still a good person. I'da probably lashed out and killed somebody by now if I'd gone through all the mess he been through, but he still wants to love and have a family and to build up his dreams real high."

The mention of dreams made me think of the cookbook I had once imagined Keith and I publishing together. Did all of those dreams have to be smashed because of the simple fact of Keith's anatomy?

"Sit here and take a moment," Aunt Gwen told me. "I know I just laid a lot on your plate."

I nodded, lost in my thoughts, and she got up and left. A while later, she returned and handed me a piece of paper. She walked away without saying anything, but when I opened the paper, I knew what she intended for me to do. I sat for what felt like hours, opening and closing the paper. I thought about my life the way it was now, trying to decide if I was happy. I thought about DJ and wondered how much my crazy life had been affecting him. No, I decided, in spite of my mess, he was a happy, well-adjusted kid, and I could take the credit for that. I knew that no matter what decision I made regarding Keith, DJ and I were going to be just fine. I checked the address on the paper Aunt Gwen had given me and got up to leave the restaurant.

"Who is it?" From behind the door, I could hear the gruffness of someone who hadn't signed up to be bothered tonight. Then I could see the peephole grow dark as someone pressed an eyeball up against it.

Keith opened the door, standing there in a wife-beater, sagging Rocawear jeans, and bare feet. He looked like I was the last person he expected to see on his doorstep, and I guess I could understand why after the way I treated him the last time we spoke.

"Hey . . ." I suddenly felt at a loss for words. Any speech I had rehearsed on my way over to his place had been forgotten. The only thoughts that registered in my brain were about how good Keith looked. When I look back on it now, it's amazing how quickly I was able to forget the shocking image of Keith standing in my bedroom with that strap-on. Looking into his eyes as we stood in his doorway now, it was like I could see into his soul, and all I saw was the person I fell in love with. It didn't even cross my mind that Keith was really a woman.

"You wanna come in? See how the other half slums it?" He opened the door wider to reveal the ultimate studio bachelor pad. A sofa bed sat in the middle of the floor, with every kind of video-game gadget spread out on top of it. DJ would love this place, I thought.

Keith cleared off the sofa, and I sat down, still unsure of what I wanted to say.

"You haven't been coming to work much lately," I said awkwardly.

"I couldn't." Those were the only words out of his mouth before he turned away.

"Because of me? Keith, you need that job." After talking to Aunt Gwen, I knew that he needed his paycheck for reasons I never would have imagined a few weeks earlier.

"I'm sorry," he blurted out. "And I don't blame you if you want to stay the fuck away from me."

"Why?" I asked now that the subject had finally been broached. "Why couldn't you tell me the truth?"

"It's just that once I started, I couldn't risk losing your friendship." His dark eyes looked so helpless and yet sexy at the same time. Damn, this was not going to be easy.

"You knew I was with a woman," I said.

"Yeah, but Tiny was a straight-up dude, yo." He cracked a smile, and I had to join him. "Nikki, this wasn't supposed to go down like this, but you just . . . I don't know. You just did something to me, and I couldn't risk losing you." He plopped down on the sofa next to me, picking up one of the game controllers and staring ahead at the television.

"And you think I was looking to fall for you?" I asked, refusing to let Keith turn this into something *I* did to *him*. "I had a relationship. I loved Tiny, and my life was going fine." It wasn't exactly the truth, because Tiny and I were having trouble, but I didn't go looking for something on the side, and certainly not something with so many issues attached.

"Why are you here?" He put down the controller and turned to me. "Is this one of those 'I'm sorry but we can be friends' conversations? If it is, I get it, and now you can leave." He stood up and motioned me to the door.

"That's it? I question you and you can't deal, so that's the way it is?" I approached him.

"Deal with it? You saying this is supposed to be easy for me? You saying you can deal with a man who doesn't have a penis?" He spat the words out, and even though he tried to be hard, I could feel his pain.

"Yeah, speaking of penises . . . What the fuck was that thing? You just walk around with a fake penis in your pants?" I guess some anger from that night still remained inside me.

"It's what they give you at the doctor's office after you begin your sex-change conversion therapy." He looked miserable.

"And did they tell you in therapy that you should tell your partner your real gender?" I knew my words would hurt, but no more than it hurt to be lied to.

"Yes." The guilt was painfully obvious in his expression.

"Then why?" I still needed to know. I wanted to hear the words from his mouth.

Finally, the truth came out. "I didn't know if you would accept me."

"Maybe I wouldn't have, but you never even gave me a chance. And now both of us have lost the opportunity to find out what might have happened."

"I'm sorry, Nikki. I would have done anything not to lose you." He stared into my eyes, unblinking.

"You mean everything except trust me?" I asked bitterly.

"I'm sorry. I should have given you more credit," he said.

"Yeah, you should have," I answered, realizing that I had become a much stronger person in the past few months. Once upon a time, I wouldn't have been standing up for myself like this, demanding trust and respect. Even though I was still angry, I had to admit that Keith deserved some of the credit for helping me to grow into this new, more confident person. Whether that was enough to forgive his lie, I wasn't sure, but it was better than all the bitterness and anger I'd been harboring.

"Nikki, can we start over?" he asked.

I only had to think about it for a second before I agreed. "Only as platonic friends, though."

My words offered enough hope to bring a small smile to Keith's face. "One day at a time," he said.

"With no promises," I emphasized.

"And the cookbook? I understand if you want to put that on hold and see how it goes from here."

"No," I said, "let's keep working. That doesn't have anything to do with all this . . ." I searched for the right word. "All this *stuff* between us. I believe in the project. I'm excited about it."

"Okay, so starting over . . ." Keith held out his hand to me. "Hi, I'm Karen, but everybody calls me Keith."

I shook his hand, and something inside of me didn't want to let go.

59

Tammy

For the past month, I'd tried everything short of throwing myself at Tim. I'd cooked him all his favorite foods, including his favorite homemade dessert—sweet potato pumpkin pie. They say the quickest way to a man's heart is through his stomach, but after a month of throwing down in the kitchen, my husband's heart and penis stayed out of my reach.

By the time he walked in the door at night, I had the children fed and bathed, in pajamas and ready for Tim to read them a bedtime story. On top of that, I made sure to be perfectly coiffed, manicured, and dressed in my most flattering dresses to highlight Tim's favorite body parts. Leaning over to serve him seconds, I made sure to brush my breasts against his shoulder. Hell, a man would have to be gay to miss the loud signals he was ignoring.

When we were alone, I made sure to do without the constriction of bras and panties. I felt the electricity between us, but instead of taking the bait, my husband always excused himself and went off to bed alone. Watching him leave the kitchen, I felt the hope of saving my family slipping through my fingertips.

"How can I lose my husband?" I asked myself. Getting him to answer one question or to even look at me was impossible. When I tried to talk about anything outside of work or the kids, he shut down and refused to continue any conversation. Sure, I could try to segue from, "What story did you read the kids?" to "Do you want to have sex?" but I knew he'd only leave the room annoyed. Tim, the man who promised to love me to the very end, now hated me.

Lying in bed at night, all I could think about was Tim, alone in our bed, and me, an outcast in the guest bedroom. I tossed and turned, sleepless with thoughts of my gigantic fuckup. This was my fault, and I was the only one who could fix it.

Finally one night—maybe it had to do with being tired, or maybe it had to do with frustration—suddenly the answer hit me over the head like a brick. Terrible Tammy was coming out of retirement. I was horny as hell, and I needed to get me some dick.

"When I whip this good pussy on him, it's gonna be a wrap," I convinced myself. I put on my sexiest negligee, one Tim had brought back from a business trip in London. I fixed my hair to give it that just-got-laid look that men love.

"Gurrrl, go and get your man!" Terrible Tammy all but hollered at me to hit it. I pushed open the door to the master bedroom. It was sad how I had taken this room for granted in the last year. Two years earlier, I'd renovated the bedroom, got all new cherrywood furniture, and did it up in a tiger and zebra motif. Yeah, I figured if there was one room where it was acceptable to act like a wild animal, it was the bedroom.

Watching Tim sleeping soundly, I almost got pissed. When the hell was the last time I slept peacefully? But this wasn't about sleeping. In fact, I wouldn't rest until I had taken my rightful place next to my husband in this bed right here, and I meant to do it that night.

I crawled under the covers, my heart beating out of my chest, and I slid my hands down Tim's leg, kissing on his neck and nibbling his ear. If there was one thing I knew, it was how to get Tim to rise to attention and salute me. I brushed my hand against his penis, feeling it grow hard.

"What the hell are you doing?" Tim jumped away from my touch as if he'd been scorched.

"I miss you, Tim. I want to be with you."

He sat up, moving to the edge of the bed, but I stayed there, waiting for him to get back under the covers.

"I can't do this anymore." He started to rise, but I put my hands on his shoulders, trying to persuade him to stay.

"I'm sorry. Please, won't you give me another chance?" I knew I was supposed to be Terrible Tammy, who didn't take no shit and always got her man, but hell, a blind man could see that approach wouldn't work tonight.

"Tammy, I meant it when I said I can't do this anymore." Tim turned on the bedside lamp. He reached across the table, picked up a manila envelope, and handed it to me. My hands began to shake, but still, I opened the envelope. I read the front page of a thick legal document labeled PETITION FOR DISSOLUTION OF MARRIAGE, and at that moment, my world crumbled and broke apart. I could not contain myself as I burst into tears, sobs wracking my body.

"Please, Tim, don't do this. I love you," I pleaded with him, but it was as if he had steeled himself from feeling anything I had to say.

"I spoke to the lawyers," he said coldly. "You can keep the house. I'll keep the business, and you'll receive a generous alimony so that you and the children don't have to alter your lifestyle. Of course, I'll no longer need you in the office. It wouldn't be good for either one of us." He rose and began pacing the length of the room, avoiding any eye contact with me.

I wanted to become hysterical, begging and pleading, but we had children, and the last thing I wanted was to wake them to see me like this.

"Tim, please, you can't leave. I need you."

"Yeah, well, you sure didn't need me when you were busy fucking Raoul behind my back, did you?" This was the first time he'd mentioned my affair since I'd moved back into the house, and it was obvious that he was still hurting deeply.

I would have given anything to rewind back to six months ago, before I had that crazy idea about threesomes and fulfilling his every fantasy. Unfortunately, I had learned the hard way that some fantasies were better left unfulfilled.

"That's not love," I tried to explain. "It was lust. I love waking up next to you every morning and taking care of our lives and our children. I love being your wife and figuring out little ways to make you happy, like wearing my hair pulled back in a ponytail so that you can take it out when you kiss me. I love watching you lick your fingers when you eat my smothered chicken. I love sitting next to you at church and believing that God has made me the luckiest woman in the world." I was crying heavily now. "Yes, I betrayed you, and I wish I could take it back. I wish I could go back to the way we used to be before I brought Egypt into our bed and started this chain of events." As I said the words, I realized that it was the first time I had taken full responsibility. Every other time we'd fought about this, I reminded him that he was the one who invited Raoul to fuck me, like somehow my affair was his fault. But now, threatened with the thought of losing him for good, I was finally taking the blame the way I should have.

I leaned close to him, lifting his chin so that he had to look into my eyes. I wanted him to see the depth of my remorse, but he still wasn't convinced.

"How do I know you won't sleep with Raoul again, or another man, for that matter? I don't even know who you are anymore."

He spoke those words with such a calm quietness that they chilled me to the bone and sent shivers up my spine. Suddenly, memories of happier times in our marriage came flooding back. It reminded me of what people say happens when you are near death and your entire life flashes before your eyes.

"You know me better than anyone. Do you really think that after almost twelve years together I could just stop loving you? I know I can't make you stay, and I can't make you love me, but I don't want this house if you're not here to come home to. This is a home because we made it together, you, me, and the kids. This is where we conceived the kids and where we celebrated every anniversary.

"I want to grow old with you," I told him. "I want to love you for the next forty years. I know I fucked up, but if you can ever forgive me and take me back, I will spend the rest of my life making it up to you. You are the only man I want, and I am so sorry I ever hurt you." As the tears dripped down my face, I knew I had told the whole truth and nothing but the truth. I loved my husband more in that moment than I ever had. All the material things we had accumulated together would mean nothing if we weren't sharing them. It hurt me to my core to know that it took the destruction of my marriage for me to realize this.

When Tim didn't say anything after my impassioned speech, I figured all hope was lost. There was nothing I could say to make him want me again. I got up off the bed, thinking I would lie awake all night in the guest room. But before I got to the door and left, I heard him say, "Do you mean all of that?" His words stopped me in my tracks.

"Yes, I do." I stared at him, waiting for him to say something, to let me know how he wanted to proceed.

"Come here," he said.

I didn't know what was about to happen, but I stepped closer to him.

"Yes?" And now I stood next to him, feeling nervous, like the young, naïve newlywed I had once been.

"I want to work this out, Tammy," he said, and I felt all the tension leave my body.

"I'll do anything, Tim. Anything you want to regain your trust," I promised.

He pulled me down onto the bed so I was sitting next to him. After a few long, silent moments, he leaned in and kissed me. At first the kiss was tentative, but then it turned into the kind of deep, passionate kiss they say you lose after the first few years of marriage. That kiss said everything we couldn't say to each other yet about the depth of our love and the power of forgiveness. And I knew in my heart that eventually, we would be all right.

Our kisses turned into wandering hands, and before I knew it, Tim was undressing me. I lay back, expecting him to get on top and enter me so we could consummate our reconciliation, but then Tim did something I thought he would never do. He dove into my pussy headfirst, licking and sucking me like a champ. Three orgasms later, my husband had graduated Pussy Eating 101, and let's just say Tim was on the fast track for the master's program. God, I love my life.

SOMETHING ON THE SIDE

CARL WEBER

ABOUT THIS GUIDE

The following questions are designed to facilitate discussion
in and among reading groups.

DISCUSSION QUESTIONS

1. What do you think about a book about plus-size women?

2. Has this book changed your idea of what sexy is or isn't?

3. Who was your favorite character?

4. Would you or have you ever had a threesome?

5. Could you deal with a mate that wouldn't perform oral sex?

6. What was your opinion of Tammy's and Raoul's affair?

7. Have you ever had two people fight over you, and if you were Isis would you have let things go as far as she did with Tony and Rashad?

8. Did you suspect that Tony was married?

9. What would you have done if the person you were dating turned out to be married?

10. Was Isis wrong for approaching Tony's wife?

11. Was Nikki ever truly gay?

12. Were you fooled by Keith?

13. Do you think Keith and Nikki will become more than friends?

14. Do you see a little bit of Coco in yourself?

15. Would you stay with a man if you found out he was a porn star?

16. Would you have given Coco the DVD if you were Tammy?

17. Do you think Coco and Mac will last?

18. If you were Tim would you have taken Tammy back?

19. If one of these characters could continue their story in another book, which one should it be?

Turn the page for a preview of Carl Weber's next book,
UP TO NO GOOD

1

James

"So, are you going to take me back to your place, or are we going to make Benny rich by running up a ridiculous bar tab?" Crystal whispered seductively.

Her eyes traveled over my body, stopping a little below my belt as she took a sip of her drink. This was her way of letting me know that she was ready. The next move was mine, and her body language was begging me to make it. She lifted her head so her eyes could meet mine as she put her drink on the bar. I smiled, giving her my own once-over. I couldn't help but respond with a devilish grin as I placed my hand on the small of her back, high enough to be respectable but low enough to have an effect. She shuddered slightly under my touch, even though her face failed to give anything away.

We hadn't seen each other in almost a year, and probably wouldn't see each other for another, unless our son Darnel's wife-to-be, Keisha, became pregnant in the next few months. Crystal had traveled back to New York from Richmond, Virginia, for Darnel's wedding the next night, and we'd met at Benny's bar, one of our old neighborhood haunts, to catch up on old times after the rehearsal dinner.

"So?" she asked again, this time with a little more desperation in her voice. She wanted me. She wanted me bad. She wanted me to do what only I could do for her—satisfy that sexual itch that nobody else seemed to be able to reach. I know it sounds rather arrogant, but I'd been sleeping with this woman off and on for the better part of twenty-eight years, so I knew what she needed in the bedroom, just like she knew what I needed.

I glanced at her again. Even in a conservative pantsuit, she had a way of enticing me. Her face was a beautiful bronze color, highlighted by a beauty mark right above the left side of her lip. She'd gained a few pounds over the years, and her hair showed a hint of gray around the edges, but hell, whose didn't? Besides, truth be told, I liked a woman with some meat on her bones and some mileage on her engine. Experience meant a lot in life, especially in the bedroom.

She turned her head slightly, exposing a small tattoo with the letters *DB*, our son's initials, on the lower side of her neck. A memory of the way she cooed when I kissed her neck came to mind. Then I looked down at her chest, and the thought of her neck was quickly replaced with an image of her large, plump breasts and the silver dollar nipples that rested atop them. My heart rate increased, and my breathing became heavier. It never mattered where I touched her; Crystal's body was so sexually in tune with mine that I didn't even have to take off my clothes to give her an orgasm. Oh, but when I did get undressed, she would return the favor like very few women I'd ever known. Having a child together bonded us, but it was the sex that kept us hungering for each other year after year.

She licked her lips and my manhood sprang to life. I flicked my wrist so I could see the time on my watch. I was wondering if Crystal was planning on a quickie or one of our all-night marathons. I'd already cancelled a date to meet with her, so an all-nighter with someone of her sexual prowess was fine by me. That, of course, left only one question.

"Where's your husband?" I asked, getting straight to the point.

Crystal looked annoyed by my question. Yes, she was married, going on five years now, and she definitely preferred that I didn't mention him when we were getting ready to get busy. We both knew that her marital status really wasn't a factor in all this anyway. We'd played this game before, Crystal and I, through countless boyfriends and two husbands. She didn't make any excuses for the fact that she was a woman who needed a man in her life. She always said that she would prefer it if that man were me, but after a while, she stopped holding her breath and moved on.

One thing was for sure: It didn't matter who she was with. If we saw each other or had the chance to talk on the phone, it was never a question of *if* we were going to get together, but rather when and where it would happen.

"He had to work third shift. He'll be here sometime early tomorrow morning." Crystal slid off her bar stool and folded her arms as if to say, "So, come on. We got time, but we ain't got all night." I knew her well, and she was not about to take no for an answer. And as good as she was looking, I wasn't about to give her an argument.

"Okay, but only if you're going to respect me in the morning," I teased.

She didn't laugh. Instead, she came back with, "Please. You my baby daddy. I ain't got to respect you." Unfortunately, I knew she wasn't joking, and her words stung like hell.

"You don't?"

"Hell no. Everybody knows you ain't shit, James. As much as I love our son, I should have never had a baby with you." She'd been using this same line on me since Darnel was a baby, and now here he was, a grown man getting ready to get married and have babies of his own. Jesus, I was getting old.

"Then why do you want me to take you home? Why do you keep sleeping with me after all these years? You tryin' to say you ain't got no love for me?"

"Please, James. You broke my heart more times than I care to remember and in more ways than I will ever forget. I'd be a fool if I still had love for you."

"If you ain't got love for me, then why are you trying to sleep with me?"

"Good dick is hard to come by," she said, like it was a simple fact of life that everyone understood. "And you've got some really good dick. Now, are you going to sit here and debate it, or are you gonna take me home and remind me why I rented a car and drove seven hours up here instead of waiting for my husband so we could drive together?"

I reached in my pocket and pulled out a twenty-dollar bill. I slapped it down on the bar, nodding my head.

"You know me. Last thing I want is for anyone to make a seven-hour trip in vain," I said with a laugh. The truth of her words could have deflated my desire for her, but I knew this was not an opportunity to waste on being overly sensitive or sentimental. Besides, I'd known this woman my entire adult life, and there wasn't a thing she could say that I hadn't heard at least a dozen times before. We were too far past that naïve stage to believe we'd ever be anything more than what we were today.

Crystal leaned in and kissed my full lips, then smiled as if I had just given her a large sum of money. The way she stared at me made my manhood grow, making it clear that I was the one about to hit the jackpot. In less than twenty minutes, we'd both be in my bed, naked as the day we were born, making love like there was no tomorrow. And as it had always been between the two of us, there would be no tomorrow; only a here and now.

Five hours later, Crystal was snoring with a purpose, her back to my chest and her round hips and ass securely resting against my lap. I'd wake her up in about ten minutes for another round. She would have to leave after that in order to make it back to her hotel before her husband showed up. Part of me didn't want her to leave because I had such a good time. I always had a good time when Crystal and I got together.

I stared at her face as I stroked her sweated-out hair. We'd gone at it for the better part of an hour—twice. The way she called out my name and told me that this would always be her dick was definitely good for the ego. It also told me that after all these years, no matter what she said, she was still in love with me.

Crystal had sacrificed most of her adult years chasing after me. We'd met right after high school. I was far from being faithful, but she was as close to a steady girlfriend as I had during those days.

She looked out for me when no one else would, sometimes even when it wasn't in her best interests. There wasn't anything Crystal Jackson wouldn't do for me. I knew that better than anyone on this earth, and the thing that haunted me the most was that she only wanted one thing in return: my love. But as much as I tried, I just couldn't give it to her the way she wanted it.

Like most women, she wanted to be a wife much more than a girlfriend. Don't get me wrong; I liked her, but I wasn't having no part of getting married. I was having too much fun with all the other women in my life. Crystal, on the other hand, wouldn't take no for an answer. As far as she was concerned, she was in love with me, and all I needed was a little coaxing and I would understand that I loved her too. She was so convinced of this that she got pregnant, hoping it would settle me down enough for us to get married. It didn't. All it really made me do was act the fool even more. It was something I wished could have been changed, but I still had no regrets. I'd had a good life, a fun life. Why would I mess it up by getting married?

"I'm sorry," I whispered.

"Huh?" She lifted her head. "What did you say?"

"Ah, nothing." I leaned over and kissed her cheek.

She rolled over to face me. "If you're gonna kiss me, kiss me right."

I smiled as I studied her face through the dim light that peeked between the curtains. She really was beautiful, and I'd never seen a woman age so well.

I pressed my lips against hers and our kiss became passionate. My hands roamed her body hungrily. Just as she mounted me for another round, my bedroom door flew open and blinding light flooded the room.

Crystal dove under the covers to hide her nakedness.

"What the—" I shouted, squinting my eyes to adjust to the bright lights as I saw what looked like a female figure standing in my doorway. In that brief moment, my mind went into over-drive, trying to understand who had just broken into my house. It could have been one of any number of women I'd been seeing over the past few months; most likely the one I had broken a date with to meet Crystal. But how the hell did she get into my house?

The woman yelled, "I knew you was here with her!" and sud-denly I knew who the intruder was. This wasn't just any woman standing in my doorway. This was a woman I loved with all my heart, but when it came to me pursuing my love life, she could be described with only one word: *trouble*.

2

Darnel

"Well, tomorrow's the big day. You're really gonna go through with it, aren't you?"

I smiled, nodding my head at my best friend, Omar, as I slid my key into the door of my hotel room, then pushed it open. We'd just left what was quite possibly the best bachelor party ever thrown, and we were both drunk. I plopped down on the first of two queen-sized beds while Omar stumbled toward the bathroom to relieve himself. I didn't know about Omar, but I was tired; both mentally and physically drained from preparing for my big day tomorrow, as well as celebrating my last night as a single man with my boys.

Omar, who was my best man, had gone all out, inviting all our friends, along with six of the wildest strippers I'd ever seen. They were more like erotic circus performers than strippers, with all the contortions and tricks they showed us. Add them to the top-shelf liquor our friend Reggie supplied and *Bam!* One hell of a bachelor party.

"You know, Dee," Omar slurred as he stood in the bathroom, "I never thought you'd really go through with it. I mean, I like Keisha and all, but . . ." He paused. I heard him say "ahhhh," followed by the sound of him relieving his over-filled bladder.

"Man, will you close the door? Don't nobody wanna hear you peeing." I loved Omar like the brother I never had, but he could really be disgusting sometimes. Some might even call him repulsive.

"Don't get your panties in a bunch. I'm done now." He walked out of the bathroom with his zipper down and his pants hanging off his ass, showing off his plaid boxers. I didn't bother to remind him to wash his hands because like I said, he could be a little raw.

"So, what were you saying about me getting married? You didn't think I was gonna do it? Man, I been with that woman since I was fifteen years old. That pussy is bought and paid for. I ain't got no choice but to marry her." I tried to sound cool for Omar, but the truth was I loved Keisha with all my heart.

"Yeah, I know that, and you been faithful to her since you was fifteen. But what I wanna know is, do you really want to die knowing you've only been with one woman?" His expression made it look as if he felt sorry for me. I hated that look.

"You act like me being faithful is a bad thing."

This conversation was nothing new to me. Omar and my boys had always thought me strange because of my faithfulness to Keisha. The way they saw it, a man was supposed to get as much experience as he could with as many women as were willing to give it up. But I viewed things differently. I had given my virginity and pledged my faithfulness to Keisha, and I wasn't about to hurt her by cheating with some woman who didn't mean anything to me. My father had done that to my mother. I grew up seeing how deeply it affected her life, saw the hurt in her eyes over and over again, so I vowed never to do that to the woman I loved. It just wasn't worth it to me.

"Nah, it ain't a bad thing," he conceded, "just unrealistic. Besides, with that chick Tia as her maid of honor, who knows what they're doing across the street at her bachelorette party?" Omar sat down on the bed across from me with a strange look on his face—like he had something important to say but he just couldn't find the words. He was starting to piss me off. "Dee, I heard Tia hired male strippers for Keisha's bachelorette party. Who knows what Keisha could be—"

I cut him off right there. "Look, bro, Keisha ain't Tia, just like I'm not you! You got that?"

"You think our strippers had big titties? Can you imagine how big those male strippers' dicks are? Stretch that tight little pussy right on out."

Omar was my boy, but he was really starting to push the limit tonight. "You're drunk, so I'm gonna ignore that. But O, you better check yourself," I warned him.

He laughed, but I wanted him to understand that I was serious. The night before my wedding was not the time for him to be disrespecting my fiancée like this. I loved that woman more than I loved myself.

"I'm just saying . . . do you really think you're the only guy Keisha has ever been with?"

I stood up and pointed my finger in his face. "Best friend or not, don't come out your face like that about her again or I'll—"

"Or you'll what? Man, sit your ass down." He laughed. "What you gonna do, fight your best man for trying to get you some pussy the night of your bachelor party?" He shook his head.

I let out an aggravated sigh. "O, I don't know why you gotta disrespect me before my wedding."

He was still smiling, but he had stopped laughing. I think he could finally see that I was upset. "Yo, Dee, I'm sorry, man. I meant no disrespect, but—"

"You need to shut that drunk-ass mouth of yours then."

"You right, I'm drunk," he admitted, still smiling at me. "And maybe I should be quiet. But just remember, drunk people usually tell the truth. So I'm telling you, Darnel, you need to get some ass before you get married. I could set it up like that." He snapped his finger.

I was amazed at how persistent Omar was. He knew damn well that Keisha was my life, so he was wasting his time trying to convince me to cheat on her.

I lay down on the bed. "Can't do it, buddy. I'm a one-woman man."

"You wasn't such a one-woman man when that stripper was giving you that lap dance in the corner, were you?" Omar's smile widened. "I saw the way you was trying to hide your hard dick once she got off of you." He imitated my actions, crossing his arms casually over his lap.

I turned my head away from him so he wouldn't see my smirk. I had indeed been turned on by the honey-colored stripper who called herself Destiny. She had coaxed me into a lap dance when I thought everyone was watching the other strippers do tricks. I'd be lying if I said I didn't enjoy it. But that still didn't mean I wanted to have sex with her.

"You saw that, huh?" I said.

"Yeah, I saw it. So did half the other brothers in the room."

"Jesus Christ." I was so embarrassed.

"What's wrong with you? It was a fuckin' bachelor party, Dee. What? Your dick not supposed to get hard when a fine-ass naked woman sits on your lap? I'd be worried if it didn't." Omar smiled as he tried once again to tempt me to get laid by another woman on the night before my wedding. "You couldn't keep your eyes off that fine-ass honey the rest of the night, could you?"

"You just don't understand. Keisha is my soul mate. I'm not supposed to be attracted to any other woman that way. I made a promise, and I'm keeping it."

"No, you don't understand." Omar paced back and forth like a lawyer delivering a passionate closing argument. "I mean, I appreciate that being faithful shit. That's what's up, but you take that shit to another level. You need to have some fun, D."

I didn't have a chance to answer him, because his cell phone rang. He must have been expecting the call because all of a sudden his eyes lit up and he looked really excited. He answered the phone in a hurry and took it into the bathroom. Unlike when he used the toilet before, this time he closed the door behind him.

He came out about five minutes later, smiling.

"Yo, I'm about to hook up with one of them strippers. Her friend Destiny asked about you. She wanted to know if you wanted to hang." He looked at me eagerly. "This is your last opportunity, man."

"Nah, you go. I'm gonna chill out right here and get some rest. I got a big day ahead of me."

"Whatever." Omar shook his head, looking very disappointed in me as he headed for the door. "If you change your mind, give me a call."

"I won't," I assured him.

Once he was gone, I pulled out my cell and dialed Keisha's number. She answered on the second ring with a sweet "Hello." I loved her voice. I know it sounds corny, but it was like music to my ears. I can't even begin to explain how much I loved this woman.

"Hey, babe," I greeted her. I was lying on my side, remembering how beautiful she looked tonight at the rehearsal dinner. I couldn't wait to make her my wife.

"Hey, boo." She sounded excited to hear from me. "You still at the bachelor party?"

"Nah, I'm in the room, bored and lonely."

"Oh, my poor baby." She was using this cute little-girl voice. "Don't worry. After tomorrow you don't ever have to be lonely again."

"I like the sound of that. So what you doing?"

"I'm about to leave the bar and go up to my room. Tia done found her some man."

"Figures," I replied. "Hey, want some company?"

"I'd love some . . . tomorrow night." She chuckled. "I know what you're up to, Mr. Black. You ain't gettin' none until after the wedding. Besides, you know it's bad luck to see the bride before the wedding."

Keisha had been holding out on me for the past three weeks. We shared an apartment together, but she'd been making me sleep in the guest room, telling me some crap about I'd appreciate it more if we waited until after the wedding. As horny as I was the past few days, I was deeply regretting the fact that I'd actually agreed to our mini-celibacy.

"Okay, okay. I guess I'll go see if I can find my other best friend."

"I just saw Omar and some woman leaving the hotel."

"It was probably that stripper he was going to meet."

"Maybe. Look, baby, I'm about to get in this elevator. If I lose the signal, I'll call you back."

"Nah, it's a'ight, babe. You go 'head. I'll see you in the morning. I love you, Mrs. Black."

"I love you too, Mr. Black. Good night." I could hear her smiling through the phone. She loved it when I called her Mrs. Black.

" 'Night, babe." I hung up the phone, fiending for my woman. I just wanted to be near her. Hell, I would have settled for a kiss and hug.

One long, lonely hour later, I found myself wishing that I had gone with Omar—not to have sex with that woman Destiny or anything, but just to do something and get out of the room. I was so keyed up. When I first got to the room, I was dead tired, but after talking to Keisha, anxiety set in and I couldn't sleep. All I could do was think of her and the wedding. Was everything going to be all right? Were the limos going to pick us up on time? Was the reception going to be decorated the way we wanted? Was Omar going to get back from screwing that woman on time? Were my father and stepfather going to get along? There were so many things running through my mind.

Whenever I had nights like this, when I had too much on my mind, Keisha was always the one who could soothe me and help me fall asleep. If I could just get one kiss, I thought, I could make it through the night. One kiss was all I wanted. Never mind all that "bad luck to see the bride" stuff; I decided to go surprise my future wife.

I got out of bed, still feeling the effects of the alcohol. I wasn't as bad as when I got back to the room, but I was still drunk.

I staggered to the elevator, punched the button, and rode down to the lobby. Fortunately, I wasn't so drunk that the lady at the front desk would give me a hard time. I told her that I had lost my key to the wedding suite. The truth was that Keisha was staying there alone tonight, and we would be there together after the wedding. But the desk clerk didn't need to know those details. As long as the name on my driver's license matched the name on the reservation, she was happy to give me a duplicate key card.

"Congratulations," she said with a smile.

"Thanks," I answered as I grabbed a handful of mints and headed back to the elevator. As I rode up to the twentieth floor, I popped a few mints in my mouth to mask the smell of alcohol on my breath. Keisha hated when I was drunk.

I couldn't wait to see her. Maybe if I played my cards right I would get more than a kiss.

When I got to the suite, I slid the card in the door and walked into the living room. The lights were out, and I didn't see any reason to turn them on as I walked from the living room into the bedroom. There were enough bright city lights coming though the space between the curtains for me to see everything I needed to. And what I saw was my worst nightmare come true.

On the bed, lying naked on her stomach, was Keisha. Now, normally that wouldn't have been a bad thing, but lying on top of her was Omar. That's right, Omar. The same Omar who was supposed to be my best friend and the best man in my wedding tomorrow, the same Omar who was trying his damnedest to get me to cheat on Keisha, was now screwing her from behind. Oh, was he having a good old time, too, pumping away like there was no tomorrow. Unfortunately for him, there would be no tomorrow, because I was going to kill him.

Like someone hit by lightning, anger swept over me in a wave. I sobered up completely within a matter of seconds. Before I could think, I took three long steps across the room, grabbed the ceramic lamp off the night table, and smashed it as hard as I could into Omar's head. The lamp shattered as Omar rolled off of Keisha, screaming out in pain.

I turned my attention to Keisha, and for a moment, time stopped. It was like our entire relationship flashed before my eyes. I saw our first date, our first kiss, the first time we made love, the prom, our apartment, the day I proposed, the last time we made love, the rehearsal dinner earlier tonight, and now her lying in front of me. I don't know how my eyes must have looked because Keisha began pleading, "Don't get crazy, Darnel. This is not what it seems."

I couldn't help myself. I slapped the shit outta her. "It's not? 'Cause it sure as hell seems like you fuckin' my best friend. That's what it seems like to me." I slapped her again, then turned to Omar.

"I'm sorry, man," Omar whimpered.

I looked down at his dick and rage filled my entire being. "Motherfucker, you ain't even wearing a condom!"

I lunged at him and start whaling on his ass. I beat him fiercely. I kicked him in the face and tried to stomp his fucking guts out.

"I thought you was my boy," I kept repeating with every punch I delivered. My blows even fell into some kind of rhythmic pattern: Fist, fist, kick, kick. Fist, fist, kick kick. "I thought you was my dog, and you gon' do me like this? Fuck my girl without a condom? I ain't even fucked her without a condom. Oh, hell naw. I'ma kill you!"

Omar never returned any blows. I guess he knew he was wrong, or else he was just too hurt to muster a defense. He covered his head the best he could, but I was relentless in my fury.

I could feel Keisha trying to pull me off. "Stop, Darnel! You're going to kill him!"

"Bitch! Get the fuck off. You fuckin' ho!" I was so full of adrenaline I threw her across the room with barely any effort. Then I returned to Omar.

I couldn't stop beating O until I got all my venom out. I've never known such pure hate. And pain. Yes, I was in just as much pain as I could assume Omar was. I wanted him to feel my agony, to know that what he did had crossed the boundaries of human decency. It reminded me of when I was a little boy and my mom would whoop me and say, "This hurts me just as much as it hurts you."

I saw Omar's nose gushing bright red blood, and his eyes were blackened and swollen. He was bleeding from his mouth. I think he was trying to say, "I'm sorry," but I didn't care. I already knew he was sorry. He was a sorry excuse for a friend and a man, that's what he was.

Keisha must have called security because two men in blue uniforms came out of nowhere and pulled me off of Omar. It took both of them to get me loose from him.

Finally, I relented and stopped kicking his ass. "Let me go. I'm cool."